THE LORD OF LUSERNA

WITNESSES OF THE LIGHT

❧ *The* LORD *of* ❧
LUSERNA

a novel of the Waldensians

D. J. Speckhals

Trade Paperback edition ISBN: 978-1-7375364-3-7
eBook ISBN: 978-1-7375364-2-0

Front cover illustration: *Blick auf Schloss Tirol bei Meran* by Wilhelm Scheuchzer
Back cover illustration: *View of Florence from San Miniato* by Thomas Cole
Maps by D. J. Speckhals
Author photograph: Following Splendor Images

5 7 9 10 8 6 4

First Edition

To my brother—

Adam Murdock

#42

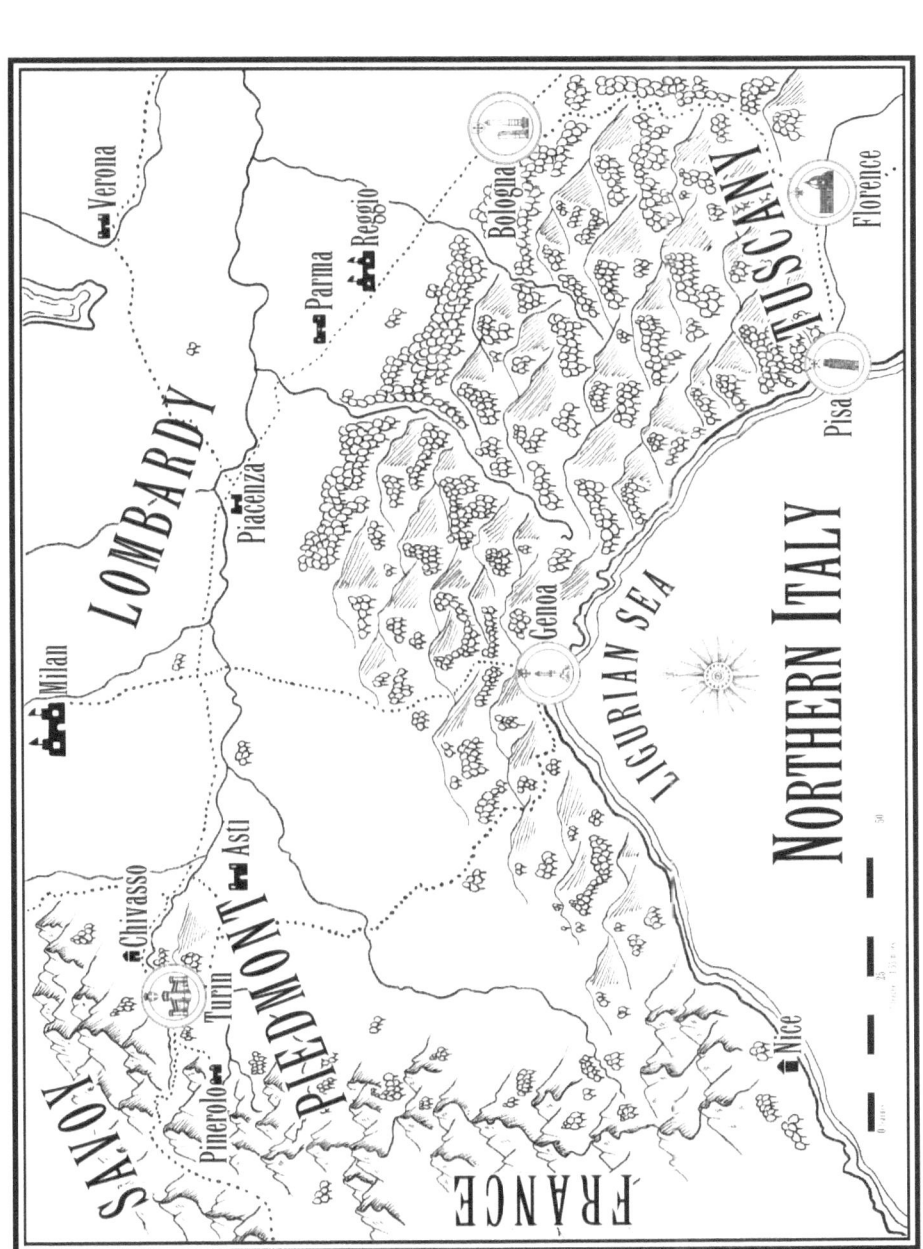

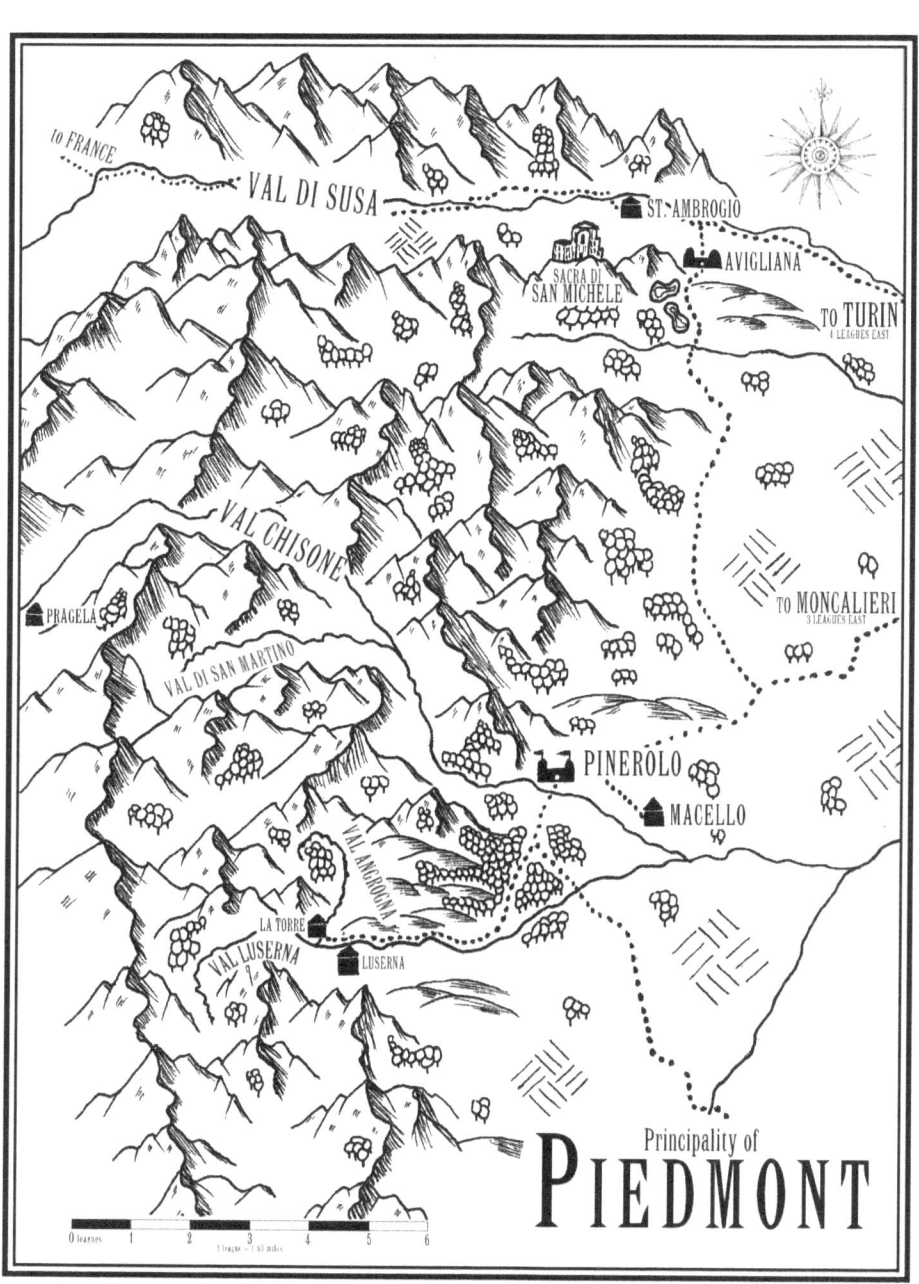

to FRANCE

VAL DI SUSA

ST. AMBROGIO

SACRA DI
SAN MICHELE

AVIGLIANA

TO TURIN
4 LEAGUES EAST

VAL CHISONE

PRAGELA

VAL DI SAN MARTINO

TO MONCALIERI
3 LEAGUES EAST

VAL ANGROGNA

PINEROLO

MACELLO

LA TORRE

VAL LUSERNA

LUSERNA

Principality of

PIEDMONT

0 leagues 1 2 3 4 5 6

1 league = 1.61 miles

VAL ANGROGNA

TO PRADELTORNO
2 LEAGUES NW

Cave

Pavarin Farm

Old Lauras Farm

Crossroads

TO LA TORRE
2 LEAGUES SOUTH

Meetinghouse

San Lorenzo

Angrogna Torrent

0 leagues   1/4   1/2

1 league = 1.52 miles

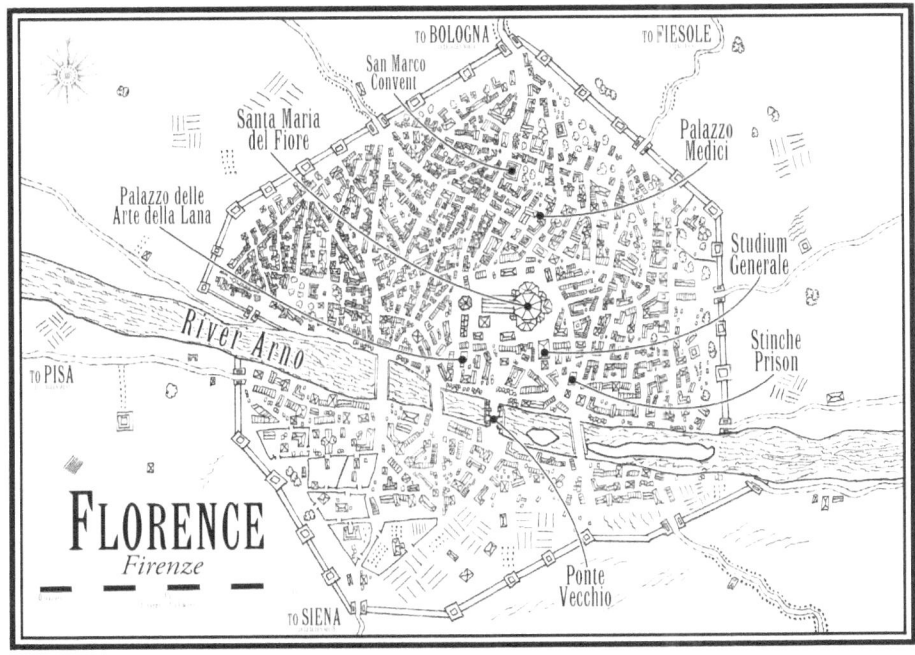

FLORENCE
Firenze

TO BOLOGNA

TO FIESOLE

San Marco
Convent

Santa Maria
del Fiore

Palazzo
Medici

Palazzo delle
Arte della Lana

Studium
Generale

River Arno

Stinche
Prison

TO PISA

TO SIENA

Ponte
Vecchio

Prologue

April 1453

THE HERALD PROCLAIMED the end of the world under the sunless midday sky. While some citizens stopped to pray and beg God for deliverance, Ioannis the philosopher rushed to escape the calamity that would soon befall Constantinople. But first, he must meet the monk.

"See, the weather itself bids us surrender to the will of God!" the herald shouted to the passersby. "Repent of your pride and submit to the one true Catholic faith of your ancestors, for only then will the holy archangel Michael save us from the legions of Satan."

Though the herald's intentions seemed pure, Ioannis ignored him and instead cast his gaze to the enormous brick structure behind the preacher.

Grandest of all the world's churches, the Hagia Sophia proclaimed the might of the city. Constantinople, the last vestige of the old Roman Empire, had endured a thousand years of treachery, despotism, and rivalry, yet she might finally fall to the Turkish hordes and their sultan.

The appointment with the monk would be brief, and then Ioannis could escape the closing jaws of slavery, torture, and death.

The paving stones under Ioannis's feet tipped and crumbled, a fitting likeness of this city, a dusty squalor that now housed only inept emperors, mystical prophets, and scheming traders. Yet it was this city and her institutions that preserved the lore of the ancients, and without her shared knowledge, the entire world might slide back into worshipping clouds and rocks.

And Ioannis Argyropoulos would not allow that to happen.

The incense struck Ioannis as soon as he entered the Hagia Sophia. Devout women cried out for deliverance while priests wearing long black robes and golden chains accepted alms from the pressing throng of worshippers. Somewhere amid the chaos was supposed to be the monk from Mount Athos, and with him, the treasures.

A firm hand grabbed Ioannis's arm and pulled him to the side. He glared at the interruption.

A wrinkled priest with weary eyes pointed to a hallway. "Follow me. What you seek is in the scriptorium."

Ioannis fumbled with his vest. "You're the monk?"

"Come, doom is upon us, and the hour is too late for introductions. The last ships embark this very night from the Golden Horn, and if you do not take the crates with you, all will be lost for eternity."

"Crates? I am here alone, and do I look as if I could carry much?"

"I have men who will transport the items to the ship for you. But hurry, our moments here must be short."

The monk hurried around sharp corners and through narrow, torchlit halls until he led Ioannis into a musty room overflowing with stacks of parchment.

Nowhere did gold sparkle, but Ioannis's jaw still dropped. He picked up the nearest piece of parchment, held it at arm's length, and read the Greek words on the first line.

Aristotle.

He rushed to the other side of the room, hands shaking, and grabbed another document. That one was from Plato. Then he found Pythagoras, Socrates, Epicurus . . .

Ioannis held a sheet, shook his head, and smiled at the monk. "You're giving all of this to me?"

"For safekeeping, of course. You are now a steward of the ancient works, and I trust you will use them wisely."

Soon a group of men carrying crates entered the scriptorium. As the men bundled and packed the stacks of parchment, the monk wandered to a brass-adorned chest, reached for his golden necklace, and unfastened a key from behind his jewel-studded crucifix. "What is contained in this chest is the most eternal, most ancient, and most precious of all. Nothing else here has been so meticulously copied and preserved."

The key clicked, the lid squeaked open, and the scent of old parchment escaped from the chest.

Ioannis scratched his white beard. "More from the ancients?"

"Indeed, but I refer not to the Greek philosophers of old. No, this codex comes from the Ancient of Days."

Decades of theological instruction told Ioannis that name referred to only one: Jesus Christ, the Ancient of Days.

The monk pulled the codex from the chest and placed it in Ioannis's hands. "The Gospels, the Acts of the Apostles, the Epistles, the Revelation of John—all written by holy men of God as they were moved by the Holy Ghost. This is no translation, my friend, for in it are the same Greek words God gave to the authors so long ago."

Ioannis laughed as he examined the elaborate illuminations on the pages. "The originals were worn into dust centuries ago. These must be copies."

"Yes, of course, copies of copies. And many like them exist. This codex, however, is in near-perfect condition and comes from a faithful lineage that weaves its path from our glorious Constantinople through Anatolia and far back to Antioch and the apostles themselves. The treasure you hold was copied at Mount Athos but came here centuries ago, where my brotherhood has since guarded it. Now, we must trust another to guard the text."

Ioannis gently turned the pages and examined each letter. "I'm sailing west to teach in Florence where the Latin Catholics and their pope reign supreme. If they discover—"

"You must never allow the Bible to fall into Latin hands, for they will stuff it into one of their libraries at best, and light it on fire at worst. Perhaps when the Muhammadan Turks are defeated and our empire is restored, you can return with it. Until then, keep it to yourself. Study it, yes, but most important of all, you must see to its preservation."

Those words weighed on Ioannis's shoulders. He had yet to hire a ship, and even then, he wasn't guaranteed safe passage to Italy. Turkish galleys prowled the Sea of Marmara, pirates stalked the Aegean trade routes, and storms always took their prey unawares. Ioannis needed to find the best sea captain left in Constantinople.

The crates and their priceless manuscripts followed Ioannis to the Golden Horn, along which lay Constantinople's renowned harbor. There the rich bartered for the few remaining spots on the Genoese and Venetian ships. But now was the moment to leave. Soon the valiant defenders of Constantinople would fix a chain across the Golden Horn to seal it off from the Turkish galleys. When that happened, there would be no escaping the apocalypse.

"One berth left on the *Perla*!"

The shout beckoned Ioannis, and he motioned for the crate haulers to follow him to the *Perla*.

Ioannis approached the shouting man. "If I pay for passage, will you also take my cargo?"

"How many crates?" the man asked in broken Greek.

"All that these men carry. Not more than twenty."

The man pursed his lips. "I'll take you anywhere you desire . . . for the right price."

"I have whatever price you demand. Anything is better than being a slave to the Turks." Ioannis opened his coin pouch and held it so the man could see.

"Gedeon Chanforan," said the man, offering a handshake. "I'm captain of this ship and the best seaman in the East . . . or the West."

The next day, the *Perla* embarked from Constantinople, turned into the Bosporus, and sailed south into the Sea of Marmara. On the shore far to the right, an enormous army sat encamped outside the walls of Constantinople.

The storm had arrived, but Ioannis and the treasures of the ancients had escaped.

1

The ocean they did not cross. Their mission field was the realms that lay outspread at the foot of their own mountains. They went forth two and two, concealing their real character under the guise of a secular profession, most commonly that of merchants or peddlers. They carried silks, jewelry, and other articles, at that time not easily purchasable save at a distant mart, and they were welcomed as merchants where they would have been spurned as missionaries.

—James Wylie
The History of the Waldenses, 1860

Six years later, July 1459

ONE DAY REMAINED, and if Andreas could endure it, he would complete the first journey of his new life and profession. The sun had just peeked its head above the horizon as he stood next to his teacher and fellow laborer, Estève Malan, scanning the throngs that bustled about the city market.

Andreas moved his eyes to the right and narrowed his gaze from the patchwork of faces to individual people, a trick Estève had taught him during their past two months of traveling through Venice, Milan, and now Turin.

So many weary faces. A smile, let alone a look of genuine joy, was rare, and though the smilers might have been the easier ones to approach, they were often closed to what Andreas and Estève had to say.

A man in his early twenties—close to Andreas's age—shuffled his feet through the crowd a few paces away. Dark stubble dotted his face, and he wore a scowl only a mother could lift. Andreas drew in a deep breath and stepped forward. He blinked quickly, his hands shaking at his sides.

Andreas turned to the left, but Estève had already found someone else. Though in his seventies, Estève had the tenacity of a young man. His back bent forward a little, but he still held his shoulders and head high. He wore a little smile, the look of true elation while sharing good news.

Andreas refocused on the scowling man, reached into his satchel, and searched for the little pouch. Each man in their profession had a unique way of initiating a conversation, and Andreas had thus far used the simplest and least suspicious: peddling. Perhaps he could learn to be a barber or a minstrel or a translator, but for someone still learning, playing the part of a merchant had to suffice.

"*Cerea*, young sir, may I show you what I bring from the East?" Andreas asked in Piedmontese, the local dialect. Sweat beaded in his palms, but the hardest part was done.

The man's eyes latched onto Andreas and looked at him from brow to ankle. And then came a chuckle.

"How about you find honest work instead of trying to sell me what you dug up from the cesspit?"

"You have never smelled a spice from faraway Persia." It all felt so unnatural, this peddling and salesmanship. "Come, I'll open this pouch and you can be the first man in Turin to experience the aroma of the Timurid courts."

The man rolled his eyes and squared his shoulders to Andreas. "Quickly now, show me."

But as Andreas fidgeted to open the pouch, a shoulder bumped him from behind, causing the exotic spice to fall onto the filthy road. He reached down to catch it but missed, and before he could pick it up, a horse's hoof smashed it deeper into the mud.

How could Andreas face the man again after that debacle? But he must. Andreas bit his lip and as he glanced up, praying he still held the man's attention.

But all he saw was the back of a wool shirt, and all he heard was a muffled laugh of amusement.

"That will be enough entertainment for me, traveler. And you should heed my advice: find proper work."

Andreas stood, puffed out his chest, and let out a long breath. *How foolish I must have looked.*

He glanced over his shoulder. There was Estève, his thin white hair nestled haphazardly under his cap. The hat alone must have been older than Andreas, but all he could do was respect the old man. For years, Estève had traveled throughout the Italian states, ever eager to proclaim the good news to anyone who would listen.

Estève was only a few paces from Andreas, but his steps were deliberate. He'd found someone. He reached into his sack and pulled from it a bolt of pure white silk. Though held by worn and wrinkled hands, the royal threads glittered in the warm sunshine.

But in front of Estève stood a woman more royal and rare than the precious silk.

Andreas blinked in rapid succession and refocused on the woman. Was she . . . could she be? Curled, dark brown hair was weaved in braids around her oval face.

Full lips surrounded her heart-shaped mouth, and those green eyes could pierce the thickest facade. The last time Andreas had seen those eyes was at his brother's wedding.

Indeed, she was Yolande of Valois, daughter of King Charles VII of France, and wife to Andreas's brother, Prince Amadeus of Savoy.

But this was bad. It was dangerous enough that Estève was approaching Savoyard royalty, but if Princess Yolande saw Andreas, she might upend his life.

Andreas slid behind the nearest pushcart, lowered the brim of his hat, and faced away. His heart thumped, but he prayed God would divert Estève away from Yolande. Of course, everyone needed to hear the gospel, but this wasn't the right time for Yolande.

Not now, Monsen Estève.

Andreas reached into his soul, pulled out a pinch of courage, and turned back. Two female escorts stood beside Princess Yolande and watched Estève as he took a step closer. The sight stole his breath, but the time to interrupt had passed. All he could do now was listen. And stay alert for any prying eyes.

"*O belle dame*, see these silks of mine?" Estève asked the princess, switching with ease to French. He held her attention, but that wasn't hard. Yolande relished the countless rarities she'd collected from Andalusia to China and everywhere between.

"Tell me, peddler, what have you draped over your arm?"

"The richest web of the Indian loom." Estève held the silk closer to Yolande, pulled a necklace from his satchel, and displayed it with his other hand. "And these pearls are as pure as your fair neck, dearest lady."

Andreas wiped his brow. The sun was oppressive, but this encounter was more so. Could Estève have found a worse person in Turin? Andreas scanned the crowd, looking for overcurious eyes.

Estève continued. "I have brought them with me a long way. Will my gentle lady buy either or both?"

Still, Yolande smiled at the worn man, and through the dark curls veiling her brow, she examined the silk and dazzling pearls.

"How much do you ask, my dear man?" Yolande's tone was soft and soothing.

"Only what my fair lady offers, and nothing more."

Yolande motioned toward an escort, who handed her a small pouch. She counted out four gold florins into Estève's hand—far more than what those items were worth. After a parting smile, Yolande whirled away with the grace of a princess.

Andreas wiped his brow and let his muscles unwind. But before he could wipe his sweaty hand on his coat, he spied three men near the fountain watching the old man and the princess. They were huddled together and spoke to each other with their chins down. One wore a red patch over his right eye.

If the conversation wasn't suspicious enough, Estève called out at a volume audible to anyone nearby. "My gentle lady, stay!"

Yolande turned back and gave a nod to the two escorts.

Andreas cringed and waited for the inevitable.

"O belle dame, I still possess a gem that casts the purest luster, more than the brightest diamond that ever shone from the lofty crown of the most magnificent king. It is a wonderful pearl of immense price, and most amazing of all, it will never decay. Even its light will be a joy to you, and a blessing on your way."

Princess Yolande motioned to the escort on her left. "The steel, if you will."

The escort fumbled in a bag, pulled out a mirror, and passed it to Yolande. She glanced at the steel as it reflected the sunlight up to her youthful yet motherly face. How many children had she borne Amadeus? Two, but by the look of her curved belly, she might carry their third.

Yolande clasped her recently purchased pearls and looked back up at Estève. "Show me this pearl of exceeding worth, old gray man. Name your price, and my escorts shall count your gold."

Andreas inched away from his cover to watch Estève and Yolande more closely while also watching the three other onlookers. He hadn't caught Yolande's eye yet, but his heart still beat quickly. Did Estève know who she was? Had he noticed the spies? To make matters worse, Estève was now coming to the most important—and dangerous—part.

As if a cloud had been lifted off the old man's appearance, he slipped a small leather-bound book from a pocket inside his shirt and shuffled closer to Princess Yolande. The book was not studded with gems, nor did it sparkle under the sunlight, yet from its pages radiated the light that could heal the soul of any man or woman, young or old, noble or peasant.

That same little book had once belonged to Raimond Durand. Since his martyrdom, Andreas had carried it everywhere, and only the day before had he let Estève borrow it after the old man gave away his own copy.

Andreas snapped his eyes wider. *No, he wouldn't . . .*

"Here, dearest lady, is the pearl of highest price." Estève held out the booklet. "May it prove as such to you."

I have to interrupt this. If those three men by the fountain witnessed Yolande receiving the Bible, they would surely tell the priest, and only terrible consequences would come from that. Andreas rose, squared himself to Estève, and weaved his way through the market crowd.

But before Andreas arrived, Yolande snapped her fingers and motioned to the escort on her left.

"No, keep your gold. I do not ask for it." Estève pushed the little Bible into Yolande's hands, clasped his over hers, and gazed into her eyes. "The Word of God is free."

Yolande smiled with half of her mouth. "*Merci beaucoup*. Thank you very much, dear man." She tilted her head ever so slightly and quieted her tone. "I have ever wanted to read the words of God myself. Yet this gift reminds me . . . my husband and I met a ship captain last month. Chanforan was his name, if I recall. He told of how he happened upon an old Greek manuscript around the time Constantinople fell to the Turks. That Bible is said to contain the words from the apostles themselves. Perhaps that would be of interest to you, old man." Yolande caught Andreas's eyes. "Or to your friend who so abruptly approaches me."

Andreas planted his feet in the dust beside Estève and relaxed his posture to appear more like a mountain peasant and less like the noble he indeed was. Did Yolande remember him? They had met only a few times, and since then Andreas had grown a beard, so surely—

"The manuscript is likely a legend, dear lady." Estève gave Princess Yolande a bow. "I often hear rumors of such things in my wanderings. But I thank you for your interest, for the Holy Scriptures are indeed precious to me. And I pray they may someday be the same to you."

Yolande handed Raimond's Bible to her escort and turned to leave, but then she glanced at Andreas one last time. Before Andreas could cast his gaze away from her, she gave him a sideways glance and left, followed closely by her escorts.

Had Andreas just seen that? His treasured Bible from Raimond—the man who'd shown him the way to God—now in the House of Savoy's hands. Of course, he wanted Yolande to read it, but that Bible was special.

But what was that about a Greek Bible? They were rumored to be scattered throughout the East, but if one had somehow found its way to the West, his people could find it, translate it—

A glimmer of red caught Andreas's eye. He glanced to the right as the three curious men ducked into the market commotion. Why were they so curious? Who were they?

* * *

Andreas motioned Estève to his side with two low and abrupt waves. Estève shuffled to Andreas while maintaining his smile. But that limp—he needed a cane. The wrinkles that creased Estève's forehead carried with them tales of labor, heartache, and sacrifice. A grand monument would never be built in his honor, nor would a scribe record his deeds in the annals of history. Yet throughout such cities as Venice, Milan, Pisa, Naples, and countless unnamed hamlets, Estève had planted seeds whose fruit would carry on through eternity

"Monsen, you gave away our last Bible."

Estève stared toward the mountains in the west. "True, our last copy of the Holy Scriptures, but if we hurry home, more will be waiting for us there."

Hurry? Estève Malan hurries only when he wishes to sleep at an early hour. Andreas shook his head and mumbled. "Bibles aren't as easy to make as you—"

"What was that?" Estève asked, holding his hand to his ear. "My hearing—"

"It takes months to copy one, Monsen."

"The Lord will provide, as always. Besides, that copy was old and worn."

"Raimond gave it to me before he died. It was . . . important."

"I didn't know Raimond gave it to you, but this morning, I read the first page. Perhaps the names written there also had something to do with it," Estève said with a nod and a wink.

"*Euh* . . . yes, that was also why that Bible was special." Over the past two months of traveling together, Estève and Andreas had entertained many conversations. Often, Andreas asked probing questions about the Holy Scriptures, while other times, their talk would drift to more . . . personal matters.

"'Copied by Constanza Pavarin,'" Estève said.

Andreas strained to keep his mouth and cheeks from the smile they wanted to show.

"Today is the day," Estève said. "Luca and Vitòria's home is on our way back to the mountains, just a short stroll outside the city." He raised both his eyebrows and his voice. "And you know who will be there."

"Since you mention that, we should move. You were too suspicious talking to Princess—" Andreas caught himself.

"Princess? That fair lady was a princess? How do you know?"

Andreas fidgeted with his coat and avoided Estève's probing eyes. He had yet to unveil his true identity to anyone save Constanza. True, he should have explained months ago, but how was he supposed to tell everyone he was the third son of their sovereign, Duke Louis of Savoy? Would they believe him? But now was not the best time.

"For my whole life, I've lived in Savoyard lands, and I'm convinced everyone knows about Yolande of Valois's beauty."

"I understand, but I didn't suspect she was a noble. I'm not privy to such court happenings as you, Andreas. Pray tell, how is she a princess?"

Before Andreas could answer, he spied a red eye patch. Andreas grabbed Estève by the arm. "Come, we should leave. I think we've been discovered."

"How?" Estève tugged his arm back, but more out of protest than trying to escape.

"Three men were watching us and the princess, and they're still curious, it appears."

Andreas pulled Estève back into the crowded market. He ducked low—as low as Estève's height—and spotted a cobblestone path packed with people shoulder-to-shoulder. That was where they needed to be: a crowded road heading south out of Turin. He raised his head and scanned the crowd, and again, the spies had disappeared.

"Andreas, I've preached under guise for fifty years, and I know when I am in danger."

Andreas released his grip on Estève's arm. "You were speaking to the wife of Prince Amadeus, and not only about silk and pearls. To her and everyone else in Turin, we're heretics of the worst kind. If the priests found—"

"I have met my share of priests. Some threw me in a dungeon, others yelled, screamed, and called me names from *heretic* and *apostate* to words I would never repeat. You must understand that this is what God has called us to do. Ridicule, mockery, spit in your face, a sore nose from a man's fist, castle dungeons—yes, even a burning pyre. Do I fear a princess? Or a few men who find us curious?" Estève cleared his throat and placed a hand on Andreas's shoulder. "If you wish to be a faithful servant of Christ, you must accept these facts, my friend."

Those words stung his heart. Andreas had listened to much exhortation and rebuke in their travels, but this was perhaps the most intense. By instinct, he turned his head away and scanned for the spies again. Another shoulder tap made him look back.

"'Be careful for nothing . . .'" Estève's wide eyes and tilted head implored Andreas to finish the passage.

"'. . . but in every thing by prayer and supplication with thanksgiving let your requests be made known unto God.'"

"Excellent. You are learning those words, but it's more important to let those words shape your feelings. Let the Holy Scriptures guide your steps, and thus will you be more like the Savior."

Andreas opened his mouth a little, remembering something else. "The princess spoke about a Greek Bible, and she mentioned the man who carried it on his ship. Chanforan."

"Yes, Chanforan. That name simmers in my memory somewhere . . ." Estève shrugged. "I can't remember, but it doesn't sound Piedmontese. It could pass as being from the mountains, perhaps even Vallense."

"Vallense isn't a language, though. It simply means us—believers in Christ who oppose the teachings of the Roman Church. Whether we're called Waldensians, Vaudois, or Vallenses, we're still Christians, no matter what language we speak."

Estève nodded. "True, but we have our own customs and names that distinctly belong to us. We build houses on land we have farmed for generations. Most of us live here in Piedmont." He passed his hand over the western horizon and the distant peaks. "In the mountains."

"Still, I haven't heard the name *Chanforan*. While we're here in Turin, we should investigate. Imagine how much more our people could accomplish with a Bible like that."

"Rumors." Estève swatted his hand to the side. "Wherever men and women gather, there you will find gossip, tales, legends, and myths. The pope says

Mehmed the Turk is the Antichrist incarnate. The Greeks claim to hold the True Cross, but so do the Latins. Let's not concern ourselves with frivolous rumors."

Andreas bit his tongue. What if the manuscript wasn't a tale? What if God was bringing His words to the West so His people could bring them to common men and women? Shouldn't they investigate? If Andreas could somehow obtain that manuscript, perhaps then the Vallenses would see him as one of their own, with the same loves, the same joys, the same goals. Estève had treated Andreas as if he were a true Vallense, but others maintained a distance. But presenting them with a manuscript could melt away their suspicions.

Andreas closed his eyes. Now was not the time to force his desires.

After Andreas opened his eyes, Estève took a step into the road and motioned for Andreas to follow. "Come, you've been anxious to see Constanza for weeks."

"How would you understand?" Andreas asked with a playful smirk.

"Ah, now you poke at the old barbe, thinking me ignorant of such matters. 'The barbe who's never been married would never understand love,' you think. Have I mentioned I once had all the girls of the Luserna Valley begging to marry me?"

Andreas rolled his eyes. "Ten or more times."

Estève rambled on, ignoring Andreas's answer. They pushed ahead through the crowd and marched on the road that led south and west.

"Turin is quite disappointing compared to Milan and Venice," Andreas said, interrupting Estève's story. A gray church rose to the right, but it wasn't worth more than a moment of admiration. "Still, I can tell the city is growing. I heard the council of nobles in Piedmont moved to Turin."

"Yes," Estève said, "*Torino*, as the locals say, represents the future of Savoy and her appanage, Piedmont."

Soon Andreas and Estève passed through the city gates and into the green countryside. Instead of buildings piled on top of one another, farmyards with pigs or sheep became more frequent. Estève continued to jabber on about the lost loves of his youth, but Andreas concerned himself with the young woman he would soon see.

Four months. That's how long it had been since he had bid her *adieu* last spring. Back then, she was off to work in a new orphanage, while Andreas embarked on his first missionary journey with Estève Malan. It had been a sweet departure back at the Pavarin farm, but much had changed since then. Andreas had learned a lifetime's worth of knowledge and skills since leaving the mountains. And what about dear Constanza? How much had she changed?

Estève led Andreas off the road and onto a narrow path that wound through the rolling hills of the Piedmont plains. "Soon, Andreas, you will experience the generosity and hospitality of the Grimaldis. They are Piedmontese, you know? Neither Luca nor Vitòria were born into believing families, but about six years ago, both were born into Christ's family. Luca was already a successful burgher—not nobility, but not peasantry either.

"Luca, though, he's no greedy merchant in pursuit of the next prestigious transaction. He and Vitòria couldn't bear their own children, so how do they spend all those riches? They take orphans off the streets of Turin and call them their own. The orphanage had grown so large that they needed extra help, and that's why your friends Constanza and Elionor are there."

Estève motioned to his right as they turned off the path into a manicured green lawn. In its midst stood a stone villa worthy of a minor lord. Though far from a castle's size, it still proclaimed the owners' prominence.

"At long last," Estève said, "the home of Luca and Vitòria Grimaldi, and our last resting place before the mountains. We cannot linger, though, for the journey home is still many miles. Our time here will be short."

Four months apart, and he would have only a short time with Constanza.

Andreas let out a long breath. But a short time was better than no time.

*   *   *

The villa rose before Andreas and Estève like a rose among clover. A brick chimney peeked through the clay roof tiles, and a stream of gray smoke trailed on the faint breeze.

Andreas's mouth watered as the breeze brought the scent of baking bread—all he'd eaten that morning was a dry barley biscuit and an old peach. Traveling food made a man wish for almost anything else. A young duck stuffed with carrots and almonds on a silver platter would be best, but unfortunately, this wasn't the wealthy Château Thonon where he had been raised.

Four children appeared around the back corner of the house. Their breathing was heavy and their faces were rosy, but when they saw their visitors, they froze. One girl of about six years raised her eyebrows, showed a half smile, and gave them a little wave.

"Cerea!" Estève called out in Piedmontese.

When they were a few paces from the children, Estève stopped and bent to their level. "*Mi im ës-ciamo Estève. Com-it us-cham-eh?*"

The little girl smiled and opened her mouth, but before she could answer, another figure rounded the corner of the house. Constanza Pavarin.

"We try to use only Romaunt in the house," Constanza said to Estève. She turned to the girl. "Go ahead, you may tell them your name. They'll understand you perfectly well. They are from the mountains as I am."

The young girl raised one shoulder and whispered, "*Me dison Valeria.*"

"Valeria." Estève placed a finger on his chin. "I once met a lady in Venice with that same name. She was so kind and had pretty black curls, much as you do.

But that was long ago." Estève rose and looked at Andreas, then at Constanza. "*Bonjorn, Madomaisèla.*"

Andreas swallowed. Constanza's smile and the sparkle in her nearly black eyes beckoned him to greet her. But how should he? A hug? No, that would be quite improper, and her father would certainly frown upon it. Perhaps he could bow. But that felt patronizing and too formal. So he stood there, silent as a stone wall.

"Bonjorn, Monsen Estève," Constanza said. "I was unaware you two would visit us today. The Grimaldis will be thrilled to see you."

Words locked up in Andreas's throat. As much as he tried to loosen them, they wouldn't budge. Nervous? Perhaps, but that wasn't why he hadn't greeted Constanza yet. Nor was it forgetfulness or lack of words. He could say bonjorn as Estève had, but four months had passed since he'd last seen her. How could he reignite their friendship after so long? Yet he must, because the time here at the Grimaldis' would pass faster than a summer rain shower.

Constanza's eyes drifted to his. Now he had to say something.

"Bonjorn," Andreas said. He smiled and bowed his head a little.

"Bonjorn." Constanza also bowed her head and smiled.

Was that it? What should he say next?

But Estève interrupted the moment before either said anything else. "Where is my friend Luca?"

"He went to the city this morning, but should return before breakfast," Constanza said. "Do you need somewhere to stay tonight?"

"Thank you for your kindness, Madomaisèla, but we must be back in the Angrogna Valley before the sun sets."

"So soon?" Constanza gave Andreas a hesitant smile. She must be waiting for him to speak.

Andreas gave an abrupt nod to Estève, then pivoted to Constanza and mouthed, "I'm sorry."

Constanza darted her eyes to the ground and tightened her lips. She turned to the children and spoke with a quivering voice. "Are your chores finished?"

"Yes," they said in unison.

"Then you may play in the gardens until breakfast. Be sure to wash your hands and feet before coming to the table." She opened her hand to Andreas and Estève. "This morning, we shall dine with royalty."

She said that playfully, but Andreas received it more as irony. They would indeed dine with royalty, though only Constanza knew the truth.

The children rushed off to play, and Constanza turned and motioned for the travelers to follow her.

"How many children are you housing these days?" Estève asked, gazing at the villa from foundation to roof peak.

"As of yesterday, one more. Monsen Luca found Alessia begging for coins in the market, and, as always, he brought her here. I picked the lice from her hair while Elionor scrubbed her skin. She's still sleeping on her fresh mat, and now we house thirteen children."

Andreas gasped. "Thirteen? Is there room for everyone?"

"It's better to be crammed into a few small rooms than on the street."

"True, true," Estève said. "You practice a pure religion, 'visiting the fatherless in their affliction.'"

"Monsen Luca and Madòna Vitòria give everything to these children: their riches, their time, their hearts. I have much to learn from them."

Estève placed his hands on his hips and nodded. "But you, dear Constanza, possess a heart far more precious than glimmering rubies."

She closed her eyes for a moment, bowed her head, and smiled before inviting them through the double doors.

Fresh air flowed through the open windows and doors, filling the vast room with scents of wildflowers and sunshine. Carved stone pillars vaulted the ceiling to an airy height, and an arched entryway led to the garden at the far end of the central room. The children's giggling and laughing drifted inside, while the noise of clanking pottery and footsteps echoed on the walls to the right.

"Is Elionor here?" Andreas said at last.

"She's in the kitchen preparing breakfast with Madòna Vitòria and the older children. We take turns helping with meals."

"Seventeen mouths to feed. How do you manage everyone?"

"It never ends." Constanza held up a finger. "Please wait here for a moment. Let me find Madòna Vitòria."

As soon as she left the room, Estève leaned close to Andreas. "Are you planning on talking to her? Our time here will end before you say more than a few empty words."

"The opportunity hasn't presented itself for more," Andreas said under his breath.

"Opportunity? Only an old unmarried man would say that."

"I'm still thinking about what to say."

"Say you end up marrying her, Andreas, and you're a barbe, gone for two or three or four months at a time while she watches over your children at home. Then you come home after a long journey and all you say is 'Bonjorn'? That's all?"

Andreas tightened his face. "I don't . . . I mean, I understand, but it's much harder in practice." He gave Estève a smile from the corner of his eyes. "Perhaps I should stop taking advice from a seventy-something-year-old bachelor."

"There, see. You know how to speak. If you want to court that charming young woman, be her friend and confidant, not her admirer from across the way."

Andreas lifted his head and nodded. Estève was right. Having preached and formed friendships longer than Andreas had been alive, Estève instinctively knew people—what made them turn like a wagon wheel on a long road.

Constanza reappeared from the kitchen with Vitòria by her side. Vitòria grinned when she spied Estève, revealing faint wrinkles on her cheeks and forehead.

"Dear friend!" She dusted off her hands on her apron and hustled toward them. "If you can forgive us for our lack of silence in this home, we would be honored to house you and—"

"Andreas," Constanza said. She looked toward him with a restrained smile, but she couldn't hide those two little creases that angled up from her nose, just above her cheeks. "Andreas de Bonomo, a close friend of mine."

"Close?" Estève said, chuckling.

Vitòria leaned toward Andreas and feigned a whisper. "I know your name, Andreas de Bonomo. For some reason, Constanza enjoys talking about you. When I saw that brown hair and beard, I knew who you were." Vitòria spun back toward the kitchen but stopped and faced them again. "Connie mentioned you would be leaving this morning. Do stay longer, at least overnight."

Andreas nudged Estève with his elbow, leaned over, and whispered, "They're inviting us."

"You are too kind, Madòna, but Andreas must hurry back to the Angrogna Valley and harvest his fields."

"Oh, fields can wait a day. And these two"—she held one open hand to Constanza and the other to Andreas—"they could use some time together."

"One meal will suffice. Thank you for offering, though."

Andreas wanted to interrupt, but he couldn't sidestep his teacher.

"Come, everyone, breakfast is ready!" Elionor Janavel shouted from the kitchen.

A stampede of little feet soon followed. Water dripped from the children's hands and faces as they streamed into the dining area, and a few dried their hands on their clothes.

"Where is Monsen Luca?" asked a girl with dirt smudged on her arms.

A strong voice answered that question from the front door. "Standing in front of you, Irene!"

Andreas turned to see a slender man jutting a hand out to him.

"I'm Luca Grimaldi. You are . . ." He winked at Constanza.

"Yes, Monsen, this is the Andreas I've told you about."

Despite his lanky form, Luca's handshake was firm.

"And my friend Estève!"

Luca gave Estève a brief but strong embrace before the clamor of children coaxed them to the dining table.

2

The Bible is worth all the other books which have ever been printed.

—Patrick Henry
Statement to his friend George Dabney, eighteenth century

ALL THIRTEEN CHILDREN GATHERED in the villa's dining area. Luca Grimaldi sat at the head of the long table, while Vitòria sat at the corner to his right. Estève sat among the children and held all their attention while he told legends from the mountains. At the opposite end of the table, Andreas sat across from Constanza. Her hair, lighter than her eyes, was parted down the middle and half covered by a white kerchief with two ribbon ties dangling below her neck. To the right sat a boy in his middle years.

Hopefully, Andreas would have time to talk with Constanza alone. But the subject of the Greek manuscript also pressed him. Perhaps Luca Grimaldi knew about that man, Chanforan.

Before Andreas could ask, Luca stood and asked for everyone's attention.

"If you have not met them yet, these are our guests: Monsen Luca and Monsen Andreas." Luca gestured toward the pair. "They will leave us soon, so please honor them. For you ambitious ones, you may practice your Romaunt with them. But now, let us thank the Lord for our dinner."

Why are they so intent on the children speaking Romaunt?

Luca sat and held his wife's hand and the hand of the boy on his other side. The rest at the table formed a circle of linked hands, including Andreas and Estève.

"Our Lord and King, we thank you for the rain and sun, which made the grain to grow so that we may now eat bread. You are merciful to each of us. In the name of our Savior, amen."

Andreas turned to the boy sitting next to him. "What's your name?"

He looked down and mumbled something unintelligible.

"Speak louder," Constanza said from across the table, stern yet with a sliver of a smile.

The boy looked up at Andreas. "Ezio Ranno, but I'm not an orphan. My mother will be away only for a short while, then she'll return, and we will buy our own house and table and maybe plant a garden and . . ."

Constanza bit her bottom lip and rubbed her cheek with her hand. "Yes, we pray every day for your mother and have hope she will return soon." But her downcast eyes indicated otherwise.

Silence came, and Andreas changed the subject. "I was wondering, why are you so eager to teach the children Romaunt? Why not let them speak their native Piedmontese?"

"That was Monsen Luca's idea before Connie and I arrived," Elionor said. "We care for both the body and soul of the children. We want to teach the children the way we do in the mountains, and much of that is from the Holy Scriptures."

Andreas nodded. "And the words from the Holy Scriptures are Romaunt. I understand."

"To be honest, I haven't missed copying Bibles," Elionor said. "I was never careful with it, and I've made my share of mistakes. I doubt there's a copy out there without copying errors."

"Even mine? The one Raimond gave me?"

"That was one of the first that Elionor and I copied," Constanza said, raising her eyebrows. "I'd be embarrassed to find how many mistakes it has."

"Had," Andreas said. "It's gone now."

Constanza drew her head back and peered down the table toward Estève. "He gave it away, didn't he? He's rumored to have that habit, though I suppose it's not so bad."

"No, it is bad, and worse, he gave it to Princess Yolande herself."

Both women widened their eyes, but then Constanza narrowed hers.

Of course she knew. Andreas acknowledged her with one subtle nod.

"Monsen Estève gave away both of our Bibles, and I'll somehow need to find another soon."

"You'll need to wait quite some time." Constanza sliced a piece of bread from the loaf. "The copiers are behind with all the new barbes traveling."

"There must be a better way." Andreas shook his head. "And as Elionor alluded to, who knows how true to the original all these copies are?"

"God gave us a promise," Constanza said. "'The grass withereth, the flower fadeth: but the word of our God shall stand for ever.'"

Any time Vallenses rattled off the Scriptures made Andreas listen with wide eyes, but to hear Constanza apply those words in the proper situations forced him to grin. If he only possessed a pinch of her knowledge . . .

Yes, the manuscript. Before he forgot, Andreas addressed Luca. "Have you heard the name *Chanforan*?"

Across the table, a flame lit in Constanza's eyes. "I work as a maid for a family with that name."

"Now I remember the name," Estève said in a long drawl, holding up his chin. "In the springtime, Luca mentioned you would work for them."

"Yes, I work in the home of Gedeon and Marta Chanforan. They're Catholics but rarely observe their rituals. They are truly honorable people, though quite lavish with their fortune. I also tutor their daughter one day per week."

Luca finished chewing and set his two-pronged fork on the table. "Working for the Chanforans makes Constanza and Elionor's mission here possible, offering a little income to help with expenses, while mostly providing cover for their real work here. A report of two mountain girls serving in an orphanage managed by heretics would cause the priests to pry. With one a maid in a respectable Catholic home, however, fewer suspicions arise."

"Monsen Gedeon often asks questions about my faith," Constanza said. "He's very curious and maybe seeking truth. He seems so hungry . . . very intelligent too. Once, we were talking about the Holy Scriptures, and he said he knows a Greek man—some sort of teacher—who owns an old manuscript of the New Testament."

Andreas dropped his jaw and caught Estève's eyes. "This is certainly the man we're looking for."

"We? I'm not looking for anyone." Estève shook his head.

"The New Testament in its original language," Andreas said to himself. He looked back at Constanza. "Did Monsen Chanforan say anything else about this Greek man?"

"No, he only mentioned him in passing, and I don't remember a name."

"Imagine what it would mean to produce a translation from the language God chose for His words, or to translate it into other languages—not only Romaunt. No more having to teach Piedmontese orphans a language from the mountains." Andreas paused and focused on Constanza. "Do you trust him? If the wrong people discovered we're barbes, they could put us in chains."

"If there's a papist you can trust, it's Gedeon Chanforan."

"You should think of a better word than *papist*. Catholics despise us calling them that."

"They call us heretics," Constanza said, shrugging her shoulders. "Besides, I used to call you a papist."

They all let out a laugh. Andreas asked, "Can you introduce Estève and me to Gedeon?"

"Yes—"

"No. Absolutely not," Estève said. "As I told you in Turin, Andreas, it's a rumor, and if we don't leave soon, we'll never reach the valley by nightfall. Either we stay here and visit for the morning"—he bounced his eyes from Andreas to Constanza and back—"or we listen to this Gedeon Chanforan tell a tale on which a novice minstrel wouldn't waste his voice. Would you dispose of your brief time with Madomaisèla Constanza for that?"

The clanking dishes from the kitchen took the place of voices. Only Andreas, Luca, Constanza, and Estève remained while the children cleared the table of its dishes. Would they have another opportunity, slim as the chance was, to see or perhaps obtain a copy of the Holy Scriptures in their original language? Yet when would he see Constanza again?

"Monsen Luca is letting Elionor and me travel home for the harvest season," Constanza said, but her voice was unsteady. "We won't leave for at least a week, but we would have plenty of time together then."

No, I can't leave her while I chase a rumor. Monsen Estève was right.

"Andreas, please don't let me hold you back." Constanza quieted her voice and nodded. "I want to see you now, but I'm thankful we have the harvest season together. I want you to go meet Gedeon and see if this rumor is true or not."

Estève gave his head a little shake and rolled his eyes at Andreas. "It's your choice, not mine. But we're still leaving today."

Andreas had a difficult time keeping his smile from growing too large. "Constanza, will you please introduce us to the Chanforans?"

3

The patriarchate of Constantinople marks the most likely place in which to look for correct copies of the New Testament. There was the native home of the Greek language, with the truest Grecian culture.

—Robert Lewis Dabney
The Doctrinal Various Readings of the New Testament Greek, 1890

B Y MIDDAY, Andreas, Estève, and Constanza had walked through the gate leading to the Chanforan villa. On either side of the gate stood lifelike stone sculptures. The one closest to Andreas was a man dressed in a toga, gazing toward the door of the house. On the other side, a woman with long hair wore a dress flowing to her ankles. A child tugged at her skirts. Additions, outbuildings, and a fountain bubbling in front of the door showcased the owner's success.

"Monsen Chanforan will be in his study. I'll fetch him.' Constanza opened a narrow door on the facade and faded through the entryway.

"I've seen villas before," Andreas said, scanning from right to left, "and this is worthy of any Savoyard noble. Do you realize how much a property like this costs?"

"More than any man should own," Estève said, staring at the door and ignoring his surroundings. "Men who live in such places think they possess everything."

"We have yet to meet Monsen Gedeon. Perhaps we should wait to pronounce our judgments."

The door opened, and out walked a well-built man who towered over everyone. He wore a genial smile and had his thin hair slicked back. His deep voice echoed from the entryway. "*Mi companhs.* My friends."

Andreas raised his brows. That was Romaunt, and with perfect pronunciation. Why hadn't Gedeon spoken in Piedmontese or French, or even Latin?

Gedeon stepped to the side. "Please, come in. The air is cool and comfortable within these walls."

"This is Estève Malan," Constanza said, motioning to the barbe, "and Andreas de Bonomo. Both are from the same valley as I am."

"Andreas," Gedeon said, holding out his hand. "I wondered if I would ever gain the pleasure of your company."

Grasping Gedeon's hand, Andreas looked up at their host, puzzled.

"Madomaisèla Constanza often speaks your name in my home." He turned to Constanza and nodded to the side. "Yet I didn't expect men of such distinction. Come, a meal is almost ready."

Before they had taken five steps following Gedeon, Estève spoke up. "Thank you for your generosity, but my friend and I have a day of travel ahead of us."

"Where are you headed?" asked Gedeon.

"To the Luserna Valley, then into the Angrogna Valley, but I doubt any rumors from our land have reached your ears."

"Madomaisèla Constanza has told me so much already. But I insist, please stay and dine with us."

Estève drooped his shoulders, stared ahead, and sighed.

They entered the dining room, and Andreas examined the decor. Though some might consider it impressive, Andreas spotted the cheapness masked as opulence. Thin gold engravings and colorful paintings covered two walls, not all four. Above the long table hung a silver ornament holding three large candles, but none were lit. Instead, behind both ends of the table, enormous windows allowed in the sunshine. Three people sat at the table: a woman with stiff posture, a girl of about sixteen, and a boy perhaps a little younger.

"My family," Gedeon said. "This is my wife, Marta, and my two children, Claudia and Addo."

Andreas bowed slightly. In truth, he shouldn't bow to them at all, for he was the son of the duke. How much his position had changed in the few years since he'd left his father's house.

"It's an honor to greet you," Andreas said. He looked toward Gedeon's wife. "Marta is an Italian name, if I'm not mistaken."

"Excellent perception. Marta is from Tuscany. We met there in my early days when I was only a dockhand, loading ships with all the rich men's purchases."

From Andreas's side, Constanza addressed Gedeon. "I spoke with Monsen Luca earlier this week, and he's allowing me to return home for the harvest. Would it inconvenience you if I returned in November? The maids can take over most of my responsibilities, but Claudia's schooling—"

"Of course you may have a furlough," Gedeon said. "We will miss you but will look forward to seeing your charm again."

"Mercé, Monsen Gedeon! I'll do as much as I can today, and I'll be back tomorrow too if that's your desire."

Gedeon held his hand up. "Do as you wish."

"Please see me before you leave," Constanza whispered to Andreas.

"You're not joining us?" Andreas frowned.

"Today, you're the honored guests of the Chanforans of Turin. And me? A mountain of dirty clothes awaits me. The sooner I care for my responsibilities here, the sooner I can leave for home"—she showed a tender smile—"and you."

At that, Constanza slipped away through the door.

The table was covered with fresh fruit: apples, dates, peaches, and bright lemons, a rare delicacy in Piedmont. Instead of wooden plates and utensils, the dishes were porcelain. Andreas hadn't seen this level of affluence since leaving his royal life behind to join the Benedictine Order. He turned his head—five years had passed since then, and eating with Gedeon and his family made Andreas long for his mother and father.

No one hurried through the meal. Except Estève. Before most had taken their first bite of bread and honey, he had cleaned his plate and emptied his goblet. He sat with his arms crossed, fidgeting. On occasion, he gave Andreas a sidelong glance then pointed his nose toward Gedeon. But Andreas ignored him. They had to be polite.

Gedeon did most of the talking. He told of his many ventures scattered throughout the Italian peninsula and beyond. Fifteen ships were registered in his name, transporting their wares from Portugal to Cyprus and each port on the way. He sounded like a man who had come into this world with nothing but, with industry and genius, had amassed an empire built on spices, silk, and precious metals.

As a servant retrieved their dishes, Gedeon's wife and children excused themselves. After a long pause, Andreas wiped his mouth, cleared his throat, and focused on the man who sat across the table.

"Monsen—"

"Please, that is what my servants call me. *Gedeon* is much more familiar."

Andreas had known many wealthy men in his life but didn't remember any willing to drop their titles. Was this man humble—a modest burgher instead of a greedy trader? Gedeon's speech was articulate but not condescending like most wealthy men. A lifetime of trades, handshakes, and business dealings must have made him that way. His voice was commanding, but not straining to the ears.

"Did Constanza mention why we wanted to speak to you?" Andreas asked.

"Yes." Gedeon took a sip from his goblet before continuing. "But first, please tell me about yourselves."

Estève leaned forward. "I'm a missionary. In Romaunt, I'm usually called a barbe."

Gedeon showed a flat, pressed smile and placed his hands on the table. "I guessed you were the ones from the market yesterday."

Andreas and Estève glanced at one another.

"Oh, you have nothing to concern yourselves about here. We are not Dominican friars. In fact, I appreciate your zeal. I wish the men I employ possessed half the passion you Vallenses do." He glanced at Andreas next. "Now, tell me about your background."

Over the past year, Andreas had honed the skill of concealing his lineage, and thus far, it had worked. But Gedeon made Andreas think twice about his words.

"A little over a year ago, I was a brother at Sacra di San Michele, if you can believe that."

"Interesting. Father Antonio is the abbot there, if I am not mistaken."

Andreas widened his eyes.

"You act surprised, but with the connections I must support, I am forced to know the names of every man above a blacksmith, at least in Piedmont."

"The Bible, Andreas," Estève said, but loud enough for Gedeon to hear.

"Yes, I mentioned that to Constanza recently," Gedeon said. "What do you wish to know?"

Andreas swallowed and gathered his thoughts. "To begin, how did you find out about it? An ancient manuscript is no trinket sold alongside cinnamon and sage."

"Oh, but it is." Gedeon nodded and looked away. "Far more than you imagine. I told you I once sailed on my ships before I employed men I could trust. May I present you with some trivia?"

Andreas looked to Estève. He still crossed his arms, but now he only stared at the table in front of him. His eyelids drooped. Was he falling asleep in a moment such as this? Andreas bit his tongue and placed his attention back on Gedeon.

Gedeon picked up a date and held it near his mouth. "What is the grandest city in all the world?" He took a bite of the fruit.

"Some would say Jerusalem, others Rome."

"I've traveled to both, and they are but dust bins compared to—"

"Paris," Andreas said, unsure of Gedeon's purpose but nevertheless amused.

"Paris is grand, but not the grandest. You would name only one city as grand if you could see Constantinople. 'Queen of Cities,' some call it. Ask any man who has visited it, and he will say the same."

"Of course, but the Greeks were defeated, cast out, vanquished by the Turks. The sultan destroyed Constantinople."

"Andreas, I like you, but let me give you a little advice: don't listen to what you hear from the clergy or nobles. They lie. The Turks may have blown a hole through the Theodosian Walls, but they are rebuilding what little they destroyed. They crowned Constantinople as their capital, and now, not seven years later, it shines brighter than it has in centuries."

"On the backs of Greek slaves, I gather."

"They lost the war, so they paid the price," Gedeon said. "Business often ends with the same outcome. There can be no sympathy, no cordiality. A trade is a trade, and money is money. Some win, and others lose." He blinked and drew his hands together in front of his face. "But I'm digressing. How does that manuscript fit into all this about ships and trade and Constantinople? I was there before Mehmed surrounded the city with his armies and navy. The clever Greeks knew what was coming, and those who could pay for passage fled like a flock of starlings. You must realize, as much as cities like Venice and Florence possess scholars, philosophers, and theologians, there is no comparison to what Constantinople had been for over a thousand years.

"I sailed into the Golden Horn and unloaded my goods. The Greeks had nothing for me to buy and transport home, other than people. So I made them pay. Did you see the statues around here? One load of cargo paid for them, and it was a ship full of refugees."

The sound of monotonous breathing flowed through the room, and as Andreas suspected, there sat Monsen Estève, sleeping through everything. True, the room was warm, his belly was probably full, and Gedeon's stories were long. But they might be listening to the most exciting opportunity for Vallenses in generations.

Gedeon smirked at Estève's snoring and continued. "As usual, it took three weeks to sail back to Genoa, and I met a few of the important people aboard. One man requested to be dropped off in Pisa, right on the Tuscany coast. He was headed to Florence to teach. Ioannis Argyropoulos was his name—very Greek, I know.

"He had an abundance of barrels and crates with him, and normally I'm indifferent to my passengers' cargo, but this time, I asked. Inside the crate he kept closest to him, right beside his hammock, was a copy of the Bible written in Greek."

"Do you think it's genuine?" Andreas asked.

Gedeon shrugged his shoulders. "I'm a trader, not a keeper of icons and relics."

"That's no icon he possessed. If it's real, those are the very words of God, preserved in the original Greek tongue. A manuscript such as that"—Andreas paused to find fitting words—"it could change the world."

"I would be more cautious with what you say here in Turin. Some might flay and burn you for thinking such a thing."

Andreas bit his lip and looked back at Estève, who now had his head resting on the back of his chair. The morning was waning, and if they didn't begin their journey soon, they would be stuck somewhere in the darkness. Estève would be sure to let Andreas know too.

"You mentioned his name. Argy-something?"

"Argyropoulos." Gedeon pronounced the name with ease. "One of those skills you learn sailing a ship on old *Mare Nostrum*."

"He's in Florence?"

"Last I heard. But listen, Andreas. I asked him how much it would be to lighten his load—that's what I do, buy and sell for a profit. I offered one hundred golden florins, and he laughed. He proceeded to call me a Latin buzzard, though

I'm not much of a Catholic. Then he said he'd sell it for no less than one thousand florins—"

"One thousand florins!" said a voice that had not previously been taking part. Few sounds could awaken Estève, but apparently a thousand florins could.

Andreas said, "That's more than . . . with that sum—"

"Indeed, I would consider an offer on my villa for one thousand florins. Of course, I refused Argyropoulos's offer. It was nothing but disintegrating parchment to me."

They all sat in silence, waiting for someone to press on with the conversation, until Gedeon said, "I will be in Florence for business in November, and I would be honored to introduce you to Ioannis Argyropoulos. Would you join me there?"

"Please, we do wish that." But then reality smacked Andreas on the back of his neck. Or was that Estève? He turned to see the barbe's wrinkled smile.

"Mercé, Monsen Gedeon," Estève said. "We appreciate your hospitality, but it would be prudent for us to make our way home now."

Gedeon leaned back in his chair and swung his gaze from Andreas to Estève and back. "You are Vallenses, are you not? Isn't the Word of God priceless to you?"

"Yes, of course. We would pay anything," Andreas said. "That is, if we had the money."

Estève pulled at Andreas's arm and whispered, "Tell him mercé. I'm ready to leave."

"I'd like to see Constanza before we leave," Andreas whispered back.

Estève's tugs showed he either hadn't heard or didn't care.

Andreas closed his eyes, sighed, and stood.

After quick handshakes, Gedeon lifted his chin. "My offer for November stands ready for your acceptance."

"We will remember it," Estève said, pulling Andreas toward the door.

That seemed rude. And why the rush?

*   *   *

Estève plodded through the villa's gateway and turned right onto the road. Andreas followed ten paces behind, not yet ready to speak with him. God had set everything in motion—He had brought them to the Chanforans, where they were treated near to nobility. Gedeon had described, in detail no less, a manuscript of God's Word—one they could verify, study, and use as a basis to sow the Holy Scriptures into the hearts of every man and woman, young and old, no matter their social status. The cost was massive, perhaps impossible, but why should they flee?

Sweat dripped from Andreas's brow and down his neck as they journeyed toward the descending sun. His hat sat squarely on his head, but he lowered it to better shield his eyes from the torch in the sky. Spending the remainder of the day walking would be miserable.

Andreas quickened his pace to catch up with Estève as they neared the crossroads where they would turn left toward Pinerolo and beyond that, the mountains.

"I'd hoped to see Constanza before we left," Andreas said.

Estève continued forward as if he didn't notice Andreas. But instead of turning left toward home, he stayed on the same path.

Andreas stopped, shaded the sun from his eyes, and peered toward the distant peaks. "That was our turn."

Estève turned to eye Andreas. "Do you assume I'm lost?"

"I've found you to be quite adept at plotting your path," Andreas said, holding out his hand, "but the mountains are that way."

"Tomorrow. Tomorrow we'll take that road. We would fail to make it to Pinerolo before sunset, and I'm not interested in tripping over my feet or yours on a night without *la luna*."

Andreas smiled. "Are we not leaving today?"

"Give your thanks to Monsen Gedeon for that. This morning's frivolity has cost us a full day, but you're unconcerned about that, I see."

Andreas tipped his head to one side, then the other, and gave a little laugh. "The Chanforans weren't as bad as you imagined, I assume."

Estève's hand flew up in dismissal. He turned his eyes back toward the road and continued forward.

"Why did you rush to leave? Perhaps you were a little drowsy."

"It had nothing to do with that. And believe me, Andreas, you'll understand in a few years."

"What was it, then? Yes, he's somewhat pretentious, but he was also friendly."

"Men like Gedeon don't impress me. The gold, the statues, the glittering shirts, and talk of all his business. It's nauseating. Give me a poor soul drenched in his own filth over Monsen Chanforan." Estève spoke in a harsh accent. "'What's the difference between Gedeon Chanforan and the man on the street?' you ask. Very little. How I see it, one finds pleasure in his filth, and the other is ashamed of it."

"That's a curious comparison," Andreas said. "Gedeon seems to possess good character."

"And the Antichrist's religion. At least the immoral and irreligious realize they are godless, and in the darkest corner of their hearts, they know they need a Savior. Gedeon Chanforan? He is the ignorant man. He spends his wealth on pleasure and prestige while he unknowingly skirts the cliffs of hell itself."

Estève was right again. Feelings, emotion, intellect—they often conflicted with spiritual discernment. "I apologize, Monsen, and I agree, in God's eyes, he is an empty man in need of a Savior." Andreas cleared his throat. "What about his offer?"

"I don't remember—"

"You mean, 'I was snoring when he was talking about that.'"

"Perhaps I was, but the price—what was it? You gasped and said, 'One thousand florins.' Then not more than a moment later, in a very low and unbelieving tone you said, 'One thousand florins.' You said it a few more times, but why belabor the point? Tonight, I will hear your voice while I sleep: 'One thousand florins, one thousand florins, one—'"

"Were you surprised by that amount?"

"No. Don't forget the phrase Gedeon recited ad nauseum: 'I'm a businessman, I'm a businessman—'"

"I understand." Andreas shrugged. "Could we raise the funds ourselves?"

"Who is *we*? If you mean me and you, perhaps if one of us married a Medici or into the House of Savoy."

If he only understood the irony.

Estève clapped his hands and stopped walking. "That's it! I'm unmarried, and now I only have to find someone to arrange a marriage."

"All jesting aside, it would require an investment from all Vallenses—every family, every hamlet, every valley."

Estève continued walking, kicking the gravel. "Do you realize how much you'd be asking?"

"It would be like a tax for every family—"

"Oh, everyone will adore that idea—a tax. As if the Lord of Luserna doesn't already burden our people with dues."

"It wouldn't be a real tax."

"You would be faced with a near impossible task trying to convince our friends in the Angrogna Valley of your idea, and that's not to mention other churches. Can you envision walking up to Constanza's brother, David—how many children does he have now?"

"Four, and one soon to arrive."

"Thus, Andreas de Bonomo asks David Pavarin, father of five, 'Pray, we heard about a genuine copy of the Holy Scriptures. All you must do is give me your farm income from now until the millennial kingdom. Your family may starve.'"

"You've made your case." Andreas stared into the distance. "I would need to convince every family, and still, we may never collect a thousand florins."

"Try to imagine it this way. God has preserved His Word for fifteen centuries, miraculous by itself. You may not recognize it, but hearing about this manuscript gives me renewed hope that one day we may see our aspirations for the Holy Scriptures realized. I agree, the Bible is for every man to read and understand with his God-created intellect. Having a pure basis from which to translate—I believe it is God's will as much as you do. Yet I also know we are sinful men who tend to jump to conclusions."

Andreas nodded. "I see, and I also know what you're going to say next."

"Pray about it. Don't just say you will—I mean, talk to God and let His will sculpt your will into his purposes."

As they walked, Andreas's thoughts wandered toward Constanza. That is, when he could divert his attention away from the yellow furnace blasting him from the sky. Tonight, perhaps, they would have a moment together.

Ahead of Andreas and Estève, two men walked toward them on the same road. Andreas examined the travelers as they approached. His muscles tensed when he spotted the red eye patch. These were two of the men from the market.

He was convinced now. Spies were on their trail. Worse, they might be here to assault him and Estève there on the road, in the light of the afternoon sun.

Andreas lowered his voice. "Monsen Estève, those men up ahead are here for us."

"You're imagining the worst," Estève said, not bothering to whisper.

"We should avoid them."

"We will do no such thing. If they wish to harm us, do you think I'll be able to run away? And if they don't, we'll look like skittish ducks running from the clouds."

"Stay close and try to appear normal."

"I am, so perhaps you should worry about yourself."

The men drew within a few paces. At first, Andreas avoided making eye contact, but he also wanted to gain a better assessment.

As the men passed on the left, the closest one eyed them. He wore a tattered leather cap atop curly hair, while his companion had nothing covering his head. Both were sweating as much as Andreas, but neither appeared discomforted.

They passed, and nothing happened. Their scuffing faded into the distance until only Andreas and Estève's plodding remained. But something was still wrong. Of the scores of people in the market, why had those two men appeared on a country byway?

Andreas looked to Estève, who curled his lips into a victorious grin.

It must have been nothing.

4

The Bible, the whole Bible, and nothing but the Bible is the religion of Christ's church.

—Charles Haddon Spurgeon
New Park Street Pulpit, 1860

WHEN ANDREAS AND ESTÈVE returned to the Grimaldis' orphanage, the children were already asleep on their mats. Estève also found his bed, but Vitòria was kind enough to wait with Andreas for Constanza.

She didn't return from the Chanforans until long after sunset.

"I believe you two wish to enjoy time alone," Vitòria said in the quiet sitting room.

Andreas and Constanza both nodded.

"The worst of the heat has gone with the sun. You should sit outside tonight. I have plenty of knitting, and I would be honored to accompany you. This is the perfect excuse for quiet time after today's exuberance. Few tasks still my spirit as threadwork does."

Soon Constanza smoothed her pleated blue skirts and sat in the grass near Andreas. She wore a loose white shirt, squared at the neckline, with ruffled sleeves ending just below her elbow. Over her shirt was a dark leather vest, laced across the front with leather strings.

Andreas and Constanza gazed toward the distant mountains. A faint orange hue filled the western sky and outlined the tall peaks above the valleys they called home. To the left, dark clouds pressed toward them. Though the air was heavy, the steady breeze cooled Andreas's brow. Crickets chirped in a hurried rhythm while a bullfrog bellowed from a pond downhill. Underneath the villa's eaves, Vitòria sat, intent on her thread and needles.

Constanza, with her eyes cast on the faraway peaks, lowered her voice and said, "I love nights like this. So peaceful."

"We might need to find a place inside if those clouds continue this way."

"You were obviously raised in a castle." Constanza glanced at Andreas and giggled. "It may look like a storm, but all farmers recognize those clouds." She peered again into the distance. "They may soon invite us to the most spectacular performance in the realm."

Andreas took his eyes off the sky and regarded Constanza. "You're speaking in riddles."

"I won't spoil the surprise. Just wait."

A moment passed, and Andreas bit his lip. He had planned what to say, but now, sitting next to Constanza, the words vanished.

After a little digging, he remembered. "Why do you sit here with me? Last year, I was nothing but a scheming papist—"

"I'm trying not to use that word anymore," Constanza said with a touch of sarcasm. "But yes, you were, yet now you're my brother in Christ."

"What did you see in me that others didn't?"

"That you're royalty." A quick burst of laughter escaped her lips. "No, I've often wondered about that. After you fell into that ravine during your boar hunt, when I cared for your wounds in my house, my papà had a stern talk with me. Did I ever tell you?"

Andreas shook his head.

"He was worried I was succumbing to an unbeliever. I denied it, of course, but that was when I realized . . . I understood—"

"When I first met you," Andreas said, "you were little more than a curiosity. But before anyone else—except maybe Raimond—you cared for my soul. You saw through my religious cloak and gave heed to my soul instead."

"It felt as if it was the only right attitude."

"In time, especially after the inquisitors captured you, I realized you were more than a Scripture-quoting shepherdess."

Constanza loosened her kerchief and moved a hairpin forward. "When you rescued me from the friar, I recognized how you differed from other men. You then revealed that you're actually 'Prince Andreas'"—her accent was playful—"but you don't act like a noble. I suppose you still speak like a noble, and the way you perceive the world is quite lofty. But not your spirit. Your character fits a Vallense farmer far more than a prince and certainly more than a celibate monk."

After a silent pause, Andreas leaned back and pressed his hands into the dry grass. "What does our future hold?"

"For as many answers as I have, there are more questions. You're training to be a barbe, and you're committed to that, for which I will always encourage you onward. Andreas, the Lord made you for this life."

"I wonder about that. I'm a son of God now, and I know He has called me to service, but our people—they still have suspicion in their eyes when I'm with them. And you should have seen me in the market yesterday. I approached a man with a pouch of spices before telling him the good news, and I dropped the pouch onto the road."

"You were trying to sell something? That can be quite challenging. Few barbes wear the cloak of a peddler. That may be where Monsen Estève has found success, but for you—each barbe has a talent God can use."

"I have yet to find that." Andreas sat up straight again. He couldn't show his discouragement to Constanza.

She lowered her voice to a hush. "You're a noble. There may be something you could do with that."

"No, Constanza. My father would be appalled simply at the sight of me sitting here with a peasant heretic woman."

Constanza smiled. "Peasant heretic woman. I might claim that title."

Andreas chuckled, then continued. "My life is tangled in the web that is the House of Savoy. Whenever I see a soldier or walk through a place bigger than a hamlet, I become alert. What if I'm recognized? And then there was Estève's conversation with Yolande in the market yesterday. Did she recognize me? I pray she didn't."

Far away, bolts of lightning flashed through the hot darkness. Andreas listened for thunder, but instead of powerful claps, it sounded like the distant grind of a millstone. As the display of summer lightning danced through the clouds, Andreas recounted his conversation with Gedeon.

"If I could bring a Greek manuscript back to the valley, perhaps then they'd see me as more than a former monk."

"That amount of money, though—outrageous."

"It feels so far from my grasp."

Now the sky was ablaze with flashes. Andreas stared into the distance. "You were right, and not a drop of rain."

"I find it both ominous and thrilling at the same time. The power behind those flashes may be unknowable to the lost, but we know the One who rules the skies."

Glancing behind, Andreas noticed Vitòria's nodding head. "I believe our time out here is coming to a close," he said, pointing at Vitòria with his chin. "Monsen Estève will want to be gone before the sun rises, so I need to sleep soon."

Constanza yawned. "Me too. But first, what should we do about . . . us?"

"Wait. Before we move further, I'll need to first gain your papà's trust."

"He loves you, Andreas. It's not you at all—it's me. I'm his youngest daughter, and he's afraid to let go, though he is softening on the matter."

"Patience will help both of us. As for now, a season of harvest awaits. In a week, we'll both be back in the Angrogna Valley binding sheaves of grain, and the manuscript will probably still be in Florence."

"Will we see each other before you leave?"

Andreas raised his eyebrows. "Before sunrise?"

"Tomorrow was supposed to be a restful morning," Constanza said in a playful tone, "but if you prefer to see me . . ."

At that, they said *bona nuèch* and proceeded to their rooms. As Andreas lay between alert and asleep, memories of lightning, Greek Bibles, Constanza, and one thousand florins drifted through his mind.

Until a sharp smell pierced his senses. Smoke.

5

They shall be seized for trial and penalties, who engage in the translation of the sacred volumes, or who hold secret conventicles, or who assume the office of preaching without the authority of their superiors; against whom process shall be commenced, without any permission of appeal.

—Pope Innocent III
Papal bull, 1215

CONSTANZA TURNED FROM ONE SIDE TO THE OTHER on her mat and sniffled. A faint whimper came from the room next to hers and Elionor's. Probably Zama with a bad dream again.

Another cry, and Constanza pried her eyes open. A knock sounded on the door, and a cough came with the voice.

"Madomaisèla!"

Valeria.

Constanza sniffled again, but this time her muscles tensed. That smell—smoke.

She shot up and strained to catch the scent again. The knock repeated as she reached to grab her dress.

"Madomaisèla, the ceiling. There's a fire up there!"

Constanza slipped the dress over her head, fastened it, and called for Elionor. "Ellie, something's on fire."

Elionor rubbed her eyes and stretched. "What?"

"A fire. There's a fire in the house."

After a quick blink and an eye rub, Elionor sprang to her feet and gathered herself while the girls' whimpering grew into a cry.

Constanza opened the door. A wall of smoke smashed into her lungs, causing her to sputter and cough. The smoke stung her eyes like a hundred angry hornets. She flung her hands up to cover her eyes as little girls ran around her into the room.

Instinct told her to flee, but she couldn't see and had to make sure the children were safe.

Valeria spoke through the crying. "Madomaisèla, there's smoke in our room, and the roof fell down, but Fosca and Ave are still in there."

Elionor bent down and held Valeria's shoulders. "Is there fire in your room?"

"I don't know . . . there's so much smoke, and we couldn't see, and my eyes hurt."

The room they were in—it had no windows. If the roof was on fire, it would collapse, trapping anyone there. They had to escape through the smoke, and someone had to save Fosca and Ave.

"I'll find the others," Constanza said. "You take the girls outside."

Six girls clung to Constanza and Elionor, but that would be no way to escape.

"Girls," Elionor said, "you remember us always telling you to obey your elders, yes?"

A few signs of acknowledgment rose above the weeping and coughing.

"Now it will be more important than ever that you do as we say. All you girls must follow me. Once we're outside, we'll be safe." Elionor gathered the girls close. "You can't hold on to my skirt out there, so we must all hold hands. And don't let go."

Constanza moved to the door while Elionor helped the girls hold hands.

When she opened the door, heat and smoke blasted into her face. Her nostrils burned, and her vision blurred. Coughs stormed from her lungs, but she couldn't stop them.

After one brief glance over her shoulder, making sure the others were on their way, she spied the girls' room through the sweltering haze. How could anyone survive the smoke? What if the roof fell? But then she tensed. Andreas and Estève were upstairs. If the roof was on fire, they would be in far greater danger. But they were grown men. Finding the two girls was most important.

She squinted and assessed the room. As Valeria had said, the ceiling burned red and orange. A pile of burning timbers smoldered in the far right corner. To the left, two bodies moved underneath a wool blanket. Whimpers trickled toward her.

Constanza lifted her neckline to cover her nose and ran toward the blanket. She slid to her knees and wrapped herself around the girls.

"Girls, it's Constanza. You're going to be fine, but we must leave."

"The smoke," Ave said, her voice muffled by the wool.

"I know, but if we don't leave, the roof will fall on us, and we'll be hurt badly."

"Can you carry me?" Fosca asked from under the blanket.

"I can't carry both of you—"

"Please, Madomaisèla Constanza, I'm—"

Something snapped far above and crashed like an avalanche onto the stone floor. Ashes and fiery splinters burst across the room and singed Constanza's cheeks and hands.

Collapsed timber blocked their one path of escape. Were there windows in the room? Constanza scanned the outside wall, but her hopes were vanquished. What could they do?

Smoke billowed from every direction. Constanza couldn't help but cough as she searched for relief, but the only comfort would be underneath the blanket. When her head slipped inside, her lungs heaved for the fresher air and her eyes begged to be rubbed.

"We're safe in here, aren't we, Madomaisèla?" Fosca asked.

But Constanza couldn't answer.

"God knows where we are, doesn't He?"

Constanza lost what little breath she had. The simple, trusting faith of a little girl.

"Girls, we're going to pray."

Sweat dripped from her brow as she begged God for deliverance. The heat and smoke charged like a bull from outside their little refuge, and though the blanket shielded them from the smoke, they couldn't survive long here.

More crashes thrashed through the room. Then a new sound came.

Chopping. Hammering. Voices.

"Constanza!"

Andreas.

Another voice rose. "Constanza, Fosca, Ave! Can you hear us?"

"Yes, yes, we're here. We're trapped and can't move."

The chopping continued, then abruptly ceased. Underneath the blanket, the girls cried and gasped for air.

A firm hand touched her back through the blanket, and a man coughed.

It was Monsen Luca.

"Come with us," Andreas said. "The path is clear for now."

Strong, confident, redeeming hands helped lift Constanza and the girls to their feet and pointed them toward the path of escape.

"I can't," Constanza said after a cough. Her lungs ached as if she'd been stabbed with a flaming sword.

"I'll lead you," Luca said. "Andreas, here, take the girls."

Andreas hoisted a girl into each arm, wobbled, and took careful steps toward the door.

Timbers suddenly fell from the ceiling. Everyone coughed. Constanza's eyes strained, then closed. Monsen Luca pulled her through the room.

When the heat was more at her back then all around, she took a full breath. Her lungs expressed their thanks, but the coughs kept coming.

"We're almost out," Luca said. "I think we're safe now, if that helps."

A cool breeze flitted across her cheeks, and all at once, the air became fresh and familiar.

She cracked her eyelids to see her surroundings. They were near the garden. Fosca and Ave sat under a tree nearby. Madòna Vitòria hugged one girl while Elionor rinsed the eyes of the other with a cup of water.

"Sit, sit," Andreas said between coughs. "I'll draw water for you."

"Is everyone . . . did anyone—"

"Everyone is alive, thank the Lord."

Constanza closed her eyes, but not because of the burning. A flood of relief washed over her soul.

"Monsen Estève is doing poorly, though. He's having trouble breathing." Andreas pointed to the right. "I figured . . . once you're able"—he coughed—"you could check on him."

Constanza covered a cough and nodded. She watched through the haze and smoke as the remainder of the villa's roof faltered and tumbled into smoldering rubble. So much love was in that home, and now it would be but a memory. Any of them could have perished. Andreas could have died. What would she have done without him?

After a rinse, her eyes no longer felt as if they were splashed with lye, but it would be days before they stopped stinging. As for her lungs, they would recover, though it would also take time.

But around the corner, a gang of men held torches as they shouted. "Leave our land, heretics! Rid us of your filth!"

Another scream. "Satan-worshippers!"

She looked at Andreas, but her eyelids forced themselves shut again from the stinging.

"We can't stay here," Andreas said.

Vitòria's voice came from behind. "Monsen Estève, though. His breathing."

Constanza opened her eyes to a slit just as a rock flew through the air and landed a short distance away. "We'll burn you with that house if we need to!"

"Are you able to walk?" Luca asked Estève.

"I . . . I think I could." His voice was weak and subdued.

"Constanza, Elionor, Andreas, gather the children," Luca said. "We cannot stay here."

6

The Waldense antagonism to the Romish church was throughout based on the Bible; the character of the Christian was, according to them, in a Christian life; and Christian life itself a gift of God.

—Alexis Muston
Israel of the Alps, 1852

How are you managing?" Andreas asked Estève.

"Managing—no more, no less. But please don't concern yourself with me." He glanced at the children clinging to Andreas's hands.

Flames glowed and flickered from atop the slope behind them. The villa—nest of hope and security for thirteen tender orphans—would soon crumble into a pile of ashes and heat-cracked stone.

Andreas peered a few paces ahead toward the Grimaldis. Their lives were upended, and the once distinguished couple now lacked a home. Who would have done such a thing to such a gentle couple? Andreas winced to think that he and Estève might have brought the calamity. Suspicious eyes in the market, two men on the road, the red eye patch—who were they?

Estève's wheezing and coughing worsened.

"Stop," Andreas said. "We need to rest."

"There's a stand of trees past the rise, so we can hide there," Luca shouted.

The children, especially the younger ones, whimpered about sore feet or tired legs, but all complied. Estève, however, had to lean over. He stopped, put his hands on his knees, and drew in three long breaths, bringing another coughing fit.

"We're almost there, Monsen."

Heated voices flew through the night air from far behind. "Are we being followed?" Estève asked.

"I . . . maybe . . . I don't know."

"Andreas, I am sorry. I should have listened to you about those men from the market."

"That's behind us now, and I pray the danger stays there too."

Estève took one more breath and struggled to stand. "I'm ready now."

Soon they entered the forest. Constanza sat and rubbed a toddler's back while Luca and Vitòria spoke in low voices. Andreas and Estève sat nearby.

"We need someplace safe to stay," Luca said, "one owned by people we can trust." He looked at Estève. "We are southwest of . . . what once was our home. Do you know anyone nearby who would take us in?"

Estève coughed and held up a finger. "Once, there was an old widow who lived along the Sangone, but she passed into eternity last winter. Otherwise—"

"What about the Chanforans?" Andreas asked.

Constanza approached from the right and said, "Monsen Gedeon would surely help."

"He may be generous, and I respect him greatly, but he's a Catholic. Also, his home is in the opposite direction, back toward our pursuers." Luca shook his head and stared at the trees. "I've been suspicious for months, which is why I try to keep an ear to the rumors in Turin. But this? I've neither seen nor heard anything pointing to violence at this scale. Sadly, I know of no one in the city whom we could trust."

"Then we must flee to the mountains," Estève said, "for only there will we find a true refuge."

Andreas dropped his jaw. "It would take us until tomorrow with all these children, and you're in no condition to travel that far."

"I can make it. I may be old, but"—he wheezed—"I'll keep up."

Vitòria gazed at her husband, then looked at the children with sympathy in her eyes. "The mountains? We'll have to travel all night."

As if to answer her, shouts drifted down the hill. But now they were closer.

"We have no other choice," Estève said. "Don't forget the One who watches over us."

After a brief prayer, they gathered the children and advanced deeper into the forest. Darkness cloaked the ground as the children tripped and struggled through the dense undergrowth.

Before long, they left the woods and came to a road.

"Turn left here," Estève said, "and soon we will come to Pinerolo. From there, the Luserna Valley is only a short distance further." He pointed his chin left and guided them forward.

Estève's breathing had become shallower, his steps more unsteady, and his need for rest more frequent. Andreas walked alongside him, but doubt settled in his mind. Estève couldn't make it—not a miles-long journey through the moonless night.

They plodded ahead like sleepwalkers on the straight, dark, uneventful road to Pinerolo. Andreas carried a girl whose name he didn't know, moving her from one arm to the other as he walked. Luca did the same. Constanza and Elionor dragged along two children each. Other than crickets and the occasional coyote, the only sounds were dragging footsteps on a dusty road.

Hours passed. Which would end first: the night or the journey?

Within sight of the Pinerolo cathedral's lamplit bell tower, Andreas turned his ears toward the north. Nothing. Their pursuers must have returned to their homes for the night. For now, the children were safe. Should they rest while they had the opportunity or trudge onward?

"They're wearing out," Constanza said, eyeing the children. "Could we not camp outdoors tonight—somewhere safe and off the road?"

Luca nodded. "We can't all continue, and with our coughing, we've likely startled all of Piedmont awake while we burn a trail through the countryside."

"I . . . can . . . stand," Estève said.

"Monsen, we have hours of walking left, and it will soon be all uphill."

"Leave me. I can find my way to the mountains once . . . once I . . . rest." More coughs.

They were so close, over halfway to the Angrogna Valley, and they couldn't abandon Estève on the roadside like a crippled horse. Andreas peered through the blackness, trying to discern the children's condition. Ezio wobbled on the balls of his feet as he waited, while the younger ones sat on the long, dewy grass with sleep-deprived eyes. No, Andreas couldn't force them to continue or their wellbeing would be at risk. They had to stop, at least until the sun rose.

They moved off the road into a field, pressed down the rye stalks, and huddled together for a moment of respite. Andreas volunteered to keep a watch on the road until dawn.

An idea came to Andreas as he sat there. Not a perfect one, but it was worth trying. An old friend lived nearby. Two springs before, Victor of Bricherasio had been far from a friend. In fact, he had robbed and abducted Andreas. But Raimond Durand had seen him converted, and Victor had helped Andreas and Constanza escape from Dominican inquisitors. Perhaps Victor and his family could help the children.

Just as an orange haze simmered over the eastern horizon, voices carried on the wind from the northwest. Andreas looked back toward the road and tensed at the sight of distant flickers. Then a shout echoed through the darkness.

If only I could give them more time to rest.

Andreas roused everyone from their slumber and whispered to Luca and Estève. "We can't stay here, but if we walk a little more, I know a friend who might help us."

After a few nods from the adults and some encouraging words for the children, they veered further away from the road and onto a farm trail.

Soon they rounded Pinerolo from the south and forded the shallow Chisone River before coming to the hamlet of Bricherasio. Despite the day being young, the townsfolk had risen from their slumber. This was a Catholic hamlet, though, and any set of eyes could relay their whereabouts to their enemies. There would be no safety until they arrived at Victor's.

Eyes drooping and feet slapping, Estève's pace slowed to a stumble.

Andreas came alongside and caught him before he fell. "Almost there."

Estève didn't respond. Andreas encouraged him along, Estève's body becoming heavier with each step.

"Help is on the other side of this bend," Andreas said. He turned and scanned the path behind them. Though there were no sounds of pursuit, he had to be sure no one followed them. The last thing they wanted was to lead their pursuers to an unknowing family's home.

Andreas helped Estève to the ground by Elionor, then approached the shack's entrance with Constanza. Dirt and moss covered the doorstep, and the windows were open to the elements.

"No one lives here," Constanza said.

"Victor was here in the spring." Andreas held a hand over his eyes to shield the sun. "There's a garden planted, a field is sown . . ."

Behind him, the children sat in circles, some sitting straight and others slouching with droopy eyes. A boy picked at grass and threw it at another. Despite the danger and uncertainty, the children found time to play.

Constanza stood with faint circles under her eyes. It had been a hard night for her too, and now that morning had arrived, they all needed real rest—more than a few moments of restlessness in a dewy rye field.

Andreas knocked on the door, but the sound echoed back at him.

"They must have left," Constanza said. "I heard talk months ago about more families from the plains moving into the mountains. It's become too risky to live out here as a Vallense."

Andreas pressed on the door, and the wood splintered and cracked. Sounds of squeaking and skittering feet reverberated through the shack.

"Rats," Andreas said to himself.

"You can open that door if you'd like, but I'm going home. If we have a little strength left in us, we could reach my family's home before dinner."

"Monsen Estève can't walk, so you all should continue and leave us here. He might gain the breath to continue later today."

"I think you're dreaming. If he were a young man, then yes, he could walk later today. Have you considered carrying him instead?"

Andreas cleared his throat. "Carry him? All the way to the Angrogna Valley?"

"No, but at least until we're among friends. You and Monsen Luca could both help him."

As they stood there, rowdy voices and shuffling echoed up the pathway. Luca gathered the children and ducked into a nearby field. Constanza and Elionor trailed behind and hushed the children, while Andreas crouched closer to the house and listened.

First came footsteps, then muffled voices, and at last, a distinct Piedmontese dialect.

"The old woman said they came this way," said a man's voice.

Andreas looked through the grass but couldn't see anyone.

"This house is abandoned," said another man.

"Furio, we've been out all night. They're just orphans, so we can find and catch them later."

"No!" said a new voice. "These heretics are sorcerers of the worst kind. Vallense spells have bewitched us and concealed their path. They also stole children from good Catholic families, so we must save them before their blood is spilled on some high mountain altar."

"Nothing here. I think the old lady lied to us."

"They're heading to the mountains, so they would've gone west," said the leader, Furio. "We'll go that way."

Andreas stood above the grass and peered toward the voices. At first he saw nothing, but then he spotted the same red eye patch and curly hair from the market the day before. Or was it two days now? The days had woven themselves together.

Before long, the voices and footsteps melted into the west. Andreas crouched again and crawled back to the group.

"One man I've seen before," Andreas said. "They're definitely trying to find us."

"And we won't let that happen," Constanza said. "We're a short walk from the valley entrance, and once we're there—"

"We carry no promises of safety. Victor's house was supposed to be a place of refuge, and we've found it's not."

"We should continue," Luca said. "I will help with Monsen Estève."

Andreas glanced at Estève, who sat with his knees up. His breathing was shallow and eyes nearly lifeless, but somehow he managed a smile—one of those smiles only a man who had seen heartache, disaster, and victory far too many times could show.

Estève forced a few words from his lips. "We'll make it."

Though Estève was small, carrying a man was far different from carrying a couple of children. Andreas heaved the old man onto his back, adjusted him upward, and staggered forward. If not for the gravity of their ordeal, he could have laughed.

The sun shone its morning rays on the mountains towering ahead. What were once distant gray figures on the horizon now dominated the landscape. Deep, misty forests blanketed the foothills under the craggy heights, and the fertile plains through which the refugees walked flowed into the wide gap in the mountains.

Last year, Andreas had walked this same road with Raimond. The first time he entered the Luserna Valley, he'd expected to encounter witches, sorcerers, and heretics. Now he came knowing he would find welcoming families, diligent farmers, and true followers of Jesus.

"Which way?" Luca asked.

Constanza, with a girl holding her arm, pointed to the left. "There's no mistaking it now—that is Mount Friouland, and the taller one shaped like a horn of silver is Mount Viso, most majestic of all peaks." Her hand moved to the right. "And Mount Vandalino stands there on the other side of the valley." Constanza closed her eyes and inhaled. "Do you smell that? Home."

The valley soon opened before them like a scroll. Smoke billowed from chimneys while barley and rye fields grew to waist height. On a rocky knoll to the right, a flock of white sheep grazed in the lily-studded grass. In this valley lived a people who had long ago found their ark of refuge nestled under the alpine peaks.

But we're not safe yet.

Instead of risking the main road, Andreas led them on a sheep path through fields, groves, vineyards, and fallow lots. Estève had become heavy, and Andreas ached from skin to sinew. Luca must have seen him struggling, for he soon came up beside Andreas and took the barbe.

"Ah, much better," Estève whispered. "You're not as bony as Andreas."

The path soon led down into a dark forest sprinkled with the occasional pine tree.

Without warning, a shout sounded out through the trees.

"Stop, heretics! This is where your road ends."

Five men descended from the rise to the left, all with crude weapons in hand. A few children cried out, and Estève mumbled a prayer. Constanza, Elionor, and Vitòria held their arms out, shielding the boys and girls.

"We don't want to harm you," said the man with the red patch. "I only ask that you follow us back to Turin."

"We've been running all night," Luca said, "and are in no condition to travel."

"Who do you think has been tracking you all night? All of us are exhausted, so please submit, drop your weapons—"

"We carry no weapons," Andreas said. "We are simply trying to reach the mountains."

"To hide as all the rest of you Vallenses do? Do you think those mountains will protect you forever?" Furio's eyes glowed with hate. "You don't know whom you're trifling with. Now please, submit and come to us."

"Where will you take us?" Luca asked.

Furio adjusted his patch and took a step toward them. "I only wish to take the children to the priest in Turin."

Andreas took a step backward and tightened his lips. They were so near to their destination. Why now, after all these miles, were they overtaken by these pathetic ruffians?

Luca stood tall and bold. "The children will not follow you back to Turin, for their place is in the mountains with us."

Furio pursed his lips and nodded to his companions. One unsheathed a sword, while another leered at Constanza and Elionor.

Depraved man. Andreas set his jaw and moved closer to Constanza. In no scenario would he allow the man to touch the women or children without a fight. He reached to his side, wishing something other than a belt were there. They had no swords, no spears, no axes. Was this how his life would end? Fighting a swordsman with his bare fists?

The blast of a ram's horn resounded through the forest. Andreas jumped.

Their pursuers' stances faltered. They cast their eyes from tree to tree, straining to find the source of the sound.

"It's a ghost," one said. "An evil Vallense phantom."

The horn blasted again. Furio said, "It's nothing but a conjurer's trick."

"We're not conjurers, but you passed a boundary you're not allowed to cross," a new voice said from behind.

Andreas glanced over his shoulder and saw a familiar face moving from the brush. Victor of Bricherasio.

"Drop your weapons and leave these people be. You're surrounded, and there's no hope of you winning this fight. Leave now and don't come back, or we'll feed your carcasses to the hogs."

"You lie," Furio said. "I see one man standing before me."

"I've got twenty crossbowmen hidden in these woods, and if you think you can outrun us, just know that we've all grown up with these trees. We know every stump, every oak, and every little stream. We'll find you."

Furio stiffened his neck. "Our priest will hear of this rebellion."

"First, you tell your priest to stop scaring little children."

Furio's gang slammed their axes, clubs, and short swords on the ground, flinching at every sign of movement from the branches and bushes. Furio made sure to spit on the ground in front of their abandoned weapons. "You may have won this time, but know this: the time of the Vallenses will soon end."

Andreas shook his head. Meaningless rambling of a defeated man.

Furio and his companions turned and marched away.

Victor waited until the men were out of sight before he spoke. "What are you doing out here, Andreas, and who are all these people?" He scanned the company until his eyes fell on Constanza. "It's a pleasure to see you again, *Tòta*."

Constanza pushed aside the niceties and motioned to Estève. "Our friend here is very sick and in need of water and rest."

Victor turned his head to the side. "And the children?"

"They are all orphans from Turin," Andreas said. He explained the villa's destruction and the night spent escaping toward the valley, then asked Victor why he had abandoned his home.

"Too dangerous. The neighbors were always threatening my wife, my boys." Victor clicked his mouth toward the trees and waved. "Boy, you can come down now."

From a thicket came a lanky youth with a quiver strapped across his back and a bow in his hand.

"That's my boy, Dino—a fine woodsman if I've ever known one."

Constanza passed her eyes over the trees. "Where are the rest?"

"That's it. Just me and my boy."

Andreas narrowed an eye and dipped his head. "I figured you were bluffing."

"Do you wish I'd told them the truth?" Victor said with a laugh. "Me and Dino are members of a Vallense group that guards the valley entrance. No man passes this way without someone knowing."

"Since when do Vallenses post their own guards?"

"After the Dominicans' crusade last summer, the men from La Torre and Luserna wanted nothing of the sort to happen again. And today you saw their wisdom."

Luca stepped forward and introduced himself. "Mercé, my friend. How can we repay the debt we owe you?"

"You can begin by moving further into the valley. It's unsafe here, and if those men come to their senses, they may guess they've been fooled."

Andreas remembered Estève. Elionor sat next to him on the forest floor with an arm around his shoulder. "He can walk no farther," Andreas said to Victor. "Do you know somewhere we can take him? We're trying to make it to the Angrogna Valley."

"Up ahead, there's a barber. He could help the old man."

"Martino Borno in San Giovanni?" Constanza huffed. "He's older than Monsen Estève."

"Better than no one," Victor said. "He helped my youngest boy through a bad fever last winter. We'll take him there, and you can be on your way."

Andreas walked to Estève and leaned down. "You need rest. Can my friend Victor take you somewhere safe and peaceful?"

Estève nodded, placed a hand on Andreas's shoulder, and smiled. "As long as he doesn't jostle me about in his arms as you did."

As they gathered the children, Luca asked, "Which way from here?"

"We are now in Madomaisèla Constanza's realm," Andreas said with a bow toward Constanza. "She will guide us the rest of the way."

Constanza stood beside Andreas and grinned. "We will sit at my father's table before the sun sets, and there we will find friends, refuge, and rest."

Exhausted plodding marked the last leg of the journey. Though they no longer fled from a phantom in the darkness, exhaustion overwhelmed them—most of all, the thirteen children. Andreas held a boy's hand. Weariness might have demanded otherwise, yet he stood straight, pulled his shoulders back, and trudged onward. By now, the sun threw all its rays at the stumbling company. Half the children whimpered and whined at each new bend or rise in the road, while the other half plodded ahead like walking statues. They passed a farm whose inhabitants gave them water, a blacksmith who filled their bellies with cheese and sausage, and others who offered beds and respite. But they had a destination, and though it was a little further, it would be exactly what everyone needed.

Soon after leaving the forest, they veered right and ascended the foothills. The flat, open fields gave way to towering oaks that stood above small stone houses and pasturelands dotted with boulders.

"Welcome to Val Angrogna—the Angrogna Valley," Constanza said. "My meme said Angrogna means 'blackthorn.' It's a flowering shrub that grows in the high meadows."

The path wound atop the crest of the valley wall. Down the hillside to the left ran a gentle stream that, during springtime, became a rushing, foaming, misting torrent. To the right, the hillside varied from steep to gentle slopes until the trees thinned and the land crested to form the natural barrier that hid the Vallenses from the outside world. Since Andreas had first ascended into the narrow defile, he had thought of it as the center of Vallense faith. Fewer families dwelt here than in the more prominent Luserna or Rorà valleys, but the Angrogna Valley trained and sent out more barbes.

In time, they came to the crossroads. Downhill was the meeting place of the church, straight ahead led to the old Lauras farm, and right would lead them to their destination. Elionor bid the company adieu and headed toward her mother's home but assured everyone she'd rejoin them tomorrow. After a quick breath, Constanza turned right, squared her shoulders, and led the group uphill one last time.

*   *   *

Before the weary company took five steps into the barnyard, Constanza's family met them with hugs, tears, and questions. The Pavarin farm was a wonder of the valley. Father Antonio back at Sacra di San Michele would be amazed if Andreas ever had the opportunity to explain Nicolaus Pavarin's methods of farming. Whether or not the rest of the Vallenses knew it, his methods of farming were the future. Nicolaus had designed a system that used terraces and ponds to capture moisture, warmth, and nutrients. To most, this land would have been an inhospitable and infertile piece of rock and fallow soil, but Constanza's father had sculpted it into a flowering hillside of plenty.

"Mamà, a man gave us something to eat, but now the children need to sleep," Constanza said. "I know it's the middle of the day, but they've been walking all night and morning."

Luca Grimaldi approached Armanda, Constanza's mother, and bowed his head. "Madòna, I will repay any costs."

"You'll need to speak to my husband about that," Armanda said, "but for now, you must regain your strength." She looked to Vitòria, but Constanza stepped toward them and made the introductions.

"These are the Grimaldis—the ones who house the orphans in Turin."

Armanda stepped forward and embraced Vitòria. "Mercé, mercé." She kissed Vitòria's brow. "You have cared for my daughter, and for that, I am indebted to you. Now, let's find everyone a place to sleep."

Constanza's older sisters and her brothers' wives must have heard the activity, for they soon were there helping as well. They sent their small children back to their houses to fetch blankets, clothes, chamber pots, and water. Before long, they had spread the orphans throughout the Pavarin home, each lying on a mat with eyes fastened shut. Armanda Pavarin offered the Grimaldis her room. At first they refused, but with a bit of prodding, they agreed and slid into bed.

Soon Armanda, Constanza, and Andreas sat at a table near the kitchen. Susanna, Constanza's oldest sister, sat down last after covering a little girl with a blanket.

"Where is Papà?" Constanza asked.

"He's with your brothers down at the old Lauras farm. They're digging a new well."

"You still call it that? Over a year has passed."

Andreas laughed without making a noise. *I still call it that too.*

"I want to see Papà soon, so I'm going to go—"

"You need to rest as much as anyone," Armanda said, putting her arm around Constanza. "He will be back when you awaken."

Constanza yawned. "Yes, I suppose I should find my mat." She yawned again. "But can I tell you what happened?"

"Was it inquisitors?" Susanna asked, concern etched into her face.

"I don't know. Perhaps." Constanza looked to Andreas for an answer, but he had none better.

Andreas's thoughts left the little stone house and rolled down the steep slope toward Constanza's father. What would he think about the danger Constanza had encountered? Andreas had to see Nicolaus and explain. He rose and stretched, and a yawn came too.

"I'm going down to the old Lauras—to the lower farm. I need to see if my planting has thrived . . . or not."

Armanda, Susanna, and another of Constanza's sisters looked at each other and smirked. "You'll need to see for yourself."

Before Andreas left, Armanda made sure to embrace him and whisper in his ear. "Mercé."

Constanza followed him, and when they were away from the others, she stiffened her posture. "If you see my papà, please don't . . . I mean, I want to tell him about the summer. There have been so many blessings." Her eyes brightened. "The manuscript, though. You must tell him about it."

Andreas nodded, said adieu, and struck off on the path downhill.

Though overgrown with summer vegetation, the path along the stream was the fastest way to the old Lauras farm—

There, he'd done it again. Old friends had once lived there. Monsen Gerald Lauras, slain in the old Roman fort by Genoese mercenaries. And Johan Lauras—other than Raimond, Johan was the first Vallense who had befriended Andreas. Soon after Gerald's death and the defeat at the fort, Johan had spiritually deteriorated until he left without so much as a word to Andreas.

With the Lauras farm abandoned, Nicolaus Pavarin had arranged a compromise with the Lord of Luserna and allowed Andreas to be the steward of that land. So, last spring, Andreas plowed, planted, and labored. The farm might never be as fruitful as the Pavarin terraces, but it was his own labor, his footprints, sweat, and blood, that cultivated the land. He lifted his chin as he came out of the forest and into the clearing.

The barley grew to his waist, too young to harvest but clearly thriving. Andreas walked into the field and pinched off a head of grain. *I thank You, my God, for Your abundance.* The former monk, son of the duke, had planted a plot of hillside land worth harvesting, thanks in part to his few years of tending vineyards at the monastery.

Clanks of metal against clay and stone came from behind the farmhouse. Andreas aimed his feet that direction and marched off to his meeting with Nicolaus Pavarin.

Andreas approached the well where Constanza's father and brothers were digging. They had dug a large perimeter hole of about a man's height, and a ladder gave them a way out. Bartholomeo Pavarin, Constanza's older brother, was the first to discover him. "Look who's returned!" he shouted to the others in the well hole. Bartholomeo wiped sweat from his brow with the back of his arm. "This is your well, Andreas. We could use your help."

Was he joking or serious? The other brother, Francesco, and their sister's husband, Abel, turned their heads upward too. Nicolaus was last.

Andreas leaned down and offered a hand to Nicolaus. "I have two months' worth of stories to tell. But Monsen Nicolaus, I need to speak with you first. It's important."

Bartholomeo and Francesco chuckled at one another.

"What is it?" Andreas asked them.

Nicolaus brushed his hands on his pants and shook dirt from his hair before accepting Andreas's grip. With what little strength he possessed after a sleepless night, Andreas pulled Nicolaus from the hole.

Francesco said, "Is it about our sister? If you're wondering, she has yet to return from Turin. But she said she might visit after harvest."

"She's already here," Andreas said.

Their expressions ranged from puzzled to shocked.

"I traveled with her and Elionor—" He caught himself. Now was not the time for all the details. He must talk with Nicolaus first. "May we speak elsewhere?"

"Certainly, but your tone concerns me."

They walked across the farmyard, which needed trimming and clearing—yet another task for the harvest time. Nicolaus limped on his left leg, shattered by Catholic mercenaries last summer. If anyone knew the forces arrayed against Vallenses, it was Nicolaus Pavarin.

When they passed out of the sons' earshot, Andreas jumped to the subject. "The orphanage in Turin is no more. Burned to the ground by . . . we're unsure who. It could have been inquisitors or someone else who hates Vallenses. Everyone is safe, thankfully."

"We can't escape the powers of this world." Nicolaus sighed. "We may see victories like last summer, but until Rome is cast down into the pit, our destiny is one of insecurity, if not violence and oppression."

They sat on the step outside the house, and for the rest of the discussion, Nicolaus said almost nothing. Instead, he shook his head and asked the occasional clarifying question. Pressed between the sweltering heat and exhaustion, Andreas's words slurred together, and his thoughts straggled behind his words.

After a long pause, Nicolaus said, "I should've never allowed her to leave."

Andreas blinked. "With all honor to you, Monsen—"

"You'll understand one day. The burdens of a father"—he caught Andreas's eyes—"and those of a husband can't be so effortlessly cast aside." Nicolaus stood and stretched his back, then helped Andreas off the step. "I'll speak with her . . . tomorrow after she's rested. But I thank you for protecting her."

"She . . . she is everything to me." Andreas turned his knees toward Nicolaus. "There is one other matter I wanted to mention. Monsen Estève and I learned about a Greek Bible that could unlock all our aspirations about the Holy Scriptures. If we—"

Nicolaus straightened his mouth and gave one abrupt nod. "That is interesting. Now, you find yourself some rest, and we'll talk about the fields tomorrow."

Andreas turned his head to the side. Did Nicolaus take him seriously about the manuscript? Though Nicolaus listened more than most, why did the Vallense men so often push Andreas's ideas aside as if he were still a novice monk? He rubbed his eyes. *I do need rest.*

After giving Nicolaus a parting embrace, Andreas opened the door and ignored anything between it and the bed. He could have washed. trimmed his beard, or downed a skin of water, but all that called his name was sleep. Sweet sleep. Answers would have to wait.

7

The Waldense language, a patois of French and Italian, is remarkably soft in expression, and well suited to those melodies of the heart of which it has long been the interpreter.

—William Beattie
The Waldenses, 1838

ONSTANZA COULDN'T REMEMBER the last time she had slept so long. Even dreams had escaped her memory. Deep into the morning, she lay on her back and stared at the plank ceiling. The same knots and grains had marked the wood since she was a little girl, bringing memories of home and laughter but also of sorrows and shattered aspirations.

Constanza turned to her side. Smoke lingered on her clothes, her skin, and worst of all, her hair. It wasn't the same scent as cooking and washing clothes over open fires. No, it was the smoke of tar, timbers, and flaming ruins.

A window poured summer sunshine into the room, inviting her to stand from the mat and take in all the day offered. Before she did anything, though—before she ate, or before she said a morning prayer—she would at least rinse her face and hair. Perhaps she might bathe more completely in the stream later in the day.

When she rose, her lungs reminded her again of the smoke. She coughed and sputtered, making her muscles shiver and ache. She took a few short breaths, steadied herself, and moved the curtain that separated her room from the rest of the house.

The room was still, and children lay scattered across the stone floor, covered in animal skins. A girl stirred, but all eyes remained closed. Mamà and the Grimaldis sat at the old dining table, sipping steaming drinks and whispering.

Constanza smiled at Mamà, Luca, and Vitòria. With a gravelly voice, she said, "Bonjorn."

She stopped and held her breath. *I must look as if I crawled from a cave filled with all manner of putrid things.* Nothing covered her head, her eyes felt puffy and sore, and her hair—she dared not imagine how it looked. *At least Andreas isn't here.*

"I made tea." Mamà held up a clay pot, the same one they'd had since Constanza was a child. "You should take some before the stampede arrives." She glanced at the sleeping children.

Constanza gave a little grin, then bit her bottom lip. To be back home with Papà and Mamà was wonderful, but with children everywhere, it would be far from the promised peaceful furlough.

"I'll drink some after I wash," Constanza said. "Is Papà awake?"

Mamà laughed and almost spilled her tea. "Why would he change? He's been awake since before the sun."

"Papà is growing older—"

"And the older he grows, the more he digs his feet into the soil. Your Papà is the same man he's always been, except more so."

"I want to tell him all about yesterday," Constanza said. "You too, of course. But first, I want to speak with Papà."

Constanza left the house and walked to the well. She lifted water from the same hole she had drawn from hundreds if not thousands of times. The splash of cool alpine water on her clammy face washed away the tears, sweat, and smoky grime. A pour of that water and the brush of her fingers through her hair removed the worst mats and tangles, but a good wash with lye and rose petals—if she could find them—would make her presentable again. But before that, she needed a kerchief. And to talk to Papà.

She scanned the farmyard for any signs of Papà and, after seeing nothing, moved her eyes to the first terrace. On the far right, a bush full of *ampoas*—raspberries—stirred, with a hat bobbing over the top. The leaves and branches shook and jolted, but not for a harvest. Instead, Papà looked to be chopping down the bush.

I should surprise him!

Constanza crept around his back and waited for a moment. He yanked at the roots, leaned back, and pulled, but although a few branches snapped, the shrub remained latched to the earth.

"Do you need any help, Papà?"

He jerked his head around and grinned from one side of his face to the other.

"Constanza!" He ran and wrapped his arms around her, squeezing hard enough to take her breath away.

She coughed. "Oh, Papà, there's nothing like your hugs."

He loosened his embrace a bit, but still, those burly arms around her and those scratchy whiskers on her cheek—it had been too long. A tear fell, but when she tried to wipe it away, her arm refused to leave its place around Papà's chest.

He held her at arm's length. "You look unhurt. And healthy. Those Piedmontese took good care of you."

"Have you met the Grimaldis yet?"

"They were still sleeping when I came outside. Your mamà told me all about them, though." He hugged her again and gave her a light tap on the back. "God has preserved you, and for that I am thankful."

"The Lord preserved us all, Papà, and we are here to serve Him another day."

"Let's go to the fourth terrace. I want to show you everything. The hogs are fattening, and your goats—they're strong, and the does are giving us rich milk."

Papà led her on winding paths past ponds and pigpens, oat fields and orchards. On the third terrace, as they passed a stand of shade trees, the air grew unusually quiet. Constanza chewed the inside of her cheek and concentrated on the tall grass nearby. This was where she had hidden from the inquisitors last summer before they abducted her, and where she had watched the evil men cripple Papà with their clubs.

Did he need to know every detail about the escape from Turin? No, she could sprinkle that in Papà's ears over the harvest season. She needed to speak with him about her future first. A barbe and his wife managed a home for widows in Asti, and in nearby Pinerolo, there was a growing church that needed a woman to train the children to read. The list continued. Small churches, some hiding in the shadows and others operating more openly, needed help.

When they reached the fourth terrace, Constanza interrupted Papà's updates about the farm. "After the harvest, there are other places for me and Elionor." She waited for his expression, but his frown brought a shadow to the hillside.

Papà shrugged and glanced to the side. "I heard men pursued you all the way from Turin. You should thank the Lord you're alive."

"I am thankful, Papà, but . . . but . . ." Andreas must have told him more than she'd asked, yet it was bound to come at some point, and there was no virtue in hiding the details. "An entire season remains to pray about this, and by the time winter arrives, perhaps danger will have subsided."

"Connie, thirteen orphans sleep at home who have been through a night of fear, uncertainty . . . pain. You can find more than enough ways to serve others here at home."

Yes, the children were precious and enjoyable, and teaching them the Holy Scriptures was truly eternal work, but they also made the days long, the washing endless, and dinnertime noisy. Constanza walked to the bush Papà had been pulling, leaned down, and gripped the base. She might not be able to do it herself, but she could help. With all her strength, she pulled and heaved. Nothing moved.

Papà stooped alongside her and wrapped his hands around the thickest branch. Together they pried the shrub from the earth.

Neither said anything. Constanza wiped her hands on her skirt, and like a looking glass, Papà did the same on his pants.

He smiled at Constanza until she said, "We need each other, Papà."

*   *   *

How could this have happened? Monsen Estève had first introduced her to the Grimaldis, and Andreas had been the one who encouraged Papà to let her go. Now she was at home again with no assurance of ever returning to the plains. Yes, the children were there, and some had not yet believed the gospel. And as the Epistle to Titus said, young women ought to be keepers at home. Still, being latched to the Pavarin farm again made her throat tighten.

Constanza rubbed her eyes, which still stung from the lingering smoke. She walked down the path to the old Lauras farm with methodical steps, eager to open her soul to Andreas. The trees swayed as a breeze danced through their leaves and branches. Beside her, the stream trickled down the slope toward the torrent far below. This was where the ruffians had captured her last summer. Andreas and Monsen Raimond had tried to protect her but were outnumbered by her captors.

From down the path, the sounds of humming—no, singing—entered her ears. It was a hymn every Vallense boy and girl learned before they were waist high. Yet this was a man's voice.

> Open the door for the Savior;
> Hear Him, forsake your sin.
> He knocks, and He pleads to enter;
> When will you let Him in?
>
> Ask not what riches you'll receive;
> Seek the Savior alone.
> Cast off the world and believe;
> Sit with Him at His throne.

Andreas's singing voice made Constanza take a deep, cleansing breath. Some remnants of his monastic chants were in the timing, but the way he formed the words and hit each note . . .

Constanza stood in the middle of the pathway until Andreas rounded the bend.

Andreas widened his eyes, and a smile followed. "A bright *angelet* on an alpine byway—what a pleasant surprise to greet the morning!"

"It's past midday now." Constanza forced herself not to grin too much. How did he express such lightheartedness after everything that had happened? Her hair was disheveled, her eyes swollen. Embarrassment would have been a natural reaction, but Andreas's tender gaze and silly grin made her sigh. Did he not see her ragged appearance? "I'm surely the most wretched angel that ever walked under the sun."

Andreas shook his head and chuckled.

"I spoke to my papà, and he said you met him yesterday."

"We talked a little, but then he must have noticed my sleepy eyes." Andreas shrugged. "He was concerned about the men who tracked us. I wish I knew who they were. They spoke Piedmontese, so they're likely from Turin. Then there was that phrase the leader said: 'The time of the Vallenses will soon end.' Your papà was most inquisitive about that. I wanted to talk about the Bible manuscript—to see what his thoughts were—but his mind was elsewhere."

Constanza closed her eyes for a moment and shook her head. "What if Monsen Estève is right? It sounds like a rumor, a myth from a mystic Greek in flight."

"I can't stop pondering it, and I still believe we should pursue it."

Another breeze swept through the forest. The mighty tree Constanza leaned against creaked while the branches far above swayed with the wind. No one had swatted away Andreas's dreams, but hers? Unrealized dreams were taken away with the wind, and her hopes buried underneath a heap of gravel. Tears welled up, and her chest tightened with uncertainty. Was she really going to cry in front of Andreas?

Yes, and she let it all out. Constanza wiped her eyes with her hand.

"Is it the manuscript? Are you upset that I'm still thinking about it?"

"No, it's not that." She looked up at Andreas. "I'm unsure if Papà will permit me to leave this valley again."

"Connie, neither of us is going anywhere between now and the first frost. We have fields and gardens to harvest, fruit to pick—"

"Goats and sheep to breed," Constanza said, sure to emphasize her responsibilities.

"And don't forget the Grimaldis and the orphans."

Constanza bobbed her head and let a slight smile show. "How could I forget?"

"They admire you far more than you realize. All those girls want to be like you. I see how they watch you walk, how they imitate your voice. You are the woman they want to be someday."

She tossed up a dismissive wave and gave Andreas a gentle nod. "Thank you for listening to me. I just needed someone to talk to."

"And cry to."

"Yes, that too." Constanza wiped the last tear from her cheek and sniffled, then ran her fingers through her hair. Why did Andreas have to see her like this? She still needed to bathe, and she hadn't put on a kerchief yet. Her cheeks warmed as she patted the sides of her dress. "What were you headed our way for?"

"I was going to ask your papà or one of your brothers for a stone to sharpen my scythe," Andreas said. "The weeds have nearly overtaken the house."

"Won't you stay and eat? Mamà has some things prepared."

"Is there enough? With all the new mouths to feed—"

"Mamà raised eleven of us, and any of my brothers could eat more than all the orphans combined."

A breeze of relief swept over Constanza as she walked with Andreas back to the farm. She suppressed the urge to dwell upon the future, despite her feelings of loss and disappointment. For now, she focused on the land and the bounty it would bring. God had allowed them to be stewards of these hillsides and terraces, but not without toil and a little pain.

8

They had received from certain lords some uncultivated lands on certain conditions; who, by indefatigable labor and constant cultivation, had made them fertile in corn and pasturage; that they knew how to endure toil and privations with patience.

—Guillaume du Bellay, French diplomat
Report to King Francis I of France, 1544

AMID THE HAY MOWING, house maintenance, and well digging, Andreas suddenly found himself in the middle of September. He gazed over his harvested barley field, whose freshly cut sheaves stood stacked and scattered across the sloped land. This was his harvest, the fruit of the earth God had given him. Each stack had started with a handful of seeds he had sown in the springtime. With sunshine and rains sent from above, those seeds had sprung from the soil and had grown to full height.

But a harvest was never guaranteed. One late frost could decimate the tender plants and bring poverty for the next year. A midseason blight could encroach on the mature plants and wither the stalks to dust. But this year, the Lord of the harvest had provided. Not for him alone, for all the farmers in the valley had harvested a bounty of rye, barley, flax, and wheat.

On the edge of the field bordering the forest, Andreas heaved an ax into a fallen tree. A few days earlier, he had noticed it leaning over the field, likely because of a windstorm. He and David Pavarin were forced to fell it, and now it would provide a stack of firewood.

When he was partway into the chopping, a cool breeze blew through Andreas's hair. He looked to the northwestern sky. Dark clouds had formed and were rolling toward him.

Andreas dropped his ax and scanned the field. Those sheaves had been drying for a day. Two days would be better. If the clouds unleashed a shower on them right now, it could mean a spoiled crop. There was no time for delay—he had to stack them in the barn before the storm destroyed everything.

He ran to the closest sheaf and hoisted it onto his back. It was dry and ready for storage. Another glance across the field made him push off with his legs and jog. His knee buckled with the pressure—a lingering pain from his encounter with the Dominicans the year before.

Reaching the barn, he threw the sheaf into the far corner and rushed to the next one. *I should have listened to Monsen Pavarin. He told me I should bring in the sheaves in the morning, and now my crop might be ruined.*

Again he looked up at the approaching clouds, and his pulse quickened. *I need help.*

Instead of picking up another sheaf, Andreas bolted into the forest. The Pavarins knew what a storm like this meant for drying grain. They had been the wise ones, cutting and binding their sheaves days before and sheltering them under barn roofs. Andreas's land was their investment too, so they would be eager to help.

After a long climb, Andreas ran into the Pavarin farmyard. Constanza stood over a kettle, washing clothes while children—a mixture of the Grimaldi orphans and her nieces and nephews—teetered somewhere between work and play.

"I need your help," Andreas said between pants.

Behind him, Nicolaus said, "Miquèl's and David's families are already on their way. We saw the clouds too."

These Pavarins—they know how to farm. "More than a hundred sheaves need to be stored. If we all head down, we'll fill the barn before sundown."

Nicolaus shook his head, laughed, and called for everyone's attention. Before long, a small force of men, women, and children from at least eight families marched back down along the creek. Andreas hurried along beside Constanza, waiting for her victorious remark. But it never came. Instead, she remained silent, but with a barely noticeable grin.

Andreas passed under the last overhanging branches and again looked over his field. He took a long breath and asked Constanza, "Can we do it?"

She placed her hands on her hips. "Not by standing here and waiting."

Andreas jogged toward the closest sheaf and wrapped his arms around it. Constanza and her niece Madalena grabbed the next. Soon everyone filed into the field and found a sheaf to carry.

Andreas would have walked faster, but with all the help, why not enjoy Constanza's company? "I never could have done this without your help," he said. "I should have started this morning—"

"We wouldn't have let you starve." Constanza gave him an indirect glance and a smile. "As much as Papà wears the cloak of an infallible farmer, he's made his share of mistakes. Three springs ago, he sowed the flax in muddy soil, thinking we would have an earlier harvest. But the seed rotted before it sprang up, and we had nothing to make linen with. I'm thankful you didn't see my dresses that year. They were quite tattered and thin."

Something wet fell on the back of Andreas's neck. "Is that—" More drops fell on his hair. They were almost halfway finished, but many sheaves remained.

Constanza adjusted her kerchief and bowed her head as the rain became steadier. Madalena looked up at the sky. "*Tanta* Constanza, we're going to get soaked."

"It's only a little water. It won't make us wilt or wash us into the river."

But soon the sprinkle had grown into a shower, and their hurried walks accelerated into jogs slowed only by the dampening ground. Andreas saddled his back with another bundle, then looked across the field. Only a quarter of the shaves remained. Yet he didn't want to lose one stalk to rot.

He could carry two. A few paces away, close to Constanza, stood a smaller bundle. With rain streaming down his forehead, Andreas ran toward them.

But a root or stone, or maybe his own clumsiness, caught his feet and jolted him forward. He stumbled and fell face-first into the earth.

What had happened? With scratchy stalks pressing his body down, Andreas closed his eyes and let out a puff of air. From above, the sounds of laughter crept into his ears.

"I will remember that tumble for all my years, Andreas de Bonomo."

He lifted his head to see Constanza cackling and Madalena frowning.

"Shouldn't you be carrying your sheaf to the barn?" Andreas said. "The grain's going to spoil."

Constanza's laughing continued. "I would pay the price of the spoilage to watch you fall once more."

Andreas pressed his hands into the mud. He would need to brush this bundle clean after all was finished, but at least his body had protected it from the worst. Constanza and Madalena slogged forward a couple of paces ahead. Andreas caught up with them and walked beside Constanza as if nothing had happened, but all she did was stare forward and hide her laughs behind closed lips.

Andreas picked up his pace. Though he carried more, his legs were longer. He would reach the barn first.

He leaped into a sprint and shot a quick glance over his shoulder. Constanza pulled Madalena along but missed the deep furrow under her feet.

And into the mud she fell. Madalena still held one end of the sheaf, but Constanza's landed on the ground. It was Andreas's turn to chuckle.

"That was unfair." Constanza stood and brushed herself off. "You tripped over your own feet, but I . . ."

"One should not laugh at a fallen brother."

Amid giggles, Constanza huffed, grabbed a handful of earth, and threw it at Andreas. It smudged underneath his chin.

Andreas couldn't let that go. He found a clump of grass and threw it back, but Constanza moved aside.

The clump landed on Madalena's feet, and she clenched her fists. "We're trying to work, and all you two can think to do is play?"

Both Andreas and Constanza looked at each other and laughed. After a few more mud slings, Andreas adjusted the load on his back and walked to the end Constanza had dropped. "I'll help you, Madalena. I wouldn't want your tanta's dirty hands all over my barley."

Madalena let her end fall to the ground. "You carry it all then."

"We were just enjoying the rain," Constanza said. "Don't assume everything to be so serious." She shook her head and helped Andreas carry the sheaf back to the barn.

By the time they arrived, the last bundles were being stacked. But all eyes were on Andreas and Constanza. His and Constanza's clothes were smattered with chaff, grass, and mud. Smears of dirt traced Constanza's cheeks and brow, and her hair was half out of her kerchief. Some Pavarins laughed, while others rolled their eyes.

"Next time," Nicolaus said, "Andreas and Constanza can manage this all themselves. They seem to enjoy the rain."

Andreas swallowed. "I can't repay all of you, except to feed you. I'm no baker, but I have wheat flour if you'd like to stay and help make bread. The hearth is already hot."

"Wheat?" said Maria, Constanza's sister. "We shall eat with our Lord Andreas amid his riches this evening."

Having grown up in the Savoyard châteaus, eating wheat instead of the peasants' rye and barley, Andreas missed the supple texture and rich taste. A few weeks earlier, he had traded for two pots of milled wheat flour. Maria's words weighed on his conscience. What would they think if they found out he was in fact a noble? Would they push him further away? Wasn't being an obscure former monk enough?

At some point, he would need to tell the full story. But today was not that day.

Andreas looked toward Constanza. A brilliance gleamed from underneath the muck that covered her from forehead to foot. Nicolaus stood next to the barley stacks and watched, wearing neither a frown nor a smile. One day soon, Andreas would speak with him about Constanza. The timing was still uncertain, but he wanted Nicolaus's blessing. Implied though the blessing might be, it was another matter entirely to take his youngest daughter.

9

The Waldenses possessed the New Testament in the vernacular. The "Lingua Romana," or Romaunt tongue, was the common language of the south of Europe from the eighth to the fourteenth century. It was the language of the troubadours and of men of letters in the Dark Ages. Into this tongue—the Romaunt—was the first translation of the whole of the New Testament made so early as the twelfth century.

— James Wylie
The History of the Waldenses, 1860

THE NEXT MORNING, Constanza rinsed her face, braided her hair, and pushed the braids under her kerchief before stumbling into the kitchen. Only one orphan, Valeria, still slept on the floor. All the other places were empty. As soon as they awoke, weather permitting, Mamà made the children go outside to work and play, for she still relished the predawn serenity after her own children had grown past the loud and riotous stage.

Constanza jerked her head back at the sight of Papà still inside, sitting at the table with Mamà. "A little late for you, Papà?"

He didn't smile, but his tone was light and playful. "I was thinking you'd linger in that bed until the Lord's Day."

"Thank you for my bed, Papà." She drew close and gave both Mamà and Papà a hug. "It's much more comfortable than that old mat."

"For certain, you're the spoiled child," Mamà said. "None of your brothers or sisters slept in their own bed."

"There are blessings to being the youngest." Constanza sat close to Papà and leaned up against him. "Why are you still inside?"

Papà shot a glance at Mamà and chuckled. "I'm an old man now. I can't manage a late night coupled with an early morning as I once could."

"You're not old, Papà."

"With thirty-six grandchildren, I'd say I'm old." Papà's hair, more white than gray now, drooped over his wrinkled forehead, and below it gazed the same strong eyes that had many times rebuked, motivated, and comforted Constanza.

The house was quiet. Too quiet. "Where are Monsen and Madòna Grimaldi?"

"They left for Turin this morning, but they'll return after a few days. Luca still has money in the bank, and he insisted on fetching it."

"Isn't it still too dangerous to go there after everything that's happened?"

"Yes, but the banks may hear rumors that the Grimaldis died and confiscate their investments, so they went to settle his finances."

Constanza reached for the leftover loaf from the previous evening, tore off a piece, and spread butter on top. Papà straightened his back. "Last night, your mamà and I spoke about you and Andreas."

Constanza swallowed. "Andreas . . . I . . . he's still saving money, but with this harvest, and if he continued to work the old Lauras farm, perhaps by next spring—"

"It has nothing to do with money," Papà said. "He's a wise, hardworking man and a quick learner. Though he was somewhat shortsighted with all those sheaves, his yield was just as much as any of your brothers', and dare I say close to mine."

Constanza refastened a pin in her hair. "He'll be a great barbe too. He may not know much of the Holy Scriptures by memory, but he understands the meaning—the plain meaning, not the esoteric Roman dogmas."

"I understand—he is very talented."

"It's not that we find him unworthy, Connie," Mamà said. "Andreas is a good man—"

"I also feel he's worthy of you," Papà said, "but there are far too many uncertainties."

Constanza narrowed her eyes.

"For one, he will be a barbe. So often they remain single. It's a hard life of dedication to our Lord, one that's seldom weighed down with other cares."

"Some barbes support a family," Constanza said. "In the San Martino Valley, Monsen—"

"We are not forbidding your courtship—quite the contrary. We want you to find what suits you best, thus the reason for not rushing further into this."

"You're still young, and he is very young," Mamà said. "Papà and I didn't marry until—"

"Papà is ten years older than you, but Andreas is just over a year older than I am."

Papà stood and held his lame knee, massaging the surrounding muscles. "You both need to be sure before falling into love and marriage. And no heavenly light will shine down upon you with all wisdom and providence, showing you God's direction. Resolve to settle that before you pursue permanence."

"Look around you," Mamà said. "Children make you smile, but you have always wanted to keep a distance. Perhaps serving here for a time will better prepare you." Mamà shook her head. "You will need an abundance of love and patience to be a wife."

"I understand your concerns, and I will think about them." Constanza's throat tightened as she pushed herself up, tore off another piece of bread, and walked to the door. She needed time alone to process everything, or better, someone with whom to talk. Not Andreas—that would be unfitting, at least at the moment. For now, she wanted her closest friend and confidant, the woman she had known since childhood.

"I'm going to find Ellie." She smiled at Mamà and Papà. "Thank you for your wisdom, though I admit it's not easy to hear."

"You have grown into a woman with a golden heart," Papà said. "I am proud of who you have become."

Constanza had to turn before the bawling came. She distracted herself by blowing up the wisps of hair escaping from her kerchief. "I'll be back this afternoon before we begin threshing."

*   *   *

Constanza found Elionor by the stream rinsing her hair—straight and shimmering, light brown in the shade but closer to blond in the sun. Elionor closed her eyes as she hummed and brushed her hair. At the Grimaldi home, Ellie had been like a workhorse, ever willing to carry the burdens of others. Last summer, she had lost her father in the battle outside the old fort, and since then, she had spent more time with the Pavarins than with her own mother.

"My sweet friend," Constanza said.

Elionor jumped and dropped the brush on the ground. When she noticed Constanza, she laughed and snatched up the brush, feigning a throw at Constanza. "I should bruise your brow for making me jump like that."

"Papà and Mamà talked with me about Andreas."

Elionor put on a wide grin and tilted her chin toward her shoulder. "What did they say?"

"Are you doing anything at the moment? I just want to talk with someone."

"It didn't happen how you expected, did it?"

"No, but would you like to go copy the Scriptures with me? It's exactly what I need to calm my soul. We can talk on the way."

"I was going to make bread at your sister's home," Elionor said, "but they can manage without me."

The path to the schoolhouse was wide and well worn from generations of footsteps. It wound its way under towering trees and across sloped farmland to the crossroads, past the schoolhouse, and eventually into the hamlet called San

Lorenzo. Here their childhood had blossomed into womanhood. The mill where they took their threshed grain was just beyond the church, and downhill from that, the girls had learned to swim. Sheep bells clanged, twigs crackled beneath their feet, and swifts called out from above the foliage.

Elionor walked with her mouth shut while Constanza recounted her conversation with her parents.

"What do you think, Ellie? I feel as though I've wandered through life since returning to the valley. Where do I go from here?" Constanza shrugged. "You, though? Near faultless—the model Vallense woman."

Elionor giggled. "Do you mock me?"

"Elionor Janavel—always performing her duty without complaint, never falling into a spirit of discontentment." A breeze blew through the forest, causing Constanza to hold her kerchief in place.

Elionor looked at Constanza, stepped closer, and lowered her voice. "I'm nearly a year older than you, but what marriage prospects have found me? I must be less than the woman you imagine." She cleared her throat. "I have something to tell you."

Constanza tilted her head.

"Do you know that man down in La Torre, the one with the handsome face who sells hemp from the plains? He enjoys my company."

"A Piedmontese farmer, Ellie? He must be twice your age."

"He's twenty-eight—not much older than I am."

"I can't believe I'm hearing this from my dearest friend. He's a worldly man whom we don't know—likely Catholic."

"It's nothing. I've only been thinking about him."

"So, it's something." Constanza kicked the gravel on the path. "Do you wish to see him again?"

"Certainly. But please don't tell your papà. Not Andreas either."

"Andreas could tell you one or two stories about worldly men. Perhaps you should listen to him."

Elionor pressed her lips together. "How can I deny my feelings for Brando—"

"Is that his name? Brando?" Constanza spat the word out as if it were sand.

"He's a goodhearted and hardworking man."

"Is he a believer?"

Elionor darted her eyes to the trees.

Constanza's breathing became heavier. This conversation reminded her too much of her past arguments with Johan Lauras. Where was he now? No one knew. She couldn't let the same happen to her closest friend. "Have you seen him alone?"

"No, never. I haven't forsaken my morals, nor do I think Brando would disrespect me. The only times I've seen him have been with you down at the market."

"Please don't do anything you would regret. I don't know Brando, but I can't imagine him being the sort of friend you should keep. Remember what we've all been taught."

They rounded the last bend and came to the empty schoolhouse. The students were all helping with their family harvests, and their lessons would not begin again until the first frost. But it was a perfect time for the peace needed to copy the Holy Scriptures, and the barbes desperately needed more copies. Both Constanza and Elionor were blessed with steady and precise hands, likely coming from a lifetime of knitting, mending, and sewing.

Some may have seen their task as a dangerous one. The Roman Catholic Church forbade any translations of the Holy Scriptures other than their corrupted Latin texts. The Vallenses had developed their own Romaunt translation from a much older and purer Latin manuscript, which had since been lost. Nevertheless, their translation had its shortcomings. Most of John's Apocalypse was missing, while other passages had faded or disappeared. Copies of copies of copies. *And that's why Andreas is so focused on that Greek manuscript*, Constanza thought.

The door creaked as Elionor opened it. Inside, dust covered the benches and tables. The smell of mildew invaded Constanza's senses, but it faded soon after they propped the door open. They walked through the room to another door that led to the Romaunt Bible. Constanza reached beneath her apron and into her pocket for the brass key. She pushed it into the lock, turned, but it didn't move. She tried again.

Elionor reached from behind and pulled the door open.

That's peculiar. I never forget to lock that door. Constanza looked to Elionor, shrugged, and stepped into the room.

Only a little light was allowed inside. It was said that the sun spoiled the old book's pages and caused the letters to fade. Constanza bent down to open the cabinet where they stored candles.

There wasn't a way to light them. In her rush to find Elionor, she'd forgotten the tinderbox and flint. "Ellie, we need to find a flame, and Andreas is the closest."

Constanza waited for Elionor's snide response about her wanting to see Andreas, but it never came. Instead, she looked up to see Elionor staring at the table.

In a hushed voice, Elionor said, "It's not here."

"And that's why we need to go to Andreas's house and—"

"No, the Bible. It's gone."

As she stood, Constanza shook her head. But then her jaw slacked. The chains that were supposed to lock the Bible to the table hung loose over the sides. Dust outlined the place where the old book had once lain.

"Perhaps . . . someone's doing work on the building," Elionor said. "And they . . . they moved it, yes, they moved it to the meetinghouse."

Constanza reached for the iron chains and let them run through her hands. The links were as broad as her palm and made her strain to lift more of the chain. When she came to a rough break, she tensed. "It's broken. Someone deliberately broke through the link. That would take a blacksmith's tools."

Elionor held up the still-intact lock with chains passing through its bolt. "They didn't bother with the lock."

"They just broke through the chain," Constanza said to herself, still thinking.

"Someone stole it," Elionor said. "What else could it be?"

"I can't think of any other reason. But why our Bible?"

"Perhaps the young boys stole it for fun."

"During harvest season? And with blacksmithing tools? No, someone doesn't want us to have that Bible."

*   *   *

They needed to find the Bible, or at least tell someone about its disappearance. With Elionor following, Constanza closed and locked both doors behind her, rounded the corner of the building, and headed north toward the old Lauras farm. With any hope, Andreas would be there. Yesterday he'd mentioned he would be working in the barn, but as with any farmer, plans changed.

Her mouth felt dry and her stomach ached. Was it her fault the Bible was missing? Had she left the door to the scriptorium unlocked? The church would blame her. They had to blame someone. That Bible had been with them for over a hundred years, and now, under her watch, it was gone—no, stolen.

Who would possess another copy? The barbes never carried a full New Testament, and no family had their own copy. Perhaps they could piece together different copies and come up with what they had before. But it would never be the same. They would be left with a patchwork of parchment copied over the years by various hands, some parts more accurate than others. They could ask another church, but their own Bible was said to be the most complete.

"My dress is going to need mending after this," Elionor said, holding a handful of her skirt at her knee. "My legs will need mending too. We could have walked to the crossroads, then over to Andreas's farm."

"Yes, I'm doubting my judgment now. I forgot that since the Laurases moved away, no one travels this path."

"Except us," Elionor said, stumbling over a hidden stump. "Andreas should pay us for reblazing his hidden trail."

Constanza shortened her stride and waited for Elionor to catch up. Then, on the path to her right, an unnatural object caught her eye. A leather sack. She reached down to pick it up and gave it a little toss.

Elionor drew close to Constanza and eyed the item. "Will you open it?"

"It's soaked from last night's rain." Constanza held it with two fingers and lifted it to her nose. "It smells like cowhide."

Elionor pointed at the sack.

"No, I can't. It doesn't belong to me."

"How will we find its owner unless we open it?"

Constanza smiled and loosened the fastening strap. Inside was a piece of parchment, which she promptly removed and unfolded. Some words were familiar, but the structure of the sentences was confusing. "I can't read this," she said, handing the parchment to Elionor.

"It's not Romaunt." Elionor tilted the note and squinted. "Not Piedmontese either. Perhaps we could ask Andreas if he knows. What else is in the sack?"

Constanza shook it and eyed the contents. "Only thread and a needle." She pulled out a dried slice of meat and held it to her nose. "Salted pork too. What do you make of it?"

"Just a guess, but I feel someone stole our Bible and dropped the sack."

"Who, though? I haven't heard of any strangers wandering around the valley. The theft was deliberate and planned. No man carries a hammer and chisel able to break that chain."

They continued walking until the underbrush thinned and the path widened. They stepped into a bean field and followed a furrow toward the barley field they had harvested the previous day.

After Constanza and Elionor rounded a stand of trees, the barn presented itself, and the sound of hammering came to Constanza's ears. She picked up her hem and jogged toward the farm.

Andreas stood on a crate, hammering a peg into a board. Breathless, Constanza said, "Sorry to bother you."

Andreas jumped and teetered. When he turned, he puffed out a breath and wrinkled his brow. "You two? I wasn't expecting . . . I mean, you're welcome to be here." He wiped his brow on his sleeve. "But you look as if you're in a rush."

"Our Bible," Constanza said. "The one in the schoolhouse—it's missing. The chains are broken."

Andreas dropped his mallet. "Stolen?"

"We couldn't think of another reason. You didn't hear about anyone taking it to mend or rebind or anything, did you?"

"No," Andreas said in a long drawl. "Why would anyone want a big, crumbling book?"

Constanza gazed at the ground. "Could it have been our enemies?"

"Stealing the Holy Scriptures from us? That seems . . . odd. Few outside these valleys know of its existence, let alone despise us enough to take it. And it wasn't in plain sight. It was deep in our valley, in a schoolhouse, behind a locked door."

Elionor cleared her throat and looked at Constanza. "Two nights ago, at your sister's home, the dogs barked through the night. We figured it was only a fox, or at worst a bear. Perhaps it was nothing, but now—"

"It had to be that." Constanza nodded. "We were there copying last Wednesday, and I doubt anyone has been in the schoolhouse since then."

Andreas shook his head. "At least we have other copies."

"Where?" Constanza asked. "The barbes? You know what Monsen Estève does with his."

"True, but we could ask the church in La Torre—"

"It's missing half the book of Acts, Paul's second letter to the Corinthians too, and I imagine more. We need our copy back. That's our reference for teaching the children and what we use to make more copies."

"You have much of it memorized already," Andreas said.

Constanza stared at Andreas and put a hand on her hip. "The Holy Scriptures are everything to us. Yes, we've tried to hide them in our hearts as much as we can—one reason is for a day like today. Without a Bible we can trust, we have no faith, no knowledge of our Savior."

After a moment of silence, Elionor elbowed Constanza and gestured toward the sack. Constanza pulled it open, removed the letter, and handed it to Andreas. "We found this on the path."

Andreas unfolded the parchment and examined it. "It's not Romaunt."

"We know that," Constanza said, smiling. "That's why we asked you."

Andreas read a few words out loud. "'*Chiedi al prete di portarti sul fianco . . .*'" He stopped and bit his bottom lip. "I don't understand it all, but it sounds like directions or instructions. Here"—he pointed at a word—"*montagna*. I think that has to do with a mountain. And here: *terrazze*. That's probably referring to your farm." Andreas looked up. "This letter must have been for the thieves."

"What language is that?"

"Tuscan. I've heard some at my father's court."

"Your father?" Elionor asked.

It will be hard to dig yourself out of this one, Andreas of Savoy.

"He . . . euh . . . had a lot of business . . . with Florentine bankers. The Medicis, you know who they are, right?"

Elionor shrugged. "No, it's only that you seldom speak of your family."

Constanza smirked and glanced at Andreas, who rolled his eyes and gave an inconspicuous smile in return. He took a deep breath and refocused on the letter. "The Tuscans seem to end many of their words with a rise in tone too—quite a pleasant dialect."

"Where could they have taken our Bible?" Constanza asked.

"If they didn't want us to have it, they likely just destroyed it. Unless they left more clues, I'm afraid I don't know where to begin looking."

Elionor nudged Constanza. "That spoils our plan for copying the Scriptures. We should tell your papà, though."

"Yes, but I don't know what he can do. It's lost."

"I'll speak with the men about it," Andreas said. "Perhaps it was some mischievous youth, and we'll see it back in its place by the week's end. If not . . ." Torches lit in his eyes.

Constanza turned her head and squinted an eye. *What is he thinking?*

10

I perceived how that it was impossible to establish the lay people in any truth except the Scripture were plainly laid before their eyes in their mother tongue.

—William Tyndale
Preface to the Pentateuch, 1530

THE DAY WANED INTO EVENING at the Pavarin farm twelve days after the Bible's disappearance. Armanda, Constanza, and Elionor took the children outside while Andreas sat with the church leaders, who had assembled to discuss the missing Bible. Would they listen to him? Would they see his discernment, or would they wave a dismissive hand at him?

Five men sat on benches around the table. Bertran Arnaldi, an olive-skinned barbe near Andreas's age, had once treated Andreas like the plague, but he had changed since a missionary trip with Raimond Durand the summer before. Next to Bertran sat David Pavarin, Constanza's brother, and beside him was Nicolaus. Paolo Stalliato, the man sitting next to Andreas, was the oldest of the group and the one who managed the church's few financial resources. Rumors said Paolo was wealthy, but his clothes were no different from those of the other men, and his home was like any other in the valley. The old barbe, Estève Malan, sat at the head of the group, fully healed from the fire and flight from Turin.

The meeting began with news that had traveled up from La Torre yesterday. David Pavarin set down a skin of water and cleared his throat. "The lord of the land is dead, they say. Nearly two weeks ago, household servants found Rinaldo Falzon, the Lord of Luserna, dead in his bed, likely poisoned."

Nicolaus Pavarin leaned back in his chair and scratched his cheek. "Lord Falzon had no sons, so the duke will appoint a new lord."

That wasn't entirely how the Savoyard feudal system operated, but Andreas wasn't about to open his mouth and reveal his expertise in the matter. The duke didn't appoint counts, marquises, and lords as he wished. It was a long, complicated chain of authority that eventually led to the pope himself. However, as insignificant as the Lord of Luserna was, this would likely be a simple ducal appointment.

"How much will our taxes and rents change with a new lord?" David Pavarin asked. "Ours have been high enough, but my wife's father says that they're higher in the San Martino Valley."

"Taxes are the least of our concerns," Estève said, brushing a tuft of his hair to the side. "More important is that we've had relative freedom to practice our religion for over a generation. But now?"

David shook his head. "High taxes will starve us. A greedy lord can take what little we possess until we're left with soot and chaff."

"Yes, but we can still meet together without fear of soldiers marching in and burning us," Estève said. "Besides, what can we do except pray and remain loyal to our rulers? We hold no more say in who will be the next Lord of Luserna than in who will be the King of France."

Nicolaus nodded along. "Estève is right. We can only pray and wait."

"Who would kill Lord Falzon, and why?" Bertran asked.

David Pavarin shrugged. "Nobles." The dismissive drawl reminded Andreas of Constanza.

But David was right—the backstabbing and intrigue amid nobility was all too common. Andreas fidgeted with his shirt and leaned forward. "It could be that another lord's honor was disgraced, and that is never taken lightly."

The men turned and looked at him. Though Andreas wasn't there to make decisions, Estève had said he could listen and offer input.

"The monk speaks," Bertran said, laughing.

"Back at Sacra di San Michele," Andreas said, "we heard about noble intrigue from almost every pilgrim who stayed in our rooms. It was a hobby of us monks to guess who the next dead or disgraced noble would be. Let me say, though: compared to the other conspiracies, a poisoned minor lord from Piedmont is nothing."

"Still, we must keep our ears to the ground," Estève said.

Bertran nodded toward Estève. "We're happy you're healed, Monsen."

Paolo shook his head. "Not the first time for him. Have you seen his scars?"

All nodded except Andreas.

"They're on his feet." Paolo motioned toward Estève. "Somewhere in Lombardy, the priest handed him to the authorities. They started burning him at a stake, saying he was practicing witchcraft."

"How did you escape?" Andreas asked.

"I didn't," Estève said. "They lit the pyre, my feet got a little hot, then the heavens poured rain onto the fire. They rescheduled the execution to the next morning, but by then, a rich man had negotiated my release."

"You told me none of that, nor did I notice your feet."

Estève tightened his mouth and shrugged.

"Now, the matter of the missing Bible," Nicolaus said. "We've asked everyone and have heard nothing. Our only clues are the letter my daughter found and the barking dogs at my son's home."

"It's gone," Estève said. "We could compile a new one. It may not be as complete as the last one, but it's better than having nothing. I no longer own a Bible, and I'll be traveling again next spring. Other barbes will also need a copy."

"We could ask the church in La Torre," Bertran said.

Estève gave a dismissive wave. "They're missing half the text, and what they have differs greatly from our own. Years ago, they tried filling in the missing parts with Jerome's Latin, but we all know how the Catholics tainted that version."

"San Martino, Rorà, Chisone, Pragela," Bertran said. "Those churches must keep copies."

Estève placed his hands on the table. "Some, yes. Others, no. Nevertheless, we'll piece together what God has given us. We've managed in the past, and so shall we continue."

Andreas's blood pulsed. He tapped the tip of his shoe on the stone floor. He had told no one of his plans, not even Constanza. What would she think? What would these men think? He cleared his throat, but before he could speak, another voice came.

"Is it not odd to you that our Bible was stolen a few miles away from where Lord Falzon was poisoned, and on nearly the same day?" David propped his elbows on the table.

"Coincidence and nothing more," Estève said. "One is the same scheme rich nobles always entangle themselves in, while the other is a petty theft."

"A petty theft?" Bertran leaned forward and stared at Estève. "To most, our Bible represents nothing more than a stack of leather and parchment. But to us? How can we know God without His commandments? Or the Psalms? Or the Gospels? Or what will transpire in the last days?"

If Andreas was going to speak, it had to be now. He straightened his posture and held his head high to show command and nobility—a lesson from his old father—and measured his next words. "How old was our Romaunt translation?"

"At least one hundred years," Estève said.

"How many copies are there?"

"Most barbes carry at least a portion," said David Pavarin.

"What about the French? Do they have a translation? And is our translation complete and accurate?"

They sat with puzzled looks on their faces until Bertran spoke. "It's . . . what we have."

Andreas let out a long breath and waited until he held everyone's attention. "What if we possessed a copy of the original, untainted and preserved through the ages? We could compare it to our copies, fill in the gaps, and develop more confidence in our translation. Once we accomplish that, we could translate the Holy Scriptures into other languages."

"We've discussed this before," Bertran said. "We don't want to teach our Romaunt tongue to Germans or French or Castilians. If we could translate the original into their language, we could make copies—"

"There is a copy. Estève and I met a burgher this past summer. Gedeon Chanforan. He told us about a scholar who possesses a Greek Bible manuscript from Constantinople itself. And that scholar now teaches in Florence."

Bertran stood and pretended to walk away. "Florence? That's in Tuscany, no? I'm prepared. Who's going with me? What is it, late September? We'll return before the first snowfall."

Everyone laughed at Bertran.

"You believe this manuscript is real?" Nicolaus asked Andreas. "This burgher, what was his name?"

"Chanforan. Monsen Gedeon Chanforan."

"Chanforan is a Vallense name," David said, narrowing his eyes. "He's from Turin, you say?"

"He once captained ships on the seas, but yes, Turin."

Estève sighed. "Unless our circumstances have changed, the Bible is beyond our grasp. You should inform these men of its cost."

Andreas smiled. "I know a way to finance the purchase. It's not a certainty, but I can't let this opportunity escape us without trying."

"How do you propose to find that money?" Nicolaus asked.

"This is where you'll need to trust me. I know someone within a day's journey whom I can compel to invest in the manuscript."

Estève's voice came from the opposite end of the table. "Who is our benevolent investor?"

With an eye roll, David asked, "Is your father rich?"

Yes, but I won't delve into that yet.

Nicolaus shook his head. "Why so mysterious, Andreas?"

"For reasons I cannot yet reveal, for all our safety, all I will say is that I have connections from my youth."

"Why ask us about it?" David pushed himself from the table. "If you know a way to buy the manuscript, why not fetch it yourself?"

Andreas laughed under his breath. "I see only Estève, Bertran, and I have traveled far from the mountains. Do you realize the target I would be, carrying a box full of gold by myself? I need help . . . and protection."

"I'll go," Bertran said. "This is an opportunity I won't let pass."

Andreas gave Bertran a quick nod. "I'd like to bring another man with me too. Do you know Victor of Bricherasio?"

"He's the one who fooled those ruffians who chased us from Turin," Estève said. "He and his son brought me to the barber so I could rest and heal."

"Victor was once a Venetian mercenary." Andreas paused, remembering Victor's criminal background too. "If I ask, he'll come. He's the type of man who would forsake everything to help."

"So, three of you—carrying enough coins to buy every farm in the valley—walking to Florence, buying an old manuscript, and bringing it back." Estève scratched the top of his head. "That sounds like a plan only you'd conjure, Andreas."

"We'll stop in Turin first and talk to Gedeon Chanforan. He said he'd be in Florence in November and introduce us to the Greek scholar with the Bible. Perhaps we can travel with him."

Nicolaus bobbed his head to the side. "I see no reason to hinder this mission."

Andreas held back a grin. "If possible, I'd like to embark in a week."

"You hold back nothing, do you?" David said.

"Better now than let the manuscript slip from our grasp."

* * *

After everyone left, Andreas walked to the hearth, stooped, and warmed his hands over the fire near a bubbling kettle. Armanda and Nicolaus were outside with the children, but Constanza had marched in with a purpose. She grabbed a rag and spoon, lifted the kettle lid, stirred, and brought the liquid to her nose.

"Will you stay for soup?" She continued to stir, then added a pinch of salt and a handful of herbs. Her eyes had not met Andreas's.

"I would enjoy that." Andreas rubbed his hands together and kept his eyes on the fire. "Constanza, what's wrong?"

She stirred so fast it seemed the spoon would break in two. "Papà told me about your plans. Your idea may prove successful, and we'll all rejoice because of it, but . . ." Her words trailed off.

"Is it that I'll be gone for so long? Are you afraid for my safety?"

Constanza gave her head a shake. "How long will the journey last?"

"First we'll walk to Turin and spend a few days there. If we can finance the trip, we'll leave for Florence, and I estimate we'll be on the road for four weeks."

Constanza stared at the soup. "Then you must journey home, and that's another full month. You won't return until snow covers the slopes and we're all huddled inside for the winter."

"Imagine, by the year's end, we may enjoy a full copy of the New Testament."

"I understand, and it brings joy to my heart. Yes, I'll long for you, but . . . but it's more than that."

Andreas took the spoon from her hand. "Haven't you stirred that enough?"

"Oh, yes." She cleared her throat, took a step back from the hearth, and patted her apron. "The children will all run in here soon."

Andreas ran his finger along the spoon and tasted the soup. The salty broth warmed his mouth. His stomach rumbled.

"Madòna Vitòria taught me to make it last summer," Constanza said, "and everyone likes it here."

"I'm surprised the Grimaldis haven't returned from Turin."

"Yes, we all are." Constanza sat at the table and made room for Andreas. "They left almost two weeks ago, saying they'd be gone for three days, and still we've heard nothing from them."

"I'll keep my eyes and ears open in Turin. Perhaps Gedeon Chanforan will have information."

Constanza stared down at her twiddling fingers. "The air is growing colder, and I'm not looking forward to that. The children play around the farmyard and terraces most of the day and seldom come inside except to eat or sleep. Soon it will be too chilly, and all eighteen of us will be indoors for the winter. And that's not to mention the sheep and goats we'll bring in on the coldest nights."

"Have you tried finding other homes for the children? They won't be moving back to Turin anytime soon."

"Our home is the largest, and Monsen Luca insists the children should stay together." Constanza shifted and turned to Andreas. "I don't mean to complain. I'm sorry . . . perhaps I'm a little jealous of you." She blurted out the words, but then she closed her eyes and nodded. "'Delight thyself also in the LORD; and he shall give thee the desires of thine heart.'"

"'Commit thy way unto the LORD; trust also in him; and he shall bring it to pass.'" Andreas lifted his chin. "See, I've learned a few lines from the Holy Scriptures."

"The Thirty-seventh Psalm—I'm impressed. Do you know it all?"

"It is long . . ."

Constanza flashed a quick smile and laughed. "You wouldn't have survived in a Vallense school."

"Since we mention the Scriptures, what do you think about my plan?"

"Papà and I spoke for only a few moments about it."

Andreas straightened his back, turned toward Constanza, and straddled the bench. "We have all we need. With the Greek Bible and one of Gutenberg's printing machines—"

"How much will that cost? And who will translate it?" Constanza plopped her hands flat on the table.

"I am willing to learn. My introduction to Greek at the monastery will offer a reasonable foundation, and with time, I could learn enough to translate it. And I'm sure Bertran will want to study alongside me. Everything works together for good, and all things are possible with Him, are they not?"

"The Scriptures you allude to—'With men this is impossible; but with God all things are possible' and 'All things work together for good'—it's not about what we want. God works in ways that are mysterious to us and often conflict with our desires." Constanza looked toward the hearth, and her voice faltered. "I watched Raimond Durand at the stake. The friar pried my eyes open and forced me to watch the godliest man I knew cough, burn, and ultimately perish. I prayed God would somehow release Barbe Raimond. 'With God all things are possible,' no? But it didn't happen. Raimond died." She wiped her eyes. "But I also know 'all things work together for good.' I may never see that good come to pass, yet I trust God's plans are far grander than I will ever be privileged to see."

Andreas ran his tongue around the inside of his lips. What could he say after that? To hear Constanza describe Raimond's martyrdom and still see God's face amid the horror forced Andreas to stop and look at her. When the flames climbed up Raimond's body, Andreas had to turn away. Constanza never had that opportunity, yet she persevered. Could he have watched the torture and maintained his belief?

The door burst open, and in ran a little boy. He spotted Constanza and came to her. "Is the soup ready?"

"Soon. Can you go tell the others?" She pulled the boy's hands to her eyes and examined them. "Please tell everyone to wash their hands and faces."

"Yes, Madomaisèla." He scurried back outside without shutting the door.

Andreas moved to the door and closed it. "You're better with the children than you think."

Constanza puffed air from her nose, asked him for the spoon, and gave the soup another stir. "My guess is that you'll ask Princess Yolande for the florins. I thought of that in Turin but kept it to myself."

"Yes, I did too, but I didn't take it seriously. If that doesn't work—" He shrugged. "Then I'll be back in two days with no Bible."

Constanza turned to Andreas, grinning with those little creases between her nose and eyes. "I would like to meet Princess Yolande and the rest of your family someday."

The door flew open again. All the children ran inside, with Nicolaus and Armanda Pavarin trailing behind them. Much of Armanda's hair had escaped her head covering, and as soon as she entered, she sighed. "Mercé, Connie. I was going to help make the soup—"

"The meal is ready, Mamà. Please sit and enjoy. You stand and serve us enough, but tonight, Andreas and I will." Constanza winked at Andreas and gave him a subtle wave to follow.

Nicolaus smirked and pulled his head back. "Who invited Andreas? I'm not sure we have enough. What do you think, children? Can he stay?"

Their voices all rose in unison. "Yes!"

Constanza paid no heed to her own comfort, but instead made sure she attended to the others before ladling soup for herself and Andreas. The table was packed elbow to elbow, so they sat on the floor with their backs to the hearth.

As everyone finished, Andreas placed his bowl on the floor. "I swear I'll return soon. And with the manuscript."

She held the bowl to her mouth, but she peered down her nose at Andreas.

"What is it?" Andreas asked.

"I swear?"

"Ah, I apologize. Old habits from the monastery."

She giggled. "I know you'll return, and I will be here waiting for you."

Suddenly one child hit another, and a scream rang out. Constanza picked up her bowl again and shook her head. "They'll be waiting too."

11

The Word of God is solid; it will stand a thousand readings; and the man who has gone over it the most frequently and the most carefully is the surest of finding new wonders there.

—James Hamilton
Sermons and Lectures, 1837

FIVE DAYS LATER, Andreas and Bertran embarked on the quest for the Greek manuscript. Constanza walked with them down to La Torre, where they stopped and said their adieus. Andreas peeked over his shoulder to catch one last glimpse of Constanza until distance and a bend in the path separated them.

Andreas focused on the road ahead. Their journey would be a long one, but the anticipation of bringing a pure copy of the Holy Scriptures back to the church kept his feet plodding forward.

Three days earlier, Andreas had asked Victor of Bricherasio to join the company. Since Victor had a wife and two sons, Andreas expected hesitancy if not an outright refusal, but to his surprise, Victor was eager to join them. The grain harvest was finished, and his boys could manage the season's remaining tasks. Thus, Victor joined as the third member of the company.

When the land flattened, they turned northeast and followed the same road on which the orphans had fled Turin in the summer. Now, instead of the thick July foliage, the trees unveiled hues of red, orange, and yellow. Andreas tightened his coat and raised his collar as a chilly wind blew down from the mountains. He touched the patches on his sleeve and the threadbare shoulders. *I hope this coat lasts the whole journey.*

"I'm thankful we'll eventually be heading south instead of north," Bertran said.

Victor walked without an overcoat, apparently more accustomed to the cooler weather. "This is better than a hot summer, if you ask me."

"Andreas, you've been so secretive about your plan to get the florins," Bertran said. "Do you plan on telling us soon?"

Andreas slowed his pace. Why wait? Further delay would only drain his companions' confidence and bring more questions. He cleared his throat. "Princess Yolande."

Victor threw his hands up and burst into a laugh. "Funny, Andreas. But honestly, how do you expect to pay for this Bible?"

"I shall ask the princess, and I believe I can convince her to invest. I hold . . . family connections with her."

"Family? Are you related to one of her servants?" Bertran glared at Andreas. "Is it this Gedeon Chanforan you spoke about? Is he providing the gold?"

"I hope we can accompany Gedeon to Florence, but he didn't give me any signs he wanted to invest in the manuscript." Andreas quickened his pace and lowered his head. He had to tell them. "I'm about to reveal something to you both that only one other person knows. Unbelievable as it may sound, please understand that I'm being completely forthright."

"Go on," Victor said in a slow drawl.

Constanza was the only one who knew, but he couldn't deceive Bertran and Victor for the entire journey. A sense of trust needed to prevail in this company, and it would begin with him. Andreas shut his eyes for a moment, prepared his mind for more questions, and finally spoke.

"I am the third son of Duke Louis." He waited for their reaction, but their mouths stayed shut, their eyes fastened on his. "My father appointed me to serve as a distinguished clergyman in the Catholic Church, which is why I once trained in Sacra di San Michele. Princess Yolande is my brother's wife."

Victor shook his head. "I wasn't expecting to hear that, nor did I expect to walk alongside royalty."

"Only Constanza knows. I haven't told Nicolaus yet." Andreas moved a few paces ahead, then turned and blocked their path. "Please don't tell that to anyone else, most of all Gedeon when he joins us."

Bertran and Victor both nodded and agreed. Andreas moved aside.

"You don't act like a noble," Victor said. "How do we know you're not playing us for court jesters?"

Andreas slowed his pace, reached into his pouch, and held up a golden ring. "Do you know this symbol?"

Victor snatched it from his hand. "I could sell this and gain a small fortune if I were still a highway robber. But I fought under this banner two summers ago." He gave it to Bertran. "It's the House of Savoy."

Bertran shrugged and gave it back to Andreas. "I suppose I believe you, but even with Princess Yolande being your brother's wife, how do you expect her to throw so much gold at our venture?"

"She enjoys having a house full of treasures and trinkets. When we propose to get the manuscript, she'll want it for herself."

"How does that help?" Victor asked.

"I'll negotiate with her. We will bring her the manuscript if she first allows us to use it for our own purposes. The process will take us perhaps two years, and then we can give her back the original. She'll agree."

"I still have my doubts," Victor said. "You may be related, but you think the princess will just give all that gold to three peasants?" He held up his hand. "I mean, two peasants and a nobleman."

"I maintain a good relationship with my brother, to the point that I believe Yolande will trust us. What's the worst that could happen? She says no, and then we head back to our homes."

"I hope not," Victor said. "I was looking forward to this little journey. At least we're not sailing to Constantinople in a ship full of stinking men."

They approached the outlying areas of Turin in the early evening. To the left, Andreas spied the remains of the Grimaldi villa. All that remained was the stone shell, blackened by smoke, cracked by heat, in no way resembling the loving home that once stood amid gardens, vineyards, and hedgerows. But where were Luca and Vitòria now?

When the men reached the Chanforans' villa, it brought back memories of its cheap gaudiness. Candlelight filtered through the windows while twilight covered the landscape. Sounds of joviality and conversation drifted out from inside, and aromas of grilled meat made Andreas lick his lips. Victor removed his hat and combed over the few strands of hair on his head while Bertran stood straighter than normal and rubbed a thumb on his palm. Andreas drew in a breath and knocked.

A servant answered in Piedmontese. "Any business with my master must wait until the morning. Monsù Chanforan and his wife are preoccupied with guests this evening."

"Can you tell him his friend Andreas de Bonomo wishes to meet with him? He'll understand."

"Andreas, you say? Were you invited to tonight's festivities?"

"No, but—"

"I will inform him, but don't expect for him to entertain you. Tonight is a glorious night for the Chanforans."

A few moments later, the door opened, and through the crack stepped Gedeon Chanforan. His posture and poise commanded the scene. If his villa's decor were more genuine, he could pass as a lord, perhaps a count. He stood a little taller than Andreas, but his thick arms and sturdy neck made Andreas feel like a scrawny youth.

Glancing at Bertran and Andreas, Gedeon fidgeted with his sleeves, then spent a moment longer on Victor, eyeing him from forehead to ankles. "Andreas,

I am . . . surprised to see you. I had wondered if you escaped from the Grimaldis'
before"—he lowered his eyes—"the fire. A tragedy, is it not? Luca and Vitòria
were both well respected here in Turin. With their death—"

"Death?" Andreas turned his head a little and narrowed an eye. "I saw them a
few weeks ago. They escaped the fire."

"I'm afraid you are mistaken," Gedeon said in a low tone, making the sign
of the cross. "Their bodies were found in the ashes and are buried in their old
garden, if you wish to see them."

"That's impossible. Everyone escaped. My companion Estève nearly died from
the smoke, and we were hunted through the night, all the way to the mountains."

Gedeon rubbed the back of his neck. "Then perhaps my information is
untrustworthy, although gravestones seldom lie. If you wish, I can probe further."

Gedeon's eyebrows were drawn together in a dark circle. And was that sorrow
in his eyes?

Andreas shook his head. "The Grimaldis returned to Turin two weeks ago,
despite the danger, to see what part of their wealth they could salvage. They
wanted to dispose of their wealth to help the children—"

"All the orphans survived, then." Gedeon rubbed his chin and peered into the
darkness beyond Andreas. "No other bodies were found in the ruins, so I'm glad
to hear it confirmed."

"That's not why we came here," Andreas said. "We want to meet Ioannis
Argyropoulos and purchase the Bible in Florence."

"You're still after that?" Gedeon coughed and glanced back inside. "Do you
have the gold?"

"Within the next few days, we will. I have an investor with whom I'll be
making a deal. Are you still planning a trip to Florence soon? We would like to
travel with you, if possible."

"Florence . . . oh, yes. I have business with the Medicis before winter."

"Can you introduce us to Ioannis Argyropoulos?"

"Of course, but how do you plan to travel?"

"We'll hike east to Parma, then south all the way to Bologna, and at last
cross the Apennines into Tuscany and Florence. It will take about a month on
foot. It's the most direct route for us, and that way we won't need to wait until
spring." Andreas paused and examined Gedeon, who tapped his fingers and
angled himself halfway to the door. Andreas needed to nail the point to the villa
door. "Are you ready to travel with us within the next few days?"

"With you?" Gedeon chuckled and shook his head. "I don't travel such
distances overland. And not to offend you, but I prefer more . . . comfortable
accommodations. What if I meet you in Florence in four weeks after I first settle
business matters here?" He glanced back at the door and gave his hands a light
clap. "Once you're there, ask for me at the *Palazzo dell' Arte della Lana*—the
Palace of the Wool Guild. They will know where to find me."

Andreas sighed as Gedeon quickly shook their hands and bid them a pleasant night. Bertran and Victor followed Andreas away from the Chanforan villa with sour looks plastered on their faces. Gedeon was supposed to help them, not place them on more uncertain ground.

They passed the ruins of the Grimaldi villa again, and the graves were as Gedeon had described. Both Luca's and Vitòria's names had been inscribed into the stone. But how? No one had died in the fire. Maybe the priests wanted the locals to believe the Grimaldis were dead.

Down the road, the men found a suitable campsite and started a fire. Bertran lay down and propped up his head. "Are you sure about Gedeon? It's almost as if we were stray dogs to him, and he threw us a piece of gristle to fill our bellies while he continued on his way."

Andreas shrugged. "I wasn't impressed this time. He was more accommodating when I met him last summer. Monsen Chanforan must be a busy man. Besides, if he never shows himself in Florence, we still know the name of the man with the manuscript."

"I don't blame him for snubbing our overland route," Victor said. "Roads are full of vigilantes, thieves—"

"You would be the one to know," Andreas said, wrinkling his brow.

Victor slapped Andreas on the back and laughed. "You too, my lord prince. But if I had known you were royalty back then, I might not have let you go free so easily."

The wind roared that night. They huddled together near the fire and took shifts to keep it burning. Andreas warmed his hands underneath his coat and blew into them to keep his blood from freezing. His thoughts shifted to the upcoming meeting with Princess Yolande. With all hope, her reaction would breathe life into their mission. But would she remember him from the Turin market? What if she was the force behind the men who had burned the Grimaldis' home and chased Andreas, his friends, and the orphans across Piedmont?

But he couldn't dwell on those possibilities. God had brought them this far, and if Yolande refused, Andreas would find another way.

12

But their address was mainly shown in selling, without money and without price, rarer and more valuable merchandise than the gems and silks which had procured them entrance. They took care to carry with them, concealed among their wares or about their persons, portions of the Word of God, their own transcription commonly, and to this they would draw the attention of the inmates. When they saw a desire to possess it, they would freely make a gift of it where the means of purchase were absent.

—James Wylie
The History of the Waldenses, 1860

MIDWAY THROUGH THE NEXT DAY, Andreas, Bertran, and Victor stood in the entryway of the Castle of Moncalieri, the primary residence of Prince Amadeus and his wife, Princess Consort Yolande of Valois. Sculptures and exotic plants sat scattered throughout the room, seemingly without thought to coordination or complement. Paintings of varying styles and artists hung on the walls, some portraits of saints and family, others colorful likenesses of nature, fruit, and cathedrals. Windows let in light behind Andreas while candles flickered in the room's corners.

Victor was the only one in their group who carried a sidearm, but the servants demanded he leave it with them. At first Victor griped, but with a little prodding from Andreas, he slammed the sword scabbard into the servant's hands.

Bertran and Victor gawked at the sights around them, but Andreas had a more learned eye. Though the art might be grand, its arrangement had been thoughtless, exhibiting no beauty or order. This room was nothing but a storage place for Yolande's collection. That hobby, however, would be the catalyst to the Vallenses having the purest copy of the Holy Scriptures.

After the majordomo entered and introduced himself, Andreas asked for Ludovicus de Romagnano, Archbishop of Turin. Odd as it might seem, he was a friend and trusted adviser to the House of Savoy but paid little heed to dictates from Rome. It had been Bishop de Romagnano who organized the Savoyard troops against the inquisitors the year before. Andreas trusted the bishop more than anyone else in this household.

Victor leaned toward Andreas and cupped his hand near his mouth. "You gave all this up so you could reap barley from a hillside?"

"It's not as impressive as it looks," Andreas said. "It's nothing more than a girl picking all the flowers that catch her eye and putting them in a box. She forgets about them, yet continues to add more to her collection, all while the first ones wilt."

"I can't imagine the cost." Bertran blinked rapidly. "It's as if they could buy anything their souls wish."

Andreas scanned the room. "They're only things. Trinkets. Oil painted on sheepskin. Chiseled rocks. They may attract your attention now, but in time they will all fade, wither, and disappear." He smiled inside—that sounded as if it came from the mouth of Estève Malan instead of a prince.

Andreas focused on a painting to the left. The Virgin Mary sat on a throne, surrounded by saints, the pope, and other clergy. A halo encircled her head as she held the infant Jesus. Kneeling around her and the saints were poor men and women, begging for Mary's intercession. This was what the artist envisioned as true religion. Andreas had thought the same not long before, but the Spirit of God had brought him to the Savior. Andreas smiled at the painting. Talented and genuine in heart as the artist had been, that painting represented nothing more than a tale, not the truth found in the Holy Scriptures.

Still gazing around the room, Bertran whispered Christ's words from the Sermon on the Mount. "'Lay not up for yourselves treasures upon earth, where moth and rust doth corrupt, and where thieves break through and steal: But lay up for yourselves treasures in heaven, where neither moth nor rust doth corrupt, and where thieves do not break through nor steal.'"

Andreas recited the rest with Bertran. "'For where your treasure is, there will your heart be also.'"

The loud click of a door latch interrupted Andreas's thoughts. He straightened his vest and hat and bowed toward the door, preparing to meet the bishop.

Two sets of little feet raced through the door.

Andreas glanced up to see two children, each younger than five years old, running through the room. A boy darted behind Victor, clutching a wood doll, as a girl chased him.

"*C'est à moi!*" the girl said in French. "That's mine!"

The boy turned and faced the girl. "*Mémé* gave it to me, not you!"

Another voice, again in French, came from behind the door as it opened. "Charles, that does not belong to you. Return it to your sister immediately."

The first thing Andreas noticed about Yolande was the child she carried. Her belly was round and her back slightly arched—he had guessed correctly in the summer. She wore a dark cap that covered her head and left no strand of hair loose. Though with child, she still walked toward Andreas with grace and agility, each of her steps precise and confident. She had certainly been reared in the court of the French king.

Andreas avoided eye contact with the princess. He wasn't supposed to meet her yet. He had planned to speak with Bishop de Romagnano that afternoon and meet Yolande later, probably the next day. He sighed. He should have shaved the scruff off his neck first.

By instinct, he bowed. "*Ma maîtresse.*"

Bertran followed Andreas's lead, but Victor fumbled an unnatural bow and uttered some gibberish that didn't translate to "my mistress." Andreas closed his eyes and waited for Yolande's response.

"Anne, Charles, this is your uncle." Her voice was low but melodic. "His name is Andreas, and he is your father's younger brother."

Andreas opened his eyes. *She remembers me.*

"He's not my uncle," Charles said, scrutinizing Andreas's clothes. "He's a farmer."

Andreas rose from his bow, and his companions followed. "Perhaps I am a farmer." He gave another bow to Charles.

Charles turned to his mother. "Why does he bow, *maman?*"

Andreas rose again and answered for Yolande. "Am I not speaking to Charles of Savoy, who will one day be Duke of Savoy?"

Charles giggled and ran away through the door.

"Princess Yolande, I was not expecting to speak with you so soon," Andreas said.

"Bishop de Romagnano is away for the winter. Golia mentioned Amadeus's brother was here, thus I guessed it was you." Yolande smiled slightly, but still with the manners of a princess. "Your other brothers . . . we shall speak of them later. And you"—she looked over his clothing—"the bishop had mentioned you had become an ascetic, but I did not quite expect this."

"If you will pardon my attire, I was planning on seeing only the bishop today. If I had known I would see you—"

Yolande held up one hand. "It is no concern of mine. I am thrilled you found your place in the world. Amadeus was worried you might shrivel into heresy or worse."

"I . . . I'm not an ascetic, ma maîtresse. I live in a hamlet a half day's journey from Pinerolo, and I manage a small farm—"

"Indeed, an ascetic, as far as I am concerned. It must run in your family, for my husband would much rather be a hermit than the Prince of Piedmont." Yolande bit her bottom lip and looked at the door. "We will soon be dining. Would you and your . . . *écuyers* care to join us?"

Andreas laughed under his breath at the word she used: squires. Bertran laughed, but Victor scratched at his temple and grimaced, obviously not understanding Yolande's French.

The men followed Yolande through the door and entered another room filled with treasures so exotic even Andreas's eyes widened. Though caught unaware at seeing Yolande so soon, perhaps it would be better this way. He would present her with his idea when they finished dining.

*   *   *

During the meal, Yolande and the servants answered every plea and summons Anne and Charles produced—a rag to wash Anne's face, a dollop of honey for Charles, and warmer stockings for them both. Yolande paid little heed to the men, turning to her right to comfort Charles one moment and helping Anne in the next. Though Yolande wore regal clothing and maintained her noble posture, her actions were those of a protective mother.

Bertran and Victor sat on either side of Andreas, smirking at the sight of a noble doing nothing but spoiling her children. The servants had prepared a simple meal of salted pork, peas, and wheat bread. Partway through eating, the servants filled the men's brass goblets with a red liquid.

Andreas lifted the cup and smelled it. Expensive wine—just as a royal would offer. The fragrance alone was both inviting and intoxicating. His mouth watered as he swirled the wine and imagined its sweetness warming his tongue. A single goblet wouldn't violate God's commandments, would it?

Victor's elbow and gruff voice disrupted Andreas. "You may not want to drink that."

Andreas reoriented himself and gave a quick head shake. "Yes, of course. I was going—"

"Trust me, Andreas, it's not worth it. I nearly lost my wife because of wine." Victor's goblet sat untouched in front of him.

Why is my temptation so intense?

"Have you any milk or water?" Bertran asked a servant girl in broken French.

"*Oui, monsieur,*" the girl said without a sign of hesitation. "Milk of cow?"

"*Oui, merci.*" Bertran held up three fingers. "*Trois.*"

The girl left and soon returned carrying three goblets sloshing with creamy whiteness. Yolande must have seen part of the exchange, for she examined the men with narrowed eyes and a timid smile. When everyone finished eating, she waved over a servant, who took the children from the room. Yolande pushed herself away from the table, stood, and took a long breath. She blinked quickly and teetered, but a servant was quick to slide beside her and grab her arm.

"I am sorry." Yolande walked toward the widest door in the room. "We shall sit somewhere comfortable, then we may speak."

Andreas, Bertran, and Victor followed Yolande and two servants into a room with a vaulted ceiling. Portraits of Savoyard counts and dukes adorned the walls while colorful banners emblazoned with coats of arms hung from the ceiling. At the far edge stood a roaring hearth with chairs arranged in a semicircle around it. Yolande sat farthest from the fire on a plush couch embroidered with horses, moons, and flowers. She folded her hands and straightened her posture—perhaps unnatural for a woman with child, but quite proper for the Princess Consort of Piedmont.

"You wish to see Amadeus, do you not?"

Andreas adjusted himself in his chair. "Yes, mistress. The last time I was here, I'm afraid the prince was sick and—"

"Yes, Bishop de Romagnano informed me. Unfortunately, Amadeus's fits have grown more frequent. More days than not, including today, he lies in bed and reads the Holy Fathers, which surprises me, for he is a poor student. But other days, he is in good health, sometimes for weeks, giving attention to both me and the children."

"Would he be willing to see me today?"

"I'm afraid not. He loves you, Andreas, do not misunderstand me. It's . . . your family. Excluding your father, they all hate us. They think me to be a pawn of my father, the King of France. Anne and Charles, my own children, they despise most. And Amadeus realizes none of this, thus he leaves me to manage the affairs of Piedmont while I must also develop an upstanding reputation for my children. I wished for none of this when I married your brother. Being the Princess Consort of Piedmont was supposed to be easy." Her eyes flickered in the firelight. "But to ensure the legacy of my husband and children, I must manage the principality myself."

Yolande's voice quivered. Not only was she managing a household, but she also carried a third child. Andreas heard the strain in her voice and saw the stress on her body. She deserved none of this. "What about my mother?" he said. "Will she not offer help?"

"She is powerless under the boot of your brother Philip."

Philip was Andreas's younger brother by one year. Hotheaded and ambitious, he had often competed with Andreas, yet seldom did he gain the victory. "Does Philip desire to take Amadeus's rights to the duchy?"

"I have no doubt," Yolande said, staring at her feet. "I fear for my husband's life . . . and those of my children. Behind our backs, Philip conspires here in Piedmont. He is trying to promote his own counts and lords in place of those loyal to my husband, which worries me endlessly."

"What does my father think of this?"

"I do not know. At times, the duke backs Amadeus against Philip, and other times he looks away while Philip connives in the shadows. The one man keeping us from Philip's schemes is Bishop de Romagnano, but he has been away for a long time now." Yolande smiled, crossed her arms, and looked at Andreas. "Then there is you—associating yourself with peasants in the mountains."

Andreas brushed his hair away from his brow. How much did she know? "It is because of them I approach you. These"—he glanced at Bertran and swallowed—"peasants wish to purchase the Greek manuscript you mentioned to me in the market . . . and this includes me."

He winced at his own voice. He couldn't turn back now. She would either throw him and his companions in a dungeon or keep listening.

Yolande widened her eyes and leaned forward. Now was the time to adorn his proposition with the jewels that could capture her attention. "We know this Bible is rare, almost priceless. Not even the Roman Catholic Church herself has a pearl of so great a price."

"Fascinating." Yolande called for a servant and whispered something to him. "You spoke to the burgher Chanforan about this relic?"

Andreas ignored the inaccuracy of the word *relic*. "Yes, he told me about a scholar, Ioannis Argyropoulos, who escaped only days before the Turks surrounded Constantinople."

The servant returned and handed a small box to Princess Yolande. After she dismissed him, she opened the box and pulled out a small book. There was no mistaking the worn leather cover. It was Raimond's Bible—the one Estève had given Yolande at the market.

Andreas's muscles tensed as blood pulsed through his wrists. He should have never brought Bertran and Victor here. They would soon rot in a cold dungeon along with rats and murderers.

Yolande tilted her head, showed a slight grin, and held out the Bible. "Do you know what this is?"

Yes, he knew, but he wouldn't tell her everything. He took the Bible and glanced at the first page. There it was: *Copied by Constanza Pavarin and Elionor Janavel.* And on the next page: *Mathio.* Matthew's Gospel. Of course he knew the book's contents—he had carried it with him for over a year, helped wear its pages, and read the wonderful words written therein.

Should he ask her to return it? Andreas thumbed through the pages, seeing a few of Raimond's scribbles beside the actual Scriptures. Estève had given it to her, and God might someday use the booklet to speak to Yolande about her soul. Andreas placed the tattered booklet back in her hands.

"I saw it is Romaunt, though many words in it are unfamiliar to me." Yolande leafed through the pages and chuckled. "Do not tell the priest, but I have read some of it."

Andreas smiled inside, though he dared not show it.

"You called that Greek manuscript a pearl, which reminded me of this little book." Yolande placed the Bible on the couch beside her, and a servant took it away.

Andreas cleared his throat and motioned to his companions. "We are on our way to Florence now to purchase the manuscript, and I would like to make a proposal. But just as with that little booklet, please don't tell the priest."

She nodded along with him.

"I live amid loyal subjects to Prince Amadeus and the House of Savoy, but they are poor mountain farmers. The Greek man who holds the manuscript, however, wants one thousand florins for its purchase, and we couldn't fathom collecting that amount."

Yolande leaned back and adjusted herself on the couch. "That is no paltry sum. And you are asking me for a . . . charitable donation?"

"No, mistress, it would be yours to add to your collection. I know you appreciate rarities from the East, and this is the greatest you will ever encounter."

Yolande waved for another servant and whispered in her ear, but this time much longer than the last. All the intrigue and subtlety made Andreas's palms itch.

He continued after the servant departed. "We ask only that you allow us to keep the manuscript until we can verify our own copies. Afterward, it will be forever yours."

"One thousand florins all the way to Florence," Yolande said in a slow and calculated rhythm. "Other than keeping the manuscript, I require a promise from you."

Andreas bit his bottom lip.

"Promise me your loyalty to my husband and children, and against your brother Philip. You enjoy some prestige among these mountain peasants, do you not?"

"I am a simple man, and none but four know of my lineage."

"Nevertheless, we require loyal subjects and allies. Would you promise to back Amadeus in the event of Philip challenging his right as heir?"

"I . . . yes, though I can offer little more than fealty and paid taxes."

Yolande held a finger to her chin. The servant returned, trailed by a man with a sword at his side and plate armor covering his chest. His eyes were set as firmly as a hilltop fort, and over his breastplate was a sash emblazoned with the red Savoyard cross.

They were being arrested. Yolande had trapped them like ignorant weasels.

Andreas looked to Victor, who met the threat with a tense torso and a hand where his sword should have been sheathed. There would be no escape from the Castle of Moncalieri. Andreas had failed his two companions and most of all Constanza. If he cooperated, Bertran and Victor might be spared a dungeon. Perhaps they could return to the valley and recount what had transpired to Constanza. Andreas cast his gaze toward Yolande, expecting the sinister smile of a victor.

But she bore no expression at all.

"Basile Halphen," Yolande said, startling Andreas. "This is the man whom I trust more than anyone to perform his duty."

The man in the armor held out his hand to Andreas, but instead of apprehending him and binding his arms in chains, Basile made a sharp bow. "*Mon seigneur.* My Lord."

Andreas slowly offered his hand, and the viselike grip almost made Andreas's eyes bulge.

"I will accept your offer," Yolande said. "I have only two conditions. First, you must stand behind Amadeus and his claim to Savoy. Second, Basile will be your escort to Florence and back. He will protect you from bandits as well as offer his experience in traveling the roads of Europe."

Victor had unwound his tenseness but grimaced as he evaluated Yolande's man. Basile stood the same height as Andreas, with a small scar just above his left eye and a firm chin. Hair grew only on the sides of his head, and firelight shimmered from the front.

Victor stood next to Andreas and hissed in Romaunt, "I can fully manage our safety. We don't need this . . . Frenchman."

Yolande must have heard him, for she said, "I will not finance your escapade without your submission. Basile will be a tremendous asset to your mission, and I trust you will find him quite agreeable if you accept his experience."

Basile's face had no smile, no sign of agreement or disagreement.

"Victor here is quite capable of protecting us," Andreas said. "He was once a mercenary for the Doge of Venice—against the Turks besieging Constantinople, no less."

Basile spoke next in French, but to Victor. "Swordsman? Archer? Cavalry?"

"Man-at-arms," Victor said in a low voice, but in Romaunt. He obviously wasn't comfortable with French. "And I served my liege with honor."

Still with the same hidden expression, Basile switched to Romaunt. "Yet you fled Constantinople, for you stand here today while most of your brothers perished before the Mohammedan hordes."

"Why perish in a dying city that wasn't mine? I was a mercenary, not a hero."

Yolande interrupted. "Basile served my father, Charles VII, from the beginning and for many years thereafter. He was wounded thirty years ago at the siege of Orléans—"

"The siege of Orléans?" Andreas locked his eyes on Basile. "You fought for the Maid of Orléans?"

Basile straightened and glanced to the side. "I fought with Jeanne d'Arc. Indeed, I marched with her before I marched with King Charles. I was one of five men who escorted her through the English patrols with the letter to Charles affirming her dreams, for God had told her to help Charles defeat the English."

The stories from France were almost mythical. Joan of Arc, the Maid of Orléans, was the heroine of legends, particularly after the Burgundians captured her and sold her to the English. Soon after, the Catholic Church burned her at the stake, saying her dreams were heresy.

Yolande folded her hands on her lap. "When I married Amadeus, I asked Basile to accompany me to Savoy, and for seven years, he has been a trusted adviser in addition to my eyes and ears in the principality."

Victor pulled Andreas aside and turned his back to Yolande.

"Pay her some respect," Andreas said, narrowing his eyes.

Victor turned his body partway back toward Yolande and lowered his voice to a whisper. "We don't know him, and he's . . . a Catholic. Did you listen to him pontificating about the Maid of Orléans? This Basile truly believes she received visions from God. He's not a man we want traveling with us."

"We have no choice." Andreas moved closer to Victor. "The final decisions about security could still be yours. Yet he may be a help to us."

"I know his type of soldier—loyal to the core but unwilling to adapt to the situation at hand. He will be a hindrance to our mission, not a help."

"You would throw away our one chance of getting the manuscript, after we've been promised the florins to purchase it, all because you don't want a French soldier in our company? That's all she asks."

"Don't forget that pledge of loyalty she demands."

"Which is nothing more than a noble family taking sides Frankly, it is not my concern, but if that's the cost of a thousand florins, I'll pledge a thousand-thousand times."

Bertran rose and stood beside them. "Will we accept the offer?"

Andreas looked at Victor, who gave him a quick nod. Victor might not be pleased with Basile accompanying them, but time would heal his concern—and two months on the road together would give them plenty of time.

"We accept your terms," Andreas said, turning to Yolande. "We will buy the Greek Bible in Florence, use it for our needs, then return it to you two years from today."

"Will this arrangement work for you?" Yolande asked Basile.

"As you wish, my mistress."

*   *   *

The next morning, the company of four departed the Castle of Moncalieri, heading south to the road that would lead them east to Asti, Piacenza, Parma, Bologna, and finally over the mountains to Florence. A crowd had gathered in the town outside the castle, and the company pushed their way through it. As they exited the crowd, Andreas took one last look behind. The castle stood halfway up the hill, while snow-capped mountains loomed like ancient sentinels far to the left.

But from the shadows underneath the eaves of a house, a man gawked in their direction. When Andreas caught his eyes, the man shifted his gaze to his hands.

"Look under the eaves," Andreas said to Victor. "He's spying on us."

"Is it inquisitors again?" Bertran asked. "I imagine they're not so enamored with you after last year."

"I wouldn't be surprised. It may have been Marco Spada or his lackeys who destroyed the Grimaldi villa. Yet it would be risky for them to operate here in Piedmont so openly. These days, the House of Savoy and the Dominican Order aren't the closest of friends. If they wish to harm us, it would be once we cross into another realm."

As Andreas scanned the surroundings, he glimpsed a familiar tuft of blond hair moving from right to left amid the crowd. Andreas held up his hand for the others to stop and drove back into the crowd, lifting his head for a better view.

The face appeared for a moment. There was no mistaking that it was Johan Lauras, Andreas's first genuine friend among the Vallenses. Andreas pushed aside anyone who stood in his path. He couldn't lose Johan.

But all the shoving was in vain. Johan had disappeared, and no combination of hopping and forcing his way helped. Andreas turned back to where the others waited.

Perhaps that wasn't Johan. Why would he be this far east, anyway? The last Andreas had heard, Johan had settled close to the mountains.

"See a ghost?" Victor asked with a smirk when Andreas returned.

"I thought . . . I saw someone I know."

"We must not begin our journey like this," Basile said in a monotone but confident voice. His Romaunt was imperfect, but it was better than teaching French to Victor. "Each delay will compound until we sit shivering in a cave months after we should have returned."

Andreas straightened his vest, readjusted his pack, and turned left toward foreign lands.

13

We have got the lamp; let us carry it. Do not find fault with the darkness—light the candle. Do not complain about there being error in the world—proclaim the Truth. And by what means can we better proclaim it than by scattering the Word of God on all hands?

— Charles Haddon Spurgeon
Speech at the Annual Meeting of the British and Foreign Bible Society, 1875

CONSTANZA SHIVERED underneath five layers of clothing as she sat on a bench during a Sunday church gathering. Today was the first bleak day of the year, and the rain outside made it all the chillier. She sat next to Papà and listened to Pastor Colletto finish his preaching from the Thirty-third Psalm.

With every beat of her heart, Constanza longed for Andreas to sit next to her once again. Only three days had passed since he left, but it felt like a month. Yet no choice remained but to wait—wait on the Lord and Andreas.

After a song and closing prayer, Constanza stood, stretched, and gazed out into the congregation. The orphans sat on the bench beside her, mostly behaving but only because she, Mamà, and Elionor flanked them. Behind them sat her sister Margarita's family. Margarita's children were young, but they sat with their hands beside them and their eyes forward.

Discipline. What the orphans need is hard work, training, and discipline.

Just then, one of Margarita's older children shoved another back into his seat and kicked him in the shin. A cry rang out across the room.

Constanza smiled and shook her head while Margarita made her way through the other children and struggled to break up the quarrel *Perhaps they're not as perfect as I imagine.*

A joyful commotion rose from the back of the room. A crowd had gathered inside the doorway. Men and boys huddled around someone, greeting him with handshakes, hugs, and backslaps while women watched at the periphery. Though

Papà had told her not to many times during her childhood, Constanza stepped onto the bench to glimpse who it was.

The sight of his feathery blond hair and chiseled jaw made her gasp. Constanza stepped off the bench and squeezed through the crowd.

An elbow prodded her side. "Do you see who it is? It's Johan Lauras."

Johan, her downhill neighbor, childhood friend, and frequent competitor. Could it be true? Had he come back? It was just like the prodigal son when he returned to his father—greetings, forgiveness, and rejoicing. Johan's father had perished by the sword, all to rescue Constanza and Raimond from Marco Spada and his inquisitors. Many good men had died that horrible day, but in the end, they had failed in their aim. Soon afterward, Johan abandoned his faith until at last he left the valley.

Now he had returned.

Johan's voice rose above the joviality. "I need a few moments of your time. It won't take long."

"You may take all the time you wish," Pastor Colletto said from behind. "We rejoice at your return."

After one last handshake, Johan moved toward the front. He didn't stand behind the podium, but in front of it. When the congregation hushed, he asked them to be seated.

"All of you know me, but in case you don't, I am Johan Lauras, son of the martyred Gerald Lauras."

Martyred? Barbe Raimond was a martyr, burned at the stake for his faith. Gerald Lauras had died honorably in battle, but not for his faith. Constanza pursed her lips and continued listening.

"As you all know, the Lord of Luserna has tragically died, and you are now without a lord."

Where is he going with this? I thought he was here to repent.

With a slight smile, Johan said, "I am here to say that I am not your new lord."

Many laughed along with him.

Johan's face straightened. "I'm employed by the man whom you will soon know as the Lord of Luserna. He will arrive in the coming months, but until then, I wanted to calm your concerns. You will soon have a just nobleman to govern your affairs, protect you, and help manage your land."

Whispers passed through the congregation, along with a few grunts and moans.

Papà turned his head slightly to the side and asked, "Who is our new lord?"

"He will soon take the surname Luserna, so you may call him the Lord of Luserna. He will meet you and introduce himself when he has the opportunity."

"And who are you?" asked a man from the back. "Who made you lord over us?"

"I am only his steward," Johan said. "You should be thankful I was once one of you, because I understand your manners, your customs—"

"Our beliefs," Papà said, loud enough for all ears.

"Indeed, your religion too."

"What if we don't want a new lord?" David Pavarin said. "We've managed ourselves without one for months now."

"Your harvest season has just ended. How many of you paid dues to your sovereign?"

A hush fell over the room.

David moved closer to Johan. "No one came to collect them as they have every year since the beginning of time. There was no way to pay them."

"Which is why you need a lord to rule over you. Who else will finance the soldiers who protect you? Who was it that stamped out the inquisitors?"

"The Duke of Savoy," Papà said. "Not the Lord of Luserna."

"How does the duke pay his soldiers? Does he maintain his own silver mine? No, his soldiers' wages come from taxes paid by loyal subjects such as you."

"Who appointed our new lord? How do we know we're not being taken by some opportunistic criminal?" David's voice was low and aggressive.

"If you wish to protest, take it to the House of Savoy, for the appointment was theirs alone."

Murmurs bubbled until Pastor Colletto approached Johan and shook his hand. "We will take your announcements into consideration, but you should know this is a house of the living God and His people, not one of secular lords and politics." He shooed Johan away and directed his words to the congregation. "We will follow the commandments given to us in the Holy Scriptures. If we have a new lord, and if Johan Lauras is his steward, then we ought to submit." He focused back on Johan, who skulked toward the exit. "Nothing has changed, though. We will always obey God before man. No king, duke, count, or prince can usurp heaven's authority, and as long as the secular authorities don't interfere with our worship, we will remain loyal."

Johan said nothing. When he reached the doorway, he turned, gave a bow, and left.

He hasn't changed at all. The same Johan Lauras I've always known.

Constanza lowered her head, slumped her shoulders, and sighed. Somehow Johan had entwined himself with nobility and found a place that suited him. How did he so easily parade into a Vallense meetinghouse, ask for an audience, and declare he was the steward of their new feudal lord? If the lord was anything like Papà described, the farmers would hear from the Lord of Luserna once per year and maybe when they exchanged land. Otherwise, the lord kept himself in his little castle, managing his household and hunting in his forest preserves.

But Johan's pride. Pride that he now had authority over them. Even the tone of his voice sounded as if he deemed the church below him. Yet he was nothing more than a child who'd been given a little responsibility and now used it as a bludgeon against his siblings.

In time, the congregation dispersed. That afternoon, Constanza had planned on helping Mamà cook while Elionor supervised the children. The Grimaldis were still gone. The children asked when they would come back, but Constanza had no answer. Had Andreas seen them in Turin or at least heard of their whereabouts? What if vagabonds on the road had accosted them? What if their enemies had captured them? Anything was possible.

The rain had slowed to a mist by the time Constanza stepped outside. Families fanned out in every direction, heading home to their hearths and dinner tables. To the right, Johan walked alone.

Constanza watched him for a moment until he turned a corner. She could at least say bonjorn to him. Perhaps she could share what had happened in the past year—her and Andreas, the Grimaldis and the orphanage, the Greek manuscript. He might be interested.

Constanza lifted her skirt from the mud and jogged to Johan's path.

A pale blue apron covered the front of Constanza's skirt, but beneath that, her dark dress showed each splash of mud. The mist had disappeared and left a biting wind in the air. She stopped to catch her breath and readjust the hold on her skirt. Why had Johan left so quickly? Constanza took another deep breath and hurried around the next curve.

At last she caught sight of Johan again. He wore a hat now and had his head tilted down, watching the road as he marched. One last jog, and she'd overtake him. "Johan Lauras! Johan, it's Constanza."

He slowed his pace and turned, but his countenance was grave. Piercing eyes made the air feel a little colder and the sky darker. Without a smile or greeting, he waved her ahead. "I figured someone was following me."

"It made me happy to see you with the church today," Constanza said as she caught up. "I hoped you'd at least say bonjorn."

"Bonjorn, Constanza Pavarin." Johan quickened his pace without saying another word.

"Will you slow down and talk or ignore me as if I'm a stranger?"

"I have too much to do today and little time for pleasantries."

Constanza planted her feet on the ground, forcing Johan to stop and face her. "Since when do you lack time, Johan?"

"Since I've found purpose and knowledge." He stopped and turned, but his eyes wandered, never settling on Constanza for more than an instant.

"Do you not wish to hear how we've fared since you left?"

"Why do I need to know? I enjoy a new life, one with meaning. I understand this world for what it is now, not what the Vallenses wish it to be."

"You're talking as if you've discovered something new. What is it?" Constanza stared at him. "Why pretend we are nothing to you?"

"I visited my mother yesterday." He dropped his gaze to the ground. "She seems to keep herself well, but I am but a phantom from her past. My sister Catherine is betrothed now, and my younger siblings are all growing." His face soured. "It's nothing, though—they've all forgotten me and treat me as a vagabond."

"Your mamà has prayed for months for your return, but she's heard nothing from you—not a visit, not a message saying where you were. You are the one who has regarded them as vagabonds."

Johan narrowed his eyes and focused on Constanza. "I now see why none of you accept the man I am. I've seen other places, met other people. The world is not as wild and wicked as I grew up believing. Happiness and honor can still be found outside Vallense churches. The barbes are all mistaken, Constanza."

Constanza's jaw dropped. He'd become an apostate. Was he a Catholic? Perhaps he had no religion at all. Someone must have filled his heart with those thoughts, or he'd birthed them from his own twisted soul and dwelled on them.

"Are you surprised?" Johan looked her over and shook his head. "Constanza Pavarin—so naive, unaware that men and women thrive outside the Vallense dictates."

"You forsook Christ then?" Constanza's voice cracked.

"No, I still believe God exists, and that He had a Son. But instead of walling out the rest of the world, I've embraced those who bring an open mind about God and religion. Your face is telling me all I need to know, Connie, so there's no need for you to quote the Holy Scriptures at me. I've heard everything you would tell me. I chose my path, and the best thing you could do for me is accept my choice."

Constanza forced a laugh, then narrowed her eyes in disgust. He said he remembered the Holy Scriptures. If those were the words of God, why pay them no heed? Johan spoke in vague subtleties with no specifics or explanation. He wanted her to listen without question, but that wasn't how Mamà and Papà had raised her. Being the youngest daughter had forced her to become astute and ready to fight for what she believed.

"What does your mamà think about your change of heart? Rather, what would your papà say?"

Johan tightened his face. "My father died outnumbered, fighting against those who would destroy his life. If more men would've chosen to fight with us that day, my father would still be alive. And your friend Andreas? What did he do but cower?"

"Andreas is your friend too. He was there the whole time, but he rescued me and Raimond instead of fighting a battle that couldn't be won with crossbows and swords."

"Yet he still failed."

Constanza's breathing quickened. "Andreas saved me, Johan. The inquisitors tortured him and tried to murder him. How dare you say he cowered! If not for his sacrifice, I would be dead." Her lip quivered. "Or much worse."

"Still, what saved him? The swords and crossbows of his father, the Duke of Savoy."

Constanza touched her parted lips. "How did . . . what do you know?"

"Have the facts not reached you yet? Andreas is the son of Duke Louis."

"I . . . knew that. He told me."

"Not me. That monk was a liar from the beginning, always pursuing his own desires, which apparently include you too."

Constanza blinked slowly and shuffled her feet. A quick turn and run would rid her of Johan's venom. Yet she couldn't let his words stand without a challenge.

"All of what you say is rubbish. It's as if you found a handful of sheep dung, and after marveling at it for a few moments, you chewed it and spewed it all over yourself. Andreas is a far greater man than you could ever feign to be. And all this." She motioned toward Johan's puffed sleeves and embroidered breeches. "You think because you wear the garments of a wealthy cosmopolitan that you are somehow not the son of Gerald and Joana Lauras? No, Johan, you are nothing but a dawdling man who found a rich noble to admire." Constanza closed her eyes and let out a quick breath.

Johan laughed. "Still the same girl I remember from my youth. You throw insults but don't realize whom I've become or whom I serve. All I will say is that you should learn to respect my lord. Please relay that message to your papà and all the other Vallenses too. The former Lord of Luserna was weak and useless, but you will find your new lord both wise and just."

Raindrops fell again in waves, and the wind picked up. Johan tilted the brim of his cap down and turned back to his path. "As I said, I have places to be. Adieu, my old friend. And tell Andreas I said the same."

Constanza turned in the opposite direction. Her heart beat against her breastbone and her throat itched with dryness. *I didn't expect a confrontation like that.* The thought of his expounding made her walk faster, but his last words made her blink. Why would Johan and this Lord of Luserna demand respect? The Vallenses of the Angrogna Valley had always honored their lord. True, they might gripe about their taxes, but they paid them.

Constanza shook her head. Johan was relishing the little stature he'd gained. A steward for a minor lord in a rural valley—he was far less than he deemed himself. Johan was wayward, but if he was truly born again, his heart might still be tender. Perhaps a few months in the valley would change his mind.

14

I want to know one thing,—the way to heaven; how to land safe on that happy shore. God himself has condescended to teach me the way. For this very end he came from heaven. He hath written it down in a book. O give me that book! At any price, give me the book of God!

—John Wesley
Preface to *Standard Sermons*, 1747

Two weeks of trudging through the autumn mud had brought Andreas, Bertran, Victor, and Basile to the gates of Parma. Each night they slept around a campfire, and though the weather warmed the farther they journeyed to the southeast, the sleep was less than satisfying. Victor and Basile were accustomed to rough campsites, so complaints were beyond them. A room with a blazing hearth would rejuvenate their bodies and bolster their strength for the last half of the journey. Andreas had had that idea on his mind since leaving Piacenza four days earlier.

The sun sat just above the mountains, far to the southwest. For a week, the Apennines had guarded the right, and though they were shorter than the Piedmontese Alps, they still dominated the distant horizon. In a week, the men would turn south and cross the range, and on the other side would be Tuscany and the city of Florence.

"We're about halfway now," Andreas said to the others. "Wouldn't a real mat, or perhaps a bed, be a treat?"

Victor huffed. "Do we have the money? I'm not so sure about this city either. What are they like here?"

"The political situation is volatile." Basile liked to insert the occasional French word, mostly as a playful insult to Victor. "The Medicis of Florence and the Sforzas of Milan are the rival families in these northern lands. The city of Parma is in the middle, and its lords sway between the two, depending on which one offers them the greatest prestige. Presently, they align with the Sforzas."

"Milan." Victor spat on the ground. "Always seeking war and power. I've opposed them in battle twice."

They soon passed through the city gate and into the dusty streets of Parma. Up ahead, the church bell tower stood far above the surrounding buildings, looking down upon its parishioners and declaring the might of the Roman Catholic Church. What day was it? By the quiet streets and closed shops, it must be Sunday. Many of Parma's citizens would have attended Mass earlier, while others would have skipped it to enjoy their one day off before the strenuous cycle of labor began once again.

Andreas longed for a Sunday gathering of believers. For the previous two Sundays, the three Vallenses huddled around the morning fire and quoted the Holy Scriptures, then prayed. Though pleasant and soul-stirring, it wasn't the church gatherings in the Angrogna Valley.

"Travelers say they enjoy good food here," Victor said, tapping his scabbard as he walked.

"When I was in the monastery," Andreas said, "we heard about a kind of cheese the monks in these lands make and sell. They age it for at least a year, and by the time it's ready, the curd is hard, crumbly, and salty. They say it makes the blandest meals bloom with life and character. The cheese is named after the city here—Parmigiano."

"I will not stoop to taste your Italian cheeses." Basile shook his head. "The cheese from France is smooth and tastes like butter instead of road dust."

Andreas lagged a little behind the other three as he examined the city. "Is it settled then? Are we staying in Parma tonight?"

"A tavern will have the cheapest rooms," Basile said in a lower pitch than usual, "but I know you Vallenses wouldn't agree."

"We all want a peaceful night," Andreas said, "and drunken, rowdy ravings won't accommodate that."

"It won't be easy finding somewhere other than a tavern," Victor said.

Bertran scratched at his beard. "Other barbes say believers live in Emilia-Romagna, which is where we are now."

Basile chuckled. "More heretics?"

"How do you know if any live here?" Victor asked.

"I don't. It's just a rumor. This is a vast region, and Parma is but one city."

Andreas turned to Basile. "Where do you suggest we start looking?"

"Find the raving lunatic preacher, and you will find heretics nearby."

"No, it's not so simple," Bertran said, ignoring Basile's jab. "If we see any beggars or orphans, we could ask them."

Basile rolled his eyes. "Asking beggars and orphans for a place to sleep—that sounds like a *magnifique* plan, Monsieur Arnaldi."

They turned a corner onto a cobblestone street, and Andreas pointed to a group of five gathered near the door of a shop. "We could ask them."

Two women wore white veils, each fringed at the bottom with two pale blue stripes and wrapped with an ornamented fillet of gold, silver, and green. Their dresses were fashioned like those of the other locals—wide, flowing, and covered by an apron. The men's attire, however, distinguished them from the other Parmensi. Their yellow hats formed a sort of short cone whose top drooped over the back of their heads. One wore a pale yellow cape over his brown wool shirt while the others wore light blue capes.

Victor narrowed his eyes. "Jews."

"God murderers," Basile said through clenched teeth, his voice low and grave.

Bertran shook his head. "They are still the people God first revealed His law to. While our ancestors worshipped stocks and stones, the Hebrews bowed to Jehovah alone."

"Except the times they forsook Him," Andreas said. "They worshiped the Egyptian gods in the wilderness, and later they bowed to Baal and Ashtoreth. In the end, they rejected Jesus the Messiah and the one true God."

"Jesus was a Jew, no?" Bertran said. "The apostles were Jews as well. Yes, their religion is false, just as much as the Catholic religion. Nevertheless, God loves the people who first called Him God." He blinked and quoted from the Holy Scriptures. "'And I will bless them that bless thee, and curse him that curseth thee: and in thee shall all families of the earth be blessed.' God hasn't abandoned the Jews, nor has He removed His promises from them."

"They steal Christian children from their mothers' arms " Basile wrinkled his nose and grimaced. "They sacrifice the children in their synagogues of Satan and use the blood in their demonic ceremonies. Jews are *la progéniture de Satan.*"

Andreas crossed his arms and watched the Jews. "Rome spreads the same tales about Vallenses, and I once believed them. But when I lived among Vallenses, I found those stories to be lies. Don't believe what the priest tells you, Monsieur Halphen. Now that you've been close to three Vallenses for days, do you still think we kidnap Catholic children?"

"You at least believe in Christ, but the Jews murdered Him. It is a different matter entirely."

"They need the gospel of their Messiah," Bertran said. "Just as much as you, Basile."

Twice since Turin, the topic of belief and religion had come up in their conversations. Basile was as staunch a Catholic as any. Around his neck, he wore a chain of beads, and each day, sometimes more than once he prayed the rosary.

"If I were less loyal to my maîtresse," Basile said with a sneer, "I'd have given you over to the Dominican friars the day we left Turin."

Was he being sarcastic, or was he mocking them? Andreas had often pondered whether Basile would fall to his instincts and betray them. For now, the only thing that kept Andreas at ease was the fact that each man carried three hundred of Princess Yolande's gold florins in a pocket tied to his belt. Early on, Basile had instructed them to each carry a quarter of the twelve hundred florins Yolande had provided. If one man carried that massive sum alone, he wouldn't be able to hide the jingling lump of coins under his coat, making him a target for robbers. If they were robbed, a bandit would have a greater challenge stealing from four men than from one. Basile's worldly wisdom had been an asset to the company.

"I'm going to ask those Jews," Andreas said.

"We could ask hundreds of other people in this city," Victor said. "Why talk to Jews?"

"They won't turn us in to the priest at that church up ahead," Andreas said, pointing with his nose toward the bell tower.

Victor and Bertran perked up their posture and smiled.

"I will not associate with those people," Basile said, "nor will I sleep anywhere they recommend."

Victor smirked. "If we find somewhere, you're welcome to sleep outside. Just stay clear of the swine, Basile. I've heard they devour men in the street at night."

Basile grunted and kept moving, while the others stopped and waited for Andreas.

The Jews greeted Andreas with whispers and subtle glances.

"My companions and I are from the northwest, near France," Andreas said in Piedmontese. It was a different dialect than what the locals spoke, but it was close enough. "We are Christians—but not Catholics—and are looking for friends who might house us for the night."

More whispers flitted between mouths and ears. At last a man with a gray beard said, "You speak of Cathars, do you not?"

Andreas bit his bottom lip and bobbed his head to the side. "That's what the pope calls us."

The elder smiled and turned to the woman beside him before looking back. "You are Vallenses from Piedmont?"

Andreas nodded.

"This is my wife, Hadassah. I am called Moshe." He held his hands out toward the others. "And these are my niece and nephews. Shalom, shalom."

"Are there others like us nearby? I heard rumors—"

"Four families once lived in Parma, but the authorities evicted them about eight years back."

Andreas looked back at the others. Bertran slumped his shoulders, and Victor kicked at the cobblestone. "Do you know of any other places to lodge other than a tavern or a monastery guesthouse?"

"You would be welcome in our home. I had pleasant experiences with the Vallenses when they lived here—always paid their debts on time and didn't make jokes about this." Moshe flipped the top of his hat to the side.

"We will pay you for your hospitality." Andreas turned. "Victor, Bertran, does this suit you?"

They both nodded, Victor a little less than Bertran. But where had Basile gone? Andreas scanned the nearby streets but saw no sign of him.

"I suppose Basile will enjoy his wish of sleeping on the street tonight," Bertran said.

Victor lowered his chin. "I'm beginning to doubt that Frenchman."

"You have since we started," Bertran said.

"No, he's becoming more . . . reclusive. He's always sneaking off by himself, only to reappear with no explanation of where he's gone. And now he's left again without telling us."

"What do you guess he's doing?"

"I don't know, but I also don't like it. We should be wary. He may swear loyalty to the princess, but given a few extra coins, he may sell us to the Dominicans and tell his maîtresse"—he said that with a parodied French accent—"that we were robbed and he was the only one to escape."

"Victor, your worries are misplaced," Andreas said. "Basile has been faithful in guiding us and keeping his eyes on the road ahead."

"I hope I'm wrong."

"If he becomes more suspicious, we'll consider our options. But for now, let's assume he believes all the myths about Jews and will sleep somewhere else tonight. Basile will find us in the morning."

That night, they shared a table with Moshe and his relations. The cheese, bread, grapes, and dried fish made Andreas lick his lips.

Before eating, Moshe prayed in an unfamiliar language. "*Barukh ata Adonai Eloheinu, Melekh ha'olam, shehakol nih'ye bidvaro.*"

"What did that mean?" Andreas asked.

Moshe picked a few grapes from a wooden plate. "It was Hebrew. We expressed our thanksgiving for this meal. 'Blessed are You, Lord our God, King of the universe, through Whose word everything comes into being.'"

Hadassah placed a sliver of hard cheese on their plates and dropped a spoonful of dark vinegar on top. "Parmigiano."

While he tasted the cheese, Andreas prayed for a way to share the love of Christ with their host, but before he could speak of those matters, everyone retired for the night.

Just before sunrise, Basile hammered on the door, ready to continue the journey. Andreas tiptoed to the door but made sure to leave a few ducats on the table to express their gratitude to Moshe and his family.

15

Thus did the Bible in those ages, veiling its majesty and its mission, travel silently through Christendom, entering homes and hearts, and there making its abode. From her lofty seat Rome looked down with contempt upon the Book and its humble bearers. She aimed at bowing the necks of kings, thinking if they were obedient meaner men would not dare revolt, and so she took little heed of a power which, weak as it seemed, was destined at a future day to break in pieces the fabric of her dominion.

—James Wylie
The History of the Waldenses, 1860

THE MORNING QUICKLY TRANSFORMED INTO AFTERNOON as the company continued the trek toward Florence. The road was mostly straight, curving or angling only to skirt a creek or pond. Locals called it the Via Aemilia and said the old Roman Empire had built it at the height of its power. It was paved with a mixture of gravel, cobblestone, and grass, but it had seen better years.

Harvested grain fields flanked the Via Aemilia on both sides. Sheep and cows grazed on the flat land stunted by the season's cool winds and shorter days. As the company passed a hamlet, worn and weathered men repaired plows while their wives cooked and washed clothes over open fires. Their clothing was ragged, more so than any Vallenses living in Piedmont.

Basile jogged up from the rear and called for the others to come close to him. "Three men follow us. They have been since this morning, and I believe it started before then."

"Why didn't you tell us before now?" Victor asked.

"I was only guessing, but I'm assured of it now."

Andreas scratched his neck. "How do you know they're following us?"

"You learn things over the years. If someone is walking the same road as you, they either pass you or drift further back. But these men keep pace with us.

When we stopped to eat, they closed the gap until they realized we'd stopped. Then they stopped. These trackers are experienced, but not flawless."

Andreas tilted his head. "If they've been following us for days, as you say, why do they linger in our shadow? Why not rob us and be on their way?"

"Because they know I am being vigilant. They will wait until we make a mistake—when we are off the main road or tired or separated."

Victor fidgeted with his scabbard. "We ought to keep a guard at night from here out."

"I have a better plan." Basile gave a crisp nod. "I'll double back on them. They are rarely together, and if I catch one by surprise, I'll interrogate him. If he's foolish enough to fight me . . . it will not fare well for him."

"Why not take another road to Florence? There are certainly others that lead over the Apennines. We could approach Florence from the west instead of the north—"

"Those roads will be narrow and less traveled," Basile said. "More treacherous for us. We will stay on the Via Aemilia until Bologna. If I don't return by the moonrise, then your safety is in Monsieur Victor's hands."

Victor leaned toward Andreas's ear. "It's never stopped being in my hands."

"Is there anything we can do?" Bertran asked.

"Stay on the road. Act normal." Basile gave a slight smile, a rare sign of emotion from the seasoned soldier. "*Et rester ensemble.* Stay together. Don't wander anywhere alone."

At that, Basile left the road and melted away into the field. How Andreas wished now for a sidearm. In royal households, the custom was for sons to learn basic swordsmanship, but years had passed. Unfortunately, the metal to make such a luxury cost more than he could afford. And even if he owned a sword, he'd be at a grave disadvantage against any veteran swordsman.

"So, he leaves us yet again," Victor said. "What if Basile's conspiring with whoever follows us? Maybe he's the one who wants us robbed and dead and is waiting for me to let down my guard." He puffed out his chest. "Not this man."

Andreas shook his head and stared into the distance. "I don't understand it all either. We're trusting Basile's word each time he comes back from one of his reconnaissance missions. What's your assessment, Victor?"

"I'd beat him, but that breastplate he has . . ." Victor blinked a few times. "It would be a hard fight."

"I don't understand," Bertran said. "What would he gain by betraying us? And Andreas . . . he wouldn't risk the wrath of the House of Savoy by killing one of their sons."

"That's if they don't already want you dead," Victor said to Andreas. "What if Princess Yolande is marching us off on a hopeless mission far from Piedmont all so she can unleash her servant on you, then claim bandits killed you? We should assume Basile is an enemy. Don't trust anything he does."

They continued walking until the sun disappeared behind the hills far to the right. They veered off the road, built a fire, and prepared a sleeping place. The nights were staying about the same temperature, but thoughts of the return trip made Andreas shiver. Instead of traveling south, they would move north as the winter chill settled upon the land. He touched his coat, tattered more by the mud, wind, and sleeping on the ground.

There would not be sunlight to hunt small game that night, so they ate a little salted pork and stale bread. Though their meal was less than filling, wild mint grew in abundance along the road. While Bertran fetched water from a nearby stream, Andreas foraged for a handful of mint leaves.

From the direction of the road, a hissing whisper smothered the sounds of scampering squirrels and rustling leaves.

Andreas looked back to the fire. Bertran was hanging the water kettle on a trivet over the fire. Victor sat leaning on one elbow as he sharpened a knife.

That hiss must have been Basile's. But why would he whisper to himself?

The whispers drew closer, but now quiet footsteps accompanied them. If it was Basile, he had another man with him. Andreas stepped backward and scanned the trees. He had no chance of fighting two men by himself. Victor was a hundred or more paces away. If Andreas could reach him, he could at least rely on Victor's sword, and as a last measure, Andreas had a knife.

"Only two by the campfire," said one whisperer in Piedmontese. "Where's the other?"

Andreas squatted and slowed his breathing, but his pulse quickened. They must not have seen him. Torchlight appeared from behind a cluster of bushes. Two men, one wearing a hat and the other with a tattered and patched coat, crept toward Bertran and Victor. Andreas had to reach the fire first. Victor was an experienced fighter, but if he was caught sitting, his sword would be useless.

Several thick tree trunks stood between Andreas and his companions. If he sneaked from one to the other, he could reach Victor without being discovered. He took a step to test the crunch of the leaves and sticks. The ground was soft, so the noise was minimal. He would make it.

His confidence swelled with each step, and he made it to the first tree undetected. He was much closer than the men carrying the torch. Andreas squinted through the twilight and examined the men's faces. Neither was Basile Halphen, but one he recognized immediately.

The man wore a red patch over his right eye, and his hair was curly. It was Furio, the man who had led the pursuit of the orphans from Turin.

Andreas's legs tensed. He locked his feet onto the forest floor. Could he alert Victor and Bertran before the attackers pounced? Where was Basile?

Furio and his companion stopped and watched Bertran and Victor. They were only thirty paces away now, but Andreas was closer. He searched for the path through the trees and forsook the plan to sneak.

Andreas leaped out from behind the tree and dashed toward Bertran and Victor. He kept his eyes forward, ignoring the ground and ignoring their enemies. "Victor! Your sword, your sword! Foes are upon us!"

Victor shot up and snapped his hand to his scabbard. He unsheathed the short sword and faced Andreas with a puzzled stare.

"Thirty paces in front of you," Andreas said between strides. "Two men, both armed." He wasn't sure they were armed, but he had to assume so. But by now, he'd lost sight of the men. He stopped and shot his gaze from tree to tree. Then two hands shoved him from behind.

Pokes and scrapes met his landing in a thicket. Thorns pierced his arms. He looked up to see a sword pointed at his neck and the one-eyed Furio standing over him.

"I found the monk," Furio announced with a chuckle. "Your little mission is finished, my lord." He bent to a mocking bow.

A body rammed into Furio's side, sending him tumbling into the same thicket as Andreas. Two swords clashed to the right. Andreas pressed his hands into the ground to stand, trying unsuccessfully to avoid the thorns. Victor fought with a man who looked half his size. The man stood no chance against Victor's swordsmanship.

Furio jolted himself up, moaning. He looked to Andreas, then back toward the sword fight. His eye patch had fallen off, revealing a lidless socket where his eye should have been. He crept backward, holding his side.

Andreas clenched his teeth and pushed himself up despite the thorns covering the ground. "Who hired you to kill us?"

Furio picked up a handful of dirt and threw it at Andreas.

Stinging eyes complemented the many scrapes and gouges from the thorns. Andreas wiped the debris from his eyes. Furio bounded away over fallen logs and roots.

Victor was still in combat to the left. With swords locked, he shoved against his opponent, then reared his sword back and sliced the man's throat.

Andreas looked away but couldn't hide from the ghastly sounds coming from the dying man. Andreas glanced back toward Furio's path of retreat, but Furio was gone.

"You saved us," Victor said, holding his sword above his head with both hands. "We'd all be dead if you hadn't spotted them."

"Where is Bertran?"

"I told him to run and wait from a distance. He'd only hurt himself in battle."

Andreas let out a long breath and wiped his forehead. He looked down at his hand to see it covered in blood and dust.

"At least you fought off the thorn bushes for me." How Victor could make a joke after slaying a man, Andreas didn't know.

"Basile's still out there somewhere."

Victor huffed. "I think those men might have killed him. Or he's out there trying to hunt us. Either way, we can't stay here."

Without bothering to extinguish the fire, Andreas, Bertran, and Victor gathered their belongings and walked away from the road. It didn't matter where they were going now, so long as they could throw any foes off their trail.

*   *   *

Andreas and his companions had to stretch as much distance as possible between them and the Via Aemilia before daylight broke. Partway through the moonless night, they happened upon a river and followed it until the sun rose.

Andreas found a sturdy tree, leaned against it, and slid his body down to the exposed roots. His muscles ached from over a day with no rest.

"I'll keep guard first." Bertran sat against his own tree. "We need Victor rested in case they overtake us again."

Andreas leaned his head on his shoulder and breathed deeply. What had seemed like the noblest pursuit now lay scattered like seeds on dry and fallow ground. Even if they made it to Florence, they didn't have Basile's portion of the gold. Had Basile fallen to Furio's men, or were Victor's suspicions about Basile correct? Andreas moved his legs and contorted his torso to find comfort, but each readjustment left him with more pangs.

Victor snored nearby. How had he fallen asleep so easily? Bertran's eyes drooped as he faced outward from their makeshift campsite. Sunlight warmed Andreas's cheek until his eyes closed and his mind slipped into emptiness.

A shoulder nudge thrust Andreas back to the present. "Someone's coming," Bertran said, his finger held to his lips. "Victor is already watching."

Through clenched teeth, Andreas said, "No rest for the prey."

Victor's voice hissed from the left. "He's not trying to hide, stomping on every stick and flapping his feet like a netted trout."

The noise came from beyond a hedgerow. The trees surrounding them couldn't be called a forest—they were a windbreak for the neighboring fields. There was nowhere to hide.

A bald head and wide-set eyes appeared from the hedgerow's corner. Andreas flinched and rose to his feet. Basile Halphen.

Victor unsheathed his sword and held it ready.

"A simple bonjour might have been more *approprié*," Basile said.

"You won't take us!" Victor shouted. "I will detach your neck from your body!"

Basile chuckled as he sauntered toward them, but his hand was nowhere near his sword hilt. "I do not understand why my companions would leave their camp without me."

Victor lowered his sword. "We thought . . ."

"We're no longer being followed. I dealt with them late yesterday."

"You dealt with them? I killed one last night, and the other—"

"The one with the red patch I killed *la nuit dernière*." Basile threw a sack at Victor's feet and held his hand out. "That is everything I found on him."

Andreas held his chin and stared at the Frenchman.

"There were more men," Victor said. "We saw only two last night."

"*Un homme.* One man. I followed him yesterday afternoon. He's an Emiliani, and the others were from elsewhere."

"They were likely Piedmontese," Andreas said. "At least, that's the dialect they spoke."

"Did you take the time to chat with them while you fought?" Victor asked with a laugh.

"I heard them before they attacked us. But why was a local with them?"

"The leader with the patch hired him."

Bertran gave Basile a sideways glance. "Where's the hired man now? Did you kill him too?"

Basile laughed and patted his sword hilt. "Everyone thinks soldiers are only killers, but Victor here knows the truth, don't you? Why risk a severed arm or gouged-out eye when you can avoid the fight altogether?"

Victor nodded along with Basile. "He's correct. No doubt there are soldiers who thirst for blood, but they're rare."

"What did you do to him?" Andreas asked.

"I paid him more ducats than Monsieur Eye Patch to stay home with his family and not get himself stabbed. After I was sure he wouldn't double-cross me, I circled back and found that the other two were gone. Later, swords clanked in the woods, so I ran in that direction and found Monsieur Eye Patch. He chose to fight me—sad for him—so I . . . dispatched his life. And that's when I found that sack."

Andreas picked it up and unfastened the tie. "What's in it?"

"I hadn't bothered to look yet. For a reason I don't yet understand, my companions abandoned me last night, and I had to track them across all Emilia-Romagna until this morning. When I found them"—he pointed his nose at Victor—"this man greeted me with a blade."

Andreas reached into the sack and found the typical supplies of a traveler: a spare set of clothes, thread, a needle, stale bread, and . . . a piece of parchment. He held it up for the others to see.

"Read it, Andreas," Victor said. "I've never been too good with letters and words."

Andreas opened the single fold and narrowed his eyes. The ink had faded to blotches, and all that remained was a red wax seal.

Bertran peered over Andreas's shoulder. "Is it a coat of arms?"

Andreas squinted at it. "Not one I've ever seen."

Basile snatched the note from Andreas, held it at arm's length, and turned it from side to side. "There's a cross here."

"Like every coat of arms in Christendom." Andreas shook his head, pulled the parchment back, and examined the seal more closely. "I see mountains, and here—letters, but they're too difficult to read." He blew dirt off the wax and held it to the sunlight. "L . . . something else . . . S . . . E . . . R . . . can't read that . . . A. Luserna."

"It looks like that to me," Bertran said. "What does it mean?"

Basile scratched his cheek. "Is it for the Lord of Luserna?"

Andreas dismissed him with a wave. "He died last summer—poisoned, or so the rumors say."

"No, there's a new lord," Basile said. "Luserna is in the principality of Piedmont, so Prince Amadeus should have been the one who appointed a new lord. But his brother Philip sold the title behind his back. It's a minor lordship, so I wasn't concerned with it—"

"That's the same place where we live," Andreas said. "It's all so . . . mysterious. The man with the red patch is the same one who led the destruction of the orphanage and chased us back to the mountains. If he worked for this new Lord of Luserna, then our people are in danger. He knows we want the Bible, and I would also guess he's the same one who organized the theft of the school's Romaunt Bible. And it seems he wants us dead too."

Basile held up his hands. "Slow down your suspicions, Andreas. You are talking about nobility. Why would they involve themselves with such petty matters as orphans and dusty peasant Bibles?"

"Whoever it is obviously knows about Vallenses and despises us. And I know only one man who would hate us to that extent—Friar Marco Spada."

"The Dominican zealot?" Basile said, pulling his head back. "Last I heard, he is still rotting in a Chambéry dungeon."

"How long ago was that?"

"Months? I do not know."

"The duke may have released him since then." Andreas glanced at the ground and thought out loud. "But appointing a Dominican friar as the Lord of Luserna? That doesn't seem right, unless my brother Philip has indeed gone rogue."

"Do not think of Philip as anything but rash," Basile said. "I would not be astonished by any action he takes. Yet I do not think he would appoint a clergyman as a feudal lord. From what I have observed, he and the Church are not on pleasant terms."

Andreas's breathing accelerated. Should they retreat to Piedmont? No, they were too close to the prize. But what would they return home to? Constanza might be in danger, and he was many days away from her. At least she had her papà and brothers.

"We should be on our way," Basile said. "We are less than a day's journey from Reggio di Lombardia. There we will gather supplies and continue to Bologna, then over the mountains into Tuscany. Ten more days, and we will be in Florence. I doubt we will have more *affrontements* with this Lord of Luserna."

By midday, they were back on the Via Aemilia, where every step brought them closer to Florence and the ancient manuscript.

16

Where copies of the Bible had, by incessant seizures, become too few to supply the wants of each, societies of young persons were formed, for the purpose of learning the Scriptures by heart, and thus preserving it, in their memory at least, from the menaced confiscation.

—Alexis Muston
Israel of the Alps, 1852

CONSTANZA PAVARIN SAT WITH TEN CHILDREN around the hearth and taught from the Holy Scriptures—not from a book, but from what she had known since her youth. Across from her sat Elionor, who helped direct the boys' attention away from their incessant motion and onto their teacher.

"*Car Dio ame enaymi lo mont . . .*" Constanza said at a methodical pace.

The children repeated the same Romaunt words, some participating more than others.

"*. . . qu'el dones lo seo filh un engenra . . .*"

Again, they recited after her. Elionor had to nudge a boy who stared at the fire instead of at his teacher.

"*. . . que tot aquel que cre en luy non perissa, mas aia vita eterna.*"

They followed her one last time, but with far less vigor than an hour earlier.

"That will be all for the evening," Constanza said, "but don't forget what we've learned. 'For God so loved the world.' When you close your eyes and fall asleep, remember, 'he gave his only begotten Son.'" She rose from her stool and clasped her hands. "Off to your mats now. Time to sleep."

A hand tugged on Constanza's apron. Little Valeria's rosy cheeks and freckles greeted her. "Madomaisèla, when will Monsen Luca and Madòna Vitòria come home?"

How many times would she ask? For the past few weeks, it had been nightly. "Soon, Valeria, very soon. When they return, Monsen Luca will throw you to the moon and catch you on the way down."

It had been over a month since the Grimaldis left for business in Turin, and they still hadn't been heard from. Something was wrong, but she dared not speak of such things with such a tender child.

"I miss them." Valeria yawned. "Madòna Vitòria bakes better bread than you and Madomaisèla Elionor."

Constanza smiled. Valeria didn't mean it as an insult, though it might have seemed so if Vitòria had not truly been a much better baker. *Lord, please let them be safe.*

The light had dimmed to candlelight and hearth fire glowing off the house's stone walls. Papà and Mamà had retired a few moments earlier, and now Constanza and Elionor finished preparing the children for the night. A week before, the cooler weather had forced the Pavarins to ask for more blankets from other families, which now kept the boys and girls snug on their mats.

Finally, when the last child had lain down and the chatter had dissipated, Constanza poured water into the washbasin, splashed her face, and rubbed her eyes. With a candle in hand, she walked toward her room and moved the curtain aside. Elionor was asleep on her mat, while Constanza's bed was empty—for now, at least. Often a little girl would hear thunder or howling wolves in the night and beg to sleep with her. Too tired to refuse, Constanza would scoot over, lift her blanket, and let the girl in. More than once, she'd awakened to five girls surrounding her, but she'd put a stop to that two weeks ago. Now only one was allowed, and never for more than a night.

Constanza crawled into the bed and pulled the blanket to her chin. As she did every night, she prayed for Andreas—that his mission would succeed and that he would return unharmed. Perhaps more, she asked God to help Papà see she was ready for marriage. Then there was her ever-present desire to serve outside the valleys. Would Papà ever let her leave again? Likely not. At first, it felt selfish to ask for such insignificant requests, at least compared to everything else in the world, but God was her Father in heaven. He would provide what He willed, and He enjoyed hearing the requests of His children.

Her thoughts drifted from Andreas to the orphans to the Grimaldis to her goats. As her eyelids relaxed and limbs lightened, three knocks sounded at the door.

Constanza's eyes flipped open. She listened for a moment, rolled to the side, and closed her eyes. Papà would answer it.

Another four knocks slammed into the door, now in rapid succession. She leaned over the side of her bed and glanced at Elionor, who continued to sleep through the pounding. Constanza propped herself up with her hands. The door unlatched, and voices echoed through the house. One was Papà's deep tone, but the other?

I know that voice. Constanza stepped from her bed, moved to the curtain that separated her room from the rest of the house, and pushed it aside.

The door slammed. Papà stood with a piece of parchment in his hand. Mamà peeked out from their curtain and asked, "Who was at the door?"

"Our lord's new steward," Papà said, shaking his head.

Mamà shushed him and motioned toward the children, some of whom the late-night visitor had startled awake.

Papà moved closer to Mamà and opened the parchment with her. He grabbed the candle from Mamà and held it to the letter. Constanza strained to angle herself and see, but alas, they were too far away. She slid back behind the curtain and listened instead.

"It must be a mistake," Papà said, trying but failing to be quiet. "That's twenty years' worth of rent and taxes."

"We can talk about it in the morning," Mamà said. "Our sons will likely receive a similar bill. We can compare ours with theirs, and then we'll see it's a mistake."

The parchment crinkled again. "Look here, it's not a mistake." Papà's voice was firm. "It explains everything. 'The land of Nicolaus Pavarin and sons has been undercharged for nine years. Provide payment immediately to avoid penalties and further fines.' Does the Lord of Luserna think we poor mountain plowmen and herders can reach into our purses and pay him with gold and jewels? I normally pay my dues with goods—grain, meat, garments—not coins."

Constanza moved the curtain aside and watched.

"You're becoming agitated," Mamà said, putting a hand on his shoulder. "Let's go back to sleep."

"I won't be able to fall asleep." He held the paper with two fingers and dangled it in Mamà's eyes.

She snatched it away and placed it back on the table. "Should we not take our burden to God?"

"It's . . . it's not a burden yet. We have other options. I'll speak with Johan Lauras myself and tell him—"

"Johan is only the steward. Does he have any say in the matter?"

"Still, he insults us. Who is he to leave his people—his God too, no less—then knock on our door at night and throw this bill at me?"

"Nicolaus." Mamà held her hand to his cheek. "Sing. Pray. You can do nothing tonight. Everyone is asleep, and you should be too."

Papà sighed, shook his head, and walked back into their room, followed closely by Mamà.

Constanza bit her lip and stared at the table where a piece of parchment lay. She glanced at the fire, then to the unlit candle at her bedside. *What does that say?*

She lit the candle, then crept to the table and opened the parchment. A broken red seal embossed with a cross and deer stood atop the word LUSERNA. Inside, the letter explained exactly what her parents had spoken about.

A mumbling entered her ears from the left—Papà's mumbling. She tiptoed to their curtain and listened. Her parents were praying. Their quiet whispers called out to the One who could provide and help. This wasn't the first time Constanza had listened to her parents pray. They had prayed for her brother Pèire's safe return, only to discover a few days later that he'd perished in an avalanche. Once, she had heard them praying for her as a youth, about a month before she believed the gospel. Papà and Mamà knew their own faults and shortcomings, but they relied on the Creator of the universe to fill the gaps.

"What are you doing awake?"

Constanza jumped. Mamà peeked through the curtain with weary eyes.

"I . . ." She still held the parchment, so she threw it back on the table and stepped in front of it. But her movement made it fall and flitter to her feet. Constanza stepped on it, swept it aside, and grinned. "What was that knock?"

"Johan Lauras dropped off our tax and rent bill, which I see you've read."

"I was curious." Constanza picked up the parchment. "What will we do?"

"It is nothing to concern yourself about," Papà said, stepping out from behind the curtain.

"How will it affect Andreas?" Constanza asked.

"I don't know yet, but please, don't worry. Andreas and I will manage it." He glanced at Mamà and raised his brows. "With God's help, of course."

They all went back to their rooms, but Constanza's mind raced with questions. And oh, how she wished for Andreas to be near. If Papà must pay the bill, then so must Andreas. And more than Papà, Andreas would have nowhere near what the lord demanded.

The patter of footsteps and a whisper interrupted her thoughts. "Madomaisèla, I heard thunder."

Constanza opened her eyes. "It was only a friend knocking on our door."

After a long pause, Irene asked, "May I sleep in your bed?"

Constanza gave a quick huff, rolled to the side, and lifted the blanket.

* * *

The next morning, after a quick breakfast of eggs and yogurt, Constanza and Elionor walked underneath the branches of the sparsely leafed forest. There they searched for willow shoots suitable for basket weaving and gathered them into bundles. Constanza found a shoot, bent it slightly, and rubbed two fingers along its length. *Perfect—not too thick, and not too green. Just as Mamà taught me.*

She placed it in her empty hand and continued searching. Elionor's bundle lay a few paces from Constanza's but so far was bigger. Constanza stooped over to inspect another stick.

"What will your papà do about the bill?" Elionor asked from under a scruffy willow tree. "Will they need to pay all of it?"

"I'm not sure, Ellie. I'm still in disbelief that Johan delivered the letter. Some may have disrespected him when he lived among us, but now, handing those letters to families he's known his whole life? I don't envy his job, no matter how much the lord pays him."

"I'm convinced we'll never experience ease in this world. Each time we find rest, more toil comes. When we have friends from the world, they eventually betray us. I fear our lives will never be comfortable."

"Yet we can find joy. And peace. 'And the peace of God, which passeth all understanding, shall keep your hearts and minds through Christ Jesus.' What greater joy can there be than serving Jesus?"

"Yes, serve Him by gathering willow shoots to make baskets," Elionor said with a laugh and head shake. "All so we can carry more things. You understand the frustration more than anyone, Connie."

Constanza bit her lip. Indeed, how was she helping bring lost sheep to their Shepherd by making baskets? Wiping a child's nose or brushing the knots from a girl's hair often didn't feel like serving Jesus. But when a girl like Valeria quoted back a portion of the Bible without mistake, or when a boy like Bino prayed with his sweet little voice, the Spirit of God brought a warm solemnity she felt from her heart to her mind and body. But many days were like today—bundling willow shoots and talking to Ellie.

Elionor wrapped twine around her bundle and tightened the knot. "Quite often, I wish for more than this life."

"I've felt the same at times, but I can't help but remember I'm supposed to be content. Sometimes I wonder what that means. I've heard it since I can remember: 'Be content, Constanza.' Paul's letter to the Philippian church says, 'For I have learned, in whatsoever state I am, therewith to be content.' But what is 'content'?"

"Weaving baskets, I assume." Elionor grinned and lifted her bundle.

Constanza carried a full bundle too, and she soon fastened hers like Elionor's. Together they walked back toward the house. Gray clouds hid every trace of the sun. For the past month, the days had been either cold and wet or dry and cloudy. And with the dreary weather came the childhood coughs and fevers. Thankfully no one had developed anything severe, but illness was a constant worry. A healthy baby on Monday could be a coughing, sweating, wailing one by Tuesday.

When they reached the barn, Constanza stared up at the still-fresh roof. The previous year's events had brought destruction to the Pavarin farm. The ragged men who called themselves crusaders had uprooted the orchards, fouled the ponds, destroyed a barn, and burned part of the house. Papà and her brothers had labored through last autumn and winter to rebuild, and though they had repaired the barn and house, years would pass before the land healed.

Constanza threw her bundle on the floor and unfastened the twine. "How long before these are ready to weave?"

Elionor laid the fresh shoots against the wall. "It will be weeks before these are dry enough. Until then, I have a few baskets I've already started back here. We can work on those today."

Constanza followed Elionor to the corner of the barn and sat on a bench. Dry withies that had already been stripped of their bark lay strewn about the room, and an assortment of unfinished baskets, shoots sticking out, sat between two wood stools.

"How many baskets do we need?" Constanza asked.

"It depends on what sizes we want."

Constanza picked up a basket not much bigger than Papà's hat. "With thirteen children, I would think the bigger the baskets are, the more content we'll be."

"Are you certain about that, Connie?" Elionor said with a smile. "The bigger they are, the more they'll hold and the heavier they'll be."

Constanza bobbed her head and gave a playful smile. "Papà can carry it for me, then—or Andreas when he returns."

She gathered a handful of withies and sat on a stool. Elionor eyed the shoots more carefully, but she soon found her own stool and sat facing Constanza.

"How many more days until Andreas returns?" Elionor asked.

Constanza's cheeks warmed, and she hid a little smile. "Unfortunately, I'm not counting days yet. Still weeks—seven, to be precise."

"I'm tired. Tired of everything." Elionor's voice changed, low and somber instead of bright and cheerful. "We were speaking about being content, but Connie, I can't be content here. I feel as if I'm wilting away. It's easy to make everyone think I'm the same Elionor Janavel as always, but in the end, I'm an outsider."

"No one thinks of you like that." Constanza threaded together the shoots that would finish the base of her basket. "We're followers of Christ. The blood in our veins doesn't make us a family. But the blood of Christ makes us sisters."

"Everyone remembers—at least those our age and older. I'm a poor wretch. My father died fighting for the pope. My mother abandoned me. Only by chance have I been raised among Vallenses."

Constanza shook her head. "You've never told me this before. I often forget the Janavels adopted you."

"Now the man who adopted me is dead, and my mother is a widow. It's difficult for me to face her. Perhaps that's why I stay here and help the orphans. I fear facing my mother."

"What do you fear? She's the only mother you've known."

"I don't remember the face of the mother who bore me, neither can I remember her name. Barbe Raimond would know, but now he's dead too. Constanza, no matter how much I try to put my doubts elsewhere, I feel as if I'm still an outsider. Do I truly belong here?"

"You're as much a Vallense as anyone in this valley." Constanza stopped weaving and put a hand on Elionor's, forcing her to stop too. "Your father loved you more than anything on this earth. Your mother too—you are her joy and greatest delight."

"I'm no longer a girl. I'm a woman, and I wish to find my own path. Don't worry about me—"

"Those are the exact words my mamà used with me last night." Constanza dropped the unfinished basket base on the floor. "Everyone tells me not to worry. I'd rather not, but how am I supposed to help if I can't know what is troubling you? Since I can remember, we've been the closest of friends—"

"You were the first one who said bonjorn to me. Do you remember? My hair was cut to the scalp because of the mats and lice." Elionor glanced to the side. "I wasn't embarrassed, because up to that point, everyone had turned their gaze away from me. I should have been ashamed, but for ignorance, I wasn't."

"I don't remember how short your hair was, nor did I care where or how you were born. What I do recall is that I met my dearest friend one day in the schoolhouse."

Elionor placed her basket on the floor as well. Though she had started after Constanza had, her weaving was much further along. "You are a true sister, Constanza Pavarin. I couldn't survive this world without you." Tears fell from her eyes, and she quickly wiped them away. "Please don't concern yourself with me. I carry feelings I must reconcile and hold many questions and doubts, but I need to handle them myself."

"Don't face your battles alone. You're surrounded by people who care for you."

"Pray for me. That's the best you can do. Pray." Elionor pressed her lips together into a slight grimace.

The way Elionor said that was troubling, but Constanza didn't press the subject.

For the next several hours, Constanza and Elionor wove withies into baskets. By late afternoon, they had finished two baskets to use for everything from carrying threshed wheat to harvesting spring greens.

As Constanza washed for dinner and the children played nearby, the ground felt as if it were shifting under her. Not an earthquake, but an instability only noticeable to the one standing in its midst. A new lord had his demands, and Papà would soon need to confront them. At the same time, Elionor—her friend and confidant—was changing, and not for the better. If Andreas were still down at the old Lauras farm, she'd ask him to her family's table that night, and then she could unfasten everything in her heart. Andreas became uncomfortable when she cried, but at least he would listen and understand, perhaps more than anyone except Mamà and Papà.

A shrill cry startled Constanza. But it was only little Valeria, sitting on the ground and pointing at Ezio. "He pushed me, Madomaisèla."

Constanza bit her lip, shook her head, and lifted her apron to dry her face. She walked to Valeria, lifted her, and carried her to the house. The little girl's head rested on Constanza's shoulder, and she couldn't help but place her hand on Valeria's back and smile.

17

The Waldense Bibles are small, plain, and portable volumes, contrasting with those splendid and ponderous folios of the Latin Vulgate, penned in characters of gold and silver, richly illuminated, their bindings decorated with gems, inviting admiration rather than study, and unfitted by their size and splendour for the use of the people.

—James Wylie
The History of the Waldenses, 1860

THE SIGHT OF THE CATHEDRAL STOLE ANDREAS'S BREATH. To the left, the sun rose over the autumn foliage of the Apennines, and to the right lay the patchwork of farms, vineyards, and villas known as Tuscany. A light fog obscured much of the walled city, but none could deny the grandeur of Florence, or as the Tuscans called it, *Firenze*.

"At last." Bertran let out a long breath and held his hands above his head.

With his jaw dropped, Basile made the sign of the cross. "I will soon partake of the Holy Eucharist standing under *le dôme*."

"It's not Sunday," Andreas said.

"Today is All Saints' Day. All members of the Holy Roman Catholic Church will commemorate the saints, past and present, known and unknown. What better place to worship than in the new cathedral—*il duomo*, as the locals say."

Even from Andreas's distant vantage point, Florence's cathedral forced him to pause and stare. Its cupola soared far above everything in the city, rivaled only by the adjacent bell tower.

"How could men build such a thing?" Bertran asked.

"Stories of so grand a structure have traveled to Paris and beyond," Basile said. "It took them more than a hundred years to build the main structure, but the cathedral was still without a dome."

"I have never seen such a marvel," Andreas said, "not even in Venice or Milan."

Basile swept his hand over the city. "No architect in the Italian peninsula knew how to build such a tall and grand dome without it collapsing on itself, but the builders chose a design by a man named Brunelleschi. They say he harnessed the genius of old Rome and applied his goldsmithing skills to craft a dome exceeding the financiers' wishes. It took them fifteen years to finish it."

Victor, his gaze still fastened to the cathedral, said, "Basile, you can worship your saints after we find Gedeon Chanforan. We came here for the manuscript, not to observe your holy days."

"I will not neglect All Saints' Day as you heathens do." Basile's tone was firm yet had a hint of playfulness.

The company descended into the valley, where tall, slender trees lined the neat cobblestone road leading to Florence. Both travelers and citizens walked the path, all heading south. For the last week, Andreas, Bertran, Victor, and Basile had trekked across the Apennines from Bologna. They had met few along the strenuous path, but now people crowded around them.

When the men passed through the gate, the guard met them with a nod. In almost every nook, merchants hawked their silks, spices, wines, and pottery to the passersby. Stone buildings with arched windows flanked the wide avenue, most rising to two or three stories. Pots of tiny orange and yellow blooms hung from windows, brightening the already charming city. Friars and monks of diverse orders—brown-hooded Franciscans, wide-sleeved Benedictines, and black-robed Dominicans—walked in clusters and followed the crowd toward the city center.

Under one alcove, a brown-robed friar with a shaved head bellowed out in Latin. "Relieve the suffering of your fathers and mothers! With just a ten-florin donation to the Church, you may lessen their time in *purgatorium*." The friar's gaze latched onto Andreas. "Come, *amicus*. You would not let your dear grandmother suffer the torments of her sin for another day, would you? She pleads to you! Come, I will offer you a special price, for the Church has compassion on your loved ones. Eight florins, and I will offer no less."

Andreas looked away, closed his eyes, and shook his head. Indulgences. Perhaps the most hideous apostasy of the Roman Church. The clergy sold slips of parchment, telling poor parishioners their family members' sins had been forgiven.

Now Andreas understood the truth: the blood of Christ and forgiveness of sins could not be bought with gold. Salvation was a gift of God, and the Savior's sacrifice was the only necessary payment for all sin. No signature from the pope affected the souls of the deceased.

But before they could leave the area, the friar lured Basile to his table. Andreas maneuvered through the crowd, but before he had the chance to object, Basile handed over some coins.

Andreas held his hands out in a plea. "Why would you spend your money on that slip of parchment?"

"See? '*Le pape Calixte III.*'" Basile pointed at the slip. "Signed by the pope himself."

"Calixtus was the last pope. He's dead now, and Pius has been the pope for over a year."

"No matter. If you were to ask me, I'd say it's better to get an indulgence from a dead pope who now sits with Christ in heaven."

Bertran chuckled from behind. "Whom did you buy it for?"

"My dear grandfather." Basile crossed himself. "He was a capable man, but he . . . did not control his anger. He beat a man to death for stealing from him."

That would be a mortal sin. The pope himself declared indulgences were meant only for venial sins. But I won't try to correct him—either way, indulgences are worth less than that shattered flowerpot across the way.

"What about your soul, Basile?" Bertran asked. "You will perish one day. Will you depend on a relative to lessen your suffering?"

"I am a faithful Catholic and have been my entire life. I am baptized and confirmed; I take part in the Holy Eucharist; I perform penance. The only times I have killed were in battle. My sins are small, and my good works are great."

Andreas nodded slowly. "I once believed the same. I knew I had sinned, and I knew Christ's sacrifice placed the grace of God on my soul. Despite that, I was an unbeliever. My righteousness is rubble compared to the purity of Christ. No sacrament could fill the void in my soul. Instead, I read from the Holy Scriptures and realized I needed God's forgiveness instead of the Church's sacraments. 'By the which will we are sanctified through the offering of the body of Jesus Christ once for all.' Once, Basile. One sacrifice is all it takes. The Holy Eucharist will not sanctify you. Only by being born again can your soul be saved."

Basile narrowed his eyes. "It may be a different day, but it's the same heresy. You, Andreas, have betrayed the Church and given yourself over to fables."

Two other times, Andreas had tried sharing the gospel with Basile, but both occasions had ended in Basile throwing up a hand and walking away. Basile might be an honorable old soldier, but he needed redemption. Andreas would try a different approach this time.

"What I say isn't a fable. It's the truth. You can read it for yourself in the Holy Scriptures. Why do you think we Vallenses place so much value on the Bible? Why risk this road when we can rest in comfort back in our valley?" Andreas caught Basile's eyes. "It's because we can know God through His Word. Without it, we Vallenses are like a swordsman without a sword, or a plowman without a plow. You cannot separate God's people from His Word."

Basile grunted. "I'm a Catholic. My *mère* and my *père* were. My grandparents were. Neither cunning nor persuasion can change *mon héritage*." He peered up toward the massive brick dome. "Behold the magnificence of the Catholic Church. I have yet to hear of any such structure Vallenses have built. You carry no love of beauty, nor appreciation of art, and you would just as soon worship in a peasant's hovel or pasture as in anything resembling a sanctuary."

Andreas blinked a few times. How could he answer Basile? What he'd said was true—the Vallenses could claim nothing comparable to Florence's cathedral. But they had something. "The mountains are our cathedral, and the boulders and trees make up our sanctuary. The Creator of the universe has fashioned our place of worship."

"Nevertheless," Basile said, "I will observe the Feast of All Saints with my fellow Christians."

Basile's sneer made Andreas clear his throat and swallow. "I was hoping to meet Gedeon today, if not our Greek friend also—"

"That will need to wait." Basile turned toward the cathedral, but Victor stepped in his path.

"You haven't been to Mass once since we left."

Basile took a step toward Victor and stood chest to chest with him. "Which is exactly why I choose to go now." He glared at Victor. "Now, monsieur, step aside."

Victor stiffened. Before Andreas could dispel the confrontation, Basile threw a right hook into Victor's cheek.

Victor winced and struggled to stand upright again, but by the time he'd collected himself, Basile had stormed off toward the cathedral.

"Filthy papist." Victor held his cheek and positioned himself for the chase, but Andreas snatched his arm and held him back.

"Let him go. Basile needs Jesus, not our fists."

"He threw the first punch, and I should have finished him. He's nothing but a slimy, creeping Frenchman."

Bertran stepped closer. "Remember, he has a quarter of the money. We can't buy the manuscript without him, nor can he go behind us and purchase it for himself. We depend on each other."

Victor spat on the ground. A little blood came along with it. He moved his jaw in a circular motion and let out a quick breath. "That'll hurt tomorrow."

The three Vallenses followed the crowd toward the center of Florence. Though they wouldn't enter the cathedral, they could at least admire it from the outside. On their way, they passed churches and convents, taverns and brothels. Inside the walls of Florence, most structures had red-orange tile roofs that resembled the hue of the cathedral's dome.

When at last they turned into the plaza surrounding the cathedral, the mass of people made Andreas's breathing quicken. From one end to the other, the citizens of Florence jammed into the plaza. Men with billowing, pleated hats stood amid peasant men whose hair rested on their heads like overturned saucers. Women wore silk dresses of every springtime color and graced themselves with more gold and jewels than Andreas had ever witnessed. Flowers and ribbons adorned their hair, and while some women covered their hair with silk head coverings, others bared their locks to the breeze. Beauty reigned among the Florentines. No doubt

Florence was a wealthy city, which was not astonishing given that the florin—the primary coinage in southern Europe—was minted in the city.

Standing before the grandeur of the Cathedral of Santa Maria del Fiore made Andreas's skin tingle. The facade was adorned with lifelike sculptures of saints and legends. To the left, the bell tower reached into the heavens, while immediately before him stood the octagonal baptistery. Each deserved its own moment of wonder, but none could be compared to the dome vaulted on the far end of the cathedral. From the distant hills, the brick dome had appeared round, but up close it was clearly an octagon.

Andreas stood on his toes and scanned the crowd. A sea of lost souls, all sinking into darkness. Like Basile, they believed their devotion to the Catholic Church was a sign of their devotion to God. *If only everyone could read the Holy Scriptures and see their desperation.* Obstacles would certainly present themselves, but he and his friends were drawing near to the Bible. From there they had only to copy it, translate it, and spread it.

The bell sounded from high above, and the mass of parishioners swept through the portal and into the cathedral. As in any Catholic church building, all would stand for the duration of the liturgy. When they finished, many would continue about their day as if nothing had happened.

As the bells tolled, the crowd thinned until only the three Vallenses and a few others—Jews with their conical hats, Mohammedans with flowing white robes, and Greek priests with bushy beards—stood alone in the plaza. They exchanged curious glances until Victor motioned to a side street.

"Let's find somewhere to sleep for the night," he said. "I've been wanting a bed since Parma."

*   *   *

While most of Florence observed All Saints' Day, Andreas, Bertran, and Victor split up to find an inn for the night.

The streets had cleared of the most respectable citizens after the church bells had rung, leaving those whom society deemed outcasts and refuse. Scantily dressed women leaned from windows in one alley and beckoned for patrons. A sickness came to Andreas's stomach at the sight, as many were so young, far too young to be used by men for the duration of their lives. *More who need the Savior.*

On another street, two signs read LOCANDA—inn. A smile crept onto Andreas's face as he knocked on the closest door. The door creaked open, and Andreas said, "Myself and my three companions—"

"*Dov'è il tuo cavallo?*" the innkeeper asked in the Tuscan dialect. He wore a floppy yellow hat and billowing purple trousers, but his face was expressionless and lacked any sign of hospitality.

"I don't have a horse. We're from far to the northwest—"

"*Niente cavallo, niente letto.* No horse, no bed. You can't afford what I offer."
He pointed over Andreas's shoulder. "Try *il convento* up on the hill. They provide
beds for the poor."

"I'm not poor—"

The door slammed and would've smashed Andreas's nose if he hadn't taken a
step back first.

Three doors down, he knocked again, and when that innkeeper answered, he
slid his gaze from Andreas's eyes down to his knees. "*Questa non è una casa di
carità.*"

Andreas took a moment to process the unfamiliar language. The man had said
something about not being a charity. Andreas reached into his hidden pocket,
pulled out a few florins, and held them up to the innkeeper.

"You stole it, and I will take no part in your crime. *Vattene!* Be gone!" And
again the door slammed.

Andreas glanced down at his clothes. Though his coat begged to be tossed
into the river and his beard was longer than usual, he was far from a beggar. *These
Florentines hold high standards!*

Bells rang out from the cathedral again, signaling the end of the Mass. Andreas
and the other Vallenses had agreed to meet in front of the baptistery to share what
lodging they'd found and wait for Basile. As Andreas approached the cathedral
plaza, the parishioners flowed past and fanned out behind him. Bertran and
Victor were already in their place, standing near a bench and gawking at the bell
tower and dome again.

"Find anything?" Victor asked.

"Only a pair of slammed doors."

Bertran shrugged. "I found only brothels and rowdy taverns along the river."

"And all I saw were shops and monasteries," Victor said. "We could leave the
city tonight and sleep somewhere outside the walls. We've been doing that for
the past month."

Andreas closed his eyes. After all the walking, he'd been looking forward to a
few nights in a proper bed. But if a tent was their only option, it would need to
suffice.

The plaza cleared except for those passing through or selling their goods. All
three Vallenses looked for Basile, but there was no sign of him.

"He does tend to find us," Bertran said in an unsteady voice.

Andreas shook his head. "Tens of thousands of people live in Florence, and it
won't be as simple as finding us sitting on a log in a one-tavern town. We should
wait here, exactly where he left us."

"Always, he abandons us in his dust," Victor said. "The only reason Monsieur
Halphen is here is for the money. He's all about himself."

"No, he's all about Princess Yolande." Andreas eyed Victor. "Whatever she wishes, he'll accomplish it and report back. At the moment, her will is for us to find the Greek manuscript, and thus we have Basile. He won't stop until the manuscript safely returns to Piedmont."

Victor's face soured. He spread his legs to shoulder width and narrowed his eyes. "Then why has he disappeared yet again? I still don't trust him. What if he lied about killing that man with the patch? What if he was with them all along and was held back only by us defending ourselves? Now we're in Florence, and all he would need to do is hire a couple of men to beat us or tell a priest who we are. Andreas, it was a bad idea to trust the princess and her man."

"Basile has been nothing but loyal to us. I agree he's stubborn, and he leaves our company without informing us, but he is the key to our venture being successful." Andreas reached into his pocket and rubbed the Savoyard ring. "Without Basile, we become enemies of Prince Amadeus and Yolande."

The sun sank behind the tiled houses of Florence, but still Basile hadn't appeared. Andreas rose from the bench and stretched. Then a voice rose from over his shoulder.

"I've been looking for you three," Basile said. "I've also found *hébergement* for tonight."

Victor jumped up and confronted Basile. "Where were you? We've been waiting here since the Mass ended, right where you left us."

"*Je fais ce que je veux, cathare.*" Basile straightened and clenched his fist.

Victor grimaced and gave his head a slight shake. "What did the *francese deficiente* say, Andreas?"

Unfortunately, Basile must have understood what Victor had called him. He took a few steps forward with eyes set like a prowling hawk's.

Andreas stepped between the two, hands up. "Is this what we want? An evening brawl between two foreigners in the middle of Florence?"

"He shames me," Basile said, "calling me a moron while I try to find comfortable beds for us."

Andreas turned his head to Basile. "You called him a Cathar, and you know that's not what we are. We can't act like this, not when we're so close to our goal. Let's enjoy a restful night, and tomorrow we'll find Gedeon Chanforan." He stepped away but kept his eyes on Victor and Basile. "Lead the way, Monsieur Halphen."

Basile stared down Victor for another moment, then turned and waved them forward. "It's near, and I think you'll find the accommodations suitable for your . . . moral tastes."

After two turns, one to the right and one to the left, they stopped at an iron gate. Inside stood a large stone building and a small outbuilding, but the steeple and rose window confirmed Andreas's suspicions. A convent.

"I'd . . . rather we not stay here," Andreas said. "The Catholic Church won't show much kindness to us Vallenses."

"They probably don't know what a Vallense is around here," Basile said. "They won't make you attend Mass, either. It's cheap and warm and they have beds."

Andreas scanned the grounds. "Which order manages the convent?"

Before Basile could speak, the seal plastered on the gate answered the question. *Ordo Prædicatorum.* The Order of Preachers, or as they were more commonly known, Dominicans.

Victor tossed Andreas a subtle glance.

But the invitation was too much to leave lying by the roadside. They would either sleep in a warm bed in a monastery or shiver again under the starry sky. What if Basile was trying—in his own way—to show kindness? He was probably correct in saying the Florentine clergy knew nothing about Vallenses.

"You hesitate?" Basile chuckled. "Is it now my chance to lodge near people with whom I'm comfortable, while you choose to sleep on the street? Better friars than Jews, I say." Without waiting for a consensus, he opened the gate. "I'm going to bed, and if you want to sleep in the street, that's your choice."

Bertran and Victor looked at Andreas. Bertran's bright eyes and tapping foot made his opinion obvious, but Victor's indifferent frown made Andreas look closer.

A cold gust of air ripped through the street. Andreas pulled his ragged coat tighter, then admired the orange glow flickering from the outbuilding—likely the guesthouse. He nodded at Bertran and Victor, and together they followed Basile into the Dominican convent.

18

How superior, then, is the humble shepherd of these Alps, who reads his Bible, and lives in observance of its precepts, to the court-bred seigneur, whose château is a miracle of good taste, but from whose conversation and closet the sacred volume is excluded.

—William Beattie
The Waldenses, 1838

THE NEXT MORNING, after a restful and uneventful night at the convent, Andreas stood with Bertran, Victor, and Basile on Florence's primary thoroughfare, facing a three-story stone building crowned with merlons. A plaque above the door portrayed a resting lamb with the words PALAZZO DELL' ARTE DELLA LANA—the Palace of the Wool Guild. Men with elaborate hats, colorful coats, and billowing pants streamed in and out of the guildhall.

Victor rubbed his cheek. "Is this the place?"

"Gedeon Chanforan told us to ask for him here, whatever that meant. He should've arrived days ago, and these men will know where to find him." Andreas looked at the other three. "I can ask, so there's no reason for all of us to enter."

The other three nodded, and soon Andreas stood amid the bustle of Florence's famed wool trade. Merchants pressed by him without acknowledgment, while traders held up papers toward a desk at the far end of the palace and yelled prices.

"*Cinque fiorini per una balla!*" a short man shouted from the left.

A young man with an accent replied. "*Rapina!* No buyer will pay such a price!"

The room swelled with more bodies. Sounds of laughter mixed with grunts and sighs as the stakes of buying and selling made the guildhall feel like a hornet's nest.

Andreas stood on his toes and searched for a quieter place where he could find someone to ask about Gedeon. At the far right, under an elaborate fresco, three old men sat at a wooden desk, scribbling on parchment and calling out names. They appeared less occupied than the rest of the hall, so Andreas pushed and weaved his way toward them through the shouting and hand waving.

"*Scusi*," Andreas said in the Tuscan dialect. "I'm looking for a man who said you would know him."

None of the three bothered to raise his eyes from the table.

Andreas leaned closer and raised his voice. "Scusi—"

"*Ti sento.* I heard you," the man on the right grunted. "Who is it?"

"He's a merchant from Piedmont—"

"Name." The man cleared his throat and spat into a bucket beside him. He still hadn't made eye contact. "I don't care where people are from."

"Gedeon Chanforan. Tall, thin hair, strong chin—"

"*Salire le scale.* Go upstairs, and you'll find the crook there."

"*Grazie*," Andreas said, but the clerk ignored him.

Andreas followed the wall to a set of stone stairs leading to the second story. When he reached the top, instead of a raucous crowd of traders and merchants, a quiet scene of men lounging on padded chairs greeted him. As they conversed, they nibbled on oranges, dates, and grapes. In the center of the room, surrounded by men in bright overgowns, gold embroidered caps, and tight breeches, sat Gedeon Chanforan.

Gedeon's voice carried through the room, and all eyes were on the tall, muscular businessman. Andreas waited in the corner as Gedeon sipped from a silver goblet adorned with emeralds.

"Family is everything to me," Gedeon said in the Tuscan dialect. "You flank yourselves with a beautiful woman on each arm, but Marta and my children are enough for me."

An oily-haired man smirked. "They will gain your inheritance and squander it as all families do. Shouldn't we invest in things that will endure? In Florence, we have built the grandest of buildings and crafted the finest arts of the age. You hold more wealth than any of us, yet you squander it in Piedmont, a poor realm ruled by a petty duke."

"In Piedmont, I may invest in what I wish." Gedeon leaned forward on his elbows. His presence commanded the room. "As we speak, I am organizing the grandest venture yet, and someday, instead of seeing me in Florence, you will travel to my land and purchase my goods. The future is in the north, my friends."

The room burst into laughter, but Gedeon formed his lips into a wry smile.

"You laugh while you sit in your luxury," Gedeon said. "Florence could maintain so much more, but you throw your gold at the Medicis and let them choose your destiny. You build your cathedrals, sculpt your statues, spin your wool, but you are slaves to the republic. I, however, will navigate my own seas."

At that moment, Gedeon noticed Andreas. He raised his brows, jerked his head back, and stood. A splash of purple liquid lopped over the side of his goblet. "*Amici*, this is . . . Andreas."

Andreas pursed his lips. *He remembered my name.*

"I . . . I did not expect to see you here so soon." Gedeon walked toward Andreas, shook his hand, and slapped him on the shoulder.

I didn't think we were that close.

"He is here on a sort of treasure hunt"—he looked at Andreas for confirmation—"and has come all the way from Piedmont on foot, if I am not mistaken."

Andreas cleared his throat. "A treasure Signore Chanforan prodded me toward, I must add."

"Always the adventurer," Gedeon said to the others, forcing a hesitant chuckle. But his countenance fell as he looked at Andreas and whispered, "I bear unfortunate news, though. I'm afraid the manuscript is not in Florence, and neither will you find Ioannis Argyropoulos here. He has disappeared."

The floorboards collapsed from underneath Andreas—or so it felt. He didn't bother to whisper. "You told us—"

Gedeon hushed him. "We will speak of these matters outside, but I assure you: your Bible is not here. Yet do not think your quest is in vain. I have something you will find"—he smacked his lips—"more suitable."

Andreas tilted his head.

"My friends, I will return in a few moments." Gedeon gave a slight bow and led Andreas to the stairs.

Again Andreas weaved his way through the shouting patrons, this time following Gedeon, until they finally found the front door. Sweat beaded on his brow at the thought of telling the men their mission had failed. All the walking, all the danger, and now they would return with their heads sagging, defeated.

Outside, Bertran sat on a bench and stared at the surrounding buildings. Victor sat beside him. Basile paced in front of them, and when he saw Andreas, he stopped and crossed his arms. "Any answers?"

"The manuscript isn't here, and Gedeon doesn't know of its whereabouts."

Basile shook his head. "A fool's journey, then. I imagined it might end this way." He glared at Gedeon, who stood alongside Andreas. "Is this your friend Chanforan?"

Gedeon stepped forward and held out his hand.

But Basile glanced at Gedeon and kept his hand to himself. "Is this some kind of trick? My maîtresse invested twelve hundred florins—"

"Who is it that financed your trip?" Gedeon asked with narrowed eyes.

Andreas looked at Basile. Should he reveal their collaboration with Princess Yolande? It didn't matter now—the manuscript was lost to them. Andreas blurted out the answer. "Princess Yolande."

Basile frowned and clenched a fist at his side. "You were supposed to keep your mouth closed, my Prince Andreas."

Andreas tightened his mouth and glared at Basile.

"Prince?" Gedeon took a step to the side and examined Andreas. "Are you . . . do you . . . is the princess . . . ?"

No use lying now. "Yes, I am the third son of Duke Louis of Savoy. You can put the rest together, though I beg you, Monsen Chanforan, keep that to yourself."

Gedeon nodded and pressed his lips together, his eyes wandering.

They stood there silent while throngs of citizens moved behind them, some heading to the cathedral and others toward the bridge over the River Arno.

Andreas slowly shook his head. He had failed not only his three companions but also Constanza and the Vallenses of the Angrogna Valley. Nicolaus Pavarin, Estève, even Bertran and Victor—they would remember Andreas for his failures, not his victories. They might never declare it, but he would always be an outsider to them.

"We have failed," Basile said, "and all for a phantom relic."

Victor stood and tightened his belt. "No reason to stay here, then. We should head out tomorrow. I need to return to my family."

"We were so close," Bertran said, his hands splayed out in front of him.

"No, it was my fault. All of it. I pursued the manuscript with such vigor. I have wanted it so much that I willed it to be true." Andreas glanced at Gedeon. "Despite the details I had been given."

Gedeon had one eye squinted, but otherwise his expression remained the same.

"So, we shall leave in the morning," Basile said. "One more night in the convent."

"Which one?" Gedeon asked.

"San Marco."

Gedeon nodded and lifted a finger to his chin. "Andreas, may I speak with you for a moment?"

"As long as it has nothing to do with my family. I cannot offer you anything, nor can I grant you any titles."

"Of course not. It is something I have been pondering since I met you in Turin in the summer." Gedeon glanced at the other men. "May we have a moment of privacy?"

Basile huffed, then motioned for Bertran and Victor to follow. "We'll be at San Marco."

Gedeon turned to Andreas as soon as they were alone. "I offer you something far grander and more prestigious than a Greek Bible."

*   *   *

The sun had risen to its apex as Gedeon led Andreas to a marble bench outside the Palazzo dell' Arte della Lana. The air was unseasonably warm, much warmer than the previous day, so Andreas took off his coat and laid it beside him.

"I'm sorry your Bible is not here," Gedeon said, "but it was folly all along. Though I had doubts, I never expressed them. For that I apologize."

"Where is the manuscript? Surely you know where this Ioannis Argyropoulos lives now."

"Perhaps in Siena. More likely Rome. Nevertheless, he probably doesn't have the Bible."

"Why didn't you tell me before we spent a month walking here?"

"Last I had heard, Ioannis Argyropoulos was here, but I never guaranteed it. I tried to dissuade you in Turin, but you refused to listen."

"Yet you still said you'd meet me here."

"Which I have, exactly as I promised." Gedeon clasped his hands together and leaned back. "I like you, Andreas. You impressed me last summer when you dined at my villa. Now you have somehow organized a team who followed you on a difficult journey. You also used your position to garner the support of royalty and obtain financing."

"Didn't you mention you had something else for me?" Andreas asked in a flat voice. "Is it a different Greek manuscript?"

Gedeon chuckled. "Don't you see? It's just scraps of paper, older than the stones on which we stand. Nothing. Perhaps you might have sold the manuscript and bought yourself a plot of land, but little more. I am here to offer you something of substance, something that will bring you far more renown than a stack of dusty religious texts."

"I led three men down here for that Bible. And my investor"—he hesitated—"Princess Yolande will be highly disappointed at our failure."

"Enough about the Bible. Don't you understand that I wish to offer you a position in my company? I want to make you a wealthy man. You are too savvy to plow fields and waste your talents on relic hunts. I will give you a life of security, comfort, ease—right here in Florence, for I need eyes, ears, and intellect to manage my investments here."

"You present that offer only now that you know my lineage." Andreas waved Gedeon off and turned to leave.

"Your family does not interest me. Besides, what fortune would I gain to employ the third son of an inept duke? As soon as the House of Savoy found out about you, they would drag you back to Chambéry and force you to marry an atrocious German princess. Or am I mistaken?"

He wasn't. Everything Gedeon said was true. Perhaps his offer was genuine. Andreas slid back on the bench.

"Madomaisèla Constanza—you wish to enjoy a future with her, no?"

Andreas waited a moment before nodding.

"Imagine living in Florence—the center of humanity, the pendulum of culture and commerce—and never living in want. I will guarantee you a stable income, and as my fortunes improve, so will yours."

"Life is more than comfort. I have a purpose, and I have chosen to follow after that."

"As a barbe?" Gedeon waved his hand toward the ground. "I see how that old man treated you at my villa. The Vallenses see you as a liability, while I see you as an asset. And if the Vallenses ever accept you, would you rather live as a rambling, aimless preacher or enjoy a life of wealth and prestige?"

"You don't understand—"

"No, I fully understand. That is the way of the barbes. If a barbe has a wife and children, they live in squalor. When he returns home after months or a year, he might bring a ducat or two with him and throw it at his wife, then blame her for the house being in disorder. Is that who you want to be, Andreas?"

Andreas fidgeted with the tattered coat beside him, not quite looking Gedeon in the eye. "It's not as you make it sound."

Gedeon shook his head. "Take your chances, then. Do as you think your deity wants, but know that you will bear eternal regrets if you refuse my very generous offer. And do not think my proposal is for the sake of compassion. I am a businessman. My job is to turn gold into more gold. You're a leader and a driven man, and I need someone like you in Florence."

Andreas bowed his head toward the ground. Most of what Gedeon said felt . . . right. There he sat, a failure in his greatest endeavor. Now a renowned merchant offered him the blessing of a position in his company. Any man lower than a king would leap at the opportunity. *I may live and worship among Vallenses, but am I one of them?* Perhaps Andreas wasn't meant to be a barbe. Vallenses who knew the Holy Scriptures, ones who could preach the good news of the Savior without stammering or fumbling, would accomplish so much more than he could.

But what would Constanza think? Would she be willing to forsake her home and family to plant roots in Florence? They could be the first believers in a growing city—the beginnings of a new Vallense church. With time, they could spread the gospel in one of the most important cities in all of Italy, if not Europe. Had God led him to Florence for the chance to work for Gedeon?

Andreas sat back and folded his hands. "We're leaving in the morning to head back to Piedmont, and I can't give you an answer by then. After you return to Turin—"

"Is it that difficult of a decision?" Gedeon straightened his back and lowered his eyebrows. "Next week, I depart on a ship north. You can find me here at the Wool Guild when you come to your senses."

Andreas gave a half smile, stood, and stuck his hand out for Gedeon to shake. "I will consider your offer."

Gedeon stood, turned, and marched through the door into the guildhall, leaving Andreas alone.

Andreas dropped back onto the bench and considered Gedeon's offer. After the disappointment of the lost manuscript, had God given him another opportunity—another path on which to travel, an open door through which he could step?

What would Monsen Estève say? Andreas laughed under his breath at the thought of Estève's reaction: rolled eyes, animated hands, a thorough scolding. If Raimond were still alive, he would smack Andreas on the back of the head and call him an imbecile for simply entertaining the offer.

Not two years before, God had rescued him from a life of sin, misery, and aimlessness. God had placed Andreas amidst people who truly believed the Holy Scriptures and lived by them. His life belonged to the Savior, not himself, and despite the life of comfort Gedeon offered, God had another purpose for Andreas's life. No, Gedeon's offer was not for him.

Standing, Andreas peered down the street to his right. The cathedral's massive orange dome peeked over the buildings. He turned in that direction and began the walk to San Marco's Convent.

19

There seems to me to have been twice as much done in some ages in defending the Bible as in expounding it, but if the whole of our strength shall henceforth go on to the exposition and spreading of it, we may leave it pretty much to defend itself.

—Charles Haddon Spurgeon
Speech at the Annual Meeting of the British and Foreign Bible Society, 1875

ONE WEEK HAD PASSED since Johan had delivered the tax and rent bill to Papà, and, as Papà had guessed, he was not the only one. Every family in the valley had received bills demanding the same or worse. Though a few men had tried, none had yet persuaded Johan to listen, let alone understand.

But Constanza and Elionor aimed to gain a different outcome. They had known Johan since childhood, and though he might have strayed from his faith in Christ, he was still the same boy they'd always known.

The women walked under barren trees along the windswept hills flanking the northern end of the Luserna Valley, heading toward Castelvecchio.

Word had come to the Angrogna Valley about the castle the new Lord of Luserna would occupy. Minor nobles had occupied Castelvecchio for generations, but over the past decades, it had fallen into disrepair. Now Johan Lauras apparently managed the efforts to put the castle back into working order.

"Will he listen?" Elionor asked Constanza.

"He'll listen, but the true question is: will he be reasonable? Johan knows as much as any of us that we are poor people and trouble no one. We'll remain loyal, but our fathers and brothers can't pay what the lord demands."

They soon passed out of the forest and onto the hillcrest. To the right, grapevines clung to trellises. Before them, the foothills of the Alps moderated down into gentle hills, and farther in the distance, the fertile Piedmont plains melted into the horizon. Constanza stopped and took deep breaths as she stared past the fields, rivers, and streams. Somewhere out there was Turin and the other cities of the plains. Four months had passed since the fire. Farther yet was Florence, where Andreas and the others had gone. A blast of cold air pushed her from behind.

Their destination rose to the left: ominous, mossy stones amid an overgrown stand of evergreens. Sounds of hammering and sawing echoed down the hillside. "This must be Castelvecchio," Constanza said.

"Not as impressive as I'd expected." Elionor slowed her pace. "At least for the dues this lord demands. I imagined something more . . . grand."

Constanza pushed up her sleeves, turned left, and quickly wound up the cobblestone path toward the villa. Near the top, two hounds greeted them with barks and howls. A whistle called them back, and Johan knelt down and let the hounds lick his face.

"I wasn't expecting such fine guests today," Johan said between slobbering kisses. "I have tea and bread if you wish to visit."

"Enough with the cordiality, Johan. You know why we're here." Constanza widened her stance and stood with one foot slightly ahead of the other, arms crossed.

"I almost forgot that we didn't leave on pleasant terms after our last meeting. I wanted to apologize for my"—he blinked a few times—"impoliteness."

Constanza took a step back and let her arms drop to her sides. An apology from Johan Lauras? "I suppose . . . I forgive you."

"Good. Now let me show you what's kept me so busy." Johan waved them ahead and coaxed the hounds to follow. Constanza and Elionor drew beside Johan and listened. "Castelvecchio—she's seen many families live under her roof, and she will soon be praiseworthy again. Today twelve men are working here, some with their wives and children. These are good, hardworking people. Your papà would like them, Connie. And the lord will reward them soon."

"Who is this lord you speak of?" Constanza asked. "We keep hearing you say *lord*, but no one has seen him. Why is he so secretive? Why not show his face? Or will he rule us from afar while he crusades across the sea and spends winters in the south?"

Johan let out an abrupt chuckle. "My lord is no crusader. You see what he is building here, and it's only the beginning. He wishes to bring prosperity to these impoverished valleys—indeed, for anyone who desires it."

"Then why does he impoverish us with taxes we can't pay?"

Johan shook his head as he focused on the ground. "I guessed your father would send you up here to beg."

"This was entirely our idea. My papà wouldn't send me to grovel, not when he is thrice the man you are." Constanza bit her tongue. *I shouldn't have said that.*

"Do you hear your friend, Elionor? Again she throws insults, always stooping to childish defamation."

Despite the biting wind, Constanza's cheeks warmed. "What would our gracious lord do if my papà can't meet his demands? Will he throw us and the thirteen orphans we house into a snowdrift?"

"Connie, we both know your father is a wealthy man. With all the land he owns, which is far more than any peasant needs, he could build his own villa and live in peace. Believe me, he can pay."

Constanza closed her eyes and held her tongue from unleashing everything she felt. Johan may have been the same person as before, but he'd become more unbearable—if that was possible. Nevertheless, she sighed and mumbled, "If you give us a year, perhaps we can—"

"A month should be plenty of time. If it takes selling part of your grain stores, then so be it."

"We gained thirteen extra mouths to feed this winter, and we don't know when their parents will return—"

"The lord didn't force you to take in so many Catholic orphans. They're not your blood, so why concern yourself with someone else's children?"

Elionor stepped forward. "The orphans are God's children first. Many have professed their own belief in Christ, and none are Catholic."

"That's not what the law says. Catholic children belong in Catholic families. They were baptized into the Roman Church, were they not?"

"We don't know," Constanza said, frowning. "Luca and Vitòria Grimaldi found most of them starving on the streets of Turin, and if the priest happened to baptize a few, it's not as if the Church owns them." She quieted her tone. "If the papists want them, perhaps they should've cared for their own instead of letting us poor heretics do it for them."

"Be careful, Constanza Pavarin. You shouldn't trifle with such weighty matters." Johan took a step toward Constanza—too close.

Constanza took a step back. "I have seen my share of atrocities, and I don't wish to see more."

"Then I suggest you let the orphans go back to their families."

"Johan, they have no families. We are their family." Constanza looked to Elionor and waited for help. Why had she said so little?

Johan shook his head again and ran his hand through his hair. "There is so much you two don't understand. The world is changing. The ground shifts under the House of Savoy. A hundred years from now, who will remember Vallenses or Bibles or orphans? No, the future has arrived for all of us. Instead of gazing up at the clouds, waiting for Christ to judge the earth, you should focus on improving your life now. And I don't mean you alone. I mean all the Vallenses. You don't want to awaken years from now to discover you have been left in the dust of history."

"All so we can transform ourselves into the model human—Johan Lauras, beloved steward of the Lord of Luserna." Constanza let out a laugh. "Perhaps you'll be the one history leaves behind—yet another who thought himself too wise or too civilized to follow God's Word."

"God's Word? You mean the stack of old parchment in the schoolhouse? Or shall I say, what was once there?"

Constanza opened her mouth, then bit her bottom lip. The look in Johan's eyes begged for further probing. "The one stolen from us? Perhaps if we had a lord to protect us from petty thieves, we would still have that old stack of parchment."

"Or perhaps if your papà paid his taxes, the lord would be more willing to provide protection."

Constanza drew her eyebrows together and lowered her voice. "I can't wait for Andreas to return and see the phenomenal man you've become."

"I wouldn't put too much hope in Andreas. Remember, he is a noble. All he has ever gained has been because of his blood, not his own wisdom or decisiveness. Besides, what is he after again? Some old Greek manuscript?"

Constanza tilted her head. "How do you know?"

"Oh, rumors tend to make their way to my ears. I also heard he may be in some degree of . . . danger." Johan shrugged and showed a disingenuous smile. Was this the same man who had grown up just down the hill from her? He had the same sandy hair and grin, but the Johan she remembered would have defended Andreas, not despised him. But somewhere, buried under this new Johan, was the boy from down the slope. God had not forsaken Johan, and neither should she. Her sharp answers and condescension would bring nothing but more spite.

Constanza looked Johan in the eye. "God has not forsaken you, and neither will we. I shall pray for you to return."

Johan gave a quick headshake, turned, and marched back toward the castle.

Elionor stood staring at the workers on the castle wall, not paying attention to the conversation. A man winked at her, and she responded with a coy smile and blush.

Constanza grabbed Elionor's arm and turned back toward home. "I hope I only imagined what I saw."

"What?" Elionor said.

"Please, Ellie. You're too good for whatever you think you like."

"It was only a little smile."

"You were giving that man something to hope for. That's what you were doing."

"I told you, Connie, don't fret over me."

First Johan, and now Elionor. Who were her friends now? Not the ones who made her laugh, but those whom she could trust?

She closed her eyes and imagined the strong, noble-hearted, God-fearing man to whom she had bid adieu last month. But then she shuddered at Johan's words. How would he know if Andreas was in danger?

She said a quick prayer for the man she loved and continued trekking along the ridge back to the farm.

*   *   *

Wind blew across Constanza's cheeks and caused her to pull her coat up. Papà swung his ax at the upright log and split it in two. Each of his swings hit its mark and splintered the wood—more fuel for the household's continual needs. Clothes must be washed, food must be cooked, and the house must be heated.

Constanza had tried splitting firewood but produced much less than Papà in more time. She stepped beside him, earning a smile from his creased and weathered face. "If you'd like, I can help stack."

"No need, Constanza. I'm nearly finished." Papà set his ax on the ground and wiped his brow with the back of his arm. Still, he sweated, though she shivered at the same time. "Where were you and Elionor this morning?"

"At Castelvecchio to speak with Johan."

Papà huffed and picked up his ax. "You shouldn't go off that far without telling me."

"It was farther than we expected. There's a sizable group of men working on the old castle, and our new lord will enjoy quite the residence by the time it's finished."

Papà chopped at the side of a log to make it shorter. "Please don't strap the burden of politics on yourself."

"The burden belongs to all of us, Papà. The rent and taxes strain you, so it strains us all . . ." Constanza paused, but before she completed her thought, Papà interrupted.

"You think I'm old." He laughed, set a log on its head, and swung down. "I can still out-muscle your brothers."

"But that leg of yours—"

"One day it will return to normal."

Papà denied reality. For over a year, he had nursed his knee, but it had improved only a little. He walked everywhere with a limp but winced through the pain. It was worse in the mornings, when it seemed he could scarcely move across the room. Whether or not Papà believed it, he would never be the man of his youth.

"I don't want to place more on your shoulders," Constanza said, "but Johan said something that worried me. Perhaps he was just saying it to scare us into paying our dues, but it's about the orphans." As Papà kept splitting wood and

Constanza helped stack, she recounted Johan's warning about Vallenses caring for Catholic children.

"Being Catholic isn't in a person's blood," Papà said. "Just as being a Vallense isn't in a person's blood. We aren't born into the family of God through our mothers and fathers, but through Christ's redemption. Even if any of the children were baptized into the Catholic Church, it means nothing."

"Are we putting ourselves in danger by housing the orphans?"

"We're always in danger, and though we participate in the world's systems, the world will never fully accept us. Doesn't Christ tell us these things?"

Constanza pulled the words from her memory. "'If the world hate you, ye know that it hated me before it hated you. If ye were of the world, the world would love his own: but because ye are not of the world, but I have chosen you out of the world, therefore the world hateth you.' The Lord of Luserna surely doesn't hate us, and neither does Johan."

Papà shook his head. "Johan won't cause any problems for us—other than the taxes, of course."

"If he goes further, then what can we do? Do we appeal to Prince Amadeus again, as Andreas did last year?"

Papà grunted and shook his head. "Please don't think about it too much, but the men of the church have spoken about these matters—"

"If our rulers turned on us we could hide." Constanza put a hand on her cheek and glanced at the firewood. "When we were girls, Elionor and I would play in the forest across the creek from the Lauras farm. There's a cave there—"

"You're imagining the worst. Don't fill your mind with the future while you live in the present. We plan in order to provide for our needs, not to step ahead of God. 'Take therefore no thought for the morrow.'"

From the time she could remember, Papà had said the same. He directed his family's thoughts to the present—not to neglect their provision but to work with and enjoy what God had given them now.

"Still, I feel we should plan," Constanza said.

Papà put another log on the chopping block. "I pray it never comes to hiding in a cave."

A cry rang out from inside the house, and Constanza groaned. "Mamà should be enjoying her own grandchildren, not managing orphans."

"True, she's weary every night, but she's the most self-sacrificing person I know. You'll rarely hear your mamà complain."

"It wears on both of you, though." Constanza lifted a split log above her shoulder and placed it on the woodpile.

"My body is not my own, which is why I don't plan too far into the future. If my wishes didn't match the reality God has set in motion, I would be disappointed daily. I can only accept the circumstances God places me in, then glorify Him regardless of my earthly desires. My flesh fights against it, but the Spirit molds me into contentment."

Constanza smiled and kept her eyes on Papà. He was an excellent farmer, but he would've made a better preacher.

"Still no word from the Grimaldis," Papà said. "You said Andreas would send a message if he heard anything in Turin, but we've received nothing. Your mamà and I feel something terrible may have happened."

"The children are everything to Luca and Vitòria, and I'm sure they wouldn't abandon them." Constanza wet her lips. "What do you think happened?"

Papà's ax glanced off the side of the log, splitting off a wood sliver. "I'm unsure. When Andreas returns—"

"He won't be back for at least another month."

"We could ask the peddlers down in the La Torre market. If anything happened to the Grimaldis, they would know."

"Ellie and I will ask. I was planning to go down to the market and sell apples and the little extra linen I have." Constanza strained to pick up the last log, but before she could heave it to the top of the stack, Papà grabbed it with one hand and stacked it himself.

"Be cautious. Strange men lurk down there—men from the plains."

"I know, Papà, but I'll be surrounded by Vallenses. La Torre is full of believers, and one of the largest Vallense churches is there. We'll leave at sunup, so we can be there before midmorning."

.

20

After the final overthrow of Constantinople, the Greek scholars and ecclesiastics, who then filled Europe with the news of their calamity, became the channels for transmitting to all the west the precious remains of early Christianity; and providence prepared the church with the new art of printing to preserve and diffuse them. It was thus that the Constantinopolitan manuscripts, the representatives of the common text of former ages, became the parents of our received text.

—Robert Lewis Dabney
The Doctrinal Various Readings of the New Testament Greek, 1890

ANDREAS LAY ON HIS MAT and gazed at the window of San Marco's Convent, waiting for the sunlight to emerge. His body ached, his eyes itched, and his thoughts drifted. The night had dragged and ground like an ungreased cart axle.

The trek back to Piedmont would be long and dreary and cold. When he returned to the Angrogna Valley, he would bear no tales of victory, no feats of glory, and no blessings to share with fellow believers. He would return as a failure, with months of not only his own time wasted but also that of Bertran, Victor, and Basile. And what would Princess Yolande do? She would never finance another quest, even if they learned where the manuscript was.

For the thousandth time, or so it felt, Basile's snores roared. Throughout the night, the heavy breathing, snorting, and throat clearing had kept Andreas tossing from one side to the other. Andreas glanced toward the window again. The slightest glint of orange in the sky signaled the new day.

Time wore on—the rooster crows became more consistent, and carts soon clattered on the cobblestone. At last the sounds of Prime, the convent's early morning liturgy, rang in his ears, beginning with the Athanasian Creed. "*Quicumque vult salvus esse, ante omnia opus est, ut teneat catholicam fidem,*" the monks chanted from the sanctuary. "Whosoever will be saved, before all things it is necessary that he hold the Catholic faith."

Andreas's lips moved to the cadence by instinct. That had been another life, like the echoes of a distant voice carrying down from the hills. Yet the words were all in vain—empty chants with which the friars sought to reconcile their souls to God. But the words of Jesus Christ dispelled the chants: *Take my yoke upon you, and learn of me; for I am meek and lowly in heart: and ye shall find rest unto your souls.*

Victor sat upright on his mat and rubbed his eyes. He groaned as he stood and reached his hands toward the ceiling. "Time to open your eyes."

Basile bolted upright, but Bertran rolled over and pulled his blanket to his nose. Andreas sat, yawned, and turned his torso. "Where were you last night, Basile? I heard you come in late."

"Roaming." Basile cracked his neck and began to pack his belongings into his sack. "I had suspicions about our encounter with Monsieur Chanforan yesterday, and those suspicions proved to be *bien fondé*—as sure as the foundation of the grandest castle."

"I don't understand," Andreas said. "Do you not trust him?"

"I trust Monsieur Chanforan as much as I would trust a lame-legged horse in battle. From the moment I set my eyes on him, I felt a bad omen. Last night, I asked around the city about our contact, Ioannis Argyropoulos." Basile tightened his belt and positioned his sword scabbard at his side. "He's here in the city and teaches Greek at the Studium Generale, the main university in Florence. It's only a short walk from here."

Andreas widened his eyes. "Gedeon must have received faulty information."

"Or he's lying to us," Victor said, scratching the back of his head. "I agree with Basile on this one." He cleared his throat. "As odd as that may sound."

"Why did you say nothing before?" Andreas asked Basile. "I would have listened."

"To me, you seemed quite enthralled by Monsieur Chanforan. May I ask, Andreas, what did he speak to you about yesterday?"

Andreas gave his head a little shake. "No, it was nothing. He . . . he asked me to join his company. I didn't give him an answer, but after thinking on it, I chose to refuse."

"I'm glad you are not *un imbécile*, Andreas." Basile gave a half smile. "I did more last night than discover Monsieur Argyropoulos's whereabouts. I also asked a few people about Monsieur Chanforan."

Andreas tapped his finger on his elbow. "And?"

"All the merchants in town love to deal with him."

"I don't understand what you're saying."

"Allow me to finish. Though the merchants enjoy his patronage, he has taken on massive debts. The Medicis—the de facto rulers here in Florence—bank for him, but they are becoming impatient. Rumor is that Monsieur Chanforan wandered into the city last week, bragging about paying off his debts all at once."

"He's a wealthy man," Andreas said, "and a shrewd merchant—"

"Or a reckless one. To our benefit, it sounds as if our treasure is here in Florence, and I propose we walk down the street and get it. Now, before we leave."

Andreas shot a glance at the door. It was far-fetched but worth trying. Perhaps Basile was right, but Gedeon had no reason to lie to them. "We should stop by the studium on our way out."

But as Andreas spoke, Victor turned his head toward the door. His hand shifted to his sword hilt, and he tiptoed to the other side of the room. Andreas must have been the only one who had noticed, for Bertran and Victor continued to speak.

"This may not be the failure we had imagined," Bertran said. "What will it be like seeing a Bible older than any other, perhaps the oldest of all?"

Basile threw a hand up. "I trust the apostles and their successors more than anything coming from the Greeks."

"How do you know the clergy are correct in what they preach? What guides them?"

"Tradition passed down from Christ Himself. Divine revelation."

Bertran shook his head. "Tradition changes, and the dogma of the Catholic Church transforms from generation to generation. How do you know the Church isn't exalting its own power and influence instead of Christ's?"

"Faith," Basile said. "Faith that God has revealed His will to us through His men."

"And that's where our differences are most obvious. We believe God has shown His will to us through His words, which He gave to us in the Holy Scriptures. All faith, all commandments, all practice must agree with His Word."

Victor stood with his ear aimed at the door. Andreas kept one eye on Bertran and Basile and the other on Victor's sly movements.

"After hundreds of years," Basile said to Bertran, "how do you imagine yourselves to be bearers of the truth? It is we Catholics who developed the doctrine of the Trinity, and it's the Church that preserved the manuscript we seek."

"No, it is God who has preserved it," Bertran said. "The Word of God is eternal. 'For ever, O LORD, thy word is settled in heaven.' And thus is the doctrine of the Trinity eternal. No council or creed can create doctrine. Men can only affirm what God has ordained from the foundations of the world. To say man has preserved the Holy Scriptures and its teachings tells only part of the truth. God has used men throughout the ages, first to inscribe His Word on papyrus and parchment, then to copy it and use it in each generation. Perhaps even you, Basile, will soon be a link in that chain, whether you know it or not."

Suddenly the door burst open. Victor took one step out, pulled a black-robed man through the door, and held his sword at the friar's neck. "Look what I trapped—a black rat."

"I . . . I . . . heard voices in the room," the friar said, shaking. "I mean you no harm."

Basile stepped forward. "Who told you to listen to us?"

The friar pressed his lips together, and Victor pressed his sword closer.

"*Obsecro ne me occidas*," the friar said in Latin.

Victor looked to Andreas. "What did he say?"

"'Please don't kill me.'"

The friar nodded, but only a little. "*Verum.* It was the abbot. I know nothing more."

"Why did your abbot wish you to spy on us?" Basile stooped down to the friar's eyes.

"*Nescio.* I don't know. I needed to listen for details about a Bible. And a man named Andreas."

Victor let his sword drop and loosened his grip on the friar. "I doubt he's lying."

"It's the Dominicans," Andreas said. He adjusted his coat and vest. "I knew staying at this convent would be dangerous."

"We leave at once," Basile said.

"I'll lock the friar in here." Victor tapped the man with his foot. "You wanted to be in here anyway, didn't you?" Victor sat the friar on the floor, commanded him to stay, and threw out a few threats, but nothing serious. They left the room and walked to the gate. The friars were all still in the sanctuary, save for the spy.

"Can we still check at the studium for Ioannis Argyropoulos?" Andreas asked.

"Yes," said Basile, "but we must keep our eyes and ears alert. Our presence in Florence is known, as well as our mission."

Despite the danger pressing down on them, Andreas's hopes simmered near a boil. Could they be so close? Perhaps the quest would be successful despite the setbacks. The massive cathedral appeared again, and Basile pointed to the left. "Past the baptistery and the bell tower, there's a narrow road. The studium is just off the plaza. If there's a time for you heretics to pray, now would be ideal."

Andreas felt for the sack of coins as he and his companions walked through the plaza and toward the ultimate goal.

*   *   *

The company of four stared at the doorway of the Studium Generale. A coat of arms above the arched doorway guarded the establishment. Six circles were arranged on a shield in a hexagon pattern, with the topmost circle containing a fleur-de-lis. Seeing that coat of arms around Florence was common, for it was the sign of the House of Medici, the rich rulers of the city.

"Do we simply step through the door," Victor asked, "or will they expect us to carry an invitation?"

"We don't need an official invitation, but we'll at least knock." Andreas hammered his fist on the hardwood door and waited.

A man with a pointy blue hat answered. "*Salve*," he said in Latin. His eyes were narrowed, and he maintained a shallow frown.

Andreas stepped forward. "Does a certain Ioannis Argyropoulos teach here? He's Greek—"

"*Sic.* He does."

Andreas turned to the others, and each man's face reflected his own anticipation. "We don't have an appointment, but we wish to speak with him, only for a few moments—"

Before Andreas could finish, the man opened the door and waved them in. "Signore Argyropoulos will teach later in the morning, but he typically prepares in his closet beforehand." He pointed down a hallway. "You will find him behind the fourth door on the left, under the stairs."

When they arrived, Andreas knocked, and after a second try, the latch clicked. A man with a neatly trimmed white beard peeked through the slit and grinned. He wore a squat, brimmed black hat and a plain burgundy vest—definitely not the flashy Florentine style. His eyes widened as he examined the company.

"I am Andreas de Bonomo, and these are my companions: Bertran Arnaldi, Victor of Bricherasio, and Basile Halphen."

The man swung the door open and thrust out his hand. "I am John Argyropoulos, Ioannis in my native tongue. *Quomodo te adiuvare possum?* How can I help you, my friends?"

Andreas cleared his throat. "We've journeyed from far in the northwest. Gedeon Chanforan, a friend"—he hesitated to call him that now—"mentioned you might possess a Greek document."

Ioannis moved aside with a skip in his step and invited them through the door. "Who is this man you speak of?"

"Gedeon Chanforan," Basile said with a gravelly voice. "He's a rich burgher from Piedmont."

"I am not familiar with that name." Ioannis closed one eye and tightened the corner of his mouth. "No, I cannot recall any Chanforans."

"He captained the ship that rescued you from Constantinople."

"Ah, the voyage where I spent everything I possessed for very poor accommodations. Yes, I remember him now. He was tall, had strong arms, and quite the imposing presence too."

Andreas raised his eyebrows and nodded.

Ioannis plopped into a chair near stacks of parchment strewn about in disorder. "Look around you. I own many Greek manuscripts—collections from Plato, others from Aristotle. For the past five years—thanks to Medicis sponsoring my work—I have been translating them into Latin, but it is unfortunate how underappreciated they are." A frown formed before he gave his head a shake and held up a finger. "Yet some of my students show promise. And I am thrilled to see that my efforts to save the ancient works have not been in vain."

Ioannis stood from his chair and rushed to a wooden crate near a window. He chuckled as he opened it. "Aristotle's *Metaphysica* is a particular favorite, though I prefer the literal Greek rendering: *ta meta ta physika*—that means 'things after the ones about the natural world.' Look at this!" He shoved a heap of papers into Andreas's hands. "What are your thoughts on causation, my friend? What makes the matter of the universe move in such miraculous order? True, God is the author of all, but how does He perform His work? Through the metaphysical world, of course!" Ioannis wrung his hands and bounced on his toes now. "Tell me, are metaphysics an interest of yours? Which university do you represent?"

"We represent no university, and though I imagine Aristotle is worthy of study, his works—"

Ioannis clapped his hands together, cackled, and bounded back to the chest. "Plato! You seek Plato! I knew when I saw your faces you were of the Platonic school of thought. His views of metaphysics are perhaps in contrast to Aristotle, but still valid and thought-provoking. The Florentines seem to prefer his school, but I—"

"I don't seek Plato or Aristotle, Dominus. What we seek is far more precious than what any ancient philosopher offers."

Ioannis scratched his head and sank back into his chair, dropping a stack of papers on his lap. He waved away the puff of dust and coughed. "I do not understand. Every genuine scholar desires to study the works of the ancients. We Greeks preserved their works while you Latins lost all traces of old Athens. You can thank us alone—perhaps the Mohammedans a little too—for preserving works such as *The Republic*, *Politics*, *On the Heavens*—"

"We seek something far more ancient—eternal words that no man or angel can destroy."

A quietness fell upon the room. Ioannis's abrupt movements and rushed speech ceased, and he replaced them with slow blinks, an open mouth, and a pondering gaze. "You seek the Holy Scriptures, the Word of God."

Andreas took a step forward and nodded. "We've journeyed for weeks to find a Greek manuscript that rumor says you possess. We also realize its value and are willing to pay with gold florins."

Ioannis crossed his arms, drew them tight into his abdomen, and sighed. "The Latin Catholics sent you, did they? You hoard our religious texts from the East, shelf them in your libraries, and forget about them."

"We don't associate with Catholics, neither Latin nor Greek. Princess Yolande of Savoy sent us." Andreas paused, not wanting to reveal more.

"Savoy?" Ioannis smacked his lips. "Last I heard, their duke is still loyal to the treacherous Latin pope."

"Our people love the Holy Scriptures, and we know you own an ancient copy."

"Is that what they're saying? You . . . or they . . . or whoever is mistaken." Ioannis chewed on his fingernails. "I am a scholar of philosophy, not a theologian. Now, unless you bring questions about logic or metaphysics, I will be of no help." He stood and drifted toward the door. "It was a pleasure to meet you, my friends, but students await me—"

"Wait," Andreas said. "You're hiding something—"

"No more details from me." Ioannis gave a quick shrug. "If you find a Greek Bible, though, please come back and tell me."

Basile stepped between Ioannis and the door. "We're able to pay up to a thousand florins."

"One thousand? Ten hundred? And you said 'gold florins'? Not cheap copper from the Castilians?"

"One thousand gold florins, minted right here in this city."

"That's unfortunate, because I had a box on the ship when I fled Constantinople. But I see no money here. And I am unwilling to inform Latin Catholics as to the whereabouts of such a holy item . . . if I know of one."

Victor loosened his belt, untied his coin sack, and slammed it into Ioannis's hands. "Three hundred. Count for yourself."

"We each carry the same amount," Basile said.

Ioannis counted on his fingers, and when he reached ten, he threw his head back and squinted. "That's twelve hundred."

Basile lowered his voice. "We offer one thousand. Accept it, or we're headed home. We aren't afraid to leave you alone and without a single coin."

Andreas bit his tongue. Was Basile willing to throw their mission to the wind for two hundred florins? *I hope it's only a negotiation tactic.*

"This manuscript that I may possess—I would not sell it for a thousand-thousand florins. I do not want to see it in a library, forsaken and forgotten until the world burns. It is beyond precious, the eternal Word of God, spoken by the Spirit, written on papyrus and parchment by holy men of old, all in the common Greek long ago spoken in the East. The Holy Scriptures are much more than a scholarly work—they are soul-transforming. No words on this earth are more powerful and true. That is why I do not trust the Latin Church, and that is why I will not separate from the manuscript."

"We are not the Latin Church." Andreas looked into Ioannis's eyes. "Rome hates our religion, in part because we love the Holy Scriptures more than their traditions. Our entire belief system is based on the written Word, and without it, we're aimless. An old translation exists in our own tongue, but it's incomplete and imprecise, which is why we have sought you."

Ioannis Argyropoulos rubbed his palms together and stared toward a closed window. As the moments passed he stood there, sometimes still as a wall, sometimes tightening his lips and closing his eyes. Would he ever come to a decision?

Suddenly the clouds broke. Ioannis stepped to the window and threw it open. Light burst into the room. He crossed his arms and smiled at Andreas and the other men. "Let me show you something." He walked to the other side of the room, stooped over, held his ear to the tile floor, and began knocking. "I cannot be too careful with what I own." His smile grew with every knock until at last he pulled up a loose tile. "Precisely where I left you, *agapité*."

Bertran leaned over and whispered in Andreas's ear. "This Ioannis is more than we bargained for."

Andreas chuckled. "He may be an odd fellow, but it looks as if he has it."

"Haha! This is what you seek, my friends." Ioannis blew the dust from the top of a bulging leather pouch. "All the Gospels, the Acts of the Apostles, the Epistles, and the Apocalypse of John."

Sunlight streamed through the window, revealing the dust that had rested on the pouch. Ioannis carried the package to a table covered in scraps of parchment and unwrapped the twine from the pouch.

"You say you love the Holy Scriptures." Ioannis pulled a sheet of parchment from the pouch. "Please read this to me."

Basile held his hands up and took a step backward. The three Vallenses looked at each other.

"I can barely read my own name," Victor said.

Bertran eyed Andreas. "You have some Greek training, Andreas."

"A little, but I can't remember much."

"Try, my friend, at least try." Ioannis pointed at the first line on the page. "Read this and tell me what it means."

Andreas glanced toward the others from the corner of his eye, then looked down at the parchment. Partway down, a golden banner framed intersecting blue circles above the block of script—an illumination style uncommon in the western world. He placed his hand on the worn parchment and squinted.

The first character was much larger than the others, but it was a common one: epsilon. And the next, nu. "*En*. The first word is *en*," Andreas said.

"Very good, but what does that translate to in your common tongue?" Ioannis asked.

"If I recall, *en* means 'in.'"

"Indeed, and what is the next word?"

Andreas focused and read the word out loud. "*Arché*. That sounds like the French word *archaïque*, which means—"

"Archaic, old." Basile puffed out his chest. "See, I can teach you something."

Andreas nodded. "Or 'beginning.' 'In the beginning . . .' And that word—*logos*. *Logos* means 'word.'"

"Excellent." Ioannis turned his head to the side and gave a half smile.

"This is the first line of John's Gospel. 'In the beginning was the Word, and the Word was with God, and the Word was God.'"

"See, you understand more than you had supposed."

Andreas scanned the rest of the page. Golden, handwritten words flowed to the bottom—the very words God had preserved from the time of the apostles until the present day. He placed his hand on the page. *Thank You, Lord.*

On the other side of the room, Ioannis counted coins from the sack, one after another, into neat stacks.

"What do you want for the pouch?" Basile asked.

"The pouch? Ten silver ducats? Does that suit you?" Ioannis rolled his head against his shoulder and laughed. "However, if you want the parchment inside—"

"All of it." Basile stared down at him, unamused.

"If I agree to sell it, will you swear on the same Bible to never give it to the Latin Church?"

"Someday, we hope to translate it into other languages," Andreas said, "but for now, we'll compare it to our Romaunt translation and fill in its gaps. After that, the House of Savoy will keep it."

Basile held up his hand. "The Prince of Piedmont and his wife, to be more exact. They are faithful Catholics, but they are not the clergy."

"Hmm." Ioannis stared at the coin stacks. "Hmm." Twice more he said it while the others waited with puzzled expressions. He positioned the last coin from the sack onto its tower and blurted out his answer. "Take it, yes, you men may take it. I like you and I trust you, though I will require much more than three hundred florins. How about one thousand and one?" He held out his hand. "Come, I have students who wait for their instructor."

Basile motioned for the others to hand over their coins.

"Why the extra coin?" Andreas asked in a murmur.

"One is not extra. It is exactly what I want—one thousand and one, and not a coin less. We are friends now, and you may never know when you will again need my services."

Victor and Basile shook their heads while Andreas blew a puff of air from his mouth. Bertran pulled a single coin from his sack, flipped it into the air, and dropped it on the table. "There is your one florin, and we'll give you seven hundred more."

Ioannis insisted on counting each florin from each sack, and after what felt like a month, he counted the last coin.

"One thousand and one. Wonderful!" He jumped up, nudged Andreas to the side, and pulled the remainder of the manuscript from the pouch. "Now you may inspect the text. Read every word, count every page. But I assure you, it is all there."

"We'll trust your word," Andreas said. "I'd like to return home before my beard grays."

"Or whitens!" Ioannis scratched his cheek. "It certainly makes me look like Aristotle, does it not?"

Andreas thumbed through the pages, beginning with Matthew and ending with John's Apocalypse. It was truly the whole New Testament. He repacked the manuscript into the pouch and tied the fastening strap.

"Do you own a lexicon?" Ioannis scurried to a shelf, pulled out a book, and pushed it toward Andreas. "I have two copies of this—*lexicon græco-latinum*. This will help you better understand those Greek words and translate them to your tongue."

Andreas bowed to Ioannis and thanked him in Greek. "*Sas efcharistó.*"

Andreas tipped his head back and restrained a grin as they left the studium. After so many failures, God had made them victorious. All that remained was to carry the Bible safely back to Piedmont.

21

Gather the riches of God's promises. Nobody can take away from you those texts from the Bible which you have learned by heart.

—Corrie ten Boom
Jesus Is the Victor, 1973

B ASILE WALKED AHEAD OF THE OTHERS, peering over the crowds and keeping his eyes on the street. "We should *séparer* until we're out of Florence."

"More French." Victor reared back and gazed upward. "As if we're all supposed to know what you said."

"Andreas and Bertran understood."

Andreas smirked at Victor. "He suggests we should separate—"

"Only until we're in the countryside and I know we're not being followed. That spying friar back at the convent still makes me uneasy."

"Would it not be better to stay together?" Andreas asked. "We'd more easily defend ourselves in a group than by ourselves."

Basile stopped and ducked into an alcove. Merchants and beggars passed them on the street, some heading back toward the cathedral and others traveling south as Andreas and his friends were. "Two groups of two—Bertran with me, and Victor will accompany Andreas. If anyone is watching for us, they'll be looking for four men together. Nothing else I see distinguishes us from anyone else in the city."

"Except this package," Andreas said, holding up the manuscript pouch.

"We'll divide the pages between us once we're out of the city, which will be less suspicious than carrying that enormous thing. Until then, Andreas, you'll need to hold it." Basile lifted the hat from his head and turned right down the road. "Make yourselves appear slightly different from yesterday. If you wore a hat, take it off or give it to someone who didn't. Remove your vest, ruffle your hair. If we had time, I would ask Andreas to shave off his beard."

"So cautious, this Frenchman," Victor said under his breath.

Basile turned. "Someone is far too curious about us, and I also don't esteem Monsieur Chanforan as highly as the rest of you do."

They entered a broad plaza, but not the one surrounding the cathedral. Instead, they stared up at a one-handed clock affixed to a narrow tower. It was part of an enormous stone building that would have resembled a castle if not for the many windows on its facade.

"That is the Palazzo della Signoria, the center of Florence's government," Basile said as they walked farther into the plaza. "Florence claims to be a democracy, but it's all about which family holds the most wealth and influence. At present, it's a family of bankers—the Medicis. It's said Cosimo de' Medici is king in all but name."

"The bridge over the Arno is just ahead." Basile stopped and waved Bertran over, but he directed his next words at Victor. "We'll meet you outside the Porta Romana, the gate at the southernmost part of the city. Take a different path to the bridge than we do and be sure we don't cross at the same time."

"Why are we leaving to the south?" Andreas asked. "The road home is north."

"If someone is searching for us, they'll surely watch the north gate. Layers of protection, Victor. Did your employers not teach you that? Or perhaps the Venetians give only the minimum training to their mercenary soldiers." Basile smirked and slapped Victor on the shoulder. "All in jest, of course."

Victor grunted and gave a nod.

When Basile and Bertran were far enough away, Victor turned to Andreas. "Is this all necessary?"

"Basile still represents the interests of Princess Yolande, and without her, we wouldn't be here. Despite the annoyances, we should follow his lead."

At a crossroads, Andreas stopped and glanced to the right. Though buildings still hugged the streets on either side, a little opening to the right revealed a shallow river reflecting the two-story houses flanking its shore like stone walls. Ahead, the road continued onward with merchants hawking their goods on both sides. The buildings were oddly shorter than those along the road behind them. "I see the River Arno, but where's the bridge?"

"I was wondering the same thing." Victor tilted his head and turned right. "Wait here a moment." He walked a ways down the intersecting road, then turned back. His eyes widened, and he gave a few slow nods before strolling back. "That's a new sight. I've seen Venice and its canals, but this bridge has shops and houses built on top. If I hadn't looked, I wouldn't have noticed it was a bridge."

"Then I guess we should make sure Basile and Bertran aren't crossing right now."

Victor peered ahead. "I don't see them. You?"

"Nothing." Andreas situated the pouch into a more comfortable position and stepped forward.

When they were halfway across, a shopkeeper held strings of shiny necklaces in Andreas's face. Another man approached before he'd waved the first off and shoved a silk garment on top of the manuscript cradled in Andreas's arms. "*Un vestito di seta per la tua signora.*"

Andreas pushed the garment away and avoided eye contact. Another man stepped in his path, but this one wore a helmet and carried a spear.

"Scusi." Andreas turned to round him, but the guard moved and blocked the path again.

"*Cosa porti tra le braccia?*" The guard's voice was flat and stern.

"I don't understand," Andreas said in Romaunt. But he understood—the guard had asked what Andreas was carrying. *Oh, yes. I'm a Vallense heretic, and I'm carrying an ancient copy of the Greek Bible. Did I mention the Catholic Church forbids me to possess this? And most heinous of all, we'll translate it into the language of the commoners so they can see the errors of your religion, reject the pope, and be scripturally baptized. But please, Signore, will you let me pass?* No, that approach wouldn't fare well.

Andreas turned to see Victor nearby. What could Victor do, though? He couldn't speak the local dialect, and starting a sword fight in the busiest street in Florence would end badly.

The guard poked at the pouch. "*Aprilo.* Open it."

Andreas took a step back and held the pouch closer. "*Non posso.* I can't." His heartbeat raced in his wrists.

The guard narrowed his eyes and reached for the pouch, but Victor stepped between them and whispered, "He's not the only one, Andreas. Three more guards are in front of us, and they're all walking this way."

Andreas looked up. It was exactly as Victor described. His legs tensed. The trap was set. The guards knew who they were and what they carried.

The sound of a sword leaving a scabbard echoed off the buildings. Three other guards converged on their position, while the first aimed his spear downward.

"Run," Victor hissed as he reached for his weapon. He rammed his shoulder into the guard, sending the spear tumbling to the ground.

Running forward would offer no escape—three guards with swords blocked the way. And they were on a bridge. Andreas's only option was to retreat.

He took one last glance at Victor, who stood like a statue and faced the three converging swordsmen. The crowd thinned, sensing an incoming duel. Victor could escape, but he would be sacrificing himself for Andreas's sake. He couldn't fight three men by himself. And Basile and Bertran were nowhere to be seen.

They should have stayed together.

*　*　*

Andreas turned his shoulders from side to side as he pushed through the crowds. His pulse galloped through his body. He part ran, part walked on the cobblestone street that bordered the River Arno, which flowed in gentle ripples to the left.

Another bridge was just ahead. *God, please clear that bridge.*

Was anyone trailing him? Sounds of rickety carts, playing children, and church bells filled the air. Midday had arrived, though he couldn't tell by the position of the sun, for a sad gray shadowed the city. Even the faces of those he passed showed melancholy expressions and downcast eyes.

He and Victor were supposed to meet Bertran and Basile at the Porta Romana, wherever that was. At least he knew it was on the opposite side of the river. Watching for any pursuit, Andreas made his way to the next bridge.

Once near it, he ducked under an empty awning and faced the bridge. No guards and no suspicious characters. The way was clear.

Andreas switched the leather pouch to his other hand and stepped onto the arched bridge. To the left, the bridge with shops on it dominated the river. Would Victor survive, or would he allow himself to be captured? Once Andreas reached Bertran and Basile, they could make a plan to rescue Victor.

The crowds were thinner on the other side of the Arno. Vines crawled up the sides of buildings, and fountains bubbled at entrances to extensive courtyards. Where was this Porta Romana?

Near the bridge, a young woman with braided hair tucked under a blue kerchief stood behind a table and sold an assortment of fruit. Andreas fumbled for a few ducats, picked up an apple, and asked, "*Dov'è la porta romana?*"

She grabbed the coins from his hand and pointed down a narrow street leading away from the bridge. Her speech was so quick Andreas didn't catch a single word. He asked again.

She rolled her eyes and held up her hand, palm facing inward, fingers pointed upward with their tips touching. The locals used the expression for various occasions, sometimes in annoyance and other times in delight. "Straight, same road, past the villas and the gardens on the left."

Andreas thanked her and continued forward. Before he stepped out of view of the river, he glanced one last time toward the first bridge and held his breath, hoping to see Victor. But there was no burly Piedmontese man strolling toward him, only the unfamiliar locals.

Though the narrow road made Andreas brush up along the buildings to avoid a hoof or cart wheel smashing his toes, he soon stood before a gate that must be the Porta Romana.

Two guards inspected those entering the city, but the exit was free of prying eyes. Should he take the risk? What if the guards saw him? Once he left Florence, he wouldn't be able to reenter without being caught. All who entered through the gates would be checked, and news of the confrontation at the bridge would soon spread. Before long, guards would examine both those coming into and leaving Florence. Now was the only time to leave.

Andreas tossed his apple core into a bush and walked toward the gate, his head held high and his stride confident.

And he walked straight through it and into the rolling countryside of Tuscany. He let out a sigh, but his heart continued to race far faster than his footsteps. Slender evergreen trees lined the road leading away from Florence.

Where would Bertran and Basile wait? To avoid the guards' eyes, Andreas walked a ways down the road. From the edge of his vision, he spotted a familiar hat, but within an instant, it disappeared behind a tree.

Andreas gasped. Basile's cap. He walked up and peered around the tree.

"We've been waiting for you," said a deep, familiar voice.

Andreas took a step backward. Gedeon Chanforan held a knife at Bertran's throat.

"Drop your package on the road, and your companion shall live."

"You . . . you were helping us."

"Yes, I helped you, and now you will deliver my prize."

"It belongs to the House of Savoy—"

"You mean Amadeus's French wench? Yolande is not the House of Savoy." Gedeon pressed the knife tighter against Bertran's neck and adjusted his stance.

Bertran mouthed something, but Andreas didn't understand.

Andreas froze. Gedeon was supposed to be a businessman, not a violent criminal. Would he truly slide that knife across Bertran's throat?

"Where is Basile?" Andreas asked.

"The Frenchman? Dead. And your idiot companion who thinks himself a soldier? Also dead, I'm afraid."

Bertran gave his head a slight shake and mouthed, "No," but Gedeon must have noticed. He slammed his boot on Bertran's foot.

"Drop the Bible, and this man will go free. Run, and he dies."

Andreas glanced behind to search for a trap, but they were alone. He held the pouch tighter and narrowed his eyes at Gedeon. Opportunistic thief, a petty man who manipulated them into spending a fortune and then snatched the prize. Just like a scavenging— "Vulture. You are nothing but a grimy, disease-ridden bird feasting on others' success."

Gedeon snickered. His eyes were deeper than the sea and as unpredictable as a wolf's. "You know nothing about me, my lord prince. Everything I possess is mine because I wanted it: my labor, my negotiating, my cunning. I once thought you had the same willpower and drive, but weakness dribbles down your chin. You, Andreas, are nobody: a cowering Vallense, a failed clergyman, and a disgraced royal."

How did Gedeon know so much about him? If Andreas had a weapon, Gedeon's blood would be pooling on the ground. But Bertran's life hung by a silk strand. One pull from Gedeon's arm, and Bertran would be gone.

Andreas closed his eyes and drew himself up to full height. He couldn't let Gedeon take the Bible. After the distance they had traveled, the danger they had faced, the obstacles God had removed—no, he wouldn't forfeit the manuscript.

The fate of the gospel and the countless souls who might accept it was at stake. Andreas glanced toward the road.

"Run, then." A few drops of blood appeared where Gedeon's knife met Bertran's neck. "His life doesn't matter to me."

Sweat beaded on Bertran's brow, but though he trembled, his face remained steady. "Flee, Andreas. Take the Bible back to our people."

Gedeon moved the knife slightly. He was killing Bertran.

Andreas turned back toward Gedeon. "You are true evil."

"Evil? You do not know what evil is. I have seen it. I have experienced the worst that man and his religions can conjure. Though I may be stern, my intentions are the purest." Gedeon glowered at Andreas. "Yesterday, I gave you a generous offer to join my company, but like an indecisive wretch, you delayed. Now I present another offer—your friend or the manuscript. And I advise you not to make the same mistake again."

Andreas looked to Bertran, the man who had once despised him but, with a little maturity on both their parts, had become a trusted ally. Both men were training to be barbes and had the same desire to spread the Holy Scriptures. Bertran had believed in the Greek manuscript before anyone else, even Constanza. They had traveled a long road together to come to this point.

The pouch weighed on Andreas's arm. In the end, it was parchment and ink, and Bertran Arnaldi was a living soul. But why would God give them the manuscript only to allow its theft?

Andreas slowly shook his head. Whatever his choice, it would alter someone's destiny. Would it be better to escape with the manuscript, or let go of it and save Bertran?

He let out a breath, bent over, and laid the pouch in the grass. He lowered his brows and his voice. "Free him."

Gedeon threw Bertran to the side and smirked, saying nothing.

Bertran ran toward Andreas. "You should have kept the Bible."

"And explain your death to your parents? No, your life is worth more."

Andreas glared at Gedeon as he pulled the manuscript from the grass and turned back toward Florence.

The Holy Scriptures and the Greek lexicon were in the hands of a robber. Gedeon Chanforan had thrown their aspirations to the earth and trampled them. Andreas clenched his fists, and his heartbeat quickened.

Men shouted from the gate. Andreas craned his neck toward the road.

Ten or more guards thundered toward Andreas and Bertran, all with swords unsheathed and matching armor—steel helmets and leather vests with billowing, crimson-striped breeches and sleeves. The guards fanned out around them.

"We can't escape this one," Bertran said.

Andreas scanned the road behind them. If they could somehow squeeze through the gap before the guards closed it, they might outrun them. He pointed his eyes, motioned for Bertran to follow, and burst into a sprint.

Andreas kept his eyes on the distant hills, where the forests might give them cover and rest. Narrow cypress trees still lined the road, making it difficult to see if any guards approached from their flanks. Up ahead, the road was jammed. He squinted to see what the commotion was but slowed when he spotted the armor.

"More guards," Andreas said to Bertran, who had nearly caught up.

Andreas veered off the road, leaped through the cypress row, and ran into a vineyard. He bent over to catch his breath, but only for a moment.

Two guards popped through the cypresses to the right. More guards came from the left. Andreas went limp.

A sandstone villa stood on the far side of the vineyard, and behind it rose a forested hill. They would need to climb over each row of vines to get there, but it was their only option.

They sprinted up to the first row and struggled over it. The Tuscan grapevines were well tended and thick, evidenced by the scratches Andreas received climbing through them. He let out a sigh at seeing at least ten more rows.

Once in the second row, they ducked and turned right, trying to find the easiest way over the next set of vines. A thinning of the vines appeared, and Andreas and Bertran climbed to the other side.

Again they turned right, but the path veered back toward the cypress trees. Andreas darted his eyes around the landscape, but his breath left him. *Why didn't I examine the vineyard's layout beforehand?*

Three guards now stood in front of them. To the right and also behind, more approached. There would be no escape.

Unarmed, winded, and without protection, Andreas slowed his pace and raised his hands. Bertran followed.

"*Fermati!*" shouted a guard from the rear. More guards appeared from the tree line, spears pointed toward them.

Andreas fumbled in his sack for his ring and moved it to an inner pocket inside his vest. *I may need it.*

The only guard with a red sash across his chest pointed at them. "*Consegna le tue armi!*"

"He wants us to hand over our weapons," Andreas said.

Bertran focused on the guards. "We have none!"

Andreas held out his hands and patted at his sides and vest. "*Guarda.* Look, nothing."

Someone grabbed Andreas's left arm and twisted it a little, sending a shot of pain through his shoulder. He struggled to loosen the hold, but it only tightened.

A grunt came from Bertran when a punch landed in his gut. His eyes widened as he struggled for breath.

Another hand latched onto Andreas, this one much looser. The guard with the sash stood in front of them and smirked. In broken French, he asked, "You are spies for the French king, no?"

Andreas shook his head and answered in the Tuscan dialect. "No, we're from Piedmont—"

"*Francese!*" The head guard glared at Andreas.

"We have friends who will confirm who we are. We are not spies, and we are not French." Andreas caught himself, remembering Basile. Better to tell the truth than be caught lying. "One of our companions is French, but he works for the House of Savoy—"

"I am not a magistrate. You are accused of committing crimes against *la Repubblica di Firenze*, and for that you must answer to the Medicis."

"We've committed no crime."

The head guard stepped up to Andreas until their noses almost touched. "*Chiudi la bocca.* Shut your mouth, or I'll break your jaw."

Andreas swallowed and complied. There was no use in asserting his rights now, but maybe once they stood before a magistrate, they could clear their names.

The soldiers yanked him back toward the road. Who would have accused them—

The realization smashed through his skull. Gedeon. But he said they would be free if they gave him the manuscript. Andreas shook his head as they walked back toward the Porta Romana.

But just before the gate, on a stony rise to the right, Gedeon Chanforan peered down at them, smiling as he held the leather pouch.

Andreas stiffened his back. There was no doubt. Gedeon had brought the accusation.

Florentines stopped and gawked as the guards led Andreas and Bertran through the streets. They walked the same road to the bridge, but now in shame. The young woman who had sold Andreas an apple cackled as he stumbled past, held by a guard on each side.

Everything—the weeks of travel, the nights of shivering by a fire, the confrontation with their pursuers outside Parma, the meeting with Ioannis Argyropoulos—it was all in vain. Now Cosimo de' Medici held their lives in his grip. They had been betrayed by Gedeon Chanforan, the man who had suggested they come here.

But the Lord of the universe is still my master. God will accomplish His purposes, though I may never see His plan blossom and bring fruit. I thought I knew God's plan, but whatever may come, I must strive to be moldable and teachable. I have tried following my heart and have failed.

As they crossed the shop-covered bridge over the Arno, Andreas remembered his friend and mentor, Raimond Durand—most of all, his off-key singing. He strained to remember the words. They were from Solomon, but what did they say? Suddenly a spark ignited the flame of Andreas's memory, but he dared not sing the words out loud. Instead, he sang them in his heart.

To every thing there is a season.

He lost the rest of the words, but amid the prods and pulls from the guards, Andreas somehow found a smile.

The voice of a preaching friar echoed off the stone buildings. In the corner of a small plaza, five or six people—peasants by their tattered clothing—surrounded him and listened. A man made the sign of the cross while the woman next to him thumbed her rosary beads and mouthed a prayer. Not long before, Andreas had been one of them. Devoted yet lost, eager yet empty. *Oh, how much God has changed me!*

The guards turned from a narrow alley and entered a plaza dominated by a windowless building. A heavy door crashed open ahead, and out of it spilled another guard. This one wore no helmet, revealing his oily, disheveled hair. The closer Andreas and Bertran walked, the more the stench of vomit and excrement pierced Andreas's senses.

"Two more," the lead guard said, pushing Andreas and Bertran toward the door.

The oily-haired jail keeper scratched under his arm. "The council had better take care of them quickly. Winter will be here soon, and I haven't got any food."

"It should be quick, but the council will want them alive for questioning."

The jail keeper swiped at his hair and patted it to the side, and somehow the thin strands stuck to his bald head. As the guards and prisoners entered, the jail keeper hacked and spit on the ground near Andreas's feet. His crooked smile showed a mouth full of yellow and black teeth. When he exhaled, Andreas winced and gagged. If the jail's stench couldn't make a man vomit, the keeper's stench could.

The guards pushed Andreas and Bertran down a damp, torchlit hall. More of Raimond's song returned. *He hath made every thing beautiful in his time . . .*

How could that be true? Andreas gazed around the jail's filth and squalor, recalling the rest of the song.

Also he hath set the world in their heart, so that no man can find out the work that God maketh from the beginning to the end.

22

Often, while wandering through these romantic defiles, the sound of mingled voices, issuing from some deep leafy recess, or falling in softened cadence from some isolated rock, meets the traveller on his way, and kindles in his mind a spirit of congenial devotion.

—William Beattie
The Waldenses, 1838

A BONE-SHIVERING GUST howled down from the slopes of Mount Vandalino. Constanza and Elionor approached the town of La Torre with a donkey pulling an apple cart. An orphan girl, Silvia, tagged along.

Another gust sent Constanza's kerchief flying backward, leaving it attached only by the tie under her chin. She let out an exasperated sigh. It felt like the hundredth time that had happened today. Constanza reattached the cloth and turned to Elionor. "Do you have an extra pin?"

"I might have one I could spare—"

"Here, Madomaisèla." Silvia ran over with pins in hand. "How many do you need?"

"Do you have two?"

Silvia placed the pins in Constanza's hand and grinned.

With her hair now in much better order, Constanza grabbed the donkey's lead back from Elionor. Compared to Turin, the La Torre market was minuscule, but it was as grand as most Vallenses would see. At the main intersection outside the town, they turned toward a collection of stone houses and ramshackle sheds.

Up ahead, a minstrel plucked and sang in Romaunt. Vallenses usually sang words from the Holy Scriptures, but occasionally they would sing a humorous children's song or songs about the creation they saw every day—ballads about snow-capped mountains, noisy torrents, or planting-ready fields. But Constanza had never heard this minstrel. She stopped and smiled as she listened to his song about an evil owl.

When the minstrel finished, the small crowd clapped and laughed while he gave a bow. Constanza squinted an eye at the ballad's grimness, but she laughed a little too.

The minstrel held out his hat, and a few copper ducats plopped in as he moved through the audience. Constanza handed him two apples—it was all she could spare today.

The man's face brightened. "Mercé, Madomaisèla. You are as heroic and charming as the tales say."

"Tales?" Constanza giggled. "What stories are told of me?"

"Of defeating the Antichrist with the sword that is the Word of God, of slaying the dragon that nests under the slopes of Mount Viso, of carrying the banner—"

"Would you like another apple?"

The minstrel pocketed the few coins, placed the hat back on his head, and let out a laugh. "No, you've blessed me enough." He bowed again.

Constanza made strong eye contact with the man. Minstrels often knew about the happenings of the world, so perhaps he'd heard something about the Grimaldis. "Monsen, do you carry any news or rumors from Turin?"

The minstrel raised his brows. "What would you like to know about? Silk prices? The new Lord of Luserna? Intrigue within the House of Savoy?"

It would be fascinating to hear about Andreas's family, but it would likely be filled with half truths. "We know a businessman from there. I once worked in an orphanage—"

The minstrel pressed his lips together and held his lute to the side. "You speak of Luca and Vitòria Grimaldi."

Constanza took a step toward the minstrel. "Do you know them?"

"No, but market rumors say they perished in a fire last summer—"

"They're alive," Silvia said from behind the cart. "They were in the valley with us . . . until they left."

"Is that so?" The minstrel scratched under his chin.

"She speaks the truth," Elionor said. "They left to handle business matters in Turin over a month ago but haven't returned."

The minstrel lowered his voice. "They had enemies in the Piedmontese trade—jealousies that have festered for years and finally burst. If, as you say, the Grimaldis survived the fire, their enemies didn't disappear."

"Their only enemies were the priests," Constanza said. "They were well respected in the community. They housed thirteen orphans who would have otherwise rotted on the street. Luca Grimaldi is a kind burgher who pays his employees an honest wage and—"

"Madomaisèla, the very best men are often the most hated." The minstrel lifted his lute from his side and cradled it. "Ambitious men bite each other's ankles like spoiled lap dogs, but when one rises above the others by virtue and industry as opposed to iniquity and conniving, he becomes the prey. Evil men cannot tolerate a rogue upending the order of their world, so you should not trust Monsen Grimaldi's reputation to keep him safe."

Constanza eyed the minstrel. "How are you so sure they died?"

"Rumors say their bodies were found and buried, and now two new graves stand on their property with stones bearing their names."

If the rumor was as the minstrel described, then someone must have devised the lie as a coverup. The entire household had escaped the flames—they'd lived for two months in the Angrogna Valley together. Perhaps the Catholic clergy had caught the Grimaldis and conjured up the story about them dying in the fire. What other explanation was there?

Constanza pulled Silvia aside after the minstrel departed. "You cannot repeat what that man said to any other children. We heard rumors, nothing else. Soon God will reveal the truth, but until then, we cannot speculate. Can I trust you?"

Silvia gave two quick nods.

Constanza, Elionor, and Silvia continued into the town square. Bright fabric swayed in the breeze at one market stand, while most others traded the bounties of the harvest season. Sacks of grain, baskets of vegetables, and crates of eggs dotted the scene. Men talked in small groups, women bargained for grain and produce, and children ran and played between the stalls.

Constanza led the donkey to a gap in the stands, unlatched it from the cart, and tied it to a post while Elionor made their apple display eye-catching. Silvia picked the ripest and most appealing apples and placed them on top of the stack, and Constanza propped up their little sign: POMS DE ANGROGNA.

Before a moment passed, their first customer smiled at Silvia and handed her a silver ducat. "How many will that buy?"

Silvia's eager eyes looked to Constanza.

"Fill your basket!" Constanza stood, walked to the other side of the cart, and handed him a few apples. Walking back, she caught a glimpse of Elionor's grin as Elionor stared at a stand across the square. A man stood near a wagon full of hay bales and flashed a smile in Elionor's direction.

Constanza shot her eyes away and coughed toward Elionor.

"What, Connie? It's all harmless." Elionor rose from her seat, brushed off her apron, and pushed a few strands of hair behind her ears. "Can you and Silvia manage the cart? I'll be only a moment."

Constanza opened her mouth to object, but Elionor was gone before Constanza could form the words. Did Ellie not realize what she was doing? The man wasn't anyone she had seen. Constanza's cheeks simmered the more Elionor trifled with . . . what was his name? Yes, Brando.

"Who is that?" Silvia asked, pointing her nose toward the man Elionor was with.

Pietat! Now I have to explain Ellie's foolish behavior to a young girl. "She's . . . visiting a friend."

"Does Madomaisèla Elionor love him?"

Constanza bit her tongue. How could she untangle Silvia's questions without insulting Elionor or feigning approval? She couldn't, so she deflected. "Are you feeling better about last night? Did Guido apologize yet?"

"He was right, though. I am fastigós." Silvia tugged on a tight curl of her hair. "The girls laugh at me too, and they say I sound like a horse when I talk."

"Does everyone, or did someone say that once?"

Silvia cast her eyes to the ground. Soon she would be eleven years old. She had a pretty smile and a pleasant demeanor but also had a few concerning tendencies. Silvia wanted to please everyone, but when she couldn't, she would turn inward and dwell on her perceived shortcomings. The older boys also had a habit of making fun of her. Her right eye sagged, at night more than other times. Last night a boy had called her *fastigós*—repugnant—after dinner, and she hadn't recovered yet. But Papà had made sure the boy went to bed with a firm reprimand.

"As soon as we return this evening, you must find Guido and tell him you forgive him. If he or anyone else continues to joke about how you look or how you talk, you must try to ignore them."

"I can't, because they're right." She sniffled and wiped her eyes with her sleeve. "It hurts."

"I know, Silvia. I don't know why children lash out at each other. Sadly, adults do as well." Constanza leaned over, looked into Silvia's eyes, and placed a hand on her cheek. "Who made you?"

"God."

"In what way did God make you?" It was a question she had taught all the orphans to answer.

Silvia peered up toward the sky and back to Constanza. "'I am fearfully and wonderfully made: marvellous are thy works; and that my soul knoweth right well.'"

"Their slurs may sadden you, but in the end, they are rebelling against God's order. His creation, His child, His girl." Constanza straightened her back and picked up an apple. "Besides, you are a beautiful young woman."

"My eye?"

The answer eluded Constanza until she examined the fruit. "What color is this apple?"

"Green, I think. Maybe yellow."

"Is it different from others in the cart?"

Silvia took the apple and compared it to the rest. "It's more yellow than most."

"Taste it, then take a bite of a perfectly green one."

Silvia did as she was told. "They taste the same. Perhaps the yellow one is sweeter."

"Is it fastigós because it's different?"

"I don't believe so."

"Neither should you imagine that because God made your one eye different, you are fastigós. Those who say otherwise are wrong. You, Silvia, are fearfully and wonderfully made."

A customer approached, but Constanza monitored Elionor. She now sat on the grass and laughed next to Brando. For the past few months, she had tried to discourage Elionor's conduct, but her words had fallen on unheeding ears. When Elionor returned, Constanza would commit herself to gentleness. Being too blunt only seemed to harm friendships.

When the market traffic slowed, Elionor finally ended her meeting and sauntered back to the apple cart. With a wide grin plastered across her face, she said, "Brando wants to meet me again next week."

"I don't believe we'll have anything left to sell next week," Constanza said, motioning to the cart. "See, not enough apples."

"We need to find something to sell."

Constanza scowled. "No. We don't."

"Oh, Connie, don't be *una prudéncia*. You should meet him. Brando will soon be employed by the Lord of Luserna."

Constanza shook her head. "I keep hearing about this lord, but see only Johan."

"Johan hired Brando, in fact. He'll be a watchman, right here in the valley."

Constanza squinted and turned her head. "Why does Johan need watchmen?"

"To maintain the peace."

"Or to collect the lord's taxes from tenants like us."

"You don't know that, and you don't know Brando. You also give Johan less respect than he deserves. Look at him—bailiff for a noble. And what is Andreas except a treasure hunter? At least Brando and Johan are forging their own futures."

Constanza gazed up at Mount Vandalino. Though her throat tightened, and her words wanted a release, Elionor needed discernment, not another tongue-lashing. "We need to head back home."

*   *   *

Soon after leaving La Torre, Constanza, Elionor, and Silvia came to the place where their track merged with another and formed a single road toward home. Their path hugged the steep hillside that dropped off toward the torrent, while the other skirted the foothills leading from Castelvecchio and the plains.

A group of travelers stood at the intersection dressed in a patchwork of threadbare linen and matted wool. Ten or so children moped around the four adults like closed daisies on a foggy morning.

"Who are they?" Elionor asked.

"I've never seen them." Constanza pulled at the donkey's reins and shielded the sun to catch a better glimpse. "Maybe they need help."

The closer they drew, the more Constanza's heart wilted. None of the travelers wore shoes, despite the chilly November air. The two women wore their hair loose and let it blow with the wind. A few children coughed, and all had bony elbows and empty, sallow eyes. They must be a new group of Vallense refugees, forced to leave their homeland for their faith. None smiled, even after Constanza greeted them.

"Where are you heading?" she asked.

A man eyed the others and tilted his head down. *"Parlës-to Piemontèis?"*

They wanted to speak Piedmontese. Thanks to her time in Turin, Constanza could understand it, but still struggled to speak it. She looked to her friend for help.

Elionor introduced herself in flawless Piedmontese. The man perked up and presented himself as Riccardo, his wife as Amalia, and the other couple as Patrizio and Mercede. They were two families from the Piedmontese plains who had uprooted their lives to replant in the valley.

Constanza beamed, giving out apples as fast as the refugees could take them. When they all held one, Constanza walked up to Amalia and hugged her. "You no longer need to"—she struggled with the Piedmontese—"fear? Live fear?"

"You no longer need to live in fear," Elionor said. She gave a quick wink to Constanza before refocusing on the families. "Where are you headed? Our cart has room—"

"To a crossroads above a hamlet—San Lorenzo, I think." Patrizio took a massive bite from an apple and continued with his mouth full. "We'll be tenants at a farm with good, plowed earth and a big house. Riccardo's family and mine will share it until he can build his own." He took another bite and chomped some more.

"None of us have farmed," Mercede said. "We are all city dwellers—from Turin, to be exact."

"Turin!" Elionor said. "We lived there for a time too."

A couple of older children had finished their fruit, and Constanza handed out more.

"If you need help," Elionor said, "we're always willing to offer assistance. We have a loving church—"

"A church?" Riccardo wore a frown and held his elbow with the opposite hand. "We heard there were no churches in these lands yet."

"Whoever said that was deeply mistaken," Elionor said. "There are three churches in the Angrogna Valley alone, and more throughout the Luserna Valley: Vilar, Bobbio, Luserna, Rorà."

"You should show us your parish. We haven't been to Mass since September—"

"Mass?" Constanza shook her head and laughed. "Are you . . . new believers?"

Riccardo and Amalia whispered to each other. Riccardo glanced back up and said, "We are Christians—followers of Christ and His Church. *Quicumque vult salvus esse, ante omnia opus est, ut teneat catholicam fidem . . .*"

He was reciting a Roman creed. Vallenses didn't do that. What type of believers were these?

Constanza interrupted Riccardo. "Haven't you . . . abandoned Rome?"

"We have not. We are baptized, our children are baptized, and we are all Catholics."

Constanza's mouth slackened. Why would Catholic peasants move into Vallense lands? And how did they come upon the finances necessary to rent land? "Elionor, can you please ask them the exact place they're headed?"

She did, and Patrizio reached into a satchel and removed a crumpled piece of parchment. He pointed at it and said, "Here. We will be the new tenants of this land."

Constanza examined the document. Beneath the ornate handwriting, someone had drawn a map. Two roads crossed, with a hamlet labeled San Lorenzo and an arrow pointing down at the words La Torre. A blot stood out at the top of the crossroads. The realization rushed into her like a snow squall. They were going to the old Lauras farm. But that was the land Andreas farmed and the house where he slept—

Questions clogged her mind, and each breath became a chore. Constanza handed the parchment back, but before it left her hand, she glimpsed the red seal—the same one she had seen stamped on the tax bill from Johan.

"Who gave . . . land . . . you?" Constanza's words were as scattered as her mind, and her attempts at Piedmontese made it worse.

"The Lord of Luserna," Patrizio said. "His steward—"

"Johan Lauras," Constanza said.

"Yes, Monsù Lauras. We heard about arable land in the mountains, and he met us and arranged the farm lease three months ago. At the price he quoted, it was a gift."

What was happening? The former Lord of Luserna had signed a document over a year ago saying Papà had the rights to the farm, and Papà let Andreas maintain it. Now Johan was giving it to strangers from the plains?

Constanza narrowed her eyes and glared. The families' language became strange and unpleasant. The children were dirtier than she had first noticed—their hair was in disarray, and their mannerisms were worse than feral swine. Amalia's and Mercede's necklines drooped far too low, and the tight fit of their shirts revealed more than any honorable woman would. The two families had become foreign—entitled strangers who invaded their land and meant to take their farms.

She had to tell Papà. He would tell the church leaders, and then they would act. The lord couldn't trample on their rights and take their land. Vallense toil had carved the fields from the mountainside, Vallense sweat had cleared the boulders, and Vallense blood had been spilled to keep their freedom. It was one matter to preach the gospel to Piedmontese in Turin or Pinerolo, but another matter entirely for Piedmontese to trespass into the valley and steal Vallense land. God had given it to Vallenses as their place of refuge, not to papists.

The donkey hee-hawed as Constanza pulled at its reins. "Ellie, Silvia, come. We must hurry home."

Elionor gave the families a parting nod and turned to Constanza. "What about them?"

"They made it this far. They can finish the journey by themselves."

"What will your papà say?"

"He can't allow it—he won't, and neither will my brothers. Monsen Estève is staying at the old Lauras farm, anyway. Whatever document those people hold is invalid."

They hurried home and arrived before dinner. The orphans scurried about the farmyard while Mamà cooked over the fire.

Where was Papà? Constanza jerked her head around and looked across the terraces, but there was no sign of him.

She sighed and plopped onto a chair outside the front door. Too much was happening. She wanted to talk to someone who understood. Elionor had no sense, Mamà was busy caring for the household, and Papà was off working somewhere.

Andreas—I wish I could sit with him, talk to him, let him listen, watch him solve these problems.

23

Like Paul and Silas, with its feet fast in the stocks, the Bible was singing sweetly the song of grace in the midst of the dark dungeons of the Middle Ages, when suddenly there was a great earthquake, and the bands of all thought, of all science, of all truth, were loosed, and then like Paul and Silas, the Bible came forth to its glorious liberty.

—Charles Haddon Spurgeon
Speech at the Annual Meeting of the British and Foreign Bible Society, 1864

THE STENCH had become as familiar as the smell of his own breath. The floor was a mixture of cobblestone, dirt, and the filth from the cell's last inmate. Even the walls were inhospitable: slimy, but rougher than two-day-old stubble.

For three days, Andreas had rehearsed all that had transpired. First, the guards had dragged Bertran in a different direction after they threw Andreas in his cell. Andreas had done nothing but accuse himself on the first day. True, he had been foolish enough to embark on the quest, but other than the failure, the worst part was leading Bertran, Victor, and Basile into the same trap. Bertran had parents, and Victor had a wife and sons. And Basile? Someone would surely mourn. They had mixed their fates with Andreas's and would suffer the same consequences.

Two sets of rapid footsteps padded down the hall outside. The door unlocked and crashed open.

"Out," said a voice.

Andreas rose from the floor. Surely if he offered a reasonable explanation, they would understand. "I'd never been to Florence until this week, and I'm not French—"

"*Stai zitto,*" said the guard. "Those words are latched to my tongue. Every prisoner is innocent, and my ears tire of hearing it. So all I say is 'shut up.'"

"My companion Bertran," Andreas spoke faster. "Ask him, and he'll confirm."

"Stai. Zitto. Now do as I say. Come."

"Are you releasing me?"

"Nobody leaves *carcere delle Stinche* unless he has rich friends. A guest has arrived for you, though."

Andreas's heart leaped. He brushed his hair to the side and walked to the door.

But his blood simmered when he stepped from the door and saw the man waiting for him. The guard pushed Andreas into a chair in the hallway, chained his hands, and strolled away.

"The manuscript and that lexicon are safe now," Gedeon Chanforan said, standing tall above him, "safely packed with my belongings and on their way to Piedmont."

"You . . . you're a *canaglia.*"

"So, you've picked up a little of the local dialect? But be assured—I am no scoundrel. I am a man with interests far outside the little world in which you live." Gedeon, clothed in an elaborate blue vest, held a clean cloth over his nose, probably to dispel the prison odor.

"Princess Yolande will show you no mercy."

"She is weak, almost as much as your sickly"—he curled his lip—"brother."

"Why steal the Bible?" Andreas's voice rattled in his throat. "You'll face the wrath of the royal family of Savoy. It was their wealth that paid for the manuscript. And what will you gain? More money to spend on fancy Florentine clothes and shiny decorations for your villa?"

Gedeon closed his eyes and shook his head. "In part, yes, but you don't know me. You, a spoiled prince striving to find himself, would never understand."

"I see you're the Dominicans' errand boy now."

"The Dominicans?" Gedeon reared his head back and laughed. "You think I'm in league with the Church, do you?"

"Why else would you be so intent on stealing the manuscript? The Church must be paying you a fortune."

"A simple opportunist—is that what you think I am? I must say, my lord prince, I'm a little ashamed you think me so base." Gedeon gave a half smile. "I admit, the manuscript is quite the lovely prize. The Holy Scriptures. The barbes say they are inspired, and have the pride to say God speaks through these ramblings, no?" He stared at the wall as if deep in thought. "If only I could purge all I was forced to memorize, but alas, I must carry it to my grave."

Andreas turned his head slightly to the side and squinted one eye. "You were a monk?"

"A monk?" Gedeon let out a brief burst of laughter, but it faded into a frown. "No, I was a Vallense."

Andreas rolled his eyes. "You mock me."

"You think you have found a lost treasure in your newfound faith. Yes, the cheerful faces, the compassionate deeds, the concern for others. I know it all."

Andreas leaned back while Gedeon paced. "I don't believe you."

"As much as you are Louis of Savoy's son, I am the son of Michele Chanforan. Did you not question my surname, Chanforan? It's as Vallense a name as any."

Andreas closed one eye and imagined Gedeon as a Vallense—sitting in a meetinghouse, swinging a scythe, quoting the Holy Scriptures. His eyes . . . something was there, but what? "Then what made you become such a canaglia?"

Gedeon gave a sidelong glance without turning his head. He flicked at a fly, then flexed his fingers. "I have a sad story to tell you," Gedeon said, his voice muffled by the cloth. He leaned back against the wall and let out a long breath.

"My father was the pastor of a thriving group of Vallenses in Turin. Indeed, my first memories were at that church, and all my friends were there."

Andreas leaned forward in his chair. The chain bit into his wrists.

"Everything seemed perfect," Gedeon said. "The church was growing, but underneath it all, a plague had developed.

"I was ten years old when I first questioned my upbringing. Papà delivered sermons to his congregants with eloquence. He would often preach against various vices: consumption of wine and ale, tavern music and dancing, women dressing in what he said was immodest apparel. But I was with Papà when he was outside the church. One day I found him lying on our floor. I was scared for his life, but Mamà quickly approached and waved me aside. 'Don't tell anyone,' she said. So I asked, 'Why is Papà sick?' She only shook her head and dragged him to bed. I asked my friends about Papà's condition, and they told me to smell his breath next time. I did and discovered the scent of ale. He was drunk.

"Papà would stand before his congregation and condemn them for the very sins he committed nightly. After I had gone to bed, he would stumble into the house drunk and demand bread from Mamà. The first time she questioned him, he beat her. I still remember that first night, which eventually blended with the rest."

Gedeon blinked rapidly and coughed through the cloth.

"Mamà resisted for the first year, but it wore on her. Her eyes sank, her hugs became cold, and she withdrew into herself. When I was thirteen, women from the church started to frequent my home, but never when Mamà was home. I was ignorant of his wiles but soon learned—not only about his appetite for women but also the hypocrisy.

"'Touch not the unclean thing,' he preached to the church. 'Marriage is honourable in all, and the bed undefiled: but whoremongers and adulterers God will judge.' Yet the more frequent his encounters, the more he shouted at the congregation."

Andreas shook his head. Gedeon's mournful eyes, his low gestures, even his muffled voice seemed genuine. "Your father was indeed a hypocrite, but no barbes I've met are like that. I've never even heard such rumors."

Gedeon laughed. "You still doubt my experiences? The church practically worshipped Papà, but my mother and I knew the truth. Evil seeped from his soul.

I was sixteen when Mamà caught him drunk, kissing her closest friend. She had tolerated the betrayal too long by the time she went before the church leaders."

"And they dismissed him as they should have," Andreas said.

Gedeon closed his eyes for a moment. "No, they were so full of piety that they ignored my mother. They refused to listen at first, believing her to be insane. The facts were obvious, though, and in time, they discovered the truth. And what did they do? They became his loyal defenders.

"Some said, 'He's God's man. We'll never rebel against the authority God has placed over us.' Others said, 'He bears the burden of the church on his back, and temptations are strong. No one is perfect.' And Papà remained a pastor. The deacons covered his drunkenness and ignored his adultery, despite a deacon's wife being involved. The rot ran deep.

"But the problems only worsened. Mamà received more than one bruised eye, and when she pleaded for help from the churchwomen, they told her to be faithful to her husband and listen closer to his sermons. Yes, that would solve our woes: listen to the oppressor's reproof.

"One night, his voice startled me awake. He yelled at Mamà and called her a wench. Then a fist slammed into flesh. I jumped from my bed, ran to the other room, and found Mamà with a bleeding forehead while Papà sat in his chair with a crooked grin. 'An unsubmissive and rebellious woman, your mother. Never marry one like her.' My rage had been pent up long enough. I hit Papà and didn't stop until he lay motionless on the floor. I carried Mamà to my bed, tended her wounds, and promised her a new home."

Andreas kept his mouth shut. What could he say? Gedeon's father deserved the divine hand of judgment. Why had the men in that church looked the other way?

"We fled to a friend's house, but they refused to shelter us," Gedeon said. "'Michele Chanforan has a good heart,' they said. We went to another church family, and they turned us away too. Some called Mamà mad and others accused her of being a menacing old witch who held Papà back from God's blessings. We were without a home and without friends, and that's when I truly changed."

A new shadow fell over Gedeon's eyes. The hatred in his voice could have been birthed only from a reality.

"We traveled a day south to my mamà's family—faithful Catholics, I may add. They took us in, fed us, and gave us a home. While the Vallenses ignored us at best and scorned us at worst, the people who supposedly hated us instead showed us compassion.

"From that moment, I became a man. If there is a God, He's not the one the Vallenses profess. Their teachings must be squashed, their Scriptures shredded and thrown to the ravens, and their God forever ripped from their desperate souls."

Andreas sat straighter. "Where is your father now?"

"I never saw him again. A year after we left, he was in prison for brawling with some noble in a tavern. And what was you Vallenses' response? You claimed Papà was persecuted. By then, a new pastor led the church, but without my father's charisma and personality, it faded into the void. My papà perished in a pool of his own vomit soon after being released from prison. Today, if you were able to ask your people about him, they would likely be ignorant, but if they were old enough to remember, they would run from the subject. Mention the name Michele Chanforan to an old barbe, and he will collapse in shame."

"You are not the man I had guessed," Andreas said. "Your zeal is as inflamed as a Dominican friar's."

Gedeon gave a quick smirk. "As I grew older, I learned how to move money. I married my wife, Marta, and gained two outstanding children who will never experience the trauma of the Vallense religion. Such a refreshing life I have made for us."

"What will you do with the manuscript? Sell it for more sculptures?" Andreas asked.

Gedeon chuckled. "No, I simply want to keep it from Vallenses. I will never allow them to hold the codex after I spent so much having the Romaunt manuscript removed from their schoolhouse."

"You stole that as well? I must say, Monsen Chanforan, I'm not surprised."

"And you, Andreas of Savoy? You are nothing but a fallen prince, and after the Medicis behead you, your name will be forgotten." Gedeon's gaze latched onto Andreas. "Just like Luca Grimaldi. Did you find their graves?"

"Those graves weren't theirs. Luca and Vitòria were in the mountains for months after the fire."

"Such a tragedy they had to suffer that fate. Luca was a talented merchant, and his dear wife was a charmer."

How had Constanza once worked for this man? "You killed them last September when they were in Turin."

"I have never killed a man, nor will I ever."

"You hired someone then, just as you hired the man with the red patch to track us."

"Ah, Furio. You met him?"

"He's dead. Basile killed him, and Victor slew the other."

"Then it was a poor investment, which unfortunately is a risk in any business." Gedeon stared at Andreas.

And Andreas stared right back. "Why would you kill the Grimaldis? They had nothing to do with your father's evil."

"You would never understand. The people of Turin were warming too much to their kindnesses—rescuing orphans from the street, feeding them. To the ignorant, it was commendable, but I saw through the deceit. They wished to poison the simple minds of those children with Vallense doctrine." Gedeon's eyes flared like glowing embers.

"You hired Constanza Pavarin as a maid. And you let her tutor your daughter. If you despise Vallenses, why let her influence your children?"

"The girl brought a certain nostalgia to me, like holding the same breed of dog I once kept as a childhood pet. She also offered a window into the Vallense plots that oozed from the Grimaldi villa, for which she served my purposes well."

"Why do you show such hatred?" Andreas's voice trembled. "We weren't seeking arms or ill-gotten wealth, but only the Word of God so we might translate it into every tongue—"

"And now it will never happen." Gedeon lowered his cloth from his nose, looked down at Andreas, and sneered.

Andreas followed the lines on Gedeon's face, from the growing crow's feet near his eyes to his clean-shaven chin. "Why did you come see me?"

Gedeon held the cloth back up. "To see your pain and to see you suffer. Considering you are a spy, they should have executed you by now, but I was thrilled to hear otherwise. For years, I have dreamed of seeing Vallenses suffer as they made me suffer, and the first bite of revenge will be the sweetest. But the rest will be the most fulfilling."

"What do you mean, the rest? Am I not enough to satisfy your grievances, or do you also seek the death of my companions? Please, if anything, spare them."

"You act the part of a genuine Vallense—pretending you value their lives over yours. No, I see through the curtain, Andreas of Savoy, and your motives are selfish."

"Is Bertran alive? At least tell me—"

"I do not know, nor am I concerned."

Andreas turned his shoulder toward Gedeon, but Gedeon stepped in front of him again.

"More will suffer, more pain will come, but it will not be death. That would be far too generous. Your friends in Piedmont will experience emotions their Holy Scriptures cannot explain. Their God won't bless them with answers when they face their worst fears. I will pull the blanket off their religion, their sect, and reveal their vilest secrets. And I want you to die knowing you could do nothing about it."

Andreas clenched his teeth. "Your pride and hatred consume you, Gedeon Chanforan. I once thought you an impressive man, though I could see through the false wealth you boasted."

Gedeon lowered the cloth from his nose again and grimaced, then dusted off his hands. "Your stench is making me dizzy. Farewell, my prince. May your death be swift." He turned and yelled for the guard, who soon returned and threw Andreas back into his cell.

The rats screeched. A drip of icy water plunked onto Andreas's ear. The cell had darkened, and another night of squirms and shivers would soon be upon him.

When would he stand before the judge? Would he receive a trial, or simply have his head lopped off? What about the others—were they alive? Worse, what did Gedeon mean about the Vallenses of Piedmont? What could one burgher accomplish that the inquisitors and their crusade could not?

*   *   *

Andreas slumped to his side and curled up like a stray dog. The few rays of light that entered the room from a high-above opening faded into the murk. For what felt like the hundredth time that day, Andreas prayed. He didn't close his eyes—the prison cell had become so familiar that it offered no distractions. On the first day, he had mouthed the words, but there was nothing to hide. Now, entering a fourth night in the prison, he said each plea, each praise, and each phrase of thanksgiving aloud. Perhaps the guards thought his mind was drifting away, but his prayers had never felt so genuine. Instead of talking to the air, he was speaking to the Father of Lights.

His lips quivered whenever thoughts of Constanza came. Why had he been so intent on seeking the manuscript? What would she think when he didn't return before winter? When the spring flowers covered the alpine meadows, would she still have her eyes set on the road, patiently waiting for him, or would she have given up all hope for his return?

Andreas gave his head a quick shake, trying to dispel those imaginations. *All things are possible with God.* Was that not what the Savior had said during His earthly ministry? Weren't all things supposed to work together for good? Then why did Andreas wilt in a prison cell on a path to execution? He and Constanza had spoken about the matter before he left for Florence. Why would Jesus say all things were possible?

Then, somewhere from the depths of Andreas's memory, the Holy Scriptures pointed him to the answer. But the words were Latin, long ago memorized at Sacra di San Michele.

Pleading in the garden of Gethsemane, Christ had agonized over His purpose to the point of asking the Father to rescue Him. There, the Savior repeated the same phrase He told His disciples: "All things are possible unto thee." Yet in the end, He said, "Nevertheless not what I will, but what thou wilt."

Submission—dying to self and becoming an instrument in God's hand. Christ Himself had done it. Andreas, however, had not followed that example. He had formulated a plan, and when he was sure of its perfection, he had called on God to bless it. "God's plan," he'd called it. With God all things were possible, and all things worked together for good. But the purpose of those teachings was not about what Andreas wanted. They were about God's kingdom, His providence throughout all ages.

Andreas let himself smile. Constanza had already explained the meaning behind those teachings, but had he listened? Yes, but had he remembered it?

A drop of water fell on his cheek. He rolled to the side but smashed his head into the wall.

Lord, how does bashing my head on stone work together for good?

Stuck like a boot in April mud, Andreas could do nothing. He was alone—without his companions, without Constanza, without a friend. He'd thought of escaping, but the dirt floor was so compacted that it might as well be rock. A single opening stood far above, but it was impossible to reach, and he'd never fit through it. No, the only hope was to plead his case in a trial, and those chances dimmed as the days rolled onward.

Raimond—what would he do? At the old fort above La Torre, he'd refused the temptations to turn inward. His eyes were on Christ, not his oppressors. But Andreas was locked in a Florentine dungeon. Was there not someone in the Holy Scriptures who experienced the same?

Andreas flared his nostrils and gave his head a quick shake. A spark flickered in his mind but didn't quite ignite.

Then he remembered: Paul and Silas were in jail and didn't plan an escape. At midnight, they sang, and God sent an earthquake to free them. Andreas chuckled. That jailor must have thought his prisoners were insane.

Andreas didn't know many Vallense songs—monastic chants occupied much of his memory—but he knew some. He could sing in his heart, but that was not what Paul and Silas had done. They sang aloud, and the other prisoners overheard them. Perhaps the guard would think Andreas had gone mad, but what did it matter? He could lift his voice to God, not in desperation or anguish, but in simple adoration.

And Andreas had plenty to sing about. God had sent His Son to redeem the world from their sins. He had seen a bitter and aimless monk, sent a messenger, and drawn Andreas to the good news of unmerited salvation. God's hand moved across time, and though the Greek manuscript was lost to Andreas, it wasn't lost to God.

Andreas's mind continued to race as he found more praise and thanksgiving. Why not sing it?

So he sang—first as quiet as an afternoon breeze. But soon the satisfaction in his soul strengthened his voice.

To his surprise, no yells came from the guard. Andreas stopped to listen for other sounds, but heard only dripping water and the faint echo of his own song.

Suddenly a shout broke the silence. *"Perché hai smesso?* Why'd you stop?"

Was it the guard? Another prisoner? *I hope so.*

He switched to another song. This time, a familiar voice joined him. As usual, Bertran's singing was off-key but filled with power. The song moved from cell to cell until Victor joined them as well. But what about Basile?

After a third song, the answer came. "I'm here too, in case you were wondering. But I'm not going to start singing."

Andreas smiled. Everyone was alive, at least for now. Perhaps the Holy Spirit would use their praise to speak to Basile's soul. Most of what they sang was from the Holy Scriptures, and God could accomplish anything through His Word.

It might have been midnight, or it might have been long after, but their songs continued. Though the Stinche Prison's foundations remained intact and the doors remained shut, God was in their midst. Whether or not they held the manuscript, God would preserve His Word. And whether they lived or died, He would accomplish His will.

But God wasn't finished with him. Death would come at some point, but it might not come now. He reached inside his vest and removed the ring he had hidden there.

Unless God sent an earthquake, it was their only hope.

24

Part of their time was occupied in transcribing the Holy Scriptures, or portions of them, which they were to distribute when they went forth as missionaries. By this, and by other agencies, the seed of the Divine Word was scattered throughout Europe more widely than is commonly supposed.

—James Wylie
The History of the Waldenses, 1860

SOAPY WATER SPLASHED ONTO CONSTANZA'S SHIRT. She opened her mouth to scold Valeria but stopped short when Valeria tilted her chin down and revealed a little smile. "Perdon, Madomaisèla."

Constanza patted the front of her shirt and continued scrubbing the clothes. Earlier, Mamà had assigned Valeria and Irene to help Constanza with the laundry, but the actual help had yet to come. Mostly they complained about the work or tried to escape from it. The few moments when they tried to help, they dropped Papà's shirt in the dirt, splashed the water, or scrubbed so lightly that the clothes might as well have soaked in the rain.

"Are we finished?" Irene asked. "My arms hurt, and the water's cold."

Constanza pulled a chemise from the suds. "After we're done with these, we still need to wash the bed linens."

"May we play first?" Valeria asked.

"No, there's too much to do. And you need to learn to finish your chores."

Irene showed a crooked grimace—a new expression Constanza had first seen a few days before, but not a respectful one. "I have chores, Madomaisèla."

"Do you think picking up your bed mat is a chore? You could be hungry, cold, and dirty, just as Monsen and Madòna Grimaldi found you, but you enjoy a warm home, clean clothes, full bellies—"

"I'm hungry," Valeria said, her eyes darting toward the house.

Constanza held her breath—and her tongue. They were still young. Valeria had turned seven the previous month, though they didn't know the exact date. Orphans seldom came with birthdates, but the only entity that might know was the Catholic parish in Turin. So the Grimaldis assigned a birthdate to the children without one.

Valeria grunted as she tried to pull Papà's breeches from the wash. Constanza dropped the shirt she was washing back in the water and helped Valeria wring the water from the pants and lay them on the grass. Valeria beamed. Her smile could melt a frozen stream.

The sun crested its zenith, and they soon finished the clothes and carried baskets back to the house to gather the bed linens. On the way, Ezio and Guido ran toward them from the forest.

"Have you finished your chores?" Constanza asked.

They eyed one another, then Ezio said, "We finished with the barn, but the grain sacks—"

"Can we play now too?" Irene said with a wide grin.

Constanza ignored her and focused on the boys. "Did you feed the animals?"

"We were about to." Ezio looked toward the trees. "But Umile wanted to show us something."

"Finish your chores now, and you can explore the woods later." She shooed them away, but their feet remained planted.

"We wanted to tell you something first."

Constanza stuck a hand on her hip and waited, but not patiently.

"Down at the old Lauras farm—"

"Madomaisèla Elionor said not to go down there by yourself," Valeria said, holding her chin high.

"I'm not so concerned about you walking down there," Constanza said, "except you should have fed the animals first."

Ezio fidgeted with his jacket. "Yes, Madomaisèla. We saw something down there, though—Monsen Estève was carrying things from the house and piling them outside."

"What things?"

"Everything. The house is probably empty by now, but that's not all. Those families—the poor ones—they were helping him. The men, their wives, and all the little ones."

Constanza had told Papà about the Catholic families soon after she had encountered them the week before. Papà said they were squatters and were only temporary nuisances. Over the years, wanderers had entered the valley, but they usually left as soon as the first winter storm blew down from the heights. Even after Constanza mentioned the note with the red seal, Papà showed no real concern.

Thankfully, the families had kept to themselves and caused no problems. Constanza had seen their little camp propped up on the edge of the land. Once she encountered a woman at the nearby stream, and Papà heard they hunted small game and foraged in the forest. But why were they helping Estève empty the house? Unless—

"Come with me." Constanza waved the boys forward.

"May we walk with you?" Valeria asked with bright eyes.

Valeria and Irene would slow them down, but it would be easier than dragging two disgruntled seven-year-olds back to the house first. "As long as you help me wash the bed linens without complaining when we return."

Both girls glowed with delight.

Ezio and Guido led the way, sword-playing with sticks as they descended toward the lower farm. Constanza plodded forward, holding Irene's right hand and Valeria's left. As they approached the forest's edge, a whistle danced in the gentle breeze. Estève appeared from behind a cluster of brambles, carrying a crate far too heavy for his age.

The boys stopped and watched, but Constanza pushed them forward. "Don't stand there and wait for the poor man to strain himself." They snapped into action, and each grabbed a side of the crate.

"The boys said you were emptying the house," Constanza said.

"Indeed," Estève said. "I'm afraid I can no longer sleep there, but it's no disaster, for I'll soon be leaving on a trip to France." He shrugged. "I was able to gather all my belongings, but Andreas's—"

"They can't take the house."

"At least they restrained themselves from violence. Last night was freezing, so I invited them into the house for warmth, but when I awoke this morning, Riccardo and Patrizio were carrying their few belongings inside."

Constanza squished her eyebrows together and raised her voice. "That house belongs to my papà and Andreas."

"Their parchment says otherwise."

"It's a fake. Papà settled the matter with the lord last autumn."

"That was the former lord, no?" Estève cleared his throat. "God blessed us with a fair lord for many years. If you were to see what the rest of the world experiences, however, you would find most people are either nobles or peasants. If the rich and powerful desire something, they take it. 'We have laws,' some say, 'but who makes the laws? The same ones who bend and break those laws whenever they wish. No, Constanza, we are strangers and pilgrims in this world, and any blessings beyond that are gifts from God."

She pulled her arms close and grew still. How could God allow such injustice? That land belonged to her family. Andreas lived in the house. He had poured his sweat on the land and had grown a bountiful harvest. By their own admission, Riccardo and Patrizio had never farmed, so how dare they claim it for themselves and toss Andreas's things into the dust?

"Andreas's belongings are still down there," Estève said, "and we'll need as many hands as you can find to haul them back to your house. And that includes all the grain he harvested."

"We'll find help, but will"—she flung her gaze down—"the papists be there?"

Estève put a finger to his chin. "I suppose so."

Did he not care? The Piedmontese were robbing her family and squatting in Andreas's house. Constanza tossed up a hand. "Then let's reclaim what we can before the papists take that too."

After sending the boys back with the crate to ask for help, Constanza, Estève, and the girls crossed the field toward the house—the same one where she and Andreas had found themselves covered in mud after the hasty gathering of the barley sheaves. Her lips crept upward into a smile, but the sight across the field squashed it. Three Piedmontese children played in the clearing in front of the house as if it were theirs, and a boy of no more than three rummaged through the pile of Andreas's belongings.

Constanza quickened her pace while Estève and the girls straggled behind. "That's not yours," she shouted in Piedmontese.

All four children jumped and ran back into the house.

Riccardo stepped from the door, brow lowered and club in hand. "This is all ours now. We'll cause no harm to you if you just leave us be."

What was the phrase she wanted to say? If only Elionor were there to speak proper Piedmontese.

But Estève spoke in her stead. "We are only gathering the rest of our things."

Constanza nudged him and whispered, "We need to demand that they leave. They're robbers."

Estève looked behind him. "Who's going to stop them? Who will throw these peasants into the elements? You?"

"Yet they tossed you out like an old chicken bone."

Amalia stepped outside and stood next to her husband. Her oily hair hung over her shoulders. "We are sorry for being abrupt, but the Lord of Luserna made us tenants of this land."

"Legally," Riccardo said. "We're willing to offer you part of next year's harvest, but we have nothing else to give you now."

"My papà can make those decisions." Constanza strode to Andreas's belongings and collected them while keeping an eye on the Catholics. Patrizio and his wife, Mercede, stepped outside with expressionless faces. Mercede's eyes sagged, and her hair was in disarray. In another time and place, Constanza might have felt pity for her.

Constanza turned toward home with her hands full, but then a voice called out to her.

"My baby is burning up," Mercede said. "He cried all night and won't eat. Do you know anyone who can help us?"

Constanza bit her lip. More than anyone else near San Lorenzo, she was the one families came to her when they needed physical help. She had set broken bones, helped deliver babies, and yes, treated childhood fevers. But what would others think if she helped this family?

Estève leaned toward her. "You know what's right."

Ezio and Guido had returned with three other boys. Constanza handed them her load and followed Mercede into the house.

The baby's cries were shallow and dry and his movements lethargic. Constanza opened his mouth and felt the tongue and lips. Dry. "He's very sick."

"What can we do? We have no money—"

"Sambucus flowers in a tea. I have some dried at my home. I'll send it down here with someone soon. Until then, try to keep him cool and fed. His mouth is parched, and he needs milk."

Constanza ran her hand along the baby's skin. Dirt and dust formed a glaze of filth that must have brought the sickness. Did these people ever bathe? By the children's scent, it wasn't their habit. No wonder the baby was sick.

"Will he survive?"

Constanza pressed her lips together and darted her eyes from Mercede to the baby. Fevers at this age often resulted in death. Perhaps if the family had kept their children clean, the sickness never would have come.

"Keep the other children away and bathe them. As for this little one, he is in God's care. There's nothing I can do."

"Thank you," Mercede said. Her husband stood behind her and gave a slight nod.

Constanza left the house. Andreas's belongings were gone except for the stack of grain in the barn. Papà and her brothers could retrieve that after she told them what had happened.

Estève stood leaning against a tree. "You did what was right, Madomaisèla."

"Or did I enable their lawlessness?" Constanza scratched her neck. "I know we should help the downtrodden, but what if they hate us? They need Christ, but if they cling to their false religion, when should we seek more fertile soil?"

"You know the answer, but your flesh fights against it. But I know how you feel, because I've experienced the same conflicts myself."

Valeria and Irene ran from behind Andreas's barn, chased by a few Piedmontese children. Constanza jumped to intervene until laughter entered her ears. Both girls smiled as they ran to Constanza.

"May we come back and play tomorrow?" Irene asked.

"Papà would never approve."

"May we ask him?"

"Come, girls. We've lost half the day, and the bed linens are still dirty."

The girls waved to their new friends as they walked back into the field, but Constanza focused ahead. They arrived home as the sun fell behind the mountains.

Estève needed a place to sleep. Constanza wet her lips and said, "Elionor and I can sleep with the girls."

Estève shook his head. "I won't allow it, forcing a woman to the floor while I rest on feathers."

"I would be insulted to allow our guest to sleep on the floor." Constanza hinted at a smile. Eventually Estève acquiesced, and Constanza and a few boys helped carry his belongings into the room.

Papà returned just after the moonrise, and Constanza ran to greet him. Her mouth moved quicker than her mind. "The Catholics—they stole Andreas's farm. Estève invited them in last night because of the cold, but they showed him their parchment and made him leave with all his things. Andreas's too."

"I know about the house. They informed me yesterday."

"You let them take it, Papà?"

"According to the law, they bear the legal right to it."

Constanza scowled. "No, it's your land."

"It's the Lord of Luserna's land, and he does with it as he pleases."

"You bear your own right to it, more than those Piedmontese families."

"I spoke with Johan yesterday, and we came to an agreement. It was Gerald Lauras, Johan's father, who cleared the land and built the house. When he died, it should have passed to Johan, but no one could find him. Then, when I approached Lord Falzon last autumn, he let me manage it, but with his death, we are beholden to the new lord and his laws. At least he allowed us to keep Andreas's grain."

"You need to do something."

"We have the grain, and for that we are thankful. But action for the sake of action is folly. We must make wise decisions instead of reacting." Papà removed his hat and hung it on the wall. "Don't concern yourself with what you can't change. Focus on what you can improve instead."

Constanza gave a halfhearted shrug and retired to her mat. *Content. I must be content.* She unfastened her hair, brushed it, then blew out the last flicker of light.

*   *   *

Long before sunrise, Mamà woke every soul in the house with her gentle prods and reassuring voice. Even the youngest children would take part in the day's activities. She handed everyone a thick slice of bread with a dollop of butter and shooed them into the predawn twilight. Papà was the last to leave the house, but when he stepped outside, his torch illuminated the children's sleepy eyes and sagging shoulders.

Constanza rubbed her eyes and yawned as she peered across the terraces. More adults and children walked in their direction—her brothers, sisters, nieces, and nephews. *I must tell Miquèl, David, Francesco, and Bartholomeo about the old*

Lauras farm. Papà might have resigned himself to the lord's dictates, but her brothers would better understand.

The men had made the preparations the day before, but today, all hands would be busy. For the past month, the hogs had fattened themselves in the forest with acorns, chestnuts, and beechnuts, but now the Pavarins would harvest the meat. Just as God provided grain, vegetables, and fruit from the soil, He blessed them with meat from the hogs—a gift for rearing them from piglets the previous spring.

When everyone arrived, Papà raised his hands and quieted the chatter. "The men will kill the hogs and bleed them out while the women prepare the water for scalding." He nodded toward Constanza. "Connie will take charge of the children under ten, and they will begin by gathering kindling for the fire. We'll need plenty today."

She shut her eyes and sighed. *Elionor could manage them better. I need to talk to my brothers.* She opened her eyes and scanned the crowd for Elionor, but she wasn't there. Odd.

Papà's voice carried through the still air. "We need to process eight hogs, so the day will be long. In the end, we will gain meat for the winter. Praise God for His providence and provisions." He bowed his head and lifted his voice to heaven.

The crowd dispersed as soon as Papà finished. Constanza spotted Mamà walking toward the firepit. "Where is Elionor? She was awake with the rest of us, but I didn't see her step outside."

"Valeria and Irene are feeling poorly. They could barely stand, so I asked her to stay in the house with them."

"Did they have fevers?"

"No, they're only weak, and they'll probably be out here with us by midday."

"Remember what I told you last night about the Catholic baby?"

"Yes, but it's not the same. Less than a day has passed since you were there." Mamà tied an apron around her waist and turned back toward the fire. "If Ellie needs you, she'll find you. Come now"—she waved her over—"let's get this water hot."

The children gathered around Constanza. "Tanta," said one of her nephews, "what are we supposed to do?"

"Euh . . . kindling. Find the driest sticks, not too big, and bring them to the fire."

Most of the children dispersed toward the forest except for two orphan girls, Fosca and Ave—the ones Constanza had helped escape from the fire. Ave asked, "Can you come with us?"

Constanza tightened her lips. *I have more pressing matters to attend.* "Nothing in the forest will harm you."

Their feet remained planted. *"Se vos plai?* Please?"

Constanza shook her head, grabbed Ave's hand, and pulled the girls toward their task.

As she gathered sticks with the girls, Constanza prayed for Andreas. Wherever he was, he needed God's help. Andreas was confident, but perhaps he needed encouragement. He should arrive in about a month, but the changes would shock him. His old friend Johan had become a noble's power-hungry *lacai*. Worse, Piedmontese squatters occupied his house—and yes, it might someday be her house too. How would Andreas respond?

The fire roared under many kettles of water. Constanza and the children carried loads of kindling until Mamà instructed them to haul logs from inside the barn.

Soon the men carried the first bled hog toward the fire as Constanza delivered her third armful of firewood. "This is the biggest," her brother Bartholomeo said. They plopped it on a layer of sticks and walked back toward the barn.

Her chance had come. Constanza ran to Bartholomeo. "Did you hear about the lower farm? The Catholics—"

"Anna needs help." Bartholomeo pointed over Constanza's shoulder with his nose.

Constanza turned to see her sister struggling with a cauldron of hot water.

"Connie, can you hold the other side?" Anna asked.

After Constanza grabbed a wool rag, they lifted the cauldron from the fire and poured it over the hog's skin. Mamà jumped into action, and with the blunt edge of her knife, she removed the coarse hair from the skin.

"More water," Mamà said.

Anna and Constanza carried over another kettle and poured it on the carcass. In an instant, Mamà was scraping again. The real work had begun, and it wouldn't finish until after sundown. But they were Pavarins, and though the task was long and arduous, they would perform it with patience and expertise.

Bartholomeo had already left by the time they finished the scalding. Pietat! Constanza gazed toward the barn. When could she speak with her brothers?

Constanza directed the children from one task to another: more firewood, more kindling, stoke the fire, fetch water from the creek. When the men delivered another hog, the work only increased. They conversed little, for the labor demanded all eyes, ears, and hands.

After they had removed the hair from the first carcass, the men hauled it back to the barn for butchering. The bustle continued through the morning and afternoon until they had prepared all eight carcasses. Though the air cooled her hands, sweat beaded on Constanza's brow. Her stomach growled, but they wouldn't feast until they had finished. She would at least wash in the creek before they began the salting, smoking, drying, and roasting. Then at last she could talk to her brothers.

On the way back from the creek, a slender figure appeared over the rise. Elionor ran toward Constanza with wide eyes, shaking her head. "Valeria and Irene are sick."

"Mamà told me this morning—"

"Both are sweating and panting. They want water but are too weak to swallow." Elionor's voice quickened and shook. "I don't know what to do."

Constanza clutched the sides of her skirt. "Are their foreheads warm?"

"I . . . maybe . . . I can't—"

"I've been managing the children here. If you take over for me, I'll stay with Valeria and Irene."

Elionor nodded, but a tear fell from her eye. "They're so sick, Connie."

"They'll be fine." *At least I hope so.*

25

When a man's cause is good, it will sufficiently plead for itself, yea, and for its master too.

—John Bunyan
The Work of Jesus Christ as an Advocate, 1688

ANDREAS COUNTED NINE NIGHTS IN PRISON —nine nights of freezing fingers, clammy clothing, and rat screeches that could shatter a man's bones. But every night since the third, he, Bertran, and Victor had sung their melodies.

A guard had mentioned their trial being postponed. Would they ever see a magistrate, or would they wither in prison? Food came in trickles—one day, Andreas received nothing, and the next, two hunks of soft bread and a bowl of pottage. Though imprisonment was miserable, it was certainly preferable to being headless. Andreas thanked God for each new day.

The morning of the ninth day came without sunlight to brighten the cell. Dampness weighed down the air, and the sound of steady raindrops poured through the window above. Andreas lay on the floor, hand propping up his head, and fiddled with his ring. The House of Savoy. Though royal blood flowed through him, how would such a trinket help free him from a Florentine prison? The relationship between Savoy and Tuscany had been cordial, but how would he prove he wasn't a French spy?

Andreas's mind wandered to Gedeon Chanforan. Why steal Princess Yolande's prize and risk her wrath? If Andreas ever felt the sun's warmth again, he would seek an answer.

A few days before, Andreas had planned to show his ring to the guards, but at the last moment, he had pulled back. The guards had thus far shown him nothing but their spit and the backs of their hands. The ring's golden sparkle would no doubt ignite their greed, and whoever saw it first would take it, then hide it from the others.

A drop of water fell into his hair. *I thought this spot was dry.* Andreas huffed and moved yet again, but he didn't see the rat dung that occupied that space and that soon occupied his elbow too. He wouldn't wipe it with his clothes, and nothing else of the like was in the cell. The wall would suffice, but after he scraped the dung off, his elbow was raw. He peered up at the window and prayed aloud.

"Father, You see me here and know what I am feeling. Your Son suffered much worse for my sake, and You have chosen this affliction for me: 'nevertheless not what I will, but what thou wilt . . . The spirit truly is ready, but the flesh is weak.'"

The emptiness of the prison offered Andreas the perfect mirror to evaluate himself. His ambitions, not the Holy Spirit, had driven him. The things he feared—inadequacy, rejection, failure—stemmed from his own selfishness. He should've learned much more from Estève on his trip last summer, but his pride had made his mind like a brick instead of a sponge. God had led him to salvation, spared his life from inquisitors, and separated him into service. And what had been his utmost concern? Whether his speech stumbled while sharing the gospel.

Selfishness, carelessness, arrogance, self-reliance—he rooted out each one and more. If only he had the chance to serve God and others with his renewed mind.

A psalm settled into his mind—Latin, yes, and Constanza would've cringed had she heard the lines from Jerome's Vulgate, but it was what he knew.

Why art thou sad, O my soul? And why dost thou disquiet me? Hope in God, for I will still give praise to him: the salvation of my countenance, and my God.

Footsteps plodded down the hall. Just as when Gedeon visited and told his terrible story, it was more than one person. The door across the hall clicked and opened. An unknown voice echoed off the stone, but the words were muffled.

A moment later, the door slammed shut. A few footsteps hit the floor, and Andreas's door clicked. Was it time for the trial? Would he breathe in the open air and sunshine, even if it was the last time? Andreas quivered as he stood.

A slender man with plain clothing stepped through the door with a torch and greeted Andreas. In the Tuscan dialect, he asked, "*Hai qualche disturbos?*"

"*Non capisco,*" Andreas said. "I don't understand."

Andreas jerked his head back when the man responded in flawless Latin. "*Habesne ægritudines?* Do you have any ailments?"

"No, but I'm starving. The guards barely feed us here."

The man opened the door further, and another man stepped in. This one wore finer clothing, but his hair resembled a mouse's nest.

"I am called Uberto," said the first man, "and my companion is Emidio. We are members of a brotherhood called *i Buononimi delle Stinche*, and we provide charity for the men in the Stinche Prison."

Andreas held out his hand, but Uberto refused it. "The captain tells me you are a French spy."

"I am not. I am from Savoy—"

"Nearly the same. *Aspirante* French, I've heard you Savoyards called."

Andreas clasped his hands together and whispered, "Please hear me."

"Every prisoner wants to plead his case to us, but we can do nothing." Uberto motioned for Emidio to step forward. "If you have any sores or sickness, Emidio will help. I also carry cured poultry that the faithful Catholics of our brotherhood have donated."

Andreas widened his eyes. "Must I pay you?" He reached into his pocket to show his lack of money, but the coolness of the ring sparked his senses.

"We only ask that you show mercy to others."

"How can I do that? My head will soon be on the chopping block."

Emidio opened a sack and placed a handful of dry meat into Andreas's hand. Andreas devoured each piece, then eyed his hand, ready to lick off every scrap. But that was below him—he would at least wait until they left. He pulled the ring from his pocket and held it toward them. "I have this as payment for your benevolence."

Uberto took a step back and held up his hands. "We cannot take—"

"Look at it. Pure gold. You won't find anything like it in the Italian peninsula. On it you will see the House of Savoy's coat of arms." Andreas held it up to Uberto's eyes. "I am Andreas, third son of Duke Louis of Savoy. I came to Florence to buy a relic from a Greek scholar, and a man who coveted the same relic falsely accused me of being a French spy, which is why I stand before you now. Please, for all that is just and good, will you show this to the Medicis and tell them my story?"

Uberto laughed. "Every prisoner has a tale that proves his innocence, but I have yet to hear a man claim he's a noble. I considered helping you, until you brought the Medicis into your scheme. We have no access to Cosimo de' Medici."

"You must know someone who will listen to me. You have been kind enough to listen, and you could find someone with the authority to intervene."

Uberto glanced at Emidio and shook his head. "We are humble citizens of Florence who strive to bring nourishment to sinners. Neither of us is in a position to help you. *Doleo.* I am sorry."

Emidio spoke up. "Do you have any friends in the city? We could present the ring to whomever you wish, and perhaps with their help—"

A face with a white beard popped into Andreas's mind. "Ioannis Argyropoulos."

Both men stared at Andreas with squinted eyes.

"He's the Greek scholar I mentioned." Andreas raised a finger to his chin. "Ioannis said the Medicis have sponsored his teaching and studies. He may be able to help." For the next few moments, Andreas explained where they could find Ioannis. His whole body lightened as he spoke, but he couldn't let his hopes compete with his reliance on God.

Uberto and Emidio turned to leave, but Andreas touched Uberto's shoulder. "Three other men accompany me—Bertran, Victor, and Basile." He motioned to the sack of provisions. "Please give them as much as you can spare."

They nodded, but Emidio extended his hand. "We need the ring."

Andreas held it out but hesitated. If they wanted, they could sell it and receive an overflowing pouch of florins. True, the ring brought him no special treatment in a prison cell, but it was still a symbol of his lineage. Without it, he was a poor heretic farmer from the Alps.

He grinned. His identity was with Christ now, not his lineage. Noble blood might bring prestige on this earth, but the blood of Christ had redeemed him and reconciled his soul to the Creator. *You alone, Lord, can move the hearts of the rulers. My fate and the fate of my companions lie in Your hands.*

Andreas opened his hand and allowed the ring to drop.

26

The Bible is the Saviour's Book. . . . And it is the book which reveals the Saviour, which tells what He is, and tells us that He is ours. Whoever has got a Bible may have the Saviour also. So that if, in respect of its authorship and origin, the Bible be the Saviour's Book, in regard of its destination and object, it is no less truly the Sinner's Book.

—James Hamilton
Sermons and Lectures, 1837

Papà stepped into the house with a pail of water. "It's freezing, but it's what you asked for."

"And it's exactly what we need." Constanza wiped the sweat from her brow and surveyed the room. The orphans lay strewn across the floor, some coughing, others whimpering, and all with rags that needed changing. Through the night, everyone in the Pavarin household had developed signs of sickness. But the younger the person was, the more severe the case.

Constanza's breath left her, and her vision spun. She reached for anything steady, but Mamà's hands found her first.

"You must rest." Mamà steadied Constanza and walked her to a chair. "Sit here. We can manage. You've pushed yourself too hard. Even the most prized horses accept their limits, and it's often sooner than we imagine."

Constanza glanced at Mamà and tried to grin. "I'm not a horse, Mamà, just a woman."

"No, not just a woman. You possess the strongest soul in this home."

"I'm far less virtuous than you suppose," Constanza mumbled, shaking her head.

Mamà smiled and gave her a pat on the cheek, then rushed back to caring for the children.

Constanza rested her arms on the table and cradled her head in them. Her eyelids yearned to shut, but she couldn't sleep. Everyone needed her.

Sounds drifted into her ears—doors opening and shutting, Elionor's comforting words, Mamà's sighs, the children. Yes, the orphans, the ones whom God loved.

"Connie!" A hand shook her awake. "Valeria is asleep, and we can't wake her. Her breath is so shallow . . ."

Constanza snapped upright and breathed in hard through her stuffy nose. "I'm coming." She stumbled from her chair, stepped over a few other children, and knelt near the corner of the room where Valeria lay.

Mamà was there, holding the girl's hand, tears falling from her eyes. "She's with the Father."

Constanza's jaw dropped. No, it couldn't be. Only a day had passed. She opened Valeria's shirt and placed her ear on the girl's chest. Though faint, her heart was still beating. Constanza put her hand close to Valeria's nose. Again faint, but still breathing. "She's alive—barely."

"What can we do?" Elionor asked.

Constanza scanned the room. Daylight streamed through the windows, forcing her to shield her eyes. Why had she allowed herself to sleep so long? "How are the others?"

Elionor shook her head. "It's difficult to know whether they're just tired or if they're delirious. Irene is much cooler than yesterday, so perhaps she's recovering. But the others? The worst may be yet to come."

"We've kept cool rags on them all night," Mamà said, "just as you instructed."

"Where is Papà?"

"Resting, and the same for Estève. We've all pressed ourselves." Exhaustion shaded Mamà's eyes, and her graying hair had mostly escaped her kerchief, falling in wisps over her cheeks.

"Mamà, you must sleep, and you too, Ellie. I'm rested now, and I will care for everyone."

"Estève and Papà will rise soon," Mamà said. "You should have plenty of water for now, and when the children awake—"

"I'll manage it. I feel much better than earlier." Constanza embraced her and Elionor, then shooed them off to bed.

Constanza moved from child to child, feeling their foreheads, covering them with blankets, and whispering a few encouraging words. When she returned to Valeria, she knelt down and listened to her heart again. Only God could strengthen her now. Valeria's eyelids fluttered and her face twitched.

Little Valeria. Constanza held her hand, cold but still pulsing with a flicker of life.

A knock sounded at the door. Constanza stretched and rose, but Papà's footsteps plodded to the door first.

"My whole family is sick," said Constanza's brother David. "Is Connie here?"

Papà turned and caught Constanza's gaze. "She is, but she's been awake most of the night already. We are suffering the same illness here, and the orphans need her too."

"Please, Papà," David said. "Catterina has been caring for the children all night and now barely stands. We are Constanza's own blood—"

"The orphans here are no less, David."

"But my children are your grandchildren, and these—"

"Are also little ones who need love and attention."

Constanza's hands shook. She couldn't bear the argument—not now. "David, a girl here is in danger of losing her life, but as soon as she is well, or"—no, she couldn't think that—"or when Mamà and Elionor are rested, I'll go to your home. But I hold no special powers. Keep them cool, make them drink water, and sit by their side." She gripped Valeria's hand tighter.

David's lips quivered, and he blinked faster than a sparrow's wings. Had she seen David weep? For the sake of her own sanity, Constanza had to look away.

Soon he was gone. He wasn't putting himself first—he was only caring for his family and had reached out in desperation.

The sickness had spread through their families like weeds in fresh soil. No doubt the papist children had ignited the *pesta*. How many would die because of their filthiness? Everyone knew sickness came from dust and dirt. When parents neglected their offspring and allowed soot and *rebut* to collect on their skin and clothes, others suffered. Not only had the Piedmontese stolen Andreas's house, but they had also brought disease and misery to the Angrogna Valley.

Papà sat at the table, head bowed, his mouth moving slightly. To others, he might have been resting, but Constanza knew her papà. Not a day passed that she didn't see or hear him speaking to God.

Irene stirred and sat up. "Valeria's still sleeping?"

"Yes, but we must pray for her, for she is very sick."

"More than I am?" Irene's eyes were brighter than a sick girl's should have been.

"Yes, I'm afraid so."

Irene stretched her arms toward the ceiling. "I'm hungry."

A wheeze escaped Valeria, then another. Her fingers slacked and grew cold in Constanza's hand. Constanza leaned over and pushed her ear into Valeria's chest. While Constanza's heartbeat quickened, Valeria's slowed.

"Madomaisèla—"

"Go find Mamà."

"What?"

"Mamà—please fetch her."

"I'm not allowed to enter her room."

"It doesn't matter now. Valeria is dying and I need Mamà."

Irene jumped up and hurried to the other room.

Constanza rubbed Valeria's cheeks and hands, but nothing warmed her. Her breaths shrank into labored wheezes, and her little eyes remained shut. Constanza placed a hand on the girl's forehead, but it was neither hot nor sweaty—nearly lifeless. But Valeria couldn't die. She had lived only seven years.

The wheezing quickened, but soon Mamà appeared. "She's failing, Mamà, and I can't do anything."

Mamà grabbed Valeria with one hand and held Constanza with the other. "The Lord is our only hope."

Mamà whispered to the Almighty for mercy. But Valeria's temporal life soon faded into the eternal. Tears fell from Constanza's eyes and onto the empty body. Now, instead of opening her eyes to sunlight, Valeria would experience the light of eternal joy. No longer would her laughter sound through the house, for a new song had entered her heart, and she sang praises to her heavenly Father.

Mamà covered Valeria with a blanket and placed her hand on top. "We will bury her today."

"Why? Why today?" Constanza's throat tightened, her voice faltered, and her shoulders shook. "Why Valeria? She was so small. We kept her clean and fed her. Why did God take her?"

"I asked myself the same questions when your brother Pèire died, and I have come to realize that I may never gain those answers." Mamà placed her hand on Constanza's cheek and gazed into her eyes. "I believe God wants us to ask questions. His Son took the sin of the world upon Himself as the same world murdered Him. Still, Jesus asked, 'My God, my God, why hast thou forsaken me?' He sees and understands our grief, though we may never understand the reasons. Perhaps in the eternal kingdom we will know, but until then, we are sure Valeria knew God's forgiveness and is in His arms."

Constanza wiped her eyes and nestled her face into Mamà's shoulder. "I'm tired. And I feel lost. Not alone, but lonely. I know God is here, but I can't sense Him."

Mamà pulled Constanza closer and rubbed her back. "The burden of grief is like none other. You've served these children for hours, and we are still in the midst of this misery. We must keep our eyes forward and not down." She hugged Constanza tighter, then held her at arm's length. "Your papà said David and Catterina need your help. Elionor, Estève, and I will care for the children while you're gone."

Constanza's eyes fell back on Valeria—or what once represented her. Her feelings toward the girl had been so much less than she wished. Why had she pushed Valeria away so often? Annoyance? Frustration? Constanza had dreamed of being more than a nursemaid, but to what end? How were her dreams more honorable than loving the fatherless? She might have given her time, talents, and energy to their care, but she hadn't given them her heart. Now she would never have another opportunity to open her heart to Valeria.

Constanza looked over the room from mat to mat. Some children sat up and rubbed their eyes, while others still slept. They might not need her physical care as much when they were better, but they needed her affection—not through action alone but also through words of love and affirmation.

27

The Bible is a treasure. It contains enough to make us rich for time and eternity. It contains the secret of happy living. It contains the key of Heaven. It contains the title-deeds of an inheritance incorruptible, and that fadeth not away. It contains the pearl of great price. Nay, in so far as it reveals them as the portion of us sinful worms, it contains the Saviour, and the living God Himself.

—James Hamilton
Sermons and Lectures, 1837

A HOWL ECHOED THROUGH THE PRISON HALLS, and then a door slammed shut. Another prisoner had been fed to the unquenchable hunger of the Stinche Prison. How often did men perish here, forgotten, forsaken, and alone? Andreas gave his head an abrupt shake. *No, I can't sink into despair.*

Andreas had waited two days for Uberto and Emidio to return, and he kept his mind sharp by quoting passages from the Holy Scriptures, praying, and remembering Constanza. Six weeks had passed since he had seen her smile or heard her laughter. *I'll never see the one I love again. Love. yes, I love her.* His greatest regret was not telling her that.

Soon more footsteps echoed through the hall. A door opened nearby. And another.

Andreas had begged for God's help and comfort in this prison, and he had come to better understand his Creator. Never would he understand all the ways of God. The words from the prophet Isaiah returned to him, committed to memory during his years as a monk. *For as the heavens are exalted above the earth, so are my ways exalted above your ways, and my thoughts above your thoughts.*

Though he had since learned about the innumerable corruptions within the Catholic Bible, the light of God's Word still shone through its foggy shadows. God's ways were indeed higher than man's.

Hollow voices, then a shout. A key clicked in the door. Andreas's stomach rumbled. Was it Uberto and Emidio?

But the guard who stepped from behind the door dashed Andreas's hopes on the stone walls.

"*Alzarsi!*" he shouted. "Up!"

Andreas rose, but his knees faltered. Another guard stepped into his cell.

"Where are you taking me?"

Neither answered.

The weakness in Andreas's limbs caused him to stumble. A guard grabbed him on each side and pulled him into the hall.

He closed his eyes and stared into the blackness of his mind. Surely they wouldn't force him to present a defense in this state. Perhaps they were skipping the show and dragging him to the executioner.

Some of the first words he had memorized from the Romaunt Bible fell on Andreas's tongue. "'Therefore if any man be in Christ, he is a new creature: old things are passed away; behold, all things are become new.'" Under the old lean-to on Francesco Pavarin's farm, Andreas had repented of his sins and believed in Christ. God had transformed him into a new creation.

Though his mouth remained shut, a little smile formed. *If I survive, I want to remember this moment for all my life. I want to experience the same reliance on God I feel now.*

A door slammed shut on the left. The guards stopped their pushing and pulling. Andreas opened his eyes as a door opened in front of him.

The sunlight he so yearned for burned holes in his vision. He pulled up his arm to shield himself, but the guards' grip dug deeper into his arms. They dragged him into the daylight as Andreas bent his head toward his shoulder and squinted his eyes as tight as his strength allowed. At least the scents were more agreeable.

He fell into a coughing fit. The previous night, the prisoners' songs had ended early. A sickness seemed to have settled in Andreas's chest, and though he had tried to sing, he couldn't without hacking uncontrollably.

Thank You, Lord, that I will gain a new body in heaven. No coughs, no year-old stripes on my back from inquisitors, only my eternal form. He whispered, "'Who shall change our vile body, that it may be fashioned like unto his glorious body, according to the working whereby he is able even to subdue all things unto himself.'"

Suddenly the guards pulled Andreas off his feet, reared him back, and threw him to the ground.

A door slammed behind him, and the air grew still. Andreas pried his eyelids open to a sliver and peered through the dust and brightness. He lay outside the prison. The buildings of Florence surrounded the prison like a fence, but people freely streamed about the plaza.

Andreas looked for a crowd gathered for the execution, but the only faces he discerned were Bertran Arnaldi, Victor of Bricherasio, and Basile Halphen. And one more—the white beard and black cap of Ioannis Argyropoulos. Andreas's heart jumped, but his muscles were too weak to do the same.

"Yes, you're free." Ioannis walked toward him. "I received your message last night."

You are gracious and merciful, God.

"Did they make you pay?" Andreas asked. "The prison, I mean."

"No, I spoke with Cosimo de' Medici himself. His son Piero is under my tutelage, and when I learned what had happened, I pleaded your case. Signore Medici was quite understanding, to my astonishment. The Medicis are always ruthless with their adversaries, but from what I can ascertain, they were as suspicious of your accuser as I was."

"You knew about Gedeon robbing me?"

"Guards making arrests on the Ponte Vecchio? Chases outside the Porta Romana? Word travels fast in Florence."

"I could've taken that whole detachment of guards on the bridge if it wasn't for the cheap blow." Victor rubbed the back of his head and gave Andreas a grin. "I almost left my poor wife a widow, holding off those guards while you ran off the bridge."

Andreas rubbed his eyes and shielded them from the sun perched in the sky above Ioannis's head. "How did you convince the Medicis we were innocent?"

"Naturally, I flashed your ring at them. Cosimo cringed at first and said Duke Louis owed him florins, but in time he relaxed. I told him I sold a Greek manuscript to the House of Savoy. He asked a few probing questions and finally told his assistant to release you."

"I don't . . . how can I thank you? I have no way to repay you—"

"Signore Chanforan. My estimation is that he plans to sell the codex—or manuscript or whatever you Latins wish to call it—to the Roman Catholics. If you are able to keep it from them, that will be payment enough. Which reminds me"—he lifted a finger—"Signore Chanforan is quite the ambitious merchant."

Andreas smirked. "I've noticed."

"No, there's more. I have friends in the Arte della Lana. Apparently Gedeon Chanforan enjoys spewing out all his accomplishments at the guildhall. One part will particularly interest you, Andreas of Savoy. Gedeon has sworn fealty to a young noble named Philip of Savoy whose plan is to overthrow the Duke of Savoy."

Andreas drew his eyebrows together. "My brother now wants to overthrow my father? I don't know what to say. Except, why would a burgher from Turin associate himself with my brother?"

Basile rolled his head around and cleared his throat. "Prince Philip will reward Gedeon in return for his loyalty. A rebellion cannot rise without support from the merchant class, and Gedeon is perhaps the most powerful burgher in Piedmont."

Gedeon's story from the prison ricocheted into Andreas's head. "Gedeon told me he wants to harm the Vallenses, and with Philip's support, no one will be able to stop him. I have a notion about what Gedeon may be scheming. He told me his life story, thinking I would never see the sun again."

"Come to my home and tell me everything," Ioannis said. "There you may rest, wash off the prison odors, and fill your stomachs."

"Only for a moment." Andreas rose and gazed over the surrounding buildings. "We must leave Florence today. Our people are in grave danger."

28

The youth who here sat at the feet of the more venerable and learned of their barbes used as their text-book the Holy Scriptures. And not only did they study the sacred volume; they were required to commit to memory, and be able accurately to recite, whole Gospels and Epistles. This was a necessary accomplishment on the part of public instructors in those ages when printing was unknown, and copies of the Word of God were rare.

—James Wylie
The History of the Waldenses, 1860

CONSTANZA RUSHED THROUGH THE DOORS OF THE MEETINGHOUSE and slid onto the last empty bench. After she brushed off her sleeves and made sure her kerchief was straight, she let out a long sigh. As much as she tried to arrive with everyone else, she so often failed. This time, they hadn't bothered to wait for her. The pastor stood before the church and spoke, meaning she had missed the singing and prayer time. Constanza tilted her ears toward Pastor Colletto.

"Most have walked through the valley of the shadow of death—some last week, others before—but our Shepherd will lead us through it."

He recited the Twenty-third Psalm. All eyes were on him as he worked to encourage the congregation after their recent storm of misery and grief. Constanza listened and shed more than one tear.

Twelve days had passed since little Valeria slipped into the Father's arms. The malady had done its worst to the inhabitants of the Angrogna Valley. It had affected children most of all, beginning with exhaustion and dizziness and ending with a boiling fever that caused them to sleep forever. Constanza had lost two nephews, and among the church, another five had fallen.

Few words left Elionor's lips, and not a smile nor laugh had come from her after Valeria's death. Elionor performed her duties, ate, slept, and did nothing else. It was as if she had resigned her life to the ashes and become a shadow of the woman who had always been Constanza's friend. Elionor hadn't come with the rest of the household today, staying in bed and complaining of a stomach pain. But there was something more there—something deeper and more disturbing.

Death-bringing disease came with life, but this time, all Vallenses realized who had brought it. Few broached the subject, but the fevers hadn't fallen upon them until the two Catholic families invaded their valley. Had Mercede's baby survived? Constanza didn't let the question concern her.

"Mourn with those who have lost a child," Pastor Colletto said, almost in response to Constanza's thoughts. "Grieve, comfort, show mercy. Let them experience Christian compassion and brotherhood."

Constanza loosened her posture as the sermon ended. The pastor's words caused her heart to ache. The pain was too much. She had spent nights staring at the ceiling, wondering why God had allowed her nephews and Valeria to die. Why not let them grow to adulthood? But then she remembered a portion of the Seventy-third Psalm. *But it is good for me to draw near to God: I have put my trust in the Lord GOD, that I may declare all thy works.*

A door opened behind Constanza, and she turned to see Johan Lauras strutting into the building. She narrowed her eyes and flung her gaze back to the pastor. What did Johan want now? What impudence to stroll into the meetinghouse during such heavy times. Her bench creaked, and when she looked left, Johan gave a nod and a lifeless smile. She glanced away without bothering to acknowledge him.

"Constanza Pavarin, always the most hospitable," Johan said in a whisper. "Today is such a pleasant day. You should find your smile, old friend." The bench lurched as he scooted toward Constanza.

"Come closer, and I'll smack that ridiculous smirk from your smooth face."

Johan widened his grin. "I'm making room for guests. Three have never entered a Vallense church, and one hasn't listened to a sermon in decades."

"Such a perfect time to bring them, now that we're nearly finished."

The church doors clicked again. A hush fell over the congregation, and Constanza turned toward the back. Her mouth fell open at the sight of the four visitors.

She had spent the most time with Claudia and Addo, but all of them she knew well. The Chanforans' clothing represented their status—brilliantly dyed fabrics, embroidered dresses, billowing sleeves, and unscuffed shoes. Monsen Gedeon Chanforan, his firm chin held high, acknowledged Johan with a quick nod and sat on the bench next to him.

Though the pastor hadn't yet dismissed the congregation, curious heads turned to study the Chanforans. But how did Johan know them?

Johan scooted closer, but by then, Constanza sat on the farthest end of the bench. She positioned herself to stand when Johan nudged her. He said nothing, but pointed his nose at the husband, who held a hand out to Constanza. But she couldn't shake his hand—his rank was too high.

Johan nudged her again.

Constanza slowly stretched the fingers of her right hand, tightened her lips, and extended her arm.

Gedeon smiled as he shook her hand. "I doubted I would see our trusted maid again. We've been anticipating this day, Claudia most of all."

Constanza glanced at Gedeon's son and daughter and smiled. It was odd to see them in a humble mountain meetinghouse instead of the grand Chanforan villa. "What . . . what brings you to the mountains?"

"Business, of course," said his wife, Marta.

Constanza held one arm tight to her body and tilted her head. "How do you know Johan? We grew up together—"

Pastor Colletto's voice rose above their conversation. "Madomaisèla Constanza, would you please introduce your guests?"

She tensed. Why must she be the one? Then again, she was the only one in the church who knew the Chanforans—save Johan, apparently, but the church men would never allow him to speak there again. The room was full, and everyone stared at her.

But as she hesitated, Gedeon stood and spoke for himself. "My name is Gedeon Chanforan of Turin, and I thank you for welcoming us."

Constanza let out a long sigh and wiped the sweat from her hands, relieved.

"We welcome you and your family, Monsen," Pastor Colletto said.

Gedeon sat, but he formed a sneer. He leaned to his wife and whispered as the pastor dismissed the church.

Papà and Mamà wound their way through the crowd and stood next to Constanza. Papà gave a slight bow and said, "Monsen Chanforan, my daughter has spoken only good about you. May I invite you to our home this afternoon for a meal?"

"That will not be necessary." Gedeon held up a hand. "Though there is a matter I wish to discuss with you, Nicolaus Pavarin."

"Here?"

"Yes, here." Gedeon jutted out his chin and motioned for Marta and the children to leave the building.

Marta took a step forward. "Constanza is a friend."

Gedeon turned, stood in Marta's path, and glared at her. "Take the children outside."

Gedeon and Marta stared each other down for a moment until Marta cast her eyes down. She waved Claudia and Addo toward her, gave Constanza a parting glance, and marched to the door.

Gedeon refocused on Nicolaus. "I hear you refuse to pay your taxes."

"My taxes?" Papà's eyes dulled and fell to the man on Gedeon's right. "Johan, why would you gossip about my finances, and to a stranger no less? I plan to settle the matter with the Lord of Luserna when he finally decides to step into his fiefdom."

"The Lord of Luserna has indeed stepped into his realm." Gedeon held out his hands and bowed. "Lord Gedeon Chanforan, newly appointed by the House of Savoy."

Constanza's jaw dropped. Was she supposed to feel relieved? Perhaps Monsen Gedeon—

Wait, what am I supposed to call him now? Lord Chanforan?

Lord Chanforan would understand Papà's situation now. He had been a just master—easy to approach, gracious, understanding. The events of the past two months pooled in her memory, beginning with the man with the red patch who had chased them from the orphanage. Constanza examined Gedeon.

"You are surprised, I see, by my presence here. But I encourage you to speak with your daughter. She knows me as a fair man." Gedeon focused on Constanza, but his eyes reflected no light or warmth. "Do not worry, for if you remain loyal to me as you did your past lord, I will ensure you live in peace."

Nicolaus cleared his throat and narrowed one eye. "Let us first discuss the farm downhill from my land."

"What is there to discuss? The matter is settled. I am sorry, for I know it was a boon to your family. But I cannot allow anarchy in my realm."

"Lord Falzon signed the lease—"

"We hold no record of such a transaction, do we, Johan?"

Papà opened his mouth to speak, but Gedeon spoke again first. "And since we speak about the house, I bear very unfortunate news that will interest you." Gedeon looked at Constanza and gave a shallow frown. "I met your friend Andreas in Florence, but the Medicis discovered a plot he had been forming for many months. I'm afraid he is a French spy. His entire act to find the Greek Bible was a ruse—"

Constanza gritted her teeth. "You lie."

"Walk to Florence and see for yourself. If you hurry, you may find him with his head still attached."

"I don't believe you." Constanza's voice shook as she turned away from Gedeon's glare.

"Just as I say about your religion—you may believe what you wish, but that does not alter the truth. Andreas de Bonomo is in prison, but I wouldn't shed a tear over him. He has betrayed the Duke of Savoy and has now crossed Cosimo de' Medici himself. Your companh was an impostor all along, and if you had any sense, you would know it as fact."

Papà grabbed Constanza's hand and pulled her toward the door. His hands shook, and his face was flushed. "We have no business with this man, Connie. Frankly, I don't understand how you worked for him. He's a liar and a thief. He wears a mask of virtue, but behind it, he's full of deceit."

Johan maneuvered around Constanza and Nicolaus, stepped into their path, and stood like a stone marker in front of the door. "Lord Chanforan hasn't finished."

Constanza curled her lip, stood on her toes, and stared directly into Johan's blue eyes. "Look what you've become."

Gedeon's low voice rose from behind. "You think I don't understand you Vallenses? You've concluded I'm an outsider who knows nothing of your beliefs or customs. No, Nicolaus Pavarin, I understand everything. I can quote the Holy Scriptures. I have prayed and have seen God work—or so I imagined. Long ago, I too was a Vallense."

Constanza shook her head. Gedeon was lying again. But his Romaunt accent was flawless—far more natural than even Andreas's. If Gedeon was being truthful, it would also explain where Johan had developed his *folet* ideas.

"Now the matter of your farm, Nicolaus, and then I will allow you to go your way." Gedeon walked over and stared down his nose. "If I don't soon receive my dues, I will be forced to partition your farm—"

"And give it to city dwellers who have no experience working the land. Do you not realize your tax revenues will plummet?"

"I am no fool. I have turned failing enterprises into quite successful ones, which is what I intend to accomplish in my new realm."

Papà's hands stopped shaking as he sighed. "I believe we could settle on some form of compromise. I wish no ill on you, Monsen. All I desire—and I believe you would discover the same with every family here—is 'that we may lead a quiet and peaceable life in all godliness and honesty.'"

"Paul the apostle's first letter to Timothy." Gedeon paused and stared at the floor.

He does know the Holy Scriptures.

"Yes, I recognize what you quoted, but what if it's you who disrupts the peace? You assume you may live as you wish and tend to your own business, all while you proselytize your young, manipulate the poor, and spread your deceit throughout the land. You quote your Holy Scriptures, trusting them as an absolute source of truth, but in reality, you cower behind them. Though you may not yet see it, the foundations of your beliefs are beginning to crumble. And far more people than you realize will watch them shrink into impotence."

Constanza's shoulders slumped as she listened. Gedeon's sentiments were exactly the same as Johan's, except more studied and shrewder. Her heart beat faster.

"As for the children you unlawfully keep—"

"They have no parents," Constanza said.

Papà held out his hand to hush her. "We are their only family, and Luca Grimaldi—"

"Luca and Vitòria Grimaldi were not their custodians, and neither are you. The only reason the Grimaldis housed them was to indoctrinate them with Vallense religion. You are free to adopt orphans of your own kind, but the ones you took belong with their own people." Gedeon crossed his arms. "Look, you stare me down with scorn. Have you never listened to an articulate assessment of your faith? So naive, you Vallenses are. Open your eyes and look into the light. Supposedly you are loyal subjects, yet you refuse to heed my pleas. I didn't write the law about children—it has been in place for generations. If you're willing to give the orphans to me, I will find them proper homes."

"Papist homes," Constanza said through tight lips.

Gedeon's grin was as bitter as horseradish. "I once thought of you as honorable, Madomaisèla, but I now see I was mistaken." He tilted his chin down. "I wouldn't hold onto those orphans so tightly."

Papà drew his eyebrows together and puffed out his chest. "You dare make threats against my daughter and the children?"

"They're in no danger." Gedeon met Papà's posture by standing taller. "I would fear only for those who rebel against their lord."

Papà shoved Johan away from the door and walked through it.

Constanza's emotions spun in tight loops. If only Andreas were there. He would know how to manage Johan and their new lord. Yet if any of what Gedeon said was true, Andreas was in trouble, and Gedeon likely had something to do with it.

She lowered her head and let out a forceful breath. *I can't allow myself to believe Gedeon's tales.* Andreas was stronger than Gedeon, and of course Andreas wasn't a French spy. Andreas would return, and when he did, he would take action.

29

Prelates are exhorted, diligently to endeavour that all heretics shall be excluded from the diocese: and also that they are enjoined, without the admission of any appeal, to coerce and punish those by ecclesiastical discipline, who transact any business, or permit any familiarity with heretics.

—Pope Innocent III
Papal bull, 1215

I CY WIND WHIRLED OUTSIDE THE PAVARIN HOME, bringing with it the winter's first snowfall. Pine trees creaked and groaned as the gale swept through the forest and farm. Though whiteness had capped the mountain peaks for weeks, the snow had yet to stick to the grass—until now.

A fire crackled in the hearth, and traces of simmering pottage wandered into Constanza's nose. She taught all twelve children a new song based on Psalm 133 while Elionor sat to the right and assisted. The orphans stared at Constanza and waited for her to continue.

"Behold, how good and how pleasant it is for brethren to dwell together in unity!"

Constanza cringed at her singing. *I sound like an old cat.* "Again, children, but it's a joyful song, so don't look so sad."

Irene stared out the window above her, and a few others followed her lead.

"Focus on the song, not the snow, however inviting it may look."

"Madomaisèla, when will we be done?" Guido asked with pouty lips.

"You can't play in the snow until you have warmer clothes. Papà will soon return with cloth from the market, and then Elionor and I will sew you each a coat."

The room let out a sigh. Elionor, though, was void of expression, as if she were in a faraway land.

Ezio turned his head toward the window. "How long will that take? The snow will all melt before we can play in it."

"You may have seen snow in Turin, but you live in the mountains now." Constanza stood and walked to the window. "This snow will stay with us until springtime."

The children jumped, cheered, and rushed to the window.

"We aren't finished yet," Constanza said with a sigh. "If you wish to attend school next month, you must all be prepared. Madòna Fraschia will show no patience to children who don't know so much as the shortest psalms."

But Constanza couldn't help but smile. Despite the Grimaldis' disappearance and Valeria's death, joy still bubbled from within the orphans' hearts. To Constanza, it felt as if Valeria was in the barn petting sheep, soon to skip back into the room and sit by Irene. She was gone, though, and they would never hear her precious singing again. How did the orphans show such resilience? Or was it forgetfulness?

Constanza couldn't explain it, nor could she point to an exact moment of transformation, but the burden she carried had become lighter. In the two weeks since the sickness had ravaged the household, sleeping on the floor next to the girls no longer rattled her mind, and when she taught the children, her patience stretched further than it had in the summer. Perhaps the Holy Spirit was transforming and renewing her mind, just as the Holy Scriptures said.

A latch clicked, and the door swung open.

"Monsen Nicolaus is back!" shouted the children, running to the door. Irene jumped like a bunny, and all cheered.

Ave ran to Constanza with bright eyes. "Can you make my coat today?"

"Mine too," Irene said.

"There's wool in the crate by your mat," Roberto said. "You can make mine with that."

Constanza gave the seven-year-old a sharp glance but also a smirk. "You were in my crate?"

Roberto looked at the wall over Constanza's shoulder.

"Besides, I'm saving that wool for when Andreas returns. He needs a new coat too."

The orphans swarmed around Constanza, some on their knees begging. But Elionor stayed in her chair with her arms crossed and stared at the ceiling.

"Wait, wait!" Constanza said. "Pull back on your reins and listen. We certainly can't make everyone's coats today. Not even by this time next week."

"I can help," Silvia said, "and you can make the others' before mine."

Constanza grinned. Such an honorable girl.

A blast of cold air blew through the front door when Papà stepped through. He stomped his shoes on the stone floor, brushed the snow from his coat, and removed his hat. "It'll be up to our knees by morning!"

Another shout rang out from the children as they clung to his legs. "The cloth, the cloth! Where is it?"

Papà straightened his mouth and asked Constanza, "Where is your mamà?"

"At the loom."

He gave an abrupt nod and wrangled the children away.

"Did you buy the wool?" Ezio asked. "We need it to make coats so we can play in the snow."

"I wasn't able to barter for any this time, but perhaps next month—"

"You said you'd bring it, though," Ave said in a sour tone.

Constanza pulled Ave toward her. "Respect Papà and trust him. We should always be content with what God has given us. Remember what Jesus said: 'Therefore take no thought, saying, What shall we eat? or, What shall we drink? or, Wherewithal shall we be clothed?' God will provide what we need."

Papà's head sank as he strolled toward the back room.

Constanza asked Elionor to watch the children, followed Papà to the side room, and arrived to see him and Mamà in an embrace.

"Was there no cloth?" Constanza asked.

"Nothing—no cloth, no tools, no seed, no livestock—only a few farmers trying to sell the same items as I was, but with no one to buy. I asked around La Torre, and apparently the merchants from the plains haven't come in two weeks. It was they who brought the goods from Pinerolo, Turin, and beyond, and without their money and goods, the market has sunk."

Mamà walked back to the loom and continued with her task while Constanza listened to Papà.

"Since I was a young man, I've sold our grain to the same trader. Sometimes I trade him for things we need, and other times he pays with silver. But he wasn't there. No one like him was. I hauled a cartload of grain down to La Torre, and no one was there to buy it. Buying textiles for winter clothes was impossible, so I had to bring the whole cartload back here."

"Nothing like this has happened in our lifetime," Mamà said. "Why now?"

"A man from Luserna said that the Piedmontese stall keepers have refused to enter the valley."

Constanza folded her hands and leaned into the conversation. "You could sell the grain in Pinerolo or Saluzzo. Maybe they'd also give you a better price."

"Paulo Stalliato tried last week, and none of the merchants in Pinerolo would barter with him. Rumor passed through the market that he was a Vallense, and they all turned him away."

Mamà wove a strand of flax through the loom. "We may need to do without winter clothes for the children. We sold most of our wool last spring, not knowing we would house thirteen"—she caught herself—"twelve children."

"Someone will help us with coats," Papà said, "but if we can't trade, worse will come. We have enough for the winter, but by spring—"

"God will provide." Mamà pulled the loom's beater down and pressed the strands together into linen. "We can still trade with other Vallenses, and though we may not have everything we want, at least we still enjoy peace."

"I also saw another Catholic family walking toward the lower farm. That's five families now. Some are even sleeping in the barn." Papà shook his head. "They're building a shack from scrap boards, but it won't keep anyone warm once the winter sets in. Everyone's going to be crammed into that one little house."

"And be sure more disease will come from it," Constanza said. "How many more will arrive before they realize? Thirty, forty people stuffed into the house? And they'll need to keep their livestock inside during the coldest days. I can't imagine how awful the stench will be."

"More have taken over other land in the valley—mostly uncultivated plots, but nevertheless, the Piedmontese continue to migrate into our valley." Papà raised his eyebrows. "Our Lord Chanforan asserts himself, but to what end?"

Mamà wove more flax through the loom. "What does he seek by pushing Catholic families into our homeland?"

"Something deep within Gedeon despises us," Constanza said, "or perhaps *hate* is a better word. I still don't understand why he showed such kindness when I worked for him."

"What did he talk to you about?" Mamà asked, her eyes still on the loom.

"Once, he asked about my praying. I'm usually discreet about it, seeing I'm working for a Piedmontese family, but he noticed. I told him, and his questions continued. He was inquisitive, never spiteful or condescending. In fact, he couldn't have been—he allowed me to teach his daughter."

"You must have challenged his notions about Vallenses," Papà said. "He seems to have concluded we're all ignorant relics lost in time."

Constanza put two fingers on her chin. "We have always been loyal subjects to our rulers, so why does he risk that loyalty? He pokes and prods as if he desires to arouse our emotions and force us to react."

"I think his impulses run much deeper," Papà said. "I've seen honorable men and women moved to evil because of long-imprisoned feelings. Jealousy, contempt, lust, bitterness, an unforgiving spirit—belittle the sins of the heart at your own peril. Let them thrive and fester inside, but they'll burst eventually. Lord Chanforan says he was once one of us, but what caused him to turn? What made him what he is today?"

Three children gathered outside the room. "It's not cold, and all of us want to play in the snow."

Constanza widened her eyes and looked down her nose. "Without coats?"

"We can use our blankets."

"What will keep you warm tonight?"

Irene furrowed her brow. "We'll dry them by the fire. Please, Madomaisèla?"

A smile crept onto Constanza's face. She looked at Mamà, who kept her eyes on her work but gave a quick nod.

"Madomaisèla Elionor said you would come with us."

"*Que siá coma aquò*," Constanza said. "So be it."

In an instant, the house was empty of children. Even Papà and Mamà stood under the falling snowflakes and watched the light diminish to a gray haze. Constanza and Estève, slow as he might be, joined opposing teams in a snow-throwing contest while Elionor stayed indoors.

As Constanza shuffled through the snow, her gaze fell on the path leading to the crossroads, looking for the man she might one day call *òm*—husband. Whatever ill Gedeon had intended, Andreas would surely escape it. He, Bertran, and Victor had likely embarked on their return trip with the prize in hand—or so her heart wished. Constanza's stomach clenched whenever she imagined where Andreas might be. Still, she trusted he would return, and when he did, she would never let him leave her side again. All they needed was Papà's approval.

Darkness settled on the farm, but the children continued as if it were a midsummer day. In the distance, a single torch flickered. The snowfall now measured above the ankles, and the figure waded through it. Constanza squinted until she recognized her brother Bartholomeo. The closer he drew, the more he quickened his pace.

"Papà, where are your sheep and goats?" Bartholomeo asked between pants.

"In the barn for the night. Why do you ask?"

"Mine are gone, all of them. All except two kid goats. David has experienced the same, but not Miquèl."

Constanza didn't finish listening. She ran to the barn and listened. Except for the muffled sounds of the playing children, all was silent. By now the moon was the only light in the sky, so she fumbled until she found the door—

Open? Constanza blinked slowly at the door swinging on its hinges. No child of Nicolaus Pavarin left a barn door flung open, especially during a snowstorm. She stepped inside but found only blackness. Stumbling through the hay, she felt for soft wool or a wet nose. But all that touched her fingers was cold air.

Torchlight soon flooded the barn. Papà gasped, but Constanza already knew the truth. Every sheep, every goat, the cow, and their horse had vanished. Constanza grasped for a beam or wall or someone to hold before Papà pulled her close and held tight.

"Stolen," Bartholomeo said as he entered the barn.

Constanza's breath escaped in trails made visible by the blazing torch. Who would have done this? But she knew, and so did everyone else. "The papists stole our land, and now they steal our animals."

Papà stared into the grain bins. "We're missing grain too—about a cart's worth."

Most would have shrugged off his concern, but Papà wasn't like other men. His mind held an exact inventory of their possessions and where they should be. "How did someone steal so much without us knowing?" Papà asked.

"We were warm inside by the fire all day," Constanza said.

Bartholomeo shook his head, then crossed his arms. "Our only choice is to take it back."

30

Each pastor being, in his turn, a missionary, the younger men thus became initiated in the delicate duties of evangelization, each being under the experienced conduct of an elder, whom discipline established as his superior, and whom he obeyed in all things, alike from the duty and from deference.

—Alexis Muston
Israel of the Alps, 1852

GENTLE WAVES LAPPED AGAINST THE DOCK as Andreas, Bertran, Victor, and Basile disembarked from the ship *Sirio* and entered the city of Genoa. Scents of salt, seawater, and freshly caught fish filled the morning air. Andreas closed his eyes and drew in a long breath. Land. The voyage from Pisa had taken three days, but his belly felt as if it had been a month. Not until they docked had he found relief, but now his limbs felt weak, and his stomach begged for a meal or three.

Twelve days had passed since their release from the Stinche Prison. On the first day, they had agreed to risk sea travel, which would bring them back to Piedmont thrice as fast as the land route. Ioannis helped them retrieve most of their belongings and gave them what gold they needed for fares. The journey from Florence to the sea took five days, and after waiting for a ship in Pisa for a week, they embarked for Genoa.

"I'm worried about this place." Victor sniffed the air. "When the Dominican inquisitors instigated the crusade, they hired Genoese mercenaries to do the work."

Basile threw up a hand at Victor. "No one knows us in Genoa, and we'll be on our way in the morning. Don't fret, *mes amis*."

Andreas scanned the shops crowding the dockside. "Can we find something to eat first?"

"So long as we don't need to sit next to you on a ship," Bertran said, and they all chuckled.

Andreas's eyes jerked from cart to shop, from dried fish to citrus fruit, from steaming pottage to buttered pasta. Every morsel pulled him like a hooked fish and made his mouth water. Underneath an awning, three weavers spun wool into thread, and beside them, a boy of about nine stood behind a cheese cart. Wheels of white cheese stood out among the softer varieties, and Andreas eyed the largest one.

He greeted the boy in the Genoese dialect, which was similar to Romaunt, and asked the cost of a wheel.

"Two silver ducats," said the boy.

Though the price was reasonable, Andreas couldn't make a purchase without a little bartering—a habit Monsen Estève had imparted to him. "Two? We can't afford that." He turned his back and stepped away, knowing the boy would offer a lower price.

But he didn't.

Andreas slowed his pace and waited, but still, nothing. A tough negotiator, this boy.

Finally the boy said, "You won't find better cheese for this price in all of Genoa. Ask any man on the street, and he'll tell you to come right here to the Corombo family's cheese cart."

Andreas turned back and grinned. "Two silver ducats it is, my boy." He approached the cart, dropped the coins into the boy's hand, and took the closest cheese wheel.

"Cristoffa!" one thread spinner shouted to the boy. "Go fetch another bale of wool and bring it here."

The boy pocketed the coins. "Yes, *Mamma.*"

Andreas smiled. "*Dio ti benedica, Cristoffa Corombo.*"

Andreas, Bertran, Victor, and Basile sat on a low wall and devoured every crumb, but it wasn't nearly enough to fill them. "I'll find a loaf of bread," Bertran said.

Victor gazed toward the produce stands. "And I can't keep my eyes off all the bright fruit here."

Andreas sat alone with Basile and watched the sailors unload cargo. Gulls flew above the ships but struggled to make progress in the steady breeze blowing off the Ligurian Sea. In the distance, towering over the endless sea, stood the Lanterna di Genova—the lighthouse.

Late the previous night, while Andreas sat topside for fresh air, the light had first appeared—at first no brighter than a distant star. The light grew while the ship kept a safe distance from the coastline to the right. Without the lighthouse, how would a ship sailing through the night know where to navigate? How could it find its harbor and refuge?

The sound of Basile sliding his knife against a whetstone interrupted Andreas's thoughts. He glanced over at the Frenchman. For weeks, they had traveled together. Even when Victor assumed otherwise, Basile had shown loyalty, honor, and strength amid their trials. Without his guidance, they might have found themselves dead. Still, Basile clung to his Roman Catholic heritage as a child clung to his mother's hand.

Andreas had been focused on the Greek manuscript and how the Vallenses could use it. Basile, however, walked alongside them. They didn't have to travel across the sea to preach to him. They didn't need to translate the Bible into French to reach him. He was in their midst, needing salvation as much as any lost soul.

The prison cell had fortified Andreas's faith and pressed him into a more zealous service for the Savior. His old perspective had been one of performance and cleverness, but serving Christ wasn't a trade or profession. It required no qualifications other than an obedient heart. And Basile Halphen was one whom God had placed in Andreas's path.

Basile felt the edge of his knife and said to himself, "Almost."

Andreas peered back at the lighthouse and remembered Jesus's teaching: *Dos se lus del mòt.* "Ye are the light of the world." But had Andreas been a light? Basile's soul was like a ship that needed direction, and other than a few brief chats, Andreas had so far failed to be that light for him. Why let Basile flounder while Andreas could show him the way?

Andreas went to the Scripture he understood best, for it was the same one that had pointed him to Jesus the summer before last. "Basile, have you been born again?"

Basile glanced up at Andreas with one eye scrunched. "I've been born once. Are you trying to be funny? Because I'm not seeing the quip."

"No, I mean born again. The Holy Scriptures tell us if we haven't been born of the water and the Spirit, we won't see the kingdom of God." Yes, he'd paraphrased the Scriptures, but he didn't remember the exact words from John's Gospel.

"I've been a Christian my whole life. The priest christened me as a baby; I received *l'Eucharistie* as soon as I understood its importance; I'm a Catholic among Catholics. I keep a short account of my sins and regularly confess them to the priest. When Jeanne d'Arc first described her heavenly visions, I was one of the first to believe her, and by God's hand, we defeated the vile English." Basile set his knife on the wall and held his hand to his heart. "The Christian religion pulses through my veins, Andreas."

"It once did for me as well. You know my background, and you also know I'm no longer a Catholic. I forsook the flesh and received salvation—not by the Church of Rome, but by the cleansing of the Spirit. Thus, I became a new creature."

"Yet you betrayed your family and noble lineage. You chose to follow a heretical religion instead of remaining true to your baptism and thus the Trinity."

"What is heresy, Basile?"

"Any teaching that usurps the authority of Christ and His Church."

"What if the Holy Scriptures challenge Rome's teachings? Does God's Word prevail or does the pope's?"

"The Bible is only part of God's Word. The rest is from the apostles, and it's by their successors, the bishops of Rome, that we know how to worship and glorify the Father."

"You imply the apostles had beliefs apart from the Holy Scriptures? No, Basile, the Bible is how God has chosen to reveal His will to us." The lighthouse drew Andreas's attention yet again. He needed to turn this debate back to the gospel. Once, Andreas had the same questions, and Raimond Durand had refused to drag the conversations into theological niceties. Raimond continually guided Andreas's questions back to the Holy Scriptures.

If only I knew as much as Raimond or Constanza. But though knowledge would indeed be helpful, he needed the Spirit more. God could make up for Andreas's inadequacies.

He looked Basile directly in the eye. "I commend you for your works, Basile. You have been a valiant and trusted friend, yet I must urge you to open your heart to the gospel. Your good deeds may make you religious, but they don't make you a child of God. Only by repentance and faith will God reconcile you with Himself."

As the clouds moved, a glimmer of sunlight reflected off Basile's knife. His gaze leaped from Andreas to the ground, then back again. "You caught me off my guard. After being around you and the others for these weeks, I appreciate you and see the joy you hold." His mouth opened and closed, but he said nothing more.

"What holds you back from believing, Basile?"

"My reputation, my career, my heritage. How could I forsake all I love for something so"—he tapped a finger on his lips—"I can't think of the word in Romaunt."

"Say it in French. I'll understand."

"*Bouleversant.*"

Andreas nodded. "Upsetting, earth-shattering—I know. I once wrestled with the same question. Should I reject what I've always known, or set aside my unbelief and be saved?"

"And that's why I cannot so easily follow your religion. I hold doubts. I . . . I can't believe I'm speaking to you about this." Basile shook his head, then looked over Andreas's shoulder. "Ah, look, the rest of our meal has arrived."

Andreas turned. Bertran walked with a loaf of bread under his arm, and Victor carried a leather sack sloshing with liquid.

"Bread and milk for us all," Victor said. "Come, tear off a piece and enjoy!"

When they had finished, Basile cleared his throat. "I've decided to part ways with you here."

Victor snapped to attention. "Why now? We're less than a week from home."

"Gedeon Chanforan is on the loose, and I must bring him to justice. He has not only betrayed us but also insulted my maîtresse. I cannot allow him to escape with her manuscript. Besides, if he has indeed aligned himself with Philip, Prince Amadeus may be in danger. I must return to Turin and unmask Monsieur Chanforan."

"Turin is on the same path we travel, and only a day's journey from the mountains," Victor said. "We'll drop you off on the way."

"No, you will take the shorter route along the coast, which would force me to backtrack. I plan to purchase a horse and ride to Turin via Alessandria. It will be the best for all of us."

"What if what we suspect is true?" Andreas asked. "What if Gedeon is in the valley as we speak?"

"Then you will see me again. But until we know, I owe the House of Savoy my allegiance, and to them I must go. I will leave before midday."

Basile gave them directions from Genoa to La Torre. Another week of traveling lay before them, and time didn't favor them. Gedeon had probably returned. He had killed the Grimaldis, tried to carry out the same with Andreas, and doubtless would do the same to others.

As the sun beamed down on their hats, Basile galloped off to the north. Andreas, Bertran, and Victor left through the western gate of Genoa and walked west along the coast. After one more day, they would turn inland toward Piedmont and whatever awaited them there.

31

I vehemently dissent from those who would not have private persons read the Holy Scriptures nor have them translated into the vulgar tongues, as though either Christ taught such difficult doctrines that they can only be understood by a few theologians, or the safety of the Christian religion lay in ignorance of it. I should also like all women to read the Gospel and the Epistles of Paul. Would that they were translated into all languages so that not only Scotch and Irish, but Turks and Saracens might be able to read and know them.

—Desiderius Erasmus Roterodamus
Introduction to *Novum Instrumentum omne*, 1516

THE AIR GREW COOLER and the wind more bitter the farther north Andreas, Bertran, and Victor walked, but after six days, Andreas finally gazed west into the familiar mountain gap. Billowing gray clouds covered the mountaintops, and the Luserna Valley beckoned them to enter. Far ahead, nestled in the narrow defile below Mount Vandalino, was the Pavarin farm, and there, Constanza would surely be waiting for him.

"*Domicili*," Bertran drawled. "Home."

Victor plopped down on a dead tree stump, leaned back, and placed his hands behind his head. "I can't walk any farther. The wind freezes my bones here. What do you say we head back to Florence for the winter?"

Andreas chuckled. "I can almost see your house from where we stand."

"Yes, but you don't need to face Celeste." Though Victor's wife had believed the gospel, she was less enthused than Victor about their new life. Victor placed all the blame on Celeste, but no doubt he had much to improve too. "She'll pinch my cheeks and kiss me when I walk through the door, but by tomorrow, she'll be nipping at my ankles again." Victor stood and cracked his back. "The warm hearth will be pleasant at least. My boy? I guess he towers over me by now."

"It's only been two months," Andreas said.

"He's fourteen. Boys that age shoot up faster than a wheat stalk."

Victor turned toward the house, but Andreas grabbed his shoulder. For months, the company had endured miles of muddy roads, scheming thieves, treachery, and a rotting prison. Though they had failed in their ultimate mission, Victor and Bertran were now like brothers.

Andreas gave Victor an embrace and two strong slaps on the back. "Adieu, my friend. May God bless and keep you until we meet again, here or in eternity."

Victor soon turned off the road toward his home. Andreas and Bertran continued into the Luserna Valley, turned right at La Torre, and ascended into the Angrogna Valley. Snow crunched under their feet while little birds jumped from branch to branch in the leafless forest. Andreas felt the front of his coat and found only holes and thin strips of fabric. *I may as well not wear it.*

He examined the landscape. "Except for the snow, everything appears the same as when we left it. But we should have passed at least a few men with carts on their way to or from La Torre."

"I guess it's the weather," Bertran said. "The farmers must think a blizzard is blowing in."

Andreas glanced up at the gathering clouds. "I suppose so."

At the crossroads above San Lorenzo, Andreas parted ways with Bertran and continued on the path toward his farm. Estève would be there with his quill in hand, writing in his journal—or napping. But Andreas wouldn't linger at the house, for as soon as he dropped off his pack, he would walk up to the Pavarins' farm. Someone would be waiting there for him, and he couldn't hold back the grin if he tried.

Smoke billowed from the chimney up ahead. After months of walking, after failures, victories, and defeats, he was back where he had begun. But Andreas had learned more about himself and his heavenly Father. No longer would he pursue his own ambitions and expect God to bless them. Soon he would ask for Nicolaus Pavarin's permission, and then he would marry Constanza. They would settle in the house, farm the land, and when it wasn't planting or harvesting season, Andreas would travel and spread the gospel.

Sounds of woodchopping grew louder as he approached the house. He stopped midstride. A smattering of wood stood nailed together into a makeshift shed, and a woman in ragged clothes stepped out of it with a baby in her arms.

When she spotted Andreas, she ducked back inside. The house door opened, and at least fifteen children spilled into the yard, none of them familiar. Andreas fumbled with his sack and shuffled backward a few steps.

A man stepped outside, wearing a sagging frown and clenching his fist as he stared at Andreas. "Ours," he said in Piedmontese.

They must be refugees from the plains. Why else would Piedmontese be this far up in the mountains? But his house—why were they in his house? Perhaps the Pavarins had let them use it until he returned.

The children scurried about in the farmyard. They kicked at the snow, rubbed their hands together, and watched their breath flow from their mouths. Patches and threadbare holes defined their clothing, and empty gazes reflected hardship and poverty. Andreas's heart sank—until the man shouted at the children. "Back inside!"

A little boy tugged on the man's pants. "I'm hungry."

"Inside!"

Andreas leaned to peek through the doorway as the last child crept back inside, but the man moved to block his view. "This is my house," Andreas said.

"No, ours."

Andreas pinched himself and felt the sting. He wasn't dreaming.

Two more men stepped into the doorway, and one tapped his palm with a thick stick.

"I'll leave." Andreas held his hands up. If he pressed them any further, they'd thrash him into a heap of broken bones. This wasn't a fight he could win.

Andreas's heartbeat quickened as he turned toward the slope that led to the Pavarin farm. He didn't want to run, though, at least not until he reached the forest. The Piedmontese might chase him. Then a suspicion came—these people weren't believers, so they must have stolen the land.

He gave the men a shallow wave and pressed toward the hill. At the tree line, he quickened his pace to a jog, leaping over roots and running around sharp corners.

What would he find at the Pavarin farm? It had been destroyed once before. Two summers ago, Friar Marco Spada had sent his hirelings to the farm. They had drained the ponds, burned the house, maimed Nicolaus, and abducted Constanza, and only by God's grace had the Pavarins overcome the terror. But had the inquisitors returned for revenge? Had they taken Constanza again? The possibilities propelled his feet onward.

The laughter of children brought a breath of hope. Cresting a hill, Andreas darted his eyes from house to barn to terrace, searching for a sign all was normal. When he caught sight of Nicolaus Pavarin placing a stone on a fence, Andreas's lips curled into a smile. Save for the snow and barren trees, everything looked the same as when he had left in October. As soon as Andreas caught his breath, he raced to Nicolaus.

"Where is Constanza?" he asked between pants.

Nicolaus jumped a little and swung around. His eyes grew enormous, and then he smiled and embraced Andreas. "You made it back."

Andreas went limp for a moment when the seasoned farmer embraced him. Had Nicolaus hugged him before? "I just came from my house—"

"We have much to discuss. As for Constanza, she took the older orphans down to the schoolhouse. She's been teaching them classroom discipline."

"Everyone is safe?"

Nicolaus's countenance sagged. "A disease swept through the valley, brought by the papists, we guess. We lost one girl, Valeria. Two of my grandchildren also perished, both infant boys."

Andreas froze. Three children, dead. He opened his mouth to speak, but nothing came out.

Nicolaus scratched under his chin and let out a long breath. "Connie will be thrilled to see you."

"I'll head down to the school soon, but can you explain what's happened? And where is Monsen Estève?"

"Estève is staying with us for now. The Piedmontese took the farm—or I should say, it was given to them. And I'm afraid there's nothing we can do, for a new lord rules over us now. Do you remember Gedeon Chanforan from Turin?"

"Gedeon is your lord?" Andreas's voice shook. His gaze wandered away from Nicolaus. He swallowed and closed his eyes.

"He arrived last week, but his steward has been asserting himself almost since you left." Nicolaus paused. "Johan Lauras."

Andreas snapped his eyes open. "Johan? He works for Gedeon?"

"The lord took the lower farm and gave it to two Piedmontese families who don't know the difference between an acorn and a grain of barley. Now more families have moved there, all Catholic. Then a week ago, our livestock disappeared, and all the evidence points to them."

Nicolaus and Andreas exchanged stories and filled in each other's gaps until the sun sat atop the mountains. It all fit neatly together now.

"Back in Florence, Gedeon mentioned his father's name," Andreas said, "and I wonder if Monsen Estève would know his family. Is he inside?"

Nicolaus nodded and called for Estève.

Andreas greeted and embraced Estève, then asked, "Do you recall the name Michele Chanforan? He was Gedeon's father."

Estève pursed his lips and gazed over Andreas's shoulder toward Mount Vandalino. "Michele Chanforan. I haven't heard that name in decades."

"Do you remember anything about him?"

"Pastor Chanforan, yes. He was a gifted preacher who knew the Holy Scriptures better than any barbe in my generation. He pastored a large church in Turin, but it's a disgraceful story."

"Did this Michele Chanforan have a son?" Andreas asked.

"I . . . I think he did. Yes, and the ages would match too. Oh"—he felt his forehead—"everything is clear now. Gedeon Chanforan is the son of Michele and Placenza Chanforan."

"What does that mean?" Nicolaus asked.

Andreas and Estève took turns telling the tale of Michele Chanforan and the Vallense church in Turin. By the time they finished, the sun had dipped below the western mountains, and Andreas wrapped his coat tighter.

"He blames us all for his father's sins." Nicolaus shook his head. "I don't understand why he can't acknowledge the hypocrisy and move past the bitterness."

Estève drew in a long breath. "Gedeon represents many shameful mistakes of the past that don't begin or end with Michele Chanforan. I remember his empty apologies, and I'm ashamed to say I believed him. Though I wasn't a part of that church, we all had connections to it. Often I would stop and attend their meetings during my travels. I was a young man then, always the junior missionary partner."

Estève paused to smile at Andreas, as if remembering their journey together last summer. "I stopped visiting the church in Turin when the rumors about Michele were proven true, but still, many refused to confront his sins. Instead, they covered them. We forsook an important principle from the apostle Paul. 'Mark them which cause divisions and offences contrary to the doctrine which ye have learned; and avoid them. For they that are such serve not our Lord Jesus Christ, but their own belly; and by good words and fair speeches deceive the hearts of the simple.' But Michele Chanforan deceived more than the hearts of the simple. He deceived the best of us, and we looked past his evil—to our own chagrin."

Nicolaus shook his head slowly. "This is the first time I've heard anything about Pastor Chanforan. I knew a Vallense church once existed in Turin, but nothing more."

"Another one of my generation's sins. We were embarrassed. No pastor wanted his church to know the details, so they buried the truth and tried to forget. We thought ourselves too holy to fall to such vices and lies."

Andreas sighed and crossed his arms. "That response reminds me more of what the Catholic Church would do."

"Precisely, and because of our misjudgments, we now have Gedeon Chanforan as a lord. I doubt he thinks all Vallenses are the same as his father. He probably sees us as his father's enablers, which is true in some sense. Lord Gedeon Chanforan, I'm afraid, is the offspring of our deepest failures."

Somewhere within Andreas, a thread of sympathy tugged on his emotions. As sinister and calculating as Gedeon might be, as deceptive as his actions were, he wasn't a simple manifestation of Satan. He was a son wounded by a wicked father, a youth forsaken by his own people, and a man bent on soothing the pain long ago planted in his soul. Could Gedeon have chosen the path of forbearance and found forgiveness? Yes, but sadly, he had followed his instincts.

Voices drifted uphill toward them, and soon a few children appeared, followed by two young women. Andreas's heart skipped. Constanza had her head bent down, talking to a girl. Andreas had waited for two months, but now his breath was buried in his chest.

Nicolaus's hand pushed him from behind. "You can talk with us if you want, but you'll enjoy her company more."

Constanza raised her head, and when she noticed Andreas, her eyes welled with tears. A smile came to her face as she lifted her skirts and ran to him.

32

I think it a great triumph and glory to the cross if it is celebrated by the tongues of all men; if the farmer at the plow sings some of the mystic Psalms, and the weaver sitting at the shuttle often refreshes himself with something from the Gospel.

—Desiderius Erasmus Roterodamus
Preface to the third edition of *Novum Instrumentum omne*, 1522

WERE HER EYES DECEIVING HER, or was it Andreas who stood with Papà and Monsen Estève? The barren trees and coating of snow, the orphans, Estève, Papà—they all vanished into the night. Her world drifted away with the wind until only she and Andreas remained.

She slowed her pace, let go of her skirts, and brushed wisps of hair back into place. "I'm so sorry, I was down at the schoolhouse with the children—"

"I've been waiting for this moment for two months." Andreas's tender gaze captured her. "I can't believe I'm with you again."

"You were in prison, I heard." Constanza stepped closer. "Is it true?"

"Thanks to your former master—"

"And our new lord. Did Papà tell you?"

"Everything, and I think we now understand who Gedeon is. His loathing of us runs deep."

The children soon went inside, and Papà sat outside on a log, carving a wooden spoon. Andreas and Constanza sat on a bench underneath the house's eaves and exchanged stories while the sun-painted sky faded into a starry night. Constanza leaned forward and listened to Andreas recount his adventures.

"Gedeon actually offered you a position in his company?" Constanza asked. "Was he genuine, or was he trying to distract you?"

"Likely both, but it wasn't until I rejected the offer and found the manuscript that he showed me ill will."

"Except for hiring men to kill you on the road."

"It doesn't all make sense to me either. When Gedeon talked to me in Florence, he was very candid. He didn't hide his opinions about our faith. Perhaps he thought he could turn me. Another ally in the House of Savoy would only further his plans."

Constanza grinned. "Andreas de Bonomo, you are a good man. Gedeon might have made you rich—comfortable, sure of the future, well respected."

"What would you have thought if I had returned and said I accepted the offer?"

"You would never do such a thing."

"I admit I was tempted for an afternoon, but God snatched me back from the brink—though I did spend nine nights in prison."

"It impresses me more that you were tempted and still resisted it, rather than not being tempted at all. You responded to the Spirit of God, and I commend you for that."

Their conversation soon turned to the orphans. A mist came to Constanza's eyes as she recalled the horrible days of the fever. "I wish we could tell Luca and Vitòria. I heard rumors about their whereabouts, but they couldn't have been true."

Andreas scooted closer to Constanza and lowered his voice. "I saw the Grimaldis' grave in Turin. They're dead, killed by Gedeon's schemes. He all but admitted it to me in Florence."

"A merchant in La Torre told me they died in the fire, but that's impossible."

"Gedeon made it look as if they died in the fire. It was a suitable cover, except for those of us who saw them here for months after the fire."

"Why would he have them murdered?" Words lodged in Constanza's throat. "The Grimaldis are the kindest and most selfless people on earth. Now what will be the fate of the orphans?"

"The Grimaldis were everything Gedeon hates about Vallenses. Perhaps more than any other, their testimony contradicts his conceptions about us. The Grimaldis cared for the outcasts when all others had forsaken them—without payment or praise and in the face of danger and persecution. They were exemplars of our Savior."

Constanza wiped away a tear. "Luca was also a wise businessman with connections throughout Piedmont."

"Which is also why Gedeon wanted him removed. My instincts tell me Gedeon has commandeered Luca Grimaldi's business for himself."

"Evil," Constanza said, narrowing her eyes.

"I don't understand Gedeon. Everything I've seen among our people has been righteous and good. Yes, I've seen the faults and shortcomings of Vallenses, but I could never imagine seeing Vallenses as Gedeon Chanforan does."

"Odd as it may sound," Constanza said, "I can sympathize with his feelings. You became a believer by your own choice. Your parents never encouraged you to memorize the Holy Scriptures, and you weren't forced to follow our ways because everyone in the church did. Instead, you saw the truth in what we preached, believed it, and accepted everything that came with it. Gedeon—and I should add Johan and me too—we've known nothing different. I've seen those with the most potential fall to sin and corruption."

"Potential," Andreas said, tapping his knee. "Raimond once told me, 'Potential is as common as a copper ducat. Everyone has it.'"

"Yes, but even among believers, the talented seem to gain the most favor. The strongest and most attractive earn the highest praise. The ones who scream the loudest and draw the most followers rise to the highest pedestals. Gedeon's father sounds as if he was one of those, and Gedeon saw the rot."

"Gedeon was given everything, though, and he didn't need to struggle with the consequences of sin as I did. I wish I had the knowledge of an eight-year-old Vallense with the Holy Scriptures. How could one be exposed to such truth and turn from it—and for what? Money? Fame? If any Vallense, young or old, wants to know what the world offers, send him to me. I'll tell him it's all folly."

Constanza shook her head. "You simplify the question, Andreas. Men like Gedeon and Johan see what they wish to. Gedeon has seen the worst in us and has concluded those evils are the Vallense identity when they are not. No logic or reason would convince him otherwise. He knows the truth but refuses to acknowledge it."

Andreas rubbed the beard on his cheek. "Other than somehow convincing Gedeon and Johan they're wrong, what can we do? Lord Chanforan has chosen to bury us. He's stolen the old Lauras farm and given it to Piedmontese families, obviously to embitter us. And he stole our Greek manuscript."

"Couldn't you ask Prince Amadeus to help us again as he did with the inquisitors? If Gedeon is aligned with your brother Philip against Amadeus and your father . . ." Constanza eyed Andreas, hunting for an answer.

"No, it's more complicated than you can fathom. So far, it sounds as if everything Gedeon has done is legal, at least in the eyes of the House of Savoy. My father or Amadeus won't involve themselves in what they regard as petty feudal matters, especially if they must side with religious dissenters like us. And we can't prove the rumor about Gedeon plotting with Philip against my father."

They paused for a moment, and the only sounds were the distant howls of wolves and the creaking of the trees. Andreas gazed up the hillside with his lips parted, and Constanza watched him. Did he still want the manuscript? Did he carry a genius plan to rid them of their woes and bring rest to the valley? Though she would have never guessed it at their first meeting—

She let out a quick chuckle. The first time she'd met Andreas, she'd threatened him with a knife. What did this handsome royal see in her, a poor mountain farmer's daughter? How could she ever match the opulence and grandeur of the noble women Andreas had known his whole life? That is, unless he wasn't impressed with any of that, which was exactly the kind of man to whom Constanza wanted to promise herself. Or had she already promised herself? She grinned. *I have, though I may not have voiced it yet.*

Andreas interrupted her thoughts. "What does Gedeon want from us? At first I thought he wanted the Greek manuscript out of greed, but it's far more sinister than that. He wanted to dangle it before our eyes, and as soon as it was within reach, he snatched it away." He leaned back and shrugged. "It reminds me of something I saw in Chambéry once. A gang of boys dangled a hunk of meat in front of a starving dog. They jeered and mocked until the dog finally snarled, bared its teeth, and leaped at them. The boys beat the dog with rocks and sticks until it was dead."

"Pain—Gedeon wants to see us suffer, but not through open violence yet."

"Except for taking your livestock."

"But he hasn't threatened us with death," Constanza said. "You're right, though—Gedeon treats us as if we're an anxious hound, poking and goading until we snap."

"Then we mustn't snap," Andreas said. "That's what he wants, it seems, and we must never give it to him."

Constanza leaned forward, caught a glimpse of Andreas's eyes, and smiled. *I adore this man.*

"What is it?" Andreas said. "Did I say something wrong? I know we can't let Gedeon starve us to death or leave us homeless, but—"

"No, it's not that. I was just admiring you." Perhaps if it wasn't so dark, and if Andreas was clean-shaven, she might have seen him blush.

Papà yawned toward them. Constanza looked toward his log, and there he stood, reaching his arms to the stars.

"You can stay with us tonight if you'd like," Constanza said.

Andreas threw up a hand and smirked. "I don't own a house, so I suppose it's my only choice."

"As long as you don't mind sleeping in the same room as Monsen Estève."

"You're going to board me with the loudest sleeper in the principality of Piedmont?"

"The barn has room too, if that suits you better. No animals will be there to keep you warm, though."

Papà walked up. "You two lovers can speak tomorrow. Andreas, seeing your housing situation—"

"Constanza already asked."

Papà tipped his chin down and looked at Constanza, then turned to Andreas with a little smile. "You will rest well here—better than in the snow, I suppose."

Andreas and Papà chatted as they walked into the house. Constanza, with a spring in her step and a wide smile, walked beside Andreas until they stepped into the house.

The floor was filled with slumbering children, and the only light was the one Papà carried. He lit one candle for Constanza and one for Andreas before wishing them a good night and retiring to his room.

Andreas gave a slight bow and said, "*Bona nuèch*, my Constanza."

Constanza blushed and returned the words to him. Her candle cast Andreas's shadow onto the ceiling of the room. Her heart sank, not out of despair, but from desire. *Andreas, if you only knew how much I want to be yours, to be your wife, to never spend another moment without you.*

*   *   *

Early the next morning, Constanza sat beside Andreas at the table. Papà, Elionor, and Estève sat on the other side of the table while the children congregated on the floor. When Papà finished praying, the children rushed up with their hands held out. Mamà brought a barley loaf from the pantry, and as soon as she placed it on the table, a line of boys and girls formed.

"Only a small piece, children."

Week by week, the orphans' manners had improved. Now, in the first week of December, they stood in a single line and politely said, "Mercé, Madòna," one after the other.

When the boys each had a piece of bread, they gathered on the floor near Andreas, wanting to be near the man who'd gone on an adventure.

"Was it a big boat?" Guido asked.

"Not big," Andreas said. "In fact, it wasn't much longer than this room."

"Can we see the Bible? Madomaisèla Constanza said you would bring a special one back."

Andreas's face sank. "We had it, but then lost it."

"How did you lose a whole Bible?" Umile asked. The boys broke into a little cackle.

"We didn't misplace it. An evil man took it from us."

"Did you try to run away?" Guido asked. "Ezio sometimes takes my spear—" He glanced at Constanza. "It's not real, though. But if I run fast enough, he gives up."

"We tried, but soldiers caught us."

Ezio's eyes brightened. "Did they have swords and shields?"

"Yes, and two of my companions also did, but the guards outnumbered us."

Constanza listened as Andreas told them tales from Parma, Florence, Pisa, and Genoa. His gestures and animated tone were perfect for the eyes and ears of little boys. He was so friendly with them, and whether or not he knew it, they saw him as a great man—maybe not as much as Constanza did, but their bright eyes and eager posture showed their love of Andreas.

A knock sounded at the door, and after Papà answered it, a familiar man stepped inside with concern etched into his expression.

"Victor!" Andreas stood to greet the man. "What brings you here of all places?"

"You heard about that rat Gedeon, I assume? His man stopped by my house yesterday, insulted my family, and left this rubbish with me." Victor slammed a piece of crumpled parchment in Andreas's hand and huffed. "Does he think I have gold to pay his bill? I say, if I did own that much, I'd take it to him and make him swallow each coin while I watched."

"Everyone received a similar note," Andreas said. "No one has what Lord Chanforan asks."

Constanza chuckled at the way Andreas said *Lord Chanforan*. His accent hinted at French but with a pinch of disgust and sarcasm.

"How much would you *scomëtte* he has our Greek Bible and that other book up at his castle? You know I can see that shack from my farm."

"I'd rather not wager anything," Andreas said, "but I imagine he's sold it by now."

"No, he still has the Bible," Elionor said.

All eyes flew to Elionor. But how would she know, unless—

"My friend Brando said it's there." Elionor dipped her head and fastened her lips.

"Who's Brando?" Victor asked.

Constanza blurted out the answer for her. "Elionor's *companh*."

"Do you still choose to meet with him?" Papà sighed. "We've discussed this before, Elionor. We love having you here, but you cannot continue to meet with this Brando."

Elionor's face turned red. "Constanza was with me, I swear."

Papà's eyes narrowed.

"It's true," Constanza said. "Last week in La Torre—"

Papà glared in Elionor's direction. "The market is empty."

"I went to visit my relatives in Luserna, and we met him on the way."

Constanza looked upward. *No, you planned to meet Brando, and you duped me into going with you.*

"He works for Lord Chanforan now," Elionor said. "He's paid a real salary and no longer has to work the land . . ." She placed her hands on the table and looked at Andreas. "Please don't tell anyone else what I told you about the Bible. I wouldn't want to hurt Brando's reputation with Lord Chanforan."

"We should go find it," Victor said, leaning back with his arms crossed. "By right, it's ours, and if you ask Basile, he'd say it's the princess's. We would be acting on behalf of the civil authority of this realm. Gedeon stole it, and now we should take it back."

Andreas propped his elbows on the table and looked at Elionor. "You're sure the manuscript is at Castelvecchio?"

"Yes . . . maybe. I think so, at least according to Brando, but please, I don't want anyone—"

"How many other guards work with your friend Brando?" Victor asked.

Elionor swallowed and looked around the table. "I shouldn't say."

"Gedeon is an evil man," Andreas said. "Though I don't know Brando's character, he is in league with a man who wants us destroyed."

"Lord Chanforan doesn't want to hurt Vallenses," Elionor said. "He only wants to reintegrate them into the realm."

Constanza squinted but didn't voice her curiosity.

"How many other guards, Ellie?" Andreas asked with a more accommodating voice than Victor. "Is Castelvecchio defended?"

She shook her head. "No one else, only Brando, and he is still learning his duties. Lord Chanforan is waiting until spring to hire more guards."

"The manuscript is at Castelvecchio waiting for us." Andreas bit his bottom lip and nodded. "After going to Florence and back, after Gedeon betrayed and defeated us, we may still see victory. Gedeon never guessed we would escape and return to Piedmont, and now we might have another chance."

"Castelvecchio isn't a real castle," Victor said, "only a villa made to look like one by a man with too much money. We could find a side door, search the most obvious places, and leave as soon as we find the manuscript." He gave Andreas a hard slap on the shoulder. "Easier than robbing a monk in the dark."

Everyone laughed—except Andreas, who gave more of a courtesy chuckle.

"We should take the Bible back while we have the chance." Andreas focused on the window.

Constanza blinked rapidly and shook her head. This all felt so hasty and unplanned.

Andreas folded his hands and looked to Papà. "What do you think?"

Papà moved his head back and forth, then rose and walked to the door. "It was stolen from us, so I suppose it would be commendable if we can get it back. At the same time, how would it sound if those in Pinerolo or Turin heard about two Vallenses sneaking into their lord's castle and taking a very expensive treasure?"

"The princess charged us with buying the Bible," Victor said. "Gedeon stole it from the princess. We're simply going to retrieve it for her."

Papà looked to Victor, then to Andreas. "If your choice is to recover the manuscript, then I pray you're certain about what this choice entails."

"Then I'll meet you at your house before dusk." Andreas gave Victor a quick nod and a handshake.

Constanza shooed the children outside after Victor left. Her jaw trembled, and she blinked back tears. "Do you feel your plan is wise?"

"I do. Is something wrong?"

"I thought I lost you in Florence, and now that you're back, I can't fathom you walking into danger again." She paused and lifted her eyes to meet his. "*T'aimi*, Andreas. I love you, and I never want to be parted from you again."

Andreas blinked a few times, gulped, and looked into her eyes. "I love you too, Constanza Pavarin."

"Se vos plai, please, ask my papà today for his blessing on our marriage."

"Today? I returned only yesterday, and I no longer have a house or farm or means to provide for you."

"We could go somewhere else. This valley offers little for us other than poverty and persecution. We could marry and settle somewhere no one knows us, somewhere we could raise a family in peace without threats from petty lords, without having to worry about the manuscript." Constanza smiled, but tears fell too. "You could still be a barbe, but somewhere far from danger. It doesn't matter where we settle, as long as I have you, Andreas."

He frowned, and his voice quieted. "Our home is in the Angrogna Valley, not in some distant, unknown land. The people who have loved and taught you since your childhood are here and in grave need of our support. When I left for Florence, I felt as though the people of this valley have kept me at a distance. Now I see how wrong I was. This is my home. We can't run at the first hints of danger, leaving your family behind, forsaking our obligations, and escaping only for our own safety and solace. And we have an opportunity to bring a pure version of the Holy Scriptures to them—"

"You have the opportunity, while I must again await news of your adventures. I must wait at home—wait for you to make decisions, to make choices that affect more than just yourself."

Andreas scratched at his beard and let out a long sigh. He stood silent for a few moments, nodding.

Had she convinced him to forget about Castelvecchio and the manuscript?

"For weeks, I've been ready to ask your papà for his blessing, and I do want you to be my wife." Andreas clasped his hands together and leaned toward her. "But getting the Bible is the right thing to do. If you saw what we went through to come to this point, you would understand. To let Gedeon keep it would be unjust."

"Everything you say is logical, and it doesn't sound as if much risk is involved. But I don't want to risk it. God ordained your release from prison, so why test Him? Why travel down the same treacherous road?"

"Because I want to give our people something of value, something they can remember and hold dear—not for wealth or fame, but for service. For generations before I became a believer, our people have dreamed of translating the Bible into languages other than Romaunt. This is our chance, and I am honored to take part in it." Andreas's eyes gleamed, and he held a fist to his heart.

Constanza's smile grew at his dedication. He had set his course, and she wouldn't be able to stop him, not without injuring their relationship. *Andreas isn't one to forsake his honor.* She bowed her head slightly. *And neither will he forsake me.*

Andreas caught her eyes again and drew closer. "Trust me, Constanza, at the first sign of trouble, we'll retreat. If there are guards, we won't enter. I have no desire to be locked in a prison cell again."

Constanza sighed and relaxed. If Andreas succeeded, they would enjoy a glimmer of assurance amid the winter's uncertainty. They could seek to understand the Greek, learn the manuscript's intricacies, and translate it into their own tongue and potentially many others. But was it worth the risk of losing Andreas? Martyrs had sacrificed their lives for their beliefs, so why couldn't the same happen for those who spread the Word of God?

She shuddered. *Not Andreas. I can't lose him.*

"I'll return to you," Andreas said, his eyes glowing like a lamp. "By tomorrow morning, you'll be looking at the Greek text long ago copied by scribes in the East."

She let out a long sigh. "Don't put yourself in danger—it's all I ask of you."

33

Although the Scriptures were written during a definite historical period, they are not the product of that period but of the eternal plan of God. When God designed the holy Scriptures in eternity, He had the whole sweep of human history in view. Hence the Scriptures are forever relevant. Their message can never be outgrown.

—Edward Freer Hills
The King James Bible Defended, 1956

"IT'S UNBOLTED," Andreas whispered to Victor, clicking the latch on a side door. The moon shone like a beacon on Castelvecchio, but since there was no sign of guards, the glow brought only welcome assistance. "You find the sitting room, and I'll find the library. The Bible should be in one of those rooms. We'll meet back at the big oak."

"No, we should stay together," Victor said. "I'd rather not have you still inside searching after I find it first."

Andreas let out a silent chuckle. "If we separate, we'll be faster. Besides, I wouldn't call this place sprawling. I'll search the far wing, and you can search the one on the other side of this door. Meet back at the oak if you can't find the manuscript."

Victor gave Andreas a quick pat on the back, then nodded at the door.

Andreas opened it and found a dim candle giving just enough light to reveal a storeroom filled with block-cutting tools, mortar, and scaffolding. Someone must have been there recently, likely a servant. An open doorway led out the opposite side. With so little light, they couldn't help but make a little noise as they wound through the clutter. They soon reached the doorway and parted ways—Andreas to the left, and Victor to the right.

The ceiling was vaulted far above Andreas. He walked through a foyer featuring a broad staircase ascending to the second level. Should he go up the stairs first? If Castelvecchio was like other castles, the lower level would house the library—the manuscript's most likely location. But he needed more light, so he went back into the storeroom and grabbed the candle, but cupped his hand near the flame to keep it from glowing too brightly.

Andreas turned left toward a set of three open doors, and at each one, he peered inside. The first was a pantry filled with milled grain sacks, smoked meat, and herbs. A long wooden table flanked with carved chairs filled the next room, and a tapestry covered the wall, bearing the same coat of arms as the seal they had seen in Parma after confronting Gedeon's men: a cross, mountains, and the word LUSERNA. The next room was a kitchen—knives, wooden utensils, and an oven.

The hall took a sharp right into a room with crates strewn about the floor. Barren shelves stood along the walls, and sheets of cloth covered what must be chairs and couches. Andreas walked to the fireplace and glanced inside but found nothing but blackened stone. Much work remained to improve this castle—if one could call it that.

Andreas held the candle over the scattered crates. He opened one to check for the manuscript but found only stacks of parchment, some stained with water and others crumpled into balls. He scanned a piece to check its purpose, but it had only numbers and Piedmontese abbreviations. These parchments must have been ledgers and receipts from Gedeon's businesses. Andreas opened another box, then another, and found the same. The manuscript must be somewhere else.

A faint shuffle echoed through Castelvecchio's halls. It could have been a house cat or only the sounds of an old house under renovation. Perhaps Victor had found the Bible and had already passed through the storage room and was standing under the oak tree, waiting for Andreas. But Andreas still had to check the second floor. He stopped and listened for any peculiar noises. Other than an owl's hoot from outside, Castelvecchio was silent.

After he crept back the way he had come, he again stood in the entryway and faced the stairs to the second level. After a slight hesitation, he ascended, but the steps were wider than he expected. At the fourth step, he tripped.

He caught himself, but the candle's flame went out. The room became as black as tar. Andreas felt for something to hold and found a railing. What would he do without a light? Could he find another flame to light the candle, or should he retreat?

Andreas took care to place his feet on level ground as he descended the stairs. One cautious step after another—one hand holding the unlit candle and the other wandering through the air—he stepped toward the storage room. At last his free hand touched cold stone. He sidestepped to his right along the wall until he felt brick, then open air. He stepped through and discovered not a storage room but a hallway, curving left with a faint light at the end. He must have miscalculated the storage room's location, but he might have found a means of reigniting the candle.

Though the hallway was still dark, the glow at the end guided him onward, growing as he rounded the curve. After another sharp turn, the light flickered, but it was too strong to be from a single candle.

Andreas tiptoed around the corner, keeping his back to the inside wall, and found a set of doors. A flickering light leaped out from one of them. The crackle of a fire filled his ears as he took a few steps toward the door.

His mind pulsed with possibilities.

Footsteps echoed down the hall behind him, growing louder with each step. More footsteps from the right. He couldn't retreat now. Andreas took a deep breath and stepped through the doorway.

Two men sat on the couch facing a roaring fire, and by the shape of his head, one was Victor of Bricherasio. But the other man Andreas couldn't recognize. Next to Victor, the pouch from Ioannis Argyropoulos sat on a pedestal. Andreas's fingers tensed.

Another man stood from behind a high-backed chair and turned toward Andreas. The tall and muscular figure was evidence enough.

"I would have invited you had you asked," Gedeon said.

A thunder of footsteps echoed from the hallway behind Andreas . He jumped and moved toward the center of the room, but by then, two armed guards had blocked the only path of escape.

"Come closer to the fire and join us, Andreas of Savoy, for we have much to discuss."

Victor lurched his head around to face Andreas, revealing his gagged mouth. The man sitting next to him yanked him back around.

Andreas scanned the room for another exit but found only walls, windows, and guards. How half-witted had he been to assume they would simply find the Bible and return?

Andreas gruffly asked, "What do you want?"

"First, please explain to your good friend why you lied to him about your past." Gedeon nodded to the other high-backed chair and lifted his hand in a rising motion. Johan Lauras rose, walked to Gedeon, and stood by his side. "Go on, Andreas. Tell him the true reason you first came to the mountains."

Andreas shook his head and said in Latin, "*Non sum qualis eram.*"

"Latin that none of us can understand." Gedeon turned to Johan. "He reverts to his monkish roots when it suits him—just as I said, Johan."

"No, what I quote is true." Andreas said. "I'm not the man I once was, and you can't hold that against me."

"Did you not unleash the inquisitors upon the Vallenses? Your mission was to spy on them—to infiltrate their society and bring them back into the Roman fold. It was you who instigated the crusade against them—"

"I tried to prevent the inquisition, not start it."

"Tell that to Johan. Tell him it was your spying and your scheming that brought about his dear father's death."

Andreas's palms moistened with sweat. True, Andreas had originally sought to spy on the Vallenses, but God had redeemed him, and his entire life had changed in an instant. Johan would remember that. He was there when Andreas testified about his salvation to the church. Johan was one of the first who stood up for him against the doubters.

"Johan, you know I'm a born-again man now. You were like a brother to me from the day we met, embracing me as a friend while most others—"

"Like all Vallenses, you are a liar," Gedeon said, "and you never told him your true identity. But be assured, I have since told him everything."

Johan crossed his arms and stared at Andreas. "You chose the wrong side in this fight, Andreas. Please don't resist Lord Chanforan, for his allies are high and many."

"Look at the man," Gedeon said to Johan. He walked to the pedestal and placed his hand on the manuscript. "Andreas trembles there, afraid to question us. He realizes he has no powerful friends who can save him." Gedeon squinted an eye and snickered. "Amadeus and his French wench won't help you this time, Andreas. Yolande's little scheme to gain this codex is the perfect picture of their ineptitude: squandering wealth, chasing trifles, and coddling heretics. Your brother Philip is much stronger, and it is he who will be the next Duke of Savoy. Soon Amadeus will be overthrown, your weak father will die, and Philip will reign. And the manuscript?" Gedeon patted the pouch. "The Vallenses will never flip through its pages."

Victor shook his head and tried to mumble something, but the man sitting next to him threw an elbow into Victor's chest.

"Let him be, Brando." Johan gave the man a sharp look. "He can't escape."

Brando—he must be the man to whom Elionor was attached.

Andreas took a step toward the hearth, but the guards shuffled at the doorway. He held his hands up. "I carry no weapons."

"So naive for a son of nobility," Gedeon said with a grimace, "entering a guarded castle as a bandit, thinking you could steal the codex from me. Did you think I would keep such a valuable item here unguarded?" He took his hand off the pouch and strolled toward Andreas. "At one time, I thought about selling it, but to see you Vallenses twitch as I rip out its pages and burn them would bring me the greatest joy. I wish it to be the last Bible on this earth, for when it perishes, so do your beliefs and practices."

Andreas let out a little chuckle. "You can't destroy the Holy Scriptures, Gedeon."

"Lord Chanforan to you," Johan said, but his voice held a tinge of hesitancy.

"I will destroy them, and you will watch. Not today, though, for first I must present you to Philip. Already I have sent a dispatch to Château Thonon, and he will do with you as he wishes—after I gain my reward, of course. Your father will certainly be interested to hear about your conversion to Catharism." Gedeon stepped toward Andreas and waved the guards over.

Victor sprang from the couch, kicked Brando, and leaped away from his captor, mumbling something from under his gag. He rushed to the pedestal, grabbed the manuscript, and heaved it toward Andreas.

The bundle of leather and parchment slammed into Andreas's forearms like a log falling from a loft. He teetered but remained standing.

"You're surrounded!" Gedeon shouted, darting his eyes between Andreas and Victor. "You can toss that back and forth all night, but in the end, you'll still be detained, and the manuscript will be back on its pedestal."

Johan stepped forward, but before he could grab Victor, Brando unsheathed his sword and held it to Victor's back.

Victor began to turn with his fist clenched.

And Brando met him with a thrust of the blade.

Victor's eyes widened and stared at Andreas as he slumped onto the couch. Johan rushed over and knelt at his side.

"Imbecile!" Gedeon screamed, running toward Victor and Brando. "I told you not to use your sword."

Brando stuttered, dropped his weapon, and stepped back, staring at what he had done.

Curses flew from Gedeon's mouth like stinging hornets. "Leave, Brando. I no longer employ you. Never show yourself in my presence again!"

Victor coughed and spat blood, but Andreas had to turn his eyes away. Then the coughing stopped.

Johan's voice shook as he yelled at Brando. "You killed him!"

"He . . . he was about to . . ." Brando trailed off, then turned and ran through the door.

Gedeon glanced back toward Andreas, then said to the guards, "Retrieve my codex, bind the thief, and put him in the corner."

Andreas turned toward the rotting window shutters and took a deep breath. How far down was the ground?

Andreas's throat tightened and his legs lost their strength at the thought of Victor, but he couldn't let himself lose the prize and be captured—not again. He'd made a promise to Constanza, and he would keep it.

Gedeon turned toward Andreas with a tear in his eye. "This is your fault. If you hadn't tried to steal the codex, that man would still breathe."

"No, Lord Chanforan, your choices caused this." Andreas's voice cracked. He blinked a few times and forced himself to look at Victor. He did briefly, but then glared back at Gedeon. "Your guilt and your assuming spirit have now made a widow and two fatherless sons."

Andreas had to tell Victor's wife and sons before Gedeon had the opportunity to lie about it. Tears tried to burst from Andreas, but he forced them back and set his jaw. He had to escape with the Bible. That was what Victor would have wanted. And he had to get back to Constanza.

A guard grabbed Andreas, but his grip was bony and loose. Andreas swallowed, held the manuscript tighter, and jerked himself from the guard's grip.

Stunned, the guard stepped back and fumbled for his sidearm.

Andreas rammed his shoulder into the guard's chest, throwing him onto the stone floor. The other guard rushed in from the left, but Andreas bolted toward the window, holding the pouch ever tighter, and braced himself for impact. *I hope those shutters open.*

He pushed at the window. The shutters refused to budge. His free hand felt for a lock or bolt, and just as the guard approached, Andreas threw up the latch, flung out a panel, and scrambled through the window.

The drop was only the height of a man, but Andreas's knee slammed into the ground and twisted while the pouch thudded beside him. He grunted, rolled to the side, and pulled the pouch into his hands.

He couldn't linger. The forest grew near the castle wall, and if he could reach it before the guards, he could escape. He struggled up, but his knee buckled as soon as he was on his feet. The pain was bearable enough to jog, though, and he reached cover before the guards appeared below the window.

"He's gone," said one guard. "Like the bandit he is."

"Track him then!" Gedeon said. "You must find that codex!"

"I'm no tracker, and you hired me to guard the castle, not chase thieves in the night."

Andreas moved farther into the forest until he could no longer make out Castelvecchio in the moonlight. All grew quiet except for the crunching leaves under his feet, the trees swaying in the wind, and his racing, uncertain breath.

34

The fact is, we sometimes read Scripture, thinking of what it ought to say, rather than what it does say.

—Charles Haddon Spurgeon
The Metropolitan Tabernacle Pulpit, 1862

ANDREAS WALKED UPHILL ALONG THE FROZEN CREEK and let the tears flow more than he ever had in his adult life. He wept for Victor, for his widow, for his two sons. His sobs shook for his warrior friend who had lost his life to . . . what? A startled recruit? Gedeon Chanforan's hatred? Or had he given his life for the cause of the Bible?

Andreas had hobbled back to Victor's farm through the moonlit night. Both the sun and the household had risen by the time he arrived, but he stood with the manuscript and shivered in the wind until he fortified himself enough to tell them. At first, Celeste's reaction had been one of denial, but then came the tears, the hugs, and the sobs.

"How will I live without my husband?" Celeste said between wails. "We'll starve!"

Andreas's jaw trembled as he tried to comfort her. "You will have want of nothing. I have grain to spare, and I will come and help your sons plow and plant in the spring."

After a morning of weeping and remembrance, Andreas had departed Victor's home and walked the long path back to the Angrogna Valley. Victor was supposed to be the strong one—the hardened mercenary, the grizzled soldier, the experienced robber—and he was the one with a family to support.

Andreas had returned to the Angrogna Valley in the afternoon. After he recounted the events to the Pavarins, he opened the pouch and examined its contents. But his heart remained heavy when he examined the bound parchment and lexicon. The pouch he had bound his hopes to felt so empty as he set it on a table near his bed. Was it worth Victor's life?

Andreas had left the house, and now, with trees towering over him, he talked to the One who knew all. God was the only one who could heal the pain throbbing from his soul.

Why did You let Victor die? What did he do to deserve death by such senseless actions?

What if Andreas had waited instead of breaking into Castelvecchio? Had his goal to gain the manuscript been misguided all along? He didn't know, but what God had been teaching him transcended that one desire. For months, he had been focused on proving himself to the Vallenses so they would fully accept him. But how could he preach the gospel without the talents of Raimond or Estève?

Then there was the present danger. Perhaps Andreas could use his position in the House of Savoy to rid the land of Lord Chanforan. Or he could walk the trail Constanza had laid out—to retreat to some obscure land and create a fresh beginning for themselves.

A single billowy cloud covered the sun and cast a shadow across the path. Andreas peered through the trees and spotted the Pavarins' first terrace, which was dotted with leafless apple and pear trees. Smoke billowed from the house's chimney, and the sounds of playing children echoed off the hillside. To the right, a faint trickle flowed over the frozen water and brought a little life back to the creek. The sun broke through the clouds and cast a warm light on the barren forest. Andreas found a boulder, sat on it, and folded his hands.

With the playful shouts of children in the background, he asked God for wisdom. Though Andreas might not understand why Victor had died, he would still praise his heavenly Father. He wept, and he laughed at the memory of Victor's banter during the trip to Florence. He cast an aimless stare at the dead and fallen leaves, then lifted his eyes in wonder at creation's beauty and magnificence. For the rest of the afternoon, Andreas recalled the Holy Scriptures, reciting what he knew and paraphrasing what he didn't.

Late in the afternoon, footsteps came from downhill. Andreas turned to see Constanza. Her cheeks glistened pink, and her moist eyes showed her grief. Though she started with a smile, her trembling lips soon curved downward. Such a tender heart. Victor might not be family, but he was the one who had found her after she escaped from the Dominicans two summers before.

As Constanza hastened toward Andreas, he rose and offered her a seat, then sat next to her.

"What will Celeste and the children do?" A tear streamed down Constanza's cheek. "They can't manage the farm by themselves. The boys are too young."

"It's my fault. It was my idea to go to Castelvecchio for the Bible. My ambitions brought—"

"No, Victor made his own choice. And it was he who first thought of breaking into the castle."

"I should have listened to your pleas. I endangered myself and nearly crushed you. Please forgive me."

Constanza dabbed her eyes with the back of her hand and sniffled, then showed a tiny smile. "I forgive you, but I must also confess my own faults. I shouldn't have pressed you about"—she glanced down—"getting married and running away."

"If we could be married today, I would. But circumstances have told us otherwise."

"We don't need much. If we must live with my parents—"

"With all the orphans? Quite the odd place for newlyweds."

Constanza bit her bottom lip. "I see. But what if we found another land—"

"I'm sure we should stay here in the valley. This is our home, and we can't abandon the Angrogna Valley in its most urgent day."

"What can we do? Wait for our freedoms to be stripped away and smashed one by one? Continue as usual while our land is invaded by people who don't speak our language, share our culture, or practice our religion?"

"I was thinking and praying about that as I sat here this afternoon," Andreas said. "From what I see, the Lord of Luserna is driving Catholics into the valley for one reason: to provoke a response from us. Not only does Gedeon want to take away our land and property, but he also wants us to despise those who differ from us."

Andreas placed his hands on his knees. "Imagine if we lashed out against them by forcing them off their land, or by burning one of their shacks. It would validate Gedeon's assumptions about Vallenses and force outside intervention."

"Filthy thieves and outsiders is what they are," Constanza said. "They belong with their own people, not among us. It's like pouring olive oil and apple vinegar into the same barrel."

"Did you think the same about me when I first came here? I was also a Catholic and likely more devout than our new neighbors."

"The Piedmontese are trespassers and pillagers, not our neighbors." But then Constanza's eyes widened.

"Not according to Jesus," Andreas said with a grin. "For once, I might outwit your knowledge of the Holy Scriptures."

Constanza let out a little laugh. "This will be your first time but probably not your last."

"When the lawyer asked, 'Who is my neighbor?' what was Christ's response?"

"He told the parable of the Samaritan, when a priest and Levite both passed by the robbed and wounded man, and the Samaritan finally stopped and showed him compassion."

"God wants us to be like the Samaritan, Constanza. Don't you see? The Samaritan didn't verify if the desperate man could repay him. He didn't make sure they spoke the same language or practiced the same religion. He cared for him, and not only that, he went beyond what anyone would ask. Jesus asked which of the three was a neighbor to the wounded man."

"'*Aqual que fey mía èluy.* He that shewed mercy on him,'" Constanza said. "I think I understand, Andreas. We should be neighbors and show mercy to the Piedmontese. But how? They show us their sticks and fists every time we approach them."

Andreas smiled slightly and gave Constanza a sidelong glance. "Did I ever tell you the words Raimond last spoke to me?"

Constanza shook her head.

"I thanked him for sharing the gospel with me, and then he said, 'Go and do likewise'—Christ's commandment after the same parable."

Constanza nodded. "We must do the same as the Samaritan. Gedeon expects us to react like the priest or Levite or worse, but we have guidance, directly from the Holy Scriptures."

"How many Piedmontese families have moved into the valley recently?" Andreas asked.

"At least ten, five alone down at the old Lauras farm."

Andreas smiled at the glimmer in Constanza's eyes. "I believe you know what we should do."

35

The Saviour who flitted before the patriarchs through the fog of the old dispensation, and who spake in time past to the fathers by the prophets, articulate but unseen, is the same Saviour who, on the open heights of the Gospel, and in the abundant daylight of this New Testament, speaks to us. Still all along it is the same Jesus, and that Bible is from beginning to end, all of it, the word of Christ.

—James Hamilton
Sermons and Lectures, 1837

FOUR DAYS AFTER VICTOR'S DEATH, Andreas, Constanza, and Silvia walked down the path along the creek toward the old Lauras farm. They each carried a basket filled with two loaves and what little butter they could spare.

Andreas lifted the cloth covering the bread he carried and took in the aroma. His stomach rumbled.

"Six loaves won't go far with so many people," Silvia said.

They had threshed and milled three baskets of Andreas's barley and baked it into six large loaves. When they approached Nicolaus that afternoon with the idea, he had shrugged. "I doubt you'll find what you're seeking, but there's no harm in being kind."

But Andreas also had to remain alert. The day after the events at Castelvecchio, Gedeon's messenger demanded that the Pavarins hand over Andreas and the manuscript, or else the Pavarins would lose their home. Before the messenger could blink, Nicolaus had turned him away. But now Andreas was *un fugitiu*—a fugitive.

How long before the lord hired enough men to march into the valley to capture Andreas and the manuscript? Andreas couldn't fret, though—he and Constanza had a new mission and purpose.

Andreas, Constanza, and Silvia soon entered a harvested field above the old Lauras farm.

"Are we going to your house?" Silvia asked Andreas.

"No, we're going to meet the family in the tent at the edge of the field. Those at the house know us and hold suspicions, but if we approach people we've never met, we may find more kindness."

Silvia tightened her lips. "Are we trying to get them to switch sides? If so, it reminds me of a game we played back in Turin. We would try to make a few of our enemies turn on their friends and join our team so we could win."

"They're not our enemies," Constanza said. "They're simply people who need to know God."

Silvia peeked into her basket. "Why are we giving them bread, then?"

"They don't know who we are or why they should listen to us," Constanza said. "To them, we're mountain farmers who practice a heretical religion, wear strange clothing, and have so far met them only with scorn. We must show them by our actions that we love them, and so much more, that God wants them to repent and believe the gospel."

"What if they don't like us?" Silvia asked.

"Then we must continue," Andreas said. "Try again, give more, find others who will listen."

"People in the church say they need to leave our land."

"The rulers of our land sway from one imprudent law to the next," Andreas said. "True, Lord Chanforan has been unjust by taking the lower farm from Monsen Nicolaus and giving it to people who didn't earn it. But these are the circumstances in which God has placed us. He doesn't instruct us to forsake our Christian duties to assert our earthly rights." He peered down the path toward the farm. "Our instincts tell us to strike back and spit upon the Piedmontese as they flee, but that's not what God commanded."

Constanza said, "For many years, we Vallenses have had little exposure to the Piedmontese. Pinerolo is a half day's journey, Turin is twice as far, and barbes travel much farther to preach. We've had to travel to evangelize, but now God has brought lost families into our own land. Why waste the witnessing opportunities for reasons of our own wellbeing? It's been difficult for me to accept, but I believe we are doing what God has commanded."

Andreas smiled while he listened. Constanza was the finest woman in the world, more precious than the brightest gems or smoothest silk. How blessed he was to have her eye and affection.

They soon came to the frozen, barren field Andreas had harvested only a few months earlier. Now he carried that same barley to people who squatted on the land he once stewarded. Were he and Constanza naive in thinking they could influence a foreign, Catholic family to convert?

Perhaps he had brushed up against Constanza's idealism too many times. But what a self-seeking rat he would be to show kindness only to gain back the farm. No, he must be as compassionate as the Samaritan man in the parable and ask for nothing in return.

They stopped at the sight of smoke trailing up from a campfire. A tent covered in patches of dull fabric stood next to it, and huddled around the fire were a woman and two young children. The woman stirred a pot over the fire while the children shivered under a blanket.

"No turning back," Constanza said.

Andreas fidgeted with the basket. "Let's pray for God's blessing."

Together, they lifted their requests to heaven. Andreas didn't have all the answers, but God's Word had given them the direction they needed. The Samaritan showed mercy—go and do thou likewise.

When they finished praying, Andreas led Constanza and Silvia toward the fire. A child spotted them first, then ran to his mother and whispered in her ear. She called the children to her, and soon a man who must have been her husband appeared from around a cluster of trees. After motioning for them to stand behind him, he stood straight and confident, though his stature was a little shorter than his wife's.

"We bring gifts from up the mountainside." Constanza lifted her basket for them to see. Thankfully, she spoke first—a young woman's voice was more reassuring than a man's. But she spoke in Romaunt.

"They can't understand you," Andreas said from behind his teeth.

Constanza showed a nervous smile and raised her chin. "Pietat, I forgot. How do you say that in Piedmontese?"

Silvia leaned over and told her in a whisper, which Constanza repeated in Piedmontese.

The man grimaced. "The lord said we're allowed to stay."

"Did he hear me correctly?" Constanza asked Andreas.

"Yes, but he's afraid we're here to harass them."

Constanza strolled forward, unfolding the cloth around the bread as she approached. Andreas jerked forward to stop her. Did she not know she was placing herself in danger? The peasants' reaction would be unpredictable.

But before Andreas could coax Constanza back, the wife stepped around her husband and walked to meet her.

Constanza placed the basket on the ground and removed a loaf. "For you."

The wife glanced back at her husband, who walked up to join her. Andreas and Silvia moved next, and when he was close enough, Andreas held out a hand to the husband. "*Bon-a sèira.* Good evening."

The man shook his head and refused to offer his own hand. "What do you want from us?"

Though the top of the man's head was below Andreas's eyes, Andreas still stepped backward. "We . . . euh . . . came to meet our neighbor and bring gifts."

"We're Catholic," said the husband, "so we don't need your charity."

The wife looked down at him and motioned toward the children.

"My sons are hungry, though." His eyes rolled, but his face softened. "We were told there would be plenty of game in the valley, but I've seen nothing except mice since we came here."

Constanza pulled the other loaf from her basket and handed both of them to the wife.

The wife handed a whole loaf to her children, who tore off enormous pieces and stuffed them into their mouths. The wife split the other loaf in half, gave one half to her husband, and scarfed down hers. The commotion was like nothing Andreas had seen.

While the family ate, Andreas and Silvia placed their baskets at the family's feet. The first two loaves were gone in moments, and soon they eyed the other two baskets.

"Save them," Constanza said, "though we can bring more later if you'd like."

The wife nodded and looked at her husband, then back to Constanza. "*Mersi.*"

Voices sounded from around the bend, and soon three men appeared. The husband snatched the two baskets and ran them to the tent, then returned with a thick stick. "Leave now. You're not welcome here again."

Andreas stepped forward, but the husband glanced over his shoulder and clenched his stick tighter. Holding his hands up, Andreas said, "What's your name? We can come back on a different day."

The husband glared down his nose. "If I see you here again, I'll bury your corpse under my tent."

"We were only trying to be friendly," Constanza said. "Perhaps tomorrow—"

"There will be no tomorrow for you," said the wife. "Please heed my husband's warning and stay away. We are loyal to the Lord of Luserna and will not betray his trust."

That statement opened Andreas's ears. How would this family betray the Lord of Luserna by talking to them? The husband took a step toward them.

"Connie, Silvia, they don't want us here." Andreas waved them back toward the path.

"That ended worse than I expected," Constanza said as they walked away.

Silvia stared at her feet as she walked. "They didn't thank us either, and it took all morning to make those loaves."

"Our first attempt at befriending the Piedmontese has ended in failure," Andreas said. "What else can we do? Find another family?"

"We should talk to my papà," Constanza said. "He might have some ideas."

But Andreas had something else to talk to Nicolaus about too.

*   *   *

The air was warm for December, enough to melt the snow from everywhere except the mountain peaks and places hidden from the sunlight. Andreas walked beside Constanza into the shed and found Nicolaus sawing on an oak log. Chisels and a mallet lay around him and sweat beaded on his brow.

"What are you making, Papà?" Constanza asked.

Nicolaus continued to saw but gave a quick nod. After a few more pulls, he stopped, wiped his brow, and let out a sigh. "A spade for David, but it's far from my best craftsmanship."

Constanza left Andreas's side, walked to Nicolaus, and embraced him. He dropped his saw and chuckled as she held him tight. "*Ma felena.* My little girl."

Andreas stood a few paces back and waited. Father and daughter showed such emotion, even in his presence. *I suppose they imagine me as one of their own now.*

Andreas had pondered the relationship between Nicolaus and Constanza. It was one of honor, love, and joy. In many ways they were opposites—Constanza's demeanor was warmer, while her father tended to be more reserved. For twenty-one winters they had woven their lives together, and now that thread seemed as strong as iron.

After a few moments, Constanza gave her papà one last squeeze and moved back to Andreas's side. Her cheeks were red, but she wore a faint smile that brightened the room more than the sunlight streaming in through the windows.

Nicolaus grabbed the saw again and set the teeth on the oak.

Andreas stepped beside Nicolaus and examined the log. "At the monastery, we would take our spades down to the blacksmith and have him cover the blades in iron. It's easier to use and wears much slower."

"I suppose, but I've been making spades all my life. This way works well enough for me." Nicolaus held the wood up to the light and used his hand to measure the width of the handle. "Besides, the nearest blacksmith is in La Torre, and I don't have the ducats to pay him."

Nothing had changed since Nicolaus tried to sell a cartload of grain in La Torre two weeks earlier. The farmers complained about breaking tools or needing to buy textiles, salt, and lye, but they had to rely on bartering, lending, and giving to one another.

Andreas fiddled with his pocket and cleared his throat. "We walked down and gave the bread to one of the Piedmontese families."

Nicolaus pushed his saw into the wood. "Did they take it?"

"They took it," Constanza said, "but they forbade us from coming back."

"As I'd guessed." Nicolaus kept his eyes on the log. "What do you suppose you'll gain from this? If you think they'll become reasonable and leave our land, you're fantasizing."

"Andreas doesn't want his land back," Constanza said, but then she glanced at Andreas. "Perhaps he does, but that's not why we're being kind. You should see them. No mother has more than skin on her bones, the children's faces are gaunt, the fathers are desperate. To survive the winter, they would need a miracle."

"Or someone else's grain," Andreas said. "The men were there too, roaming with clubs and sticks. And they weren't smiling. They know our farm, and if they're desperate to feed their wives and children, they'll steal more than livestock."

Nicolaus rubbed his hand along the rough edge of the spade. "If they choose that path, then we must defend ourselves. We outnumber them—"

"Is it so inevitable?" Andreas asked.

"If they're hungry, then yes, they'll hold back nothing."

"No, I'm saying, could we soothe their hunger and avoid their desperation?"

Nicolaus shook his head and chuckled. "Was this your idea, Connie?"

"It was Andreas's, though it was my idea to bake the bread. He had to convince me we should be their neighbor, using Jesus's parable of the man who fell among thieves."

"The world is more complicated than you imagine." Nicolaus blew sawdust from the spade, grabbed a chisel, and angled it into the oak. "We face more than a simple story can explain."

"Don't they need to hear the gospel?" Constanza asked.

"Yes, but by moving here, they also threaten our way of life. If the Lord of Luserna and the foreigners he's brought in trample our beliefs and traditions, then we'll never have the chance to preach Christ to them or anyone else."

"Monsen, I respect your wisdom," Andreas said, "but from what I've read in the Gospels, Jesus never taught that. He didn't teach His disciples to evangelize only when they weren't being threatened and oppressed. They were to preach the gospel with no qualifications."

Nicolaus chiseled off one strip after another from the blade. "You're correct, but what if they won't listen? Did you speak to them about the gospel today?"

"No," Constanza said, "which is why we came to seek your wisdom."

Nicolaus chiseled without saying a word. With a trained eye, he placed the tool at precise angles, hammering it with his mallet and adjusting as he progressed. Lords and scholars might gloat about their knowledge, but men like Nicolaus Pavarin held a true understanding of the world.

Finally Nicolaus set down the chisel. "Even with your grain harvest, Andreas, our supplies will be scarce without milk."

"It will work," Andreas said. "God will supply what we need."

"What happens when all the Piedmontese learn we're handing out food? They'll empty our grain bins, then ask for more."

"God provided for our family through many barren winters," Constanza said. "Couldn't He do the same again?"

"Don't take what I say and forsake your mission. I believe in what you are doing and am only sharing my opinion. Just be sure to leave enough food for our own."

"We need more help too," Andreas said.

"Twelve children are inside," Constanza said. "Mamà and I would be thrilled if they were occupied with something other than running around the house and fighting all winter."

Nicolaus held the shovel out in front of him, closed an eye, and peered down its handle. "The Pavarins aren't the only believers in the Angrogna Valley."

Andreas scratched his beard. "Will the church be willing to help?"

"If you can convince me, you can convince them." Nicolaus placed the shovel on the bench and looked at Constanza. "I'm proud you two thought of this but can't promise you the outcome you want—in fact, I don't expect much success."

"What if one Piedmontese family believes?" Andreas asked. "What if we convince them we are friends instead of enemies? They'll think us strange at first, but God will bless our obedience to His commandments."

"They may hate you," Nicolaus said, "and they may spit in your eye or stomp on your toes. Expect it, but don't falter. What you begin, you must finish. It might be like tending an apple sapling, watching for those pink blossoms to form into fruit. Don't be disappointed when you don't see results. More than anything, don't surrender after one failure."

Constanza's eyes brightened. "If we see one convert, then God has completely overthrown Lord Chanforan's plans."

"And the greatest victory of all would be another soul added to God's kingdom," Nicolaus said.

"Do we have your blessing?" Andreas asked. Then he gulped. It sounded too much like the other matter. Should he wait, or was now the time?

Nicolaus nodded and placed his hand on Constanza's shoulder. "I will help in whatever way you ask, but this is your endeavor." He focused his gaze on Andreas. "Constanza's wellbeing is in your hands."

Andreas glanced at Constanza, and his heart hurried to a sprint. He had no farm, no house, and no stable income without crops.

"I'm going to ask him now," Andreas whispered.

Constanza bit her lip and grinned.

"Ask me what?" Nicolaus asked as he scraped and oiled the spade handle.

"Nothing related to what we've been talking about." Andreas stood straighter, held his chin up, and cleared his throat. "I desire to marry your daughter."

Nicolaus picked up the spade and pushed its blade into the dirt. His face was expressionless. "How do you think this will work?"

Andreas walked to the spade, pulled it up, and handed it back to Nicolaus. His heart thumped and his hands shook. "You really should try to take this to the blacksmith."

"Not the spade, about being married. You two have my blessing, but the old Lauras farm was supposed to have been the dowry."

"I don't ask for any of your property or wealth, only Constanza." He'd said it, and his heart nearly beat from his chest. Constanza's smile caught him—the corners of her mouth slightly upturned, sparkling teeth peeking out from behind her lips, those little creases angling up from her nose to her eyes.

Nicolaus smiled and stuck the shovel in the ground again. He pulled Constanza to him with one arm, motioned for Andreas to come to the other, and tightened his strong arms around them. "I suppose I should thank you for offering to take my youngest after twenty-one long years of misery."

All three laughed, but the weight fell on Andreas's shoulders. He was a man in hiding—not only from Gedeon Chanforan but also from his own family. If his father discovered Andreas was married to a peasant, he'd declare the marriage void because it wasn't performed by a Catholic priest, then drag Andreas back to Chambéry. How could he force sweet, upright Constanza into the life of a runaway noble?

Andreas's breath escaped him, but as Nicolaus released them from his hug, Constanza's voice lifted his worries from the depths.

"I've dreamed of this day for far too long."

"I'm not your husband yet. I still need to—"

"I know you will do what you must, and I love you for it, Andreas. And I couldn't be happier than serving by your side as we try to reach our papist friends down the hill."

"Papist?"

"They are, no?"

Andreas shook his head and let out a little laugh. Constanza Pavarin, the woman who had once threatened him with a knife, would be his wife. But first there was much to accomplish. Somehow—without property or provision, with a hostile lord, with the surety the duke would learn of his son's conversion and betrothal—Andreas had to arrange a peaceful life for Constanza, all while showing Christlike love and compassion to the Piedmontese.

36

With little time for idle indulgence, and so many opportunities for instruction—rendered doubly effective by the example handed down, and the "living example" of their teachers—we cannot be surprised that the Waldenses have so long maintained a marked superiority of morals and shown themselves to be a people who are "doers of the word, and not hearers only."

—William Beattie
The Waldenses, 1838

A MONTH LATER, Constanza rubbed her hands together and blew into them. *I should have worn my mittens!* The wind stung her cheeks like a thousand tiny pinpricks as she crunched through the thin layer of snow toward the forest. Towering pines swayed in waves, but when she passed under them, a warmth returned to her body. As on every afternoon for the past month, she thought through what she would say.

Though some knew her purpose, she always left the house alone for this *rendetz-vos*. The situation was delicate, and she prayed every morning for both wisdom and boldness.

From down the hill, the sound of chipping ice entered her ears. Amalia slammed a rock into the ice as Constanza approached the usual meeting spot. The ice cracked but didn't shatter.

Amalia glanced up at Constanza. "Finding water would have been easier if Ricardo had let Andreas finish the well before the ground froze. He still hates all of you Vallenses."

"The cold is cruel today," Constanza said in her best Piedmontese, which had improved since she and Amalia had first met. At first they had said little, but after four weeks, their cordialities had transformed into genuine conversations.

Amalia shook her head and hit the ice again. This time it shattered, and a trickle of fresh water bubbled up from the cracks. A child of about a year lay in the snow, bundled in wool but not enough to warm her.

Constanza walked to the baby, removed her own coat, and wrapped the child. "Let me do that now," she said to Amalia.

"It's almost broken." Amalia huffed and tossed the stone aside in frustration.

"If there's not enough flowing water, you might need to bring ice back and melt it."

"We can't afford to melt ice. Our firewood is almost gone."

Constanza chuckled under her breath. It wasn't their firewood. Andreas had cut it all last summer and stacked it in the barn. But perhaps God knew these people needed it. "Can Riccardo chop more?"

"There's one ax, but it's too dull to be useful."

"My papà could sharpen it."

"No, my husband will have no dealings with your people."

From the outset, the Piedmontese had resisted the Vallenses. The men in the old Lauras farmhouse had shouted curses the first time Andreas and Constanza brought the squatters a pot filled with milled flour. Afterward, Andreas and Constanza enlisted the help of others in the church. Some were hard to persuade, but the church soon united around the cause. Children threshed barley before their mothers baked bread. Papà showed men a game trail where they might find rabbits. Mamà helped a mother comfort her colicky infant. And Andreas helped Piedmontese men build shelters for the winter. In time, the Piedmontese had warmed to the Vallenses—all except the four families crammed in the farmhouse.

Constanza took the rock from Amalia's hand and hit the ice herself. Her hand and forearm shook from the dull thud, but the ice remained intact. "If you bring the ax here tomorrow. I'll bring it back sharpened the next day. I don't want your family freezing to death this winter."

Amalia nestled the baby under her coat. "I considered what you said yesterday, but I don't understand how forgiveness can be free. What if a man murders another? What if he forsakes his own family and takes another wife? Does God still accept him?"

"God never accepts sin," Constanza said, "but He accepts a repentant sinner." She slammed the rock into the ice again, and that time, the rock shattered it into pieces.

Amalia scurried to Constanza with the bucket. "But you said all God requires is faith. How does He want us to both believe and repent? That sounds no different from what the priests teach."

Constanza filled a bucket with water, slush, and ice chips. "Sin separates us from God, and the sacrifice of Christ paid for those sins. Repentance isn't our merit—it's the work of God. If we were required to work for the salvation offered through the cross, we would never meet the standard. Trusting in Christ's finished work is what changes us, not our own righteousness."

Amalia nodded. "It all sounds too wonderful. I want to believe, but I'm afraid Riccardo would throw me into the cold and keep the children for himself."

Constanza grabbed the other bucket and filled it too. "I confess, it would be easy for me to say, 'Pray and trust God, Amalia. That's all you need to do, and God will bless you.' But Jesus said affliction would come to those who believe in Him, so I can't promise peace, nor can I deny Riccardo might hate you for your faith. When I became a believer at a young age, almost everyone I knew had already done the same."

"I wish I had been born into a family like yours," Amalia said. "I never knew such peace existed. I doubt your father has ever drunk himself into a stupor. Did your mother ever scream at you or smack you across the face when you misbehaved?"

"We're nothing except peasants with God-given grace, free and undeserved." Constanza lifted both buckets and carried them back to Amalia.

"If I were to convert, would your people accept me? Look at me—I conceived my oldest son before I was married. And before we moved here, I often stole from the market. I'm a liar—"

"God wants to accept you. If you realize your sins have corrupted your soul and believe Jesus died for those sins, was buried, and rose from the tomb after three days, then all you must do is confess with your mouth and believe in your heart." Constanza would have quoted the Holy Scriptures, but Amalia wouldn't understand the Romaunt, so she paraphrased.

Amalia stood with her baby and moved to Constanza. Her voice quieted, and she showed a slight smile. "I believe all you've told me, and I know only faith in Christ can save my soul."

Constanza dropped the buckets. "You . . . you realize your family and everyone in your house would consider you a heretic?"

"I know." Amalia maintained her smile. "I thought about everything last night and only wanted to ask a few more questions."

"You're saying you trust Christ alone—not the Eucharist or your baptism or almsgiving?"

"Yes, and you can't convince me otherwise. I believe in the Savior alone."

Constanza's jaw dropped, and her toes curled in her shoes. The first convert—God had saved Amalia from her sin. Andreas had been right about the Piedmontese, and she couldn't wait to tell him. Constanza wanted to slap her own cheek and be sure she wasn't dreaming.

"In time, I will tell Riccardo and perhaps the others, but I must be careful."

Constanza eyed the buckets. For weeks, she had helped Amalia fill them, but never helped her carry them back to the house for fear of her husband.

"I'll carry the water this time," Constanza said.

Amalia shook her head. "Only to the yard, or else Riccardo might see you."

"We've become acquainted with all the other Piedmontese families in the valley, except those in your house. Surely the men have softened since we first met."

Amalia stared at the ground for a few moments. "I suppose you could come, but don't let their reaction surprise you."

Constanza lifted both buckets and followed Amalia across the path to the old Lauras farm. If not for Elionor's departure soon after the first ill-fated bread delivery to the Piedmontese, she probably would have been carrying the other bucket. Elionor said she was off to visit her mother, but not a word had come from her in over three weeks. A haze of concern hung over Constanza, but the bustle of her current endeavor often made her forget. Surely Ellie would return soon, and Constanza could tell her all about Amalia's conversion.

By the time they entered the yard, Constanza's shoulders and arms burned like fire. She placed the buckets by the door just as Riccardo appeared.

"Who is that?" he asked Amalia.

"A friend from uphill. She helped me—"

Riccardo spat on the ground in front of Constanza's feet. "The witch can't be here."

Constanza widened her eyes but held her tongue.

"She's tried to show us kindness. Please, she's only here to help."

"No, she's trying to convert you." He gave a quick whistle toward the house.

Constanza gulped and pushed her hair under her kerchief.

"Has she spoken to you?" Riccardo asked.

Amalia tightened her lips.

"Speak, woman. What has she said to you?"

"Only kind words, nothing to harm our family."

"You're a liar. You listened to her poison, and I see it in your eyes."

Amalia flinched back, but Riccardo grabbed her by the shirt and pulled her forward while she struggled to hold the baby. Another man appeared at the door, glassy-eyed and staggering.

"You've been drinking," Amalia said. "Please, I'm holding a baby, don't—"

Riccardo shoved Amalia into the side of the house, slamming the back of her head into the stone.

Constanza took a step backward. She couldn't help, not with those men in the house.

"Leave, Constanza!" Amalia shouted.

Riccardo pulled Amalia forward again, looked into her eyes, and slurred, "Constanza? Is that the wench's name?"

"Yes, but she's an honorable woman with a kind soul who only wants to help us. Other families have formed relationships with these people. They don't wish us ill. Indeed, they're helping others build and giving them bread. Haven't you heard about their deeds?"

Riccardo's face hardened, and two other men stumbled from the doorway. Riccardo pushed Amalia to the side and turned to Constanza with clenched fists. "Talk to my wife again, witch, and we'll cook you alive and feed your flesh to the rats. The Lord of Luserna will hear about your bewitchments." He stumbled back into the house, but the other men hesitated.

Constanza gathered her skirts and prepared to leave, then caught one last glimpse of Amalia and the baby.

But she had no words for them. What could she say to one in such a dire place? She could tell Amalia she would pray, or she could encourage her to trust God, but that felt so trite and uncompassionate now.

Finally something came to her. "I'm always here, whenever you need me." God would have to do the rest.

Amalia gave an abrupt nod and disappeared through the doorway. The other men soon followed.

All grew quiet outside, while rage thundered from inside the house. Constanza listened for a moment, which only caused a cold tear to crip down her cheek. What could she do now? Wait? Try to meet Amalia anyway and risk her own safety?

Her mind drifted to Andreas. She had to tell him everything.

37

So you hold the text, now received by all, in which is nothing corrupt.

—Abraham Elzevir
Preface to the Textus Receptus, 1633

ANDREAS HAMMERED A BOARD INTO PLACE while Bertran Arnaldi held the other end. "Two more," David Pavarin said from inside the newly framed hut. "Tomorrow we'll place the roof."

Nearby, two Piedmontese men sawed a plank to the correct length as their wives and children watched. "Six feet?" asked one man.

"Six," Andreas said. "Same for the last one."

Guido, one of the orphans, grabbed a handful of daub and slapped it into the gap between the boards, and the rest of the men followed. The seventh house was almost finished, and another family would have shelter for the rest of the winter. Though the huts were primitive—pine logs, mud, thatch roof, and dirt floor—they would at least prevent frostbitten toes and fingers. Though none of the Piedmontese had converted over the past month, most had softened—and that was fruit.

Threats came from Lord Chanforan about taxes, land, and the orphans, but without anyone to enforce the demands, the Vallenses continued their winter routines. They mended fences, spun wool, cared for newborn lambs, and repaired tools for the fast-approaching spring.

David hooted from inside the building. "Someone's here for you, Andreas."

Bertran and the Piedmontese men cackled as Andreas turned toward his betrothed. She was running, and though she smiled, her eyes also bore a certain sadness.

"I didn't know you would visit today." Andreas set down his hammer.

"I couldn't wait." Constanza's voice was quick and breathy. "I was at the old Lauras farm—"

"You mean Andreas's farm," David said. "The one meant to be his dowry."

Andreas shrugged. "The farm never belonged to me. Though I had my own purposes for it, they must not have aligned with God's."

David laughed. "I try not to spend too many days with Andreas, for I fear I'll experience the same fate."

"I'm content with Andreas alone." Constanza smiled at Andreas. "He'll find where God wants us, then plant us there."

"You two deserve one another." David rolled his eyes. "If we must, we could always build you one of these huts."

"And we'll content ourselves with that," Andreas said.

Constanza cleared her throat and glared at David.

"I apologize, Connie," David said after one last laugh. "You were at the old Lauras farm . . ."

"Yes, I was helping Amalia fill her water buckets at the creek, and she became a believer—right there in the forest. Amalia is born again now."

"Are you certain?" Andreas asked. "She wasn't trying to gain your favor for more food?"

"Without a doubt, she believed the gospel. She's concerned about her family and the others in the house, though. Amalia hasn't told them yet, but she wants to."

Andreas's blood pulsed with warmth, and his vision misted. God had worked through them, and now a soul had been saved from sin's punishment. Was that why God had brought the foreigners into their land?

"Praise God for His mercy and providence"—he looked at Constanza—"and for His faithful witnesses."

"I did nothing except show her the Holy Scriptures and answer her questions."

"You obeyed God's commandment. Your willingness to follow Christ's example changed the life of a young mother. And we pray this is only the beginning."

"And not the end." Constanza's smile sagged into a frown. "Four men threatened me when I left Amalia. They knew why I was there and said if I returned, they'd kill me. Riccardo was drunk and yelling at Amalia, then he pushed her, even though she was holding a baby. I want her to join our church, but Riccardo will beat her if he learns about her conversion." Her eyes glistened. "I'm afraid for her life and others who might convert. Those men want to intimidate others into not believing, and now I don't know if I'll see Amalia again. Why would God separate her from His people the day she became a believer?"

"God didn't separate her," Andreas said. "Those men did."

"Riccardo also said he'd tell Gedeon about me."

"Gedeon is powerless. Other than a pair of dispatches, both he and Johan have been silent. They send their empty threats but enforce nothing. Perhaps he's invested too much into his alliance with Philip."

"Andreas, there's a reward for your capture. If you leave this valley's protection, the first man who recognizes you will turn you over. Don't underestimate Gedeon."

"He doesn't frighten me. When his guard killed Victor, that set him back. You should have seen his grief that night. The entire ordeal pained him."

Constanza lowered her voice. "Papà received another demand from Gedeon yesterday, now about the orphans."

"Again," Andreas said, "he's trying to shake us and see if we'll snap. Gedeon is afraid of us."

"What if he's preparing instead? What if as soon as the snow melts, he marches his army—"

"He has no army. Gedeon Chanforan is a conniving burgher who happened to gain enough wealth to buy his own lordship, and then he had to swear allegiance to my landless, twenty-one-year-old brother."

Constanza relaxed her posture. "How can I help Amalia, though? The families in that house have almost no food—"

"Did you see signs of your livestock while you were there?"

"I didn't pay attention, but I would have noticed. So no, I saw nothing."

So strange. How could a herd of sheep and a pair of goats disappear? "Have you met other women from the house?" Andreas asked.

"Only Mercede, but she never comes to the creek, and Amalia says she's a devout papist. If I approach her, it will need to be in secret."

"We should continue. I believe more will be born again. Bertran and I have had conversations with men about the gospel, and though they hold their objections, they're opening. Before the week is spent, we may see others profess Christ."

"When Lord Chanforan hears we've been evangelizing the peasants, he'll be irate," Constanza said. "I'm afraid he'll try to shut down our work. Gedeon would rather the Piedmontese starve than convert."

"We can't control our earthly lord, but we can trust in the Lord of the universe. The kingdom of God is not about us—it's about eternity. We have a chance to preach the gospel to those nearest us, and we should use that opportunity while we can."

Constanza smiled and nodded. "You're a different man than you were last winter, and I love you all the more for it."

"The Stinche Prison will do that to a man. God taught me much in that dark cell, and more since then."

Guido ran up to Andreas from the hut. "Are we finished for today?"

Constanza put her hands on her hips and gave him a grin. "Do you enjoy working with Monsen Andreas all day?"

"Yes! Did you see what we built?" Guido pointed his chin toward the house and showed a confident smile.

"It's perfect. The Grimaldis gave you everything. And now look—you're giving to others too."

Andreas tilted his head slightly. The orphan boys often made more work than they accomplished, but their pride in their work let him know it was worth bringing them. He gave Guido a nod and a closed-mouth smile. "Let's wash up then and head home. I suppose the ladies will have a warm meal ready by the time we get there."

Constanza's eyes widened. "Pietat! Mamà must be scorning my name. I was supposed to help with dinner." She rushed up the path and waved. "I'll see you there when you're finished."

Soon Constanza passed into the forest. She deserved so much, but he could offer little other than his love and loyalty. But God had given him more than enough: serving their neighbors and preaching the gospel to them, seeing other Vallenses do the same, studying the Greek Bible every evening, and being betrothed to Constanza. His chest fluttered at the thought.

Andreas glanced back at the hut. The next day, they would set the roof, and the family could sleep under it the day afterward. But on a stool outside the doorway, Bertran sat with Ulrico, a Piedmontese man who had been helping them. They bowed their heads, and after a few moments, Ulrico opened his eyes and hugged Bertran.

Ulrico walked toward Andreas, but by then it was obvious—the Savior had found another lost sheep.

38

Do not condemn us without hearing us, for we are Christians and faithful subjects; and our barbes are prepared to prove, in public or in private, that our doctrines are conformable with the Word of God. True, we have not followed the transgressors of the evangelical law, who have so long departed from the tradition of the apostles; we have rejected their corrupt precepts and refused to recognise any other authority than that of the Bible; but we find happiness in a pure and simple life, wherein alone the Christian faith takes root and flourishes.

—John Campo and John Desiderio
Address to the archdeacon at Pinerolo, 1487

G EDEON CUT FIVE RIBS from the roasted lamb rack at the center of the table. Marta sat to the right, and Claudia and Addo sat farther down. On the left sat Johan, sawing into his portion of meat with a furor. Gedeon tore off a rib, slurped the juices, and took a generous bite while the five guests sitting on the opposite side of the table stared at his mouth.

Fernand, the leader of the emissaries, made the sign of the cross, followed by the other four. Together they said, *"Benedic, Domine, nos et hæc tua dona quæ de tua largitate sumus sumpturi, per Christum Dominum nostrum. Amen."*

Gedeon chuckled when they made the second sign of the cross and cut off their own portions from the lamb. "We also practice the Catholic faith in this household, though you may not see as many signs as on the other side of the mountains."

"Philip will demand loyalty to the Church and the Holy See," Fernand said, "for he does not tolerate the heresy in these lands like Amadeus and Yolande."

Gedeon finished chewing, then swallowed. "You know I will not tolerate the Vallenses, which is why the soldiers will enable me to enforce the realm's laws."

"So long as they assist you only as mercenaries and volunteers, not as soldiers employed by the House of Savoy. Philip cannot risk open conflict yet."

Gedeon sucked the remaining meat from the bone and tossed it onto the plate. "What difference will it make? If you allow them to wear the insignia of the duke, the Vallenses will respect them more and my task will be simpler."

"The men will still wear insignia, just not the duke's. Instead, they will wear regalia from their native Swiss lands, which won't inflame any political turmoil."

"May I use them however I wish?" Gedeon ripped off another rib and took a bite.

"Philip trusts you to levy your taxes, and if the peasants do not submit, you may imprison them."

"If they resist?"

Fernand narrowed his eyes. "Then they are enemies of the duchy."

Gedeon finished what was in his mouth, then grabbed a goblet and gulped the wine. "My steward, Johan, will accompany the contingent. He understands the Vallenses more than anyone, and soon they'll submit to their new lord."

Marta placed her elbows on the table and looked up at Gedeon. "They have submitted."

"They broke into my home, stole my property, and threatened my family."

"The children and I were in Turin—"

Gedeon shushed her with a wave and refocused on Fernand. "Peasants more loyal to me have settled in the land now, and by this time next year, our coffers will be full."

Johan leaned toward his ear and whispered, "I must speak to you after the emissaries leave. Some grim news has reached me from the Angrogna—"

"Speak now," Gedeon said, loud enough for all to hear. "We hide nothing from the rightful ruler of the duchy or his representatives."

"I would find it more prudent," Johan said from behind clenched teeth, "if we spoke in private."

Gedeon swallowed another mouthful of wine, then let the empty goblet topple and roll to the ground. It clanked a few times before rolling under his chair. "I'm not drunk."

"My lord, can we please wait until later?" Johan pointed his jaw at the emissaries.

Gedeon glared down his nose at Johan. "No, now."

Johan sighed and darted his eyes from the emissaries to Gedeon. "I have ears among our Piedmontese friends, and there are rumors. I'm unsure whether they're true. Perhaps it's hearsay from peasants, but there might be some—"

"Stop mumbling, Johan, and make your point." *I must maintain myself, especially before Philip's men.* If he had drunk a few too many sips of wine, he couldn't show it.

"First, I heard about a young mother, and she's been talking to my old friend Constanza Pavarin."

"Pavarin, Pavarin, Pavarin." Gedeon slapped his hand on the table. "That name is like an untuned bell to my ears. I should have disposed of that woman when she was our maid."

"I rather liked her," Claudia said from the right.

"Silence!" Gedeon said. "This discussion is far above your simple mind."

Marta's nostrils flared. "Do not speak to our children—"

Gedeon glared at his family, pushed himself from the table, and pointed to the door. "Leave and retire to your rooms. All of you."

Marta stared for a moment, but Gedeon had the greater fortitude. Soon Marta motioned for Claudia and Addo, and they stomped away.

Gedeon's tone had been more harsh than he intended, but he couldn't entertain his imprudent wife and children while he worked to improve their status in the world. Marta and the children didn't appreciate how far they had risen, how rich they had become, or how prestigious the name *Charforan* would soon be. Claudia and Addo would marry nobles with land and wealth, and Gedeon would never again bear the shame of his father's name. *I am a success without a church, without religion, and without God.*

"I apologize for their manners." Gedeon looked at Fernand. "The move from Turin has been difficult." He placed his hand on the table in front of Johan. "Now, Constanza Pavarin, what has she done?"

"It's not her alone, but she and Andreas are apparently the leaders."

"Is this Andreas our Philip's brother?" Fernand asked. "We read about his heresy in your dispatch. Duke Louis crumpled up the parchment and wept when he read it."

"Yes, the same Andreas. The Vallenses look to him for guidance and wisdom, but he is weak. They haven't yet seen his folly as I have. What ridiculous enterprise is our Andreas involved with now? Tell me, Johan."

"It's difficult to explain. Please understand, Vallenses take certain actions based on what their Holy Scriptures say—"

"I know exactly what they believe, far more than you do, in fact."

"A week ago, a husband came to me sputtering about his wife talking to Constanza. He claimed she had converted to their religion."

Gedeon drew his eyebrows together and pursed his lips, but he let Johan continue.

"At first I waved off the rumor. These Vallenses enjoy their tales and gossip, and if I told you everything, it would overwhelm you. But then more rumors came—whole families converted."

"How did this happen? The Vallenses hate anyone who doesn't believe as they do."

"It's not so simple," Johan said. "They've somehow befriended many of the Piedmontese. They build huts for them, give them grain, even invite some into their homes."

Gedeon's breathing quickened, and his veins pulsed. The canny Vallenses had duped his peasants. How had he not anticipated that? They were supposed to hate each other, not become friends. But though the Vallenses had always been adept at convincing the poor, they couldn't outwit a man who had experienced what he had. Cut the leaders off, and their entire edifice would come crashing to the earth. And it would begin with the Pavarins.

Gedeon tore off another rib and held it up to his guests. "Vallense lamb." He bit off a piece and chewed, with his mouth closed, of course—he was a nobleman now. After swallowing, he said, "They refused to pay their taxes, and I seized their livestock. I figured they would blame the Piedmontese for their disappearance, but it must not have been obvious enough." He pushed the plate closer to them. "I have plenty more sheep in my fields. Please eat until your bellies are full."

The emissaries looked at the plate for a moment, and after a little more prodding, they took the rest of the meat.

"I have a mission for my Swiss soldiers," Gedeon said. "The Angrogna Valley is a quarter day's journey from here, and there's a certain farm there with terraces on the hillside. They will confiscate all grain from anyone with the name Pavarin—and anyone with family ties to them. Not a single husk will be left. In time, the soldiers will disperse it among the loyal Piedmontese families. I am far more generous than the Vallense witches, they will see, for I will not speak to them about religion or require them to dress in drab attire or indoctrinate their children. No, I will give freely to all who reject the Vallense lies, and then we will see how many of those conversions were genuine. By this time next week, you will hear of no more conversions."

But a lack of grain and an inability to proselytize wouldn't deter the Pavarins. He glanced to the right, where Claudia and Addo had sat. Children. A nest of little orphan children.

"Do you know the law about Catholic orphans?" Gedeon asked Fernand.

"Tell me."

"Parentless Catholic children must be raised only by other Catholic families." Gedeon pushed his plate full of bones forward. "The family we speak of has hidden Piedmontese children for many months, and the moment has finally arrived for us to rescue their unfortunate souls from abuse. While the soldiers confiscate their grain, they will also retrieve the children, Andreas, and my Greek codex."

"What if they refuse?" Johan asked.

Gedeon grinned. "Swiss pikes will convince even the strongest men."

39

The Old Testament in Hebrew and the New Testament in Greek, being immediately inspired by God, and by his singular care and providence kept pure in all ages, are therefore authentic; so as in all controversies of religion, the church is finally to appeal to them.

—London Baptist Confession of Faith, 1689

Mornings began early at the Pavarin home. Everyone had finished breakfast, but Papà, Mamà, Estève, and Constanza still sat around the table while the children ran about the open area. Constanza sat next to Andreas, listening to him talk about another Piedmontese family who had believed the gospel.

Fosca tugged at the shoulder of Constanza's dress. "Madomaisèla, I'm still hungry."

"We will eat again tonight."

"Tonight? Why did we stop eating at midday?"

"It's winter, and we don't need as much as in the warmer months." It was true, but not fully—they had rationed meals because of shortages and decided to eat only twice per day until the first vegetables sprouted.

Fosca sighed. "Is it because we're giving all our food away?"

Constanza put a hand on Fosca's cheek. "God has blessed us with enough to feed ourselves and our friends, and we should be thankful. Yes, your belly may want more, but remember: a slice of bread or salted pork is only a half day away. But if we didn't help the Piedmontese, they would have nothing, perhaps for days and weeks. The Holy Scriptures say, 'He that hath a bountiful eye shall be blessed; for he giveth of his bread to the poor.' God will provide what we need."

Constanza jumped when a fist pounded on the door.

Being closest, Mamà rose and strolled to the door. The knock sounded again. "One moment," she said, shaking her head. But when she opened the door, a man with a bald head spoke in a French accent.

"Andreas of Savoy. Is he here?"

"Savoy?" Mamà said. "Do you mean Andreas de Bonomo?"

Constanza tensed. It must be one of Gedeon's men here to arrest Andreas. She looked toward the back door, hoping Andreas could outrun the man.

Andreas stood, but instead of running, he greeted the man with a handshake followed by a firm embrace. "What brings you to the mountains, and in winter no less?"

"There's no time to explain—"

Andreas pulled the man through the door. "This is my friend Basile Halphen, one of my companions on the journey to Florence."

Papà bowed slightly and gave Basile a pat on the shoulder. "Andreas has spoken highly of you."

But Basile ignored Papà and gave Andreas a firm look. "Swiss pikemen are marching into the valley as we speak. They will be at this farm before *la troisième heure*."

Andreas translated for the Pavarins. "Before the third hour."

"Everyone must leave, especially the orphans. Those soldiers mean them harm."

"How do you know?" Andreas asked. "I haven't seen you in two months and now you come with such dire news."

Basile furrowed his brow. "I am showing you great preference by coming here. If it were anyone else, I would have stayed away and let fate take its course. I came here because I care for your safety." He snapped his head forward. "Go, I am not exaggerating. Swiss soldiers will be here soon, specifically for the orphans and the manuscript."

"I will not leave my house," Papà said.

"That's your risk, not mine, but I advise you to remove the orphans and the manuscript far from this valley. Gedeon means to take them from you."

"Why should we trust you?" Constanza asked. "Are you not a Catholic yourself?"

"I am not here because of your religious feuds. It is in my interest to see Andreas, the children, and Princess Yolande's investments safe."

Andreas whispered in Constanza's ear. "We can trust him, perhaps more than anyone."

Papà glanced at Andreas and then the children.

Andreas gave a few gentle claps. "Gather everything you can. We're going to David and Catterina's house."

"Who is David?" Basile asked.

"A son of this household, and his home is across the terraces—"

"No, it won't be safe. You must leave the valley entirely. But you cannot go south toward La Torre. The soldiers are marching up both the upper and lower roads. You must go over the mountains."

"In winter?" Papà raised his voice. "That's impossible, more so with the children."

"You cannot stay here or anywhere near this valley."

"Basile, you're asking us to abandon our homes and flee." Andreas threw his hands up. "Does Amadeus know about Gedeon and Philip yet?"

Basile clenched his lips together, then scanned the room and gave a quick nod. "Your brother and his wife are both aware—"

"Brother?" Mamà asked, narrowing her eyes.

Andreas cleared his throat. "I was meaning to tell you more about myself . . . and my parents . . . and my family."

"Andreas is a prince," Basile said without chagrin, "third son of your duke, and brother of Amadeus, Prince of Piedmont."

Papà and Mamà both shot grave looks at Andreas, then at Constanza. She remained expressionless and avoided eye contact.

"Did you know about this?" Mamà asked.

Constanza swallowed. "Yes, for over a year now."

"I'll explain everything soon," Andreas said, "but please understand, I was only trying to protect myself and the people in this valley."

Papà shook his head and chuckled. "That explains your lack of disappointment about not receiving a dowry."

"I'm as ducatless as any peasant now. Any hope of an inheritance died when I became a believer."

Prospera tugged on Constanza's sleeve and whispered, "Is Monsen Andreas truly a prince?"

"Yes, he is." Constanza turned to the girl and smiled. "But you and any other girl whom God has adopted are daughters of a much greater ruler—the King of Kings. I suppose that makes you and me princesses too."

Constanza glanced back up to the men's conversation.

"Do not expect help from Turin," Basile said to Andreas. "The prince cannot risk open conflict with Lord Chanforan. The political situation is too *précaire*."

Papà straightened his stance. "When the Dominicans launched their crusade—"

"Those events were much different," Andreas said. "This is all about noble succession, and we're in the center of it. Gedeon Chanforan is on the side opposing Amadeus, and he's using his newfound power against us. These circumstances are often the most dangerous: one rogue lord can have his way with no one countering the rashness."

"It's graver than you realize," Basile said. "My sources tell me Gedeon Chanforan plans to erase the name *Vallense* from the earth, and violence is not beyond him. Despite how reasonable he may seem, the Lord of Luserna is ruthless and will not stop pursuing you until your religion is vanquished."

Andreas crossed his arms and shook his head. "Basile is right. We can't risk losing"—he looked at the orphans, then to Constanza—"them. The only way is over the mountain."

Constanza scanned the room. The youngest children scurried behind curtains, across the mats, and under the table, while the older children stood nearby listening. She looked to Andreas. "The children don't have warm coats."

"Have you tried to climb over the ridge in winter?" Papà asked Andreas. "I did once, and I'll never do it again. There must be another way."

Constanza clasped her hands and thought through all the nearby escape paths. West over the torrent would lead them toward Mount Vandalino, the most inhospitable route of all. North would take them deeper into the valley, but the mountains also rose higher there—even in the summer months, trekking over the northern passes was difficult. The trails eastward above the terraces were the simplest, but they'd never traversed that route in the winter.

"The eastern path is our only option," Constanza said. "With pleasant weather and enough provision, we'll reach safer lands by nightfall tomorrow."

"Are you sure?" Andreas asked in a barely audible whisper.

The children were strong, and if not, they would learn. Constanza gave a single quick nod to Andreas.

"Children, all of you, listen," Andreas said. "Gather your warmest clothes and blankets. We're going on an adventure beyond the fourth terrace and over the ridge."

Constanza held her breath as Andreas finished. She was supposed to help one of the new Piedmontese converts mend blankets that morning, but now she would hike over the mountain ridge. They wouldn't stay there for more than a few weeks, would they?

The household became a flurry. While Mamà gathered provisions to last a few days, Estève grabbed the flint and iron. Papà and Andreas packed the bags, then discussed the safest route over the ridge. Constanza packed a pot for cooking, a bucket for water, and some writing instruments—just in case.

She stuffed a blanket into a sack. Then another. They would need to carry enough for everyone. And if one fell in the snow, it would be useless. She hustled into the room where the children slept and froze as she stared at the mounting pile of blankets. *We can't take twelve children over a mountain in the middle of winter. If we don't freeze first, Gedeon will find us, take the orphans, and punish any who have harbored them.*

Constanza ran to Andreas, tears pooling in her eyes. "We can't do this, not without more help, not over the mountain—"

Under his arm, Andreas held the pouch containing the Greek manuscript. "We will do what we must in order to protect the children, whether over a mountain or through a swamp. We won't let Gedeon take them."

Constanza sniffled but held back her cries. "I'm afraid, Andreas."

"Your parents are coming with us, and far more than that, we have our heavenly Father. Gedeon is only a man, and he can't defeat the God of the universe, no matter how strong he may seem." He took a step toward her. His gaze was steady and his tone confident. "You will always have my protection, and I will not allow any harm to come to you. T'aimi, Constanza Pavarin."

She parted her lips and took deep breaths. "*T'aimi tanben*, Andreas."

As Andreas went to gather supplies, Constanza stuffed the last few items into a sack and grabbed an armful of blankets. When she opened her crate, the new wool coat she had been making for Andreas sat on top. She ran her hands over the front and sleeves and felt the unfinished fringes. Her smile crept upward as she called for Andreas.

He arrived in a hurry.

"I made this for you." Constanza handed the new coat to Andreas. "I still need to finish the cuffs and tails, but it will keep you warm today."

Andreas widened his eyes and smirked. "Was my old one so bad?"

"I already used it to stuff a bed mat."

Andreas unfolded the coat, held it up, and shook his head. "You could've used the wool for the children."

She gave Andreas a half grin. "I wanted to make it for you."

Basile's voice boomed through the house. "Silence, everyone. The forest out front is moving, so you'll need to leave through the back."

"What about you?" Andreas asked.

"Leave now and don't worry about me. Take the children, take the manuscript, and flee as fast as you can away from this land."

Andreas formed the children into a line at the back door and counted. "Ten . . . eleven . . . twelve, plus Monsen Nicolaus, Madòna Armanda, Monsen Estève, and"—he winked at Constanza—"you. Everyone is here."

Before they departed, Estève prayed for protection. Constanza peeked partway through and smiled. Even Basile bowed his head while keeping a watch out the window. Constanza's throat tightened, but she straightened her posture and held up her chin. She had to be strong for the children and, most of all, for Andreas.

*   *   *

Papà opened the back door of the house and held it until everyone passed. Wet, fluffy snowflakes stuck to Constanza's cheeks. Instead of a chill, they brought warmth to her heart. As long as the snowfall continued, their tracks up the mountain would be invisible.

Before Papà shut the door, Basile called from inside. "Whoever is out there is watching the house, but they haven't stepped out of the forest yet."

"The path along the creek is beyond their view," Papà said to Andreas. "If we take it instead of winding up the terraces, they won't spot us."

"I'll scout the path ahead." Andreas turned his attention to the children and slung a pack over his shoulder. "No noises, no talking, no whistles, and move as quiet as a bunny. Soon we'll be safe, but until we tell you, say nothing."

Silvia, her mouth fastened shut, gave a nod and grabbed Ave's and Zama's hands. The older boys, with faces as firm as old mountaineers, stood straight and ready, yet their eyes provided a window that revealed their fear and uncertainty.

Constanza wanted to shed tears, to let her hands tremble, to glance skittishly up the hillside, but no, she must remain steady.

Papà led the way to the trail, and soon they trudged up the steep path along the frozen creek while Andreas surveyed far ahead.

The higher they climbed, the more the snowflakes intensified until all was as white as a swan. Constanza's legs ached as she plodded upward. Her footprints became deeper, and some children walked nearly to their knees in snow. Estève struggled most of all, so Papà walked alongside and offered a hand during the steepest ascents. The children coughed and shielded their eyes from the constant stream of icy wind, but somehow, they remained calm and followed silently.

They were finally near the high pastures but still less than halfway up the mountain. No one voiced it, but they couldn't continue much longer. On a day of sunshine and calm air, they could have persevered, but not today.

Up ahead, from the frozen wasteland, a white shadow appeared. At first it blended into its surroundings, but then specks of brown hair stood out, then boots, then an ice-covered new coat. Andreas shook the snow from his head and rubbed his hands together.

"The path ahead is too treacherous, to the point where I couldn't take another step. The snowdrifts are as high as my shoulder, and the wind blows harder. Our only choice is to turn back."

"We can't." Constanza motioned to the children but turned her face so they wouldn't hear. "Those soldiers will find us."

"Andreas is right," Papà said. "Death would follow us if we continued. We're far from the top, and we still must descend the eastern slope."

Estève sat with his arms wrapped around his torso. He would never admit it, and he would struggle forward if they needed to, but it would be cruel to keep dragging him onward.

"We can decide our next steps once we escape this weather." Andreas waved everyone back down the path.

They stepped from footprint to footprint back down the ridge. Soon the wind calmed and the snow became only flurries.

Again Andreas scouted the path, and when they neared the farm, he returned with a smile. "Everything is normal at the farm. I saw no signs of danger there, but we still can't go back. Not with me, the children, and the manuscript."

Mamà waved to the children and led them away from the discussion. They didn't need to hear all the adults would talk about.

Papà stared through the trees and wiped the melting snow from his brow. "Maybe we could all remain at the farm except Andreas and the children. Lord Chanforan wants them, not us. We would only slow your escape."

"That may be the wisest choice," Andreas said, "though I'm unsure I can watch all twelve by myself."

Constanza looked at Andreas. His hair and beard were wet, his hands were red and puffy, but still he stood strong and steadfast. Even if they faced all of Satan's legions, she would stand with this man and the children.

"My place is beside Andreas. Besides, who will wash all their clothes and prepare their dinner?" She grinned. "Surely not him."

"We may be gone for months, though," Andreas said. "Until the situation here is calm, we can't risk the children being in the open."

Constanza raised her brows. "The cave, Andreas. We should go to the cave."

"What cave?"

"The one across the creek from your farm, but I suppose I've never mentioned it to you."

"A cave? I could camp outside for a few nights in the winter, but the children . . . and you?"

"It's warmer there than you might guess," Papà said. "It may be damp, and you'll hear bats through the night—"

"Any cave is better than facing Gedeon," Estève said, "no matter how damp."

Andreas paused for a moment and looked over the children. "Then that's where we'll go."

Constanza called for the children and gathered them in a circle. She widened her eyes and tried to make the decision as appealing as possible. "Tonight we're going to spend the night in a cave—"

Fosca gasped. "I've never been in a cave, and I don't wish to—they're dark, and evil spirits live there."

Constanza closed her eyes and shook her head. In her youth, she had heard the same tales and had probably added her own myths. Passed down from one generation of children to the next, the legends of the Vallense youth only grew more absurd. "There are no evil spirits in caves. We'll all be together—"

"But Monsen Estève, Mamà, and I will stay here," Papà said. "We must watch over the farm and lead the soldiers away from your trail—if they come."

"Andreas and Constanza will be with you, though," Mamà said. "You have nothing to fear, and soon we'll all be together again."

"When will the Grimaldis return?" Silvia asked.

Constanza's heart sank. They had to tell them, but when? Why frighten them while they had to flee to a dark cave? Perhaps another day.

"The supplies we packed should last a few days, but we'll bring more tonight or tomorrow," Papà said. "Bread, eggs, meat, firewood. You'll have plenty."

Hugs, tears, and prayers accompanied their departure, and soon Andreas and Constanza walked with twelve orphans down the hillside.

*   *   *

A deer fed among twigs and branches on the hillside to the right. It raised its head to watch the spectacle of fourteen people winding along the hidden trail. Except for the light padding of feet on fresh snow, all was silent. Even the wind was still.

Constanza led the way, followed by the youngest children first and the older ones last. Andreas took up the rear and watched for stragglers or any spying eyes along the old route leading downhill around boulders, ravines, and ancient trees. They couldn't risk anyone seeing them, not even a Vallense. If their enemies discovered the hiding place, they would have no chance of escape.

Constanza lifted the edges of her skirts to keep them from snagging on the undergrowth. Walking down the mountainside was a slow process, more so with the orphans. The children stepped through the snow, over rocks, and around exposed roots. Silvia held little Ave's hand and guided her forward, while Ezio tagged alongside Andreas and tried to match his every step.

Did Andreas realize how much the boys admired him? He was strong, and of course handsome, but it went much deeper than that. The children knew they were in danger, and whether or not they voiced it, Andreas was their rock. Though uncertainty swirled in the chilly air, he maintained his steadiness and fortitude. Was it possible for Constanza to adore him more than at that moment?

Soon they crossed another trail—right would lead them deeper into the Angrogna Valley toward Pradeltorno, and left bent toward the old Lauras farm. But the path also continued straight ahead, though only an eye familiar with the surroundings could have seen it. Constanza stopped and listened while the rest caught up and gathered around her. Andreas stepped by her side and peered in both directions.

"Are we almost there?" he asked in a hushed tone.

"It's a short walk downhill from here, but the path is treacherous. The children should hold hands when we descend."

Far above, on a rocky outcrop, a great bird called out. Its wings unfurled to display a beauty only the Creator could have designed. Golden brown feathers glowed in the morning light, and its white tail feathers reflected the hues of the snow. The eagle leaped from the rock, flapped its wings, and gained height until it soared high above the trees.

"Majestic," Andreas said. "We would often spot them at Sacra di San Michele. They seem both vulnerable and fearless at the same time."

"If only we had wings to fly wherever we wished." Constanza drew her attention back to the trail. "It looks as if we're safe to descend. I've seen no one since we left the farm."

They instructed the children to gather, then crossed the path and found the switchback trail down the mountainside. The trail took a sharp turn and dipped beside a rock wall that rose on the left. At what appeared to be the trail's end, they made a hard right and walked at the base of another massive cliff. Three more times they made turns, all while keeping a free hand on the rocks to avoid rolling down the hillside.

Constanza rounded the towering cliff and made the last turn, but instead of bending right as a switchback would have, the trail curved left into the hillside and opened into a clearing covered with flat, mossy rocks and dead leaves. A few paces ahead, massive boulders taller than any house lay piled on top of one another in a pattern untouched since the formation of the world. The cliff angled over them and formed a narrow canopy.

"I don't see a cave here," Fosca whispered.

Constanza pointed to the lower boulders. "In there. When I was a girl, Madomaisèla Elionor and I would come here and pretend to be Deborah the prophetess." A lump formed in her throat. In many ways, she and Elionor were those same two ten-year-old girls, but their lives seemed to have taken diverging trails. How she longed for the simplicity of those long-ago summer afternoons.

Fosca asked, "Must we sleep outside, though?"

"It will be cold, but with a fire, we'll be comfortable enough. Besides, the cave will be warmer than the open air and shield us from the wind."

Andreas cleared his throat. "Estève had the flint and iron and I forgot to grab it from him."

Fosca's shoulders dropped. "No fire, then?"

"We can try sticks," Constanza said. "I've never been successful, but I've seen Papà start a fire that way."

"Is there no flint among all these rocks?" Andreas asked.

"Not here. When the market was open, we would buy ours from traders."

"I suppose I could try rubbing sticks together." Andreas turned to three boys—Ezio, Roberto, and Umile. "Find the driest sticks, but stay within sight of the cave. Keep silent too."

After they nodded and scurried off, Constanza pointed her nose at the lower boulders. "We should see what the cave offers us this afternoon."

The orphans and Andreas followed Constanza upward, stepping from rock to rock until they stood before the dark opening. Even Zama, the shortest of the orphans, stood taller than the entrance. It was smaller than Constanza remembered, but then again, she hadn't wandered down to the cave in years.

Andreas weaved through the children until he stood next to Constanza. "I'll go first."

"Good. If any bears are sleeping inside, they'll chase you first." She flashed a grin at Andreas, but he maintained his straight face.

"A torch would be helpful if I had thought to bring one. At least I remembered the Bible." Andreas set his pack on the ground, knelt to all fours, took one more look back, and crawled through the opening. His voice soon echoed from inside. "This cave is enormous."

"Any bears?" Constanza looked at Fosca. "Or evil spirits?"

"Not even a bat," Andreas said. "It's safe to bring the children."

Guido was the first to crawl through, followed by the rest of the boys and a few girls. Fosca and Irene, however, stood behind Constanza.

"Can you go first?" Irene asked Fosca, who then glanced up at Constanza.

"You have nothing to fear. Andreas is in there, and he'll keep us safe."

Irene reached for Constanza's hand. "I want you to go with me."

Constanza grinned, shook her head, then stooped over and crawled through the opening, followed closely by the two girls.

The entrance unfolded into a soaring cavern—narrow at its breadth, yet deep and lofty. The sun streamed through fissures in the high ceiling, letting in just enough light to welcome them into the grotto. The children shouted and listened to their voices bounce off the rock.

Constanza reached for the nearest child. "Silence. We mustn't shout in case someone hears us."

Few heard her, and the echoing shouts increased.

A whistle bounced off the walls. All eyes locked on Andreas, who stood on a rock, awaiting everyone's attention. In a hushed voice, he said, "After the danger passes, we'll take all of you back here to explore, but until then, we can't speak with loud voices. If our enemies hear us—"

"Who are our enemies?" Silvia asked. "Why do they care about us?"

Constanza answered. "The Lord of Luserna is a cruel man who hates Vallenses."

"We're not Vallenses," Guido said. "All of us orphans are Piedmontese."

"Then neither am I a Vallense," Andreas said. "The only one among us born in these mountains is Madomaisèla Constanza. But it's not our blood or birthplace Lord Chanforan hates, it's our belief in God and His Word."

"The Lord of Luserna was once one of us," Constanza said. "He sat under wise teachers, memorized the Holy Scriptures, and attended church gatherings. But he saw evil men, including his own father, abuse their positions and shame the name of Christ. They scarred him, and Lord Chanforan has since blamed his past troubles on all Vallenses."

"We didn't do anything to him," Silvia said.

"Perhaps that's the saddest part," Andreas said. "Lord Chanforan shows a cloak of heroism and strength, but underneath it he wears tragedy and heartache. Men like him often turn to the most villainous acts. For what reason? I've tried to understand but haven't found an answer other than man's sinful state."

Sounds of cackling boys filtered into the cave. Andreas walked in that direction and hushed the three.

"We found what you asked for." Ezio held out an armful of twigs and other forest growth.

Andreas glanced at Constanza and gave a hesitant smile. "Time to try starting this fire."

All the boys and a few girls huddled around Andreas while he rubbed the sticks together, blew air into the kindling, and did the same again. He answered their every curiosity with a smile and a genuine answer.

Constanza relaxed her muscles, sat on a smooth rock, and watched. Yes, she would have welcomed a hearth, roof, and warm bread, but God had placed them in a shelter He had formed in ages past. What better place to be than here with Andreas and the children?

40

But because these original tongues are not known to all the people of God, who have a right unto, and interest in the Scriptures, and are commanded in the fear of God to read and search them, therefore they are to be translated into the vulgar language of every nation unto which they come, that the Word of God dwelling plentifully in all, they may worship him in an acceptable manner, and through patience and comfort of the Scriptures may have hope.

—London Baptist Confession of Faith, 1689

ANDREAS STIRRED IN THE PREDAWN DARKNESS. The embers from the night's fire had dimmed, making it hard to distinguish rock from the thirteen people sleeping on the cave floor. Beside him, hidden in the pack, was the Greek manuscript. Would he have an opportunity to put it to use?

Andreas, Constanza, and the orphans had spent four nights shivering, tossing, and turning. Constanza had split the rest of the bread into hand-size portions in the morning, but everyone had lain down that night with hunger pangs.

Where were the promised provisions? Since they arrived at the hiding place, no one had come and no one had left. Nicolaus Pavarin had promised to come, but something must have happened. He wouldn't have forsaken his daughter and the orphans.

The previous evening, Andreas and Constanza had chosen to seek help. They couldn't survive without food and more blankets—a flint stone would also be convenient. While Constanza stayed with the children and the Bible, Andreas would rise before the sun, find the path along the creek, and walk to the Pavarin farm for supplies.

Andreas sat up and ran his hand across his cheek. Four days without trimming made for a scruffy appearance and a bit of scratching. He stood and stretched, peering across the floor where the children slept, but their breathing was the only sign they were there. Somewhere in the tarry darkness, likely snuggled up with a few little girls, slept Constanza. The thought of leaving her alone with the children made him tense, but they needed supplies. And though Constanza knew the forests better than Andreas, he wouldn't risk her life—not when Gedeon's men likely prowled the area.

A boy stirred at his feet. Ezio.

Andreas stretched out his hand and felt for anything hard, but found only air. He took a step forward, keeping his foot low to avoid disturbing anyone, and this time his fingers touched the smooth cavern wall. He felt his way along it until he came to the small opening that led outside. Turning one last time, he envisioned everyone strewn across the floor. *God, please protect them.*

Andreas ducked and crawled through the hole and into the wild alpine woodlands. Eerie twilight revealed a fresh layer of snow coating the ground. Nothing moved, not even the wind. Far above, an owl hooted, and to the right, the distant howling of wolves came in waves. Andreas let out a long breath, stepped into the hollow, and made his way toward the switchback trail.

He walked on the edge of the trail and made the most inconspicuous steps his feet would allow, for a line of footprints would attract curious eyes. When the switchback ended, Andreas turned right onto the main trail and crossed the creek.

A smoke trail rose over the trees. *My old house.* While Andreas, Constanza, and the orphans slept in a freezing cave, the Piedmontese slept in comfort. But God had chosen their circumstances—He had ordained both the cave's inhabitants and the house's. How was Amalia, the young mother Constanza had befriended? Did her husband tolerate her new beliefs, or had he tossed her into the snowdrifts? And how were the other converts faring? Perhaps Gedeon had discovered their newfound faith and threatened them as well.

The black sky turned gray as the sun rose behind the clouds. Andreas turned left and walked up the creek path toward the Pavarin farm, passing through the same place where the Dominicans had abducted Constanza two summers before. Never again would Andreas let anyone harm her.

He continued up the trail to the edge of the forest, where the Pavarins' chimney billowed thick smoke—a pleasant sign amid the uncertainty. A trace of roasted lamb drifted into his nostrils—

No, something was wrong. All the Pavarin livestock had been stolen, so there was no meat to roast.

Andreas slid behind a tree and faced the opposite direction. *I need to find them, and I need to get food for the orphans, but I can't risk soldiers discovering me or my tracks.*

He ducked low and moved from tree to tree, maneuvering until he could see the door. He knelt behind a briar and peered through the branches toward the barn. One . . . two . . . three . . . twelve horses, all muscular, clean, and well-fed. They were tied to a fence and neighed when Andreas transferred his weight to the other knee. *They know I'm here.*

He scanned the barn for any sign of their riders but saw nothing until the door burst open. Two men strode out, each wearing a crimson cloak emblazoned with a square white cross. The regalia was similar to the House of Savoy's, but a trained eye knew the difference. While Savoy's white cross was rectangular and reached the sides of the uniform, the Swiss cross was square and centered.

Swiss mercenaries owed their allegiance to whoever hired them. Men who opposed them—horsemen most of all—cowered at their long pikes and poise in battle. How had Gedeon afforded such a force?

The soldiers laughed as they gnawed meat off mutton bones. They must have stolen a sheep from another farm. Where were Nicolaus, Armanda, and Estève? Had the soldiers captured them and taken them away? No, they would have fled to David's or Francesco's farm.

Andreas's pulse quickened. The Pavarin sons' farms were just across the creek, but would he find the same situation there? He let out a dejected sigh. He needed to find food.

Another soldier left the house and strolled to the horses. He ran his hands through a horse's mane, touched its nose, then said something foreign. Though Andreas had grown up near Swiss lands, he had never learned their coarse Germanic language.

All three soldiers went inside but soon returned holding pikes.

Andreas ducked lower while the pikemen walked closer. If he stayed, they would discover him. He crawled backward until he found a massive oak. He slid behind it, and when the soldiers passed by, he slowly breathed out and waited for them to step inside.

The German voices became distant mumbles until the door slammed shut. Andreas listened for a few more moments, then crept from tree to tree toward the other Pavarin farms, his heart galloping.

The door of the house burst open, and the yelps of two hound dogs barreled toward him. Andreas froze. His breath quickened and his hands shook.

Paws scampered over the forest floor, sending dead leaves flying. Andreas peeked from around the tree. Two dogs prowled, noses lifted. They were small and unthreatening except for their keen ability to track. But they would catch him if he didn't run.

Andreas braced against the tree, scanned for a clear path, and leaped from cover. The dogs could outrun him, but that wasn't their duty—their task was finished, and now the Swiss pikemen would chase the prey

Andreas scurried through the forest, unconcerned about leaving footprints in the snow. German voices called out from behind, but they grew farther away. He might not know the forest like Constanza, but at least he knew it better than the soldiers.

By the time he crossed the creek, the barking had ceased. He collapsed near a rock outcrop and tried to muffle the coughs from his exhausted lungs, which still felt weak from nine days in the Stinche Prison.

He had escaped, but to what end? Had Gedeon unleashed his fury on the entire valley?

*   *   *

Muffled voices drifted from Francesco Pavarin's house as Andreas crouched under a window. The words brought a sigh of relief—all Romaunt and no harsh German. Still, he had to be sure. The soldiers could easily track him once they found his prints on the other side of the creek, and he couldn't risk leading them here.

Andreas scanned the tree line to the southeast and listened. To the left stood the old lean-to with a pair of sheep nestled underneath it. The lean-to brought warmth to his heart and a smile to his face, for there he had read from Raimond's pocket-sized Bible, and through it, God's Spirit had shown him the way of salvation. From that moment, God had transformed Andreas into a new man—the man who now sat under the eaves and remembered that rainy summer evening.

Estève Malan's smooth voice floated into Andreas's ears. He was inside the house. *Thank You, Lord.*

Andreas rose but kept his attention on the forest. He walked around the corner and knocked on the door.

Francesco Pavarin answered. "Brother! You're safe"—he peered toward the tree line—"but you're in danger. Come inside."

Andreas ducked through the door and found Nicolaus with one of his grandchildren on his lap, while Estève had a quill in hand, writing on a sheet of parchment.

"Constanza and the children—are they safe?" Nicolaus asked.

"Yes, but we've eaten nothing since yesterday."

"We're no better here," Francesco said. "The soldiers took all Papà's grain. Yours too. It's gone."

"They took our farm the day you went to the cave." Nicolaus took the child off his lap and approached Andreas. "I hear soldiers are housed there now."

Andreas nodded. "I saw them just now, and they chased me across the creek."

"They want you more than anything, Andreas. As soon as the soldiers arrived, they asked about you and the Greek Bible."

"The orphans?"

"Yes, them too," Nicolaus said. "After the soldiers took the grain, they demanded we bring them the children."

"We told them you escaped over the northern passes." Estève glanced up from his parchment. "As far as they're concerned, you're far from here."

"Are you sure they believed you?" Andreas asked.

"No, but in time, they'll stop searching," Nicolaus said.

Armanda entered the room with Francesco's wife, Martha. Nicolaus looked at them and said, "Gather all the food we can spare and pack it for Andreas, Connie, and the children."

"Is everyone—"

"All are well," Andreas said. "A little cold, which reminds me—may I take a flint and iron?" He showed them his raw palms.

"Please tell me," Armanda said, "how are the children?"

"By God's grace, we're all healthy, but we soon hope to be somewhere comfortable again."

Armanda took a deep breath and tightened her lips. She and Martha went to work gathering bread, cheese, and dried meat.

"We've tried to bring supplies," Nicolaus said, "but we can't leave the farm without soldiers seeing us. They prowl the path along the creek, they're always at the crossroads, and they forbade us from gathering in the church meetinghouse."

"Have you heard from the Piedmontese? How are they reacting?"

"I don't know." Nicolaus shrugged. "Lord Chanforan has forbidden us from speaking to them. My guess is he's learned about your dealings with them and wants it stopped." He found a chair and motioned for Andreas to do the same. "Come, we should talk."

"I've already left Constanza and the children for too long," Andreas said. "I need to hurry back as soon as the supplies are ready."

"You can't go back there now," Francesco said. "If the soldiers discover you're nearby, they'll hunt you as if you're a mad wolf."

Andreas shook his head. "I can't leave them alone without food. I saw no soldiers on this side of the creek."

"You'll see them once they discover your trail."

"Which is why I must hurry. We trekked downhill from here to the cave with the orphans, and I intend to take the same path back."

Armanda placed two sacks in Andreas's hands. "Enough for a few days. We packed some extra blankets too." She embraced Andreas and whispered, "You are a good man."

Nicolaus crossed his arms and glanced up at Andreas. "I know I once advised the opposite, but tomorrow morning, take everyone and leave the valley. The mountain passes are less dangerous than Lord Chanforan and his men, and the weather is looking more hospitable. Find somewhere far from here and wait until we send word it's safe to return."

Andreas opened his mouth and froze. What if another storm blew in? Where would they flee? Who would shelter twelve orphans, a fugitive, and a young woman? But if they escaped, they and the precious manuscript would be free of Lord Chanforan.

"I'll speak to Constanza and the children about it when I return."

"If you choose to leave," Nicolaus said, "you would be making a wise decision. But don't delay. Every moment you stay in that cave risks someone seeing you. One hound's nose, one curious soldier, or one Catholic man eager to please his lord could put you in a trap you can't escape."

Andreas nodded. He could risk his own safety, but not Constanza's and the children's. With God's help, they could make it over the mountain, and somewhere they would find Vallenses to house them.

Andreas slumped his shoulders and sighed. After all the recent victories, they would need to retreat. But hadn't mighty men such as Moses, David, Samson, the apostle Paul, and even Christ done the same? To escape was not defeat; it was only a bend on the trail. But what about the new believers they would leave behind? Who would continue the ministry when Andreas and Constanza were gone?

Andreas slung the sack of bread over his shoulder. The ministry didn't belong to him or Constanza—it belonged to the Holy Spirit. God would accomplish His will with or without them.

After saying his adieus, Andreas opened the door, and a gust of snow whipped his cheeks and battered his eyes. *Lord, please calm the storm so we can leave.*

But at least the snow would cover his steps back to the cave. Andreas scanned the landscape as he descended the same path from four days earlier, but the only sign of life was a pair of squirrels chasing each other through the tree branches. He soon came to the switchback trail to the cave and wound his way through the cliffs and boulders.

As he approached the entrance, a little light flickered from inside the cave. Faint laughter of children bounced off the rocks. Andreas let his head fall back in relief.

Then the sun burst through the clouds, and the snow stopped falling. He glanced back. An icy shiver raced down his spine. His own footprints led down the trail he had taken.

41

Behold the kings of the Earth how they oppress
Thy chosen, to what highth thir pow'r unjust
They have exalted, and behind them cast
All fear of thee, arise and vindicate
Thy Glory, free thy people from thir yoke.

—John Milton
Paradise Regained, 1671

HEAT RADIATED FROM THE HEARTH and warmed the back of Gedeon's padded chair. Johan sat to the right, cupping his chin in his hand as his elbow rested on the chair.

The Swiss captain stood before Gedeon, straight as a pillar. "We followed the fugitive's tracks to a garden of boulders. They led into a cave."

"How do you know it was the fugitive?" Gedeon asked.

"When we listened at the cave entrance, which is shorter than my knee, we heard muted voices. My lord, he is in there, hiding with all the orphans."

Gedeon squinted an eye. "Why did you not flush them out?"

"Because you commanded us to leave him and the children unharmed."

Gedeon stood and paced to the right with his chin bowed. "Are there any exits from this cave?"

"A pair of slits at the ceiling, but no man or child could fit through them."

"I know the cave," Johan said. "It's a short walk across the creek from my old home."

Gedeon, still pacing, nodded and glanced back at the soldier. "Did they know you were prodding around?"

"No, their speaking continued the entire time we investigated, but when we were near the entrance, I heard the man talk about leaving. They intend to escape over the mountains in the next few days . . . at least from what I could decipher from his Romaunt."

"Did you post a detachment nearby in the event they attempt to flee?"

"Yes, I posted two men to guard the path."

"We must act quickly." Gedeon spun on the ball of his foot and paced back toward the hearth. "We will extinguish the Vallense flame at the cave. The scribes, if they bother to mention Vallenses, will record tomorrow as the day of their demise." He flung up his hand. "Johan, I need you to gather the family heads of our Piedmontese friends. Tell them we will provide grain for the winter, and that we will distribute it at the cave. Their wives and children may come too if they wish."

"What's your plan?" Johan asked.

"All will witness the hypocrisy of these sectarians, and the Vallenses will not escape the trap we will set for them. And having the Piedmontese there to witness everything will bind them to our cause."

Gedeon stopped and focused on the mercenary. "Captain, have your men gather the confiscated grain and bring it to the cave. I need all your men there too. And bring kindling and enough dry wood to make a fire roar."

Johan jumped from his chair. "You can't burn Andreas . . . or Constanza . . . no one."

Gedeon smirked. "An inquisitor I am not. I don't burn heretics, I cause them to lose their faith. I sow seeds of despair and suspicion, then watch them sprout into doubt and rebellion against their God."

His own family would also watch the spectacle. Marta, Claudia, and Addo would at last see the Vallenses through his eyes. No longer would they sympathize with them or question his passion. They would realize a woman like Constanza wore virtue and honor as a disguise, but when exposed to the quandary of her own beliefs, she would react like any other human. The Vallense religion was a farce propagated by the barbes and their Bibles to control the mindless and insecure.

Johan gave Gedeon a sidelong glance. "So long as you don't harm anyone. I want to see their religion buried in the grave as much as you, but they're still people I know. They've always shown me kindness, Andreas and Constanza most of all."

"Except for all you've told me." Gedeon stood nose to nose with Johan until he could smell Johan's breath and feel the air pulsing from his nose. "Constanza's moralizing about every choice you make, her judgments about your lifestyle, her calling you lazy, her manipulating of your emotions. Then there is Andreas. Remember who he is and how he used you. He turned you against your beloved father, and when you defended your family and fought against the crusaders, he refused to participate. And did any of Nicolaus Pavarin's sons stand beside you in battle? No, they cowered. They made you and your father take up arms while they watched from their peaceful homes."

Johan pursed his lips and took a step back. "You swear you won't harm Andreas and Constanza?"

Gedeon rubbed the inside corners of his eyes. *I won't personally, but I employ men who might.* Nevertheless, he placed his hand over his heart. "I swear on my mother's pitiful soul."

"What do you want me to do about the families who claim to have converted?" Johan asked.

"They didn't convert. The Vallenses enticed the Piedmontese with their open hands. When we provide grain without judgment, they'll see my benevolence and recant whatever professions they made." Gedeon turned to the mercenary. "At first light, you will take me and my family to the cave."

The mercenary gave a quick bow. "At first light, my lord."

Gedeon's breath quickened. After all those like him had experienced, the Vallenses would pay for their deeds. But he had one more man to add to his plan—the one who would prove the Vallenses didn't believe what they preached. "Prepare our prisoner for the journey too. Bind his hands, tie him to a horse, and assign two of your best men to guard him on the road. He is a dangerous man."

Again the mercenary bowed.

"Johan, you will begin your journey earlier. Everyone must arrive at the same time."

"I will arrive with everyone," Johan said.

Gedeon peered at the pedestal beside the hearth, where the codex from Florence had lain . . . before Andreas stole it. Years before, Gedeon had vowed to never again allow religious books to contort his intellect and maim his soul. But long-forgotten memories still drummed against his soul. Once he had cherished the words in that old book. They had comforted him in the dark corners of his house as he listened to his father raging against his mother; they had lifted his mind toward heaven; they had told the stories of Noah, David, Nehemiah, and Daniel. Indeed, the words of Jesus once seemed both real and supernatural. Though the horrors at home had singed his conscience, he still felt as if God loved him.

But the world was cold and dark, and only by ambition, justice, and self-worth could a man manifest his life into something worthy of remembrance. Humility, meekness, and contentment—unnatural relics of a dying belief system.

Tomorrow, he would show Andreas, Constanza, and all other Vallenses the Bible's utter uselessness.

42

The aspect of this land, both terrible and sublime, which served as the asylum of truth when almost all the world lay in darkness—the recollection of the faithful martyrs of old—the deep caverns into which they retired to read the Bible in secret, and to worship the Father of Light in spirit and in truth—every thing tends to elevate my soul, and to inspire it with sentiments difficult to describe.

—Felix Neff
Ladoucette, 1825

CONSTANZA ROLLED ONTO HER BACK, let out a long sigh, and stared at the cave ceiling. It must have been the hundredth time. Between moments of dozing, she had passed the night turning, readjusting, and adding more fuel to the fire. Now all slept soundly except for her.

When dawn arrived, she and Andreas would gather the children and begin the journey over the eastern ridge. How long would they walk? How bitter would the wind be? Then there was the matter of finding someone who would give them shelter. She looked at the cave wall. *We're vagabonds now—wanderers without a home.*

Last summer, she had left the valley victorious and full of life. After years of waiting, she had pursued her dreams of service and Christian charity. Serving those in need hadn't been so glorious. It was work—grinding, daily labor, which may or may not have earned her a *mercé* from a needy eight-year-old. Yet that labor, the daily investment in the lives of others, was what mattered for eternity.

The fire crackled and popped nearby, bringing just enough light to perceive the difference between the children laying on the cave floor. Ave slept at Constanza's side, and Silvia lay beside her. Irene, Fosca, Alessia, Zama, and Prospera made up the rest of the girls. Beyond them, nestled under blankets on the other side of the fire, slept the boys: Ezio, Guido, Roberto, Bino, and Umile. Twelve young souls the Grimaldis had rescued from a life of rejection and destitution. If only she had a heart and arms as open as Luca and Vitòria.

Farthest from the fire and closest to the door, curled up without a blanket, lay the man who would soon be her husband. Dear Andreas, born a son of royalty, giving up his blanket so orphans could sleep in warmth. He had kept them safe and risked his life to bring them food, and now he would try to lead them over the mountain again. Nevertheless, he seemed to be dreaming in comfort.

Constanza propped her head up with her elbow and stared at the fire. She had tried praying herself to sleep, but the concerns of life shadowed her mind. She quoted from Paul's epistles and mouthed David's psalms, but still she lay awake. Her arms and neck ached from so many nights on the hard ground. She was thankful she lacked a looking glass for fear of her own reflection.

Still, the way Andreas looked at her made her heart flutter. Though he had seen her at her most vulnerable, he showed her the deepest admiration. God couldn't have brought a more honorable man to her. Had she ever dreamed of marrying a papist monk, or, for that matter, a prince? She closed her eyes and laughed on the inside but didn't reopen them.

Constanza's eyes snapped open at the sound of a wolf—or perhaps a dog—yapping outside the cave. She had fallen asleep. *Thank You, Lord.*

She stretched and yawned, but the air had grown cooler. She rose and walked to the log pile, grabbed an armful, and placed them on the fire. Soon it cast an orange glow on the cavern walls. She lay back down and covered herself with a blanket, but her eyelids refused to relax. Dawn had not yet come, and again, she stared at the ceiling. Thoughts flew through her mind in an endless stream—not worrisome or fearful, but expectant.

She had a quill, ink, and a few sheets of parchment in her sack. Sometimes on the coldest winter days, she would write her thoughts down in a song or prayer, but she had never shared them with anyone, not even Papà and Mamà. The fire provided enough light, so she pulled the instruments out, dipped the quill, and placed it on the paper.

The first line was often the hardest, and the quill refused to move. Constanza peered around the cave for inspiration and found only rocks—cold, gray, unwelcoming rocks. But couldn't she praise God for those rocks? And the hills? Even the creatures of the forest were worthy of thanksgiving. She moved the quill and formed the ink into letters, words, and lines.

> For the strength of the hills we praise You,
> Our God, our fathers' God!
> You have made Your children mighty
> By the touch of mountain sod.
> You have fixed our ark of refuge
> Where the spoiler's foot ne'er trod;
> For the strength of the hills we praise You,
> Our God, our fathers' God.

We are watchers of a beacon
Whose light must never die,
We are guardians of an altar
'Midst the silence of the sky;
The rocks yield founts of courage,
Struck forth as by Your rod;
For the strength of the hills we praise You,
Our God, our fathers' God.

For the dark resounding caverns,
Where Your still small voice is heard,
For the strong pines of the forests
That by Your breath are stirred,
For the storms on whose free pinions
Your Spirit walks abroad;
For the strength of the hills we praise You,
Our God, our fathers' God.

The royal eagle darteth
On his quarry from the heights,
And the stag that knows no master,
Seeks there his wild delights;
But we for Your communion,
Have sought the mountain sod;
For the strength of the hills we praise You,
Our God, our fathers' God.

For the shadow of Your presence
Round our camp of rock outspread,
For the wheat and for the harvest
That bestows our daily bread;
For the snows and for the torrents,
For the free hearts' burial sod;
For the strength of the hills we praise You,
Our God, our fathers' God.

A stirring on the opposite side of the cave made Constanza lift her eyes from the parchment. How long had she been writing? Andreas sat and rubbed his eyes before standing. He gazed at everyone asleep on the cavern floor, then closed his eyes and leaned against the wall in what looked like a praying posture. Had he noticed her?

Constanza took one last look at the parchment and laid it aside. Though her muscles were sore and her mind was exhausted, God had blanketed her with heavenly confidence and security. The trail up the mountain would be long, and the day longer, but with Andreas, the children, and her Savior, she would both endure and thrive.

"Bonjorn, boys," Andreas said. "The sun is rising, and the road is long."

Constanza roused the girls, and before long, everyone was bundling their few items together for the journey. She yawned near the cave's back corner, ten or more paces from where the children were.

Andreas approached her. "Did you not rest well?"

She squinted an eye and showed a half grin. "Is my lack of sleep so obvious?"

"Euh . . . no, I saw you awake early by the fire."

"I was trying to sleep but couldn't."

"Was it too cold? I would've asked one of the boys to—"

"No, I feel better now. I wrote—" She caught herself and cast her eyes to the side.

"Is that it?" Andreas nodded toward the parchment.

Constanza stepped in front of it. "It's nothing that matters, only something to occupy my mind."

"May I—"

"Not right now. I was tired, and it would seem muddled and senseless to you. Perhaps someday I'll let you read it."

Andreas shrugged. He gave a few commands to the children, then turned back to her. "We'll be in a safe place soon."

"I'm afraid for my family," Constanza said. "Where will they flee if Gedeon takes Francesco's farm too?"

"Your papà is both smart and godly. He'll know what to do."

Constanza nodded and smiled at Andreas. "Like my future husband."

Andreas looked away for a moment and shook his head. "I'm more uncertain than I look. I try to show confidence around the children . . . and you, but I've faced nothing like this." He took a step closer to Constanza, eyed the children, and whispered, "A few days ago, I imagined I was protecting the orphans by obligation. I thought long about it, but . . . I love them. Perhaps when our circumstances level out, we could—"

"You want the children to stay with us—me and you." She stared beyond Andreas, curious but not stunned.

"Am I absolutely mad for thinking about it?"

Constanza wet her lips and swallowed. She had thought the same as Andreas but had thrown the idea aside, assuming he would think her folet—crazed. She cared for the children too, but to be their mother? She wasn't a mother. One day she and Andreas might have their own children, and yes, they would call her Mamà, but was she ready for so many at once?

Mamà and Papà were too old to manage twelve by themselves. Perhaps she and Andreas could take one or two. But how could they split the children? She could say, "Let's pray about it," or "If God tells us." But why reason themselves into or out of a decision they knew was right?

Constanza leaned close to Andreas and made sure she was turned away from the children. "You suggest we marry and adopt twelve children all at once?"

"Yes." Andreas bit his lip and smiled. "I am mad, aren't I?"

Constanza smiled back. "I suppose I am too."

A light sprang from Andreas's eyes. "You're the only woman in the world who would do such a thing."

"As I said once, I'm mad."

"We should wait to tell the children, at least until we have a place to live. And of course, we have to be married too."

Constanza nodded. "Those in the direst circumstances take the boldest actions."

"Perhaps a better way to say that is: virtue is born from necessity."

Silvia walked up and stood next to Constanza. "Everything is packed."

"Except this." Andreas picked up the pack containing the manuscript. "Now we're ready."

Constanza held out the coat she had made for him. "You nearly forgot."

Andreas snatched it with a smile, put his arms into the sleeves, and nodded. He waved them forward, dropped to all fours, and crawled through the opening.

As Constanza followed him under the boulder, she recalled a phrase from her parchment. *The rocks yield founts of courage, struck forth as by Your rod.*

43

The history of the New Testament text is the history of a conflict between God and Satan.

—Edward Freer Hills
The King James Bible Defended, 1956

FLUFFY SNOWFLAKES FLOATED through the crisp air and fell on the rocks outside the cave. Once through the opening, Andreas stood, adjusted his pack, and gazed at the surroundings, where the snow had covered all the tree branches in a sparkling white powder.

A cluster of footprints had disturbed the snow partway down the hill. *Odd. No one left the cave yet this morning.*

Constanza crawled out behind him, followed by two girls.

A pair of dogs barked from up the hill. Andreas froze and motioned for the children to stop leaving the cave. The dogs likely belonged to a nearby farm, but it wasn't worth the risk.

"Go back inside," Andreas said to Irene and Ave.

A growl came from around a boulder to the left. A helmeted Swiss mercenary stepped out, then another.

Andreas darted his eyes to the trail. A group of mercenaries carrying torches appeared around the cliff. At their head strode Lord Gedeon Chanforan.

Andreas flinched and scanned the area. The first two men guarded the forested slope to the left, Gedeon's force stood straight ahead, sheer cliffs towered on the right, and behind him was the cave—with no exit.

His muscles tensed, but there was nowhere to run. They were snared like weasels.

Two more hounds growled behind Gedeon. He glared at Andreas and Constanza.

Andreas glanced over his shoulder to see Ave crawling back into the cavern. The children were safe for now but were still trapped inside.

"We can't run," Constanza whispered.

"Crawl back inside," Andreas said. "I'll talk to Gedeon."

"He'll chain you and send you to prison like the Grimaldis."

"No, he won't." Andreas raised his voice for Gedeon to hear. "He's afraid of what my father would do."

Gedeon chuckled and strolled forward, shaking his head. "Do you believe I'm here for you, Andreas? I hold no conflict with you or the House of Savoy unless you choose to block my path, for my feud is with the Vallenses."

"I am a Vallense." Andreas narrowed his eyes and raised his chin. "We are here as one family, and you won't take the children from us." The pack with the manuscript weighed on his shoulder.

"You are breaking the laws of the realm." Gedeon eyed Andreas's pack. "Nevertheless, I'm not here for the children either. I am here for a purpose that will continue far beyond my lifetime. One day I will die, but I want it said that Gedeon Chanforan unmasked the Vallense abuses and ended their festering from these valleys. I won't need a crusader army and inquisitors to vanquish you. I need only confront you with your own convictions."

Gedeon gave two quick waves toward the trail, and man after man carried full grain sacks and stacked them on the ground.

Andreas squinted at the growing stack. The bags had brown stripes around the bottoms. *That's my barley harvest.*

He glanced at Constanza and pointed her toward the cave again, but she kept her feet planted next to him.

Gedeon walked to the stack of grain sacks and stepped on one. "You thought you would defeat me by bribing my peasants with food, and I admit you are competent. But you know why they supposedly converted to your religion. It wasn't for their sin or supposed need for Christ. They didn't find new life or redemption. No, they responded because they wanted your grain and your labor and your experience. You thought you had outwitted me, and perhaps if I were a common man, you would have. But I know your ways all too well."

Again Gedeon waved toward the trail, and a stream of peasants filtered into the clearing. Their clothes were tattered, their faces dirty, and their expressions desperate. Andreas recognized some, including a few for whom he had built shelter.

Constanza gasped. "Amalia."

"See, I can also force conversions with bribes. Yet I won't require them to practice any religion. In fact"—he directed his voice to the peasants—"I will feed all of you through the winter with no stipulations. I apologize that I allowed the Vallenses to trick some of you into rejecting the Roman Church. But come, take all the grain you want and forsake the Vallense teachings."

No one moved—at first.

Then a scurry of men and women grabbed for the sacks. They carried them back toward the trail until Gedeon held up a hand.

"I have something else to show my faithful subjects _n case any still hold doubts about following the Vallense ways."

Gedeon motioned to the nearest soldiers, who rushed toward the cave entrance.

"Connie, crawl back inside!" Andreas shouted. He yanked the pack from his shoulder, pushed it into Constanza's hands, and stepped in front of her. "Go!"

Andreas widened his stance to block the soldiers' path and allow Constanza to crawl back through the entrance. *Please let her make it, God.*

A soldier lowered his shoulder and rammed into Andreas like an enraged bull, while the other jumped over them and lunged for Constanza.

The soldier pinned Andreas to the ground and punched him in the jaw. His head smashed into the ground.

He strained his neck to find Constanza, but her scream bounced off the cliffs. A soldier had her by the leg and was pulling her and the priceless manuscript from the cave.

Andreas grunted and struggled, but two massive hands had him pinned to the ground.

"*Ich beiße dir die finger ab,*" mumbled the soldier before he punched Andreas just below the eye.

The rocks spun in arcs at the corners of his vision.

* * *

Children wept with hollow cries of fear and uncertainty.

Andreas blinked, but sparks and blurs overwhelmed his vision. He tried to rub his eyes, but his hands wouldn't move. They were tied behind him.

"I can't see."

A single laugh broke out in front of him. "You've been blind since you let these people trick and conjure you."

A torrent of memories returned. The cave, the grain, Piedmontese, the manuscript.

He gasped. Constanza.

He was sitting on something cold. Rock. Ice crystals coated his eyelashes and hair. Andreas wiggled his hips, but nothing loosened.

Gedeon spoke in German, and hands latched onto Andreas's arms and yanked him upward. His head spun and his limbs buckled, but those viselike hands forced him straight.

With each blink, his surroundings became clearer. Amalia, the first convert. Other Piedmontese. He clenched his bound fists—Gedeon.

Behind him, muffled cries came from the cave. Where was Constanza?

He turned to the left. Only armored men.

But straight ahead, two figures faced him, kneeling a few paces apart from one another. He blinked the snow from his lashes. His chest heaved.

A dusting of snowflakes covered Constanza's chestnut hair. Her eyes glowed with defiance, but behind those embers was an ashy dread. She spoke, but a gag muffled her words into gibberish.

No! I promised to protect her.

Another figure knelt next to her. Basile Halphen, loyal servant of Princess Yolande. Basile's bald head was wet with sweat, and snow lingered there for less than a blink before dripping down his brow. A face seasoned with war, intrigue, loyalty, and servitude glanced at Andreas but remained expressionless.

"We found your French spy lurking about a few mornings ago, and though he fought with a tenacity few have seen, my men captured him." Gedeon walked in front of the prisoners and stood between them. "A friend of yours, no?"

Andreas glared at Gedeon but kept his mouth shut.

"Does your jaw still hurt? I suppose it does, but it will heal." Gedeon held his hands up and motioned toward the surrounding landscape. "All will heal. For too long, you have been allowed to pollute this land with your teachings, but today the Vallenses' demise begins." He turned to the crowd of Piedmontese gathered behind him. "Today you will witness one of many contradictions buried within these people's souls, and I will prove they do not believe what they preach."

Andreas scanned the crowd. So many familiar faces—men who had held a board while Andreas hammered a nail, women and children for whom he had built a house. At the edge of the crowd stood a group in much finer attire: Gedeon's wife, his son, his daughter, and—

He narrowed his eyes and stared at Johan Lauras, giving his head a little shake. How far that man had fallen. Johan had gone from furiously defending Vallenses to working for Gedeon Chanforan. What had dragged him to this depth?

Gedeon's voice rose above the whispers and chatter. "I have asked for what is due to me—many times. It was supposed to be a simple matter, but the Vallenses have betrayed my trust. They say they submit to the realm's authority, but they mock my steward and ignore my pleas. They say they love you but call you papists and trick you into joining their sect. Vallenses claim morality and virtue but commit sins no honorable man would dare mention."

Gedeon turned up his nose and focused on Andreas. His eyes pierced Andreas like a spear. "Hypocrites, every one of them. And what do Solomon's Proverbs tell us about hypocrites? Do you spiritual Vallenses know?"

Gedeon snapped his eyes to Constanza. "Surely you, the perfect, innocent Madomaisèla Constanza would know. Or does that not fit your beliefs? Did they never teach you those words from your Holy Scriptures? But I remember them. Far back in the darkest halls of my memory, I remember."

Andreas struggled against his captors and frowned at Gedeon. What point was he trying to make? It was no surprise Gedeon had grown up in the home of a preacher, because preaching was exactly what he was doing now.

"Since neither of you know, I'll quote it. 'An hypocrite with his mouth destroyeth his neighbour: but through knowledge shall the just be delivered.'" He lifted his voice to the crowd. "The Vallenses have tried to destroy you with their words. They want you to be estranged from your families. Just as they have for those poor orphans in the cave, they want your children filled with their poisonous teachings—indoctrinated beyond hope of repair. They want to destroy your intellect and pride, your conscience and agency. They hope to squash you"—he demonstrated with his hands—"to abolish your self-determination and replace it with mindless obedience and submission."

Gedeon paused, bowed his head, and lifted a hand. "But you can be delivered through knowledge. And that is my gift to you today—knowledge, awareness."

The air was still. Snowflakes continued their gentle descent while Gedeon paced in front of Constanza and Basile, leaving his footprints in the snow. Andreas squished his eyebrows together and waited until Gedeon faced him.

Gedeon flipped his hand up again and said something in German, and immediately the soldiers untied Andreas's hands. He wiped his eyes and brushed the snow from his hair.

"Today, Andreas of Savoy, I offer you what should be a simple choice." Gedeon held his hand out to Constanza and Basile. "These two are my prisoners, and as the Lord of Luserna, I maintain the right to do with them as I wish. Yet I will allow you to choose which criminal lives . . . and which one perishes by the sword."

Andreas's mouth fell open. He stared at Constanza and again struggled to escape from his bonds.

Marta Chanforan gasped and marched toward Gedeon. "Are you mad? She's a young woman and has shown us nothing but kindness."

Gedeon rolled his eyes. "Watch, and you'll understand. This is what I've been telling you about for years." He grabbed her cheeks and pinched them together, but not gently, then whispered in her ear and threw her aside.

Gedeon turned back to Andreas. "I already know what you're going to ask. 'Why Constanza? What crime has she committed?'"

"She has done nothing I haven't done myself." Andreas swallowed and bowed his head. "Take me instead."

Gedeon's chest heaved as he laughed. "You? No, that would be too easy. You are a son of nobility, which is why I am offering the choice to you." He stopped his pacing and held up a finger. "If you choose the woman, I will allow you, her, and the orphans to leave in peace. You may leave my realm and dwell somewhere safe. I also hold another item I will add to the offer." He waved Johan over, who carried the pouch to Gedeon and placed it in his hands. "Your precious codex on which you spent a fortune—enough to feed the peasants here for a century. It is yours if you choose the woman."

A warm hope pulsed through Andreas's veins. They could live—everyone—and gain the Bible too. Yes, they would have to live somewhere else, but it wouldn't be forever. Gedeon's power would eventually wane and they could return. Basile's death would be a tragedy, but what other choice did Andreas possess? He had promised Constanza that no harm would come to her, and he would hold to that.

He opened his mouth to speak, but Gedeon interrupted.

"Before you choose your beloved Constanza, let me remind you who this man is." Gedeon held his hand out toward Basile. "A Frenchman, a Catholic, and now I have discovered he is a spy." He directed his voice toward the crowd. "But the choice is not so easy as it may sound, for our friend Andreas also has a certain belief that will not allow him to let this man perish."

Gedeon pulled the gag from Basile's mouth but held it in his hand. "What is your religion?"

"Catholic."

"What do you think about Andreas's religion? Did he ever speak to you about it, or did he keep it to himself?"

Basile's eyes darted from the rocks to Gedeon then back. "*À quoi veux-tu en venir?* What are you getting at?"

Gedeon responded in French, but loud enough for all to hear. "*Éternité.*"

Andreas took a step back as his heartbeat quickened. He pressed his tongue into the top of his mouth.

"The Vallenses believe their way is the only way to know God, and without being converted to their religion, you are bound for an éternité in the torments of hell. They claim to love the souls of Catholics and all others they see as unbelievers. Yet if Andreas were to choose the woman, he would condemn the Frenchman to everlasting torture. The woman, however, is a believer. If she were to die this instant, her soul would be blissfully united with God in heaven."

A few stray flakes were all that remained of the snow shower, and the only sound in the clearing was Andreas's rushed breathing. He couldn't let Constanza die, but despite Gedeon's evil intentions, he was right about Basile. Andreas recalled the conversation with Basile at the Genoa wharf. He couldn't let Basile die without God's forgiveness, but neither could he let Constanza die.

"Do you see the anguish?" Gedeon asked the crowd. "Can you smell the conflict raging within him? Do you know why he is conflicted? It's because he doesn't believe what he preaches." He spat those last words out as if they were bile. "As disturbing as it sounds, if Andreas truly followed his religion, he would choose to let the criminal Frenchman live. He wouldn't send this man to hell. But look into his eyes. He doesn't believe that. His raw human emotion drives him to let the Frenchman die and thus save the woman he loves."

Andreas latched onto Constanza's eyes. Though her mouth was gagged, her alert gaze and resolute jaw told him what she wanted. It was nonsensical to someone like Gedeon, but to a believer, it was everything. Christ had given His life for her, and she would do the same for others.

But Andreas couldn't let her die, not when he had promised her otherwise, not when they could take the Bible and orphans and live in peace.

He sighed and focused on Basile next, but Basile's eyes were closed, and his head was bowed.

The Piedmontese, some with mouths hanging open and others with blank stares, watched the scene. Johan leaned against the cliff with his bow propped nearby. Marta, Claudia, and Addo all had tears in their eyes.

Andreas peered back to the cave and listened, but no sounds echoed out. A pile of logs as tall as a man had been stacked there since the soldier had punched him.

Dear God, I can't make this choice. I am at Your mercy—we are all at Your mercy.

"Would you abandon your life with Constanza for one old Frenchman? Would you let your Bible fall into the hands of infidels, all to let this man live his life of debauchery?" Gedeon shot his gaze directly at Andreas. "Or would you sacrifice a man's soul for the one you love?"

Andreas blinked and swallowed. Both Constanza and Basile grunted through their gags. What were they trying to tell him? Were they both willing to sacrifice their lives?

Sweat beaded in Andreas's palms. He couldn't make this choice. Gedeon was a shrewd man, so surely he would be willing to negotiate.

"What is it you want, Lord Chanforan?" Andreas spoke resolutely.

Gedeon tightened his lips and shook his head. "I want everyone to see you and weep. I want no one to suffer, but if it's necessary to free the naive from the snare of your beliefs, I am more than willing. No one should be forced to experience the misery I have."

Andreas narrowed his eyes as an idea entered his conscience. It might not save any lives, and it might infuriate Gedeon, but it was better than bowing to this evil man's whims. God was the judge of the earth, not Andreas, and certainly not the Lord of Luserna.

He pulled his shoulders back and raised his voice for all to hear. "You stand there, haughty and enlightened, imagining you're performing a noble deed for the world, yet you don't see the futility of your efforts. No, Gedeon Chanforan, I won't step into your trap, and I will not choose for you."

Gedeon burst into laughter. "You have no other choice than to appoint either the woman or the Frenchman to live."

"No, I refuse." Andreas's chest tightened. He would soon know if it was a foolish decision, but he couldn't let either die. Not by his choice.

Perhaps Savoyard soldiers would arrive at exactly the right moment, streaming down the path and throwing Gedeon and his mercenaries off the cliff—God's mighty arm of vengeance, wiping their oppressors from the earth. Andreas prayed for deliverance—for swords and shields, for a host of angels, for victory.

"You refuse?" Gedeon's voice grew louder. "Is it not simple to save the woman and be done with this?" He walked to Andreas and stood over him as his face tightened. "So it shall be. All will die—the woman, the orphans, the Frenchman . . . and you."

Gedeon spoke to the guards in German, and their grip tightened. Ropes fell on Andreas's hands, and gloved hands wrapped them around his wrists. Andreas grunted and struggled, but another soldier kicked him in the knee.

Pain radiated up to his chest and down to the heel of his foot. Tears fell from his eyes. The guards threw him to the ground, held his legs, and fastened them like his wrists.

Gedeon's voice growled through the struggle. "Your unwillingness to choose will make everyone suffer. You will burn, but you will not stand in the fire like a martyr. No, I will stuff your mouth with rags and hang you by your limbs like a hog. You will roast over the fire while the smoke from your flesh suffocates the orphans in the cave. Yes, I will throw your beloved Constanza in with them too."

Andreas shook his head to dispense of the tears and lurched to catch a glimpse of Constanza. Where was she? Where had they taken her?

"I know what you're thinking. 'The slits in cave ceiling will allow the smoke to escape.' Don't fret, though. My men have sealed the whole grotto."

Marta Chanforan screamed, but Gedeon shot a poisonous look at her. The guards dragged her around the corner of the cliff face.

"The children are innocent," Andreas said desperately. "Take my life. Leave them."

"Better for them to die young than suffer through Vallense abuses."

"Duke Louis will be enraged when he hears you killed his son." Andreas had to find something to deter Gedeon. "Marta and your children—they don't want you to do this either. You're being irrational—"

"Irrational? Look at yourself. You are willing to burn to avoid a decision. That, my prince, is irrational. I'm thrilled I didn't hire you back in Florence."

"And that would have been the worst decision of my life," Andreas said as the mercenaries lifted him off the ground.

"No, today you have made your worst decision." Gedeon smirked and motioned toward the cave.

The mercenaries tied Andreas's wrists and ankles to a pole, but his heart thudded through the silence. His limbs jolted when they dropped the pole onto the sticks suspending it above the stacked wood. Men stuffed rags into his mouth, taking what little moisture was left.

Faces passed through his vision—the Piedmontese, the Chanforans, Johan. Andreas closed his eyes, and his soul looked up into heaven. God might rescue them, or His will might be for them to die. But Andreas had condemned no one to their death, including himself. Gedeon Chanforan was the murderer.

A muffled scream came from the cave entrance, which was only a pace away from the pyre. Two soldiers forced Constanza through the opening and blocked it. Unless Gedeon showed mercy, smoke would soon suck the air from the cave and fill it with choking fumes.

Gedeon approached with Andreas's pouch in one hand and a torch in the other, wearing a grave smile. He would send Andreas up in flames while the innocents slowly died in the cave. But Gedeon would never be gratified. The empty chambers of his soul would only grow wider.

When Gedeon stood no more than ten paces away, he removed the manuscript and showed it to the crowd, then to Andreas. "What could be more fitting than to burn you with your vile book?"

Andreas squinted as Gedeon held the torch to the pages.

A small flame flickered near the back cover and quickly engulfed it. Gedeon still held the manuscript in his hand, rolling it around to avoid the heat. "You will die, your manuscript will die, your indoctrination will die." He tossed the manuscript under Andreas and scowled. "And your God will die."

The codex raged in flames, and one after another, the parchment pages curled and burned into glowing embers.

Gedeon kicked it toward the pyre, but none of the logs caught fire. Grimacing, he kicked it closer.

The stinging, dusty smell burned Andreas's nostrils. He braced himself for the coming heat.

Soon flames lapped at his back. His legs jerked, and his jaw clenched. He couldn't let himself and the Bible perish like this. Maybe he could break free, crawl to the cave, and spend his last moments with Constanza instead of being roasted on a pole. He opened his eyes and gathered his courage for one last, desperate surge of energy.

Andreas heaved and tossed with every muscle and tendon until one side of the pole rolled from its cradle.

His feet hit the ground first. The other end of the pole cracked, dropping Andreas directly onto the burning manuscript.

Flames launched upward from both sides of his coat, and then everything under him cooled. He rolled away from the pyre, and there lay a heap of ashes, but no flame. He brushed his bound arms across the coarse new wool. The coat had smothered the fire.

Gedeon narrowed his eyes, stepped toward Andreas, and called for the guards. "*Hilfe!*"

But a woman blocked his path.

It was Amalia, the peasant woman Constanza had seen converted. "You will not burn him," she said, staring up at Gedeon.

Gedeon chuckled and shoved her aside.

Amalia stumbled back, but now her husband stood with her.

Gedeon glowered at the couple. "After all I have done, you dare betray me?" He spat on the ground near their feet and shrugged. "So be it. Die with the rest of them."

Three more Piedmontese stepped between Gedeon and Andreas. Soon at least ten men and women surrounded Andreas.

"The Vallenses have bewitched you all," Gedeon said. "Do you not see? They hate you."

A voice rose above the crowd. "We were poor and had nothing. We stole their land and still they gave us bread. The Vallenses loved our children, and they gave us shelter."

Andreas didn't recognize the voice, but it boomed off the nearby rocks.

"Lord Chanforan, you are a liar." It was Ulrico, one of the new converts. "What the Vallenses believe is true, and what they practice is real. We have not only heard it but also seen and experienced it."

Andreas smiled.

Gedeon shouted in German again, but the mercenaries hesitated. They glanced at each other, then back at their lord.

Veins protruded from Gedeon's neck. "All of you will burn, and your children too. You aren't worth the air you breathe." He glanced back at the guards, closed his eyes, and screamed, "I pay your salary! Do what I say!"

Three mercenaries stepped forward with their pikes pointed toward Andreas and the Piedmontese.

Andreas winced and prayed for deliverance. The peasants were greater in number, but they couldn't fight Swiss pikemen.

A twang, followed by a thud and grunt, echoed through the commotion.

The crowd grew silent, and the pikemen stood and stared at Gedeon. He dropped to his knees with an arrowhead protruding from his chest, blood pouring from the wound.

At the corner of the cliff face, next to Marta Chanforan and her children, stood Johan Lauras, shaking with a bow in his hands.

A Piedmontese man grabbed Andreas's wrists and sawed at the ropes, while another cut through those at his ankles. When they finished, they lifted Andreas to his feet. His arms lightened, and his neck muscles gradually relaxed.

He peered toward the pile of parchment ashes. The manuscript was gone. Forever.

The mercenaries lowered their pikes and backed away.

Amalia stood by her husband's side and gave a half smile to Andreas. "You're safe now."

44

But I say unto you which hear, Love your enemies, do good to them which hate you, Bless them that curse you, and pray for them which despitefully use you.

—The Holy Bible
Luke 6:27–28

CONSTANZA'S HANDS TREMBLED as the children listened and prayed near the cavern entrance. Some eyes were wet with tears, while others were dry with fear.

The younger children asked questions: "Where's Monsen Andreas? Why is that man yelling? When are we leaving?" But the words were buried in Constanza's throat. It was better they perish in ignorance than in fear.

She rubbed her freezing fingers together as she waited for the smoke, but it never came. Then the noises outside quieted to a hush.

A voice called into the cave like a dream, yet it was full of life. "We're saved! We're all safe, and you can all come out."

Constanza's heart stilled. Had the wind deceived her?

Fosca hugged her tighter and looked up. "Are we still going over the mountain?"

"Yes, if God allows."

Someone crawled through the opening, and Constanza tensed. She stood in front of the children and blocked them from the intruder.

The figure became clear. His cheek was bruised, but still he smiled at her. "Lord Chanforan is defeated."

Andreas.

Constanza's eyes widened, and her entire body warmed. All fear and all dread vanished. "How did—"

"The Piedmontese—all of them, and Amalia's husband—"

"Riccardo?"

"Yes, everyone." Andreas held out his hands and let a few children embrace him. His coat was singed. "They wouldn't let Gedeon light the fire. After all he promised them, they stood beside us."

"The soldiers let them?"

"Many hesitated, but when a few came at the peasants with their pikes, Johan Lauras shot Gedeon in the back."

Constanza's jaw dropped. "Where is he? Is it bad?"

"Yes." Andreas swallowed and squinted one eye at her. "He will die if he hasn't already."

Constanza tightened her lips. Gedeon Chanforan was reaping what he had sown.

Andreas waved them toward the cave opening. "The soldiers are gone. No one is left to pay them, so they're probably heading home."

"The Bible," Constanza said, ducking under the rock. "Do you still have it?"

Andreas didn't answer until they were outside. He pointed to a pile of ashes near the pyre as the breeze carried some of them into the air. "That was once our manuscript."

His monotone voice told of his resignation. After all Andreas had given to find that manuscript, the swirling wind now spread its gray ashes across the snow. Such precious words, written so long ago, would now sift back into the earth.

The Frenchman Basile approached and gave a bow to Andreas. "You are an imbécile, my friend." He threw his arms around Andreas, but for only a moment. "After living a long and memorable life, I was ready to die, and you should have allowed me."

"It must have seemed reckless—"

"I am not finished," Basile said. "I thought you had forsaken your senses, but when I saw you stand nose to nose with Monsieur Chanforan and choose to give your own life, I knew you were different. When these peasants stood with you, I saw your religion was real—engraved in your soul. Everything you told me in Genoa, I believe it now. God has forgiven my sins."

Tears streamed down Constanza's cheeks. She wiped them away and sniffled. Andreas's words had sown the seed, his actions had watered the ground, and God had brought the harvest. God indeed used His disciples to accomplish His will. They had not prayed for oppression, but God had brought it, and they now had the privilege of glimpsing His divine providence.

Constanza scanned the crowd. Amalia stood talking with her husband, while her children tugged at her apron. Other men and women, both strange and familiar, talked, smiled, or stood in awe, but none wore the armor of a soldier.

Under the shadow of the rocks, a woman and two children knelt beside a man lying on the ground and writhing in agony. Gedeon's mouth was open, and his eyes blinked in slow beats.

Would anyone tend to him? After everything Gedeon had done, after all the evil he had promised, was it worth offering any sympathy? Could she not forget about Gedeon Chanforan forever and leave him to the fate spawned by his own choices?

But then Christ's words flooded her conscience. *Love your enemies, do good to them which hate you.* Instead of contempt, revenge, and hatred, He preached honor, forgiveness, and love—not the feeling of love, not tolerance of sin, but the action and sacrifice true love demanded. *And as ye would that men should do to you, do ye also to them likewise.*

Gedeon, Marta, Claudia, and Addo were alone. While Constanza, Andreas, and the orphans rejoiced, a family of four wept without hope. She sighed and looked to Andreas. "We should help them."

Andreas bit his lip. "He won't want to see me after everything that's happened."

She swallowed. "I'll go alone."

Constanza briefly closed her eyes and took the first step toward the Chanforans, but her breathing quickened. This man had tried to kill her. What would she say, and how would they respond? She didn't know, but it was what the Spirit wanted her to do.

Gedeon caught Constanza's eyes when she was within a few paces and pointed his gaze to the ground.

"May I see the wound?" Constanza asked.

Marta, shaking with silent sobs, nodded and scooted back.

"Let me die in peace," Gedeon said, spitting the words out with his own blood.

Scrapes, burns, and broken bones Constanza had treated, but not a battle wound. Her mind told her to look away, but she couldn't. The arrowhead protruded from his chest. Her hands shook as she grabbed the shaft to snap it—Papà had done that after a deer kill, so—

Gedeon swatted her hand away. "I'm dying. You pull that arrow through me again"—he wheezed and coughed—"I'll . . . the pain."

"I want to help you, Monsen Gedeon."

"No, you hate me, and you're here to gloat."

Thou shalt love the Lord thy God with all thy heart, and with all thy soul, and with all thy strength, and with all thy mind; and thy neighbour as thyself. Long ago, a lawyer asked Jesus about the latter commandment: *And who is my neighbour?*

Constanza put a hand on Gedeon's cheek. "I am here to show you mercy."

The anger and conceit fled from Gedeon's face. He didn't smile, but somewhere beneath the veneer of this conflicted man, a light glimmered.

"Care for my family." Gedeon choked and placed his hands flat on the ground. "I want . . . I want . . ."

Marta drew close and held her husband's arm while Claudia and Addo sat on Gedeon's other side.

"We will watch them," Constanza said. "Whatever they need—"

"Teach them . . . show them"—his eyelids closed and popped back open—"the cross."

Gedeon's mouth fell open and his eyes stared into the snow-specked sky. But they didn't blink again. The Lord of Luserna was gone.

Marta stared in disbelief for a moment, then Claudia and Addo held her as they sobbed over Gedeon's body. They had no hope, no peace, and no comfort. Constanza could offer no words for them, but she could be there for the Chanforans. She could honor Gedeon's last wish. They would never be homeless, never live in want, and forever enjoy friends among the Vallenses.

*   *   *

"That farm is rightfully yours," Riccardo said to Andreas.

While the orphans sang a psalm, *boscarlas* chirped amid the snow-covered pines. Sunrays warmed Andreas's cheeks as he helped the Piedmontese men return the grain to the stack. God had worked in Riccardo's heart both to accept Christ and to reconcile with Andreas about the old Lauras farm.

"I'll help you build whatever shelter you need," Andreas said, "and you're welcome to stay on the land as long as necessary." He squinted one eye and glanced down. "As long as you help plow and plant when the ground thaws."

At the other side of the clearing, Johan Lauras leaned against the rock face, staring into the forest and shivering. His bow lay snapped in two pieces near his feet.

Andreas bit his bottom lip and blinked rapidly. Johan needed him—he needed to understand that Andreas forgave him.

"I've been wrong all along," Johan said as Andreas approached, "and . . . and . . . I killed him. I killed Lord Chanforan."

"Johan, it's finished now."

"I couldn't stand to watch you die—you didn't deserve it. Gedeon promised he wouldn't harm you, and when I saw his lies, I couldn't think of a better way. What if I hadn't—"

"Stop asking, 'what if?' It's more important what you choose to do next."

"I swore myself to Gedeon and his family. In my darkest hour, they took me in and helped me. They grieved with me after I lost my father and after I left my people. But I see the other side. I saw the pain Gedeon caused and wanted no part in it."

Andreas looked at his old confidant—the first Vallense to treat him like a friend instead of a worldly outsider, and one of the first to accept him after his conversion. When Andreas had questions, Johan answered them. Not all of Johan's advice had been wise, nor had all his motivations been pure, but he had shown Andreas kindness when others looked down their noses at him.

And Andreas now had to do the same for him. "Johan, God always welcomes you into His arms. He has not rejected you."

"I know, but will everyone else? I've betrayed them and used them. Who would dare show me goodwill?"

"If you come back, some will despise you, but don't dwell on them. Focus on your relationship with God and your obedience to Him, and when some avoid you, then they bear their own sin to settle."

Johan sighed, collapsed his shoulders, and put a hand on Andreas. "You are like a brother."

"I'm unsure of what to do next. Gedeon is dead, our people are free, the manuscript is gone."

"I saw you drop yourself on that fire and smother it."

Andreas shook his head and pointed to the pyre. "It's all in ashes now."

"Some might have survived."

Andreas peered beyond Johan, then turned and walked to the pyre.

When he pushed a foot through the pile, ashes swirled, but he felt nothing but air. Again he kicked at the ashes, but this time his shoe hit something. Andreas kneeled and brushed away the debris with both hands.

At first there was only blackened parchment. But the more he peeled away, the more the pages were intact.

Letters. I see letters. And words!

Andreas lifted what remained and held it to his eyes. The words were upside down, so he turned the still-warm parchment. There at the top of the page were two Greek words: *PRAXEIS APOSTOLON*. After a moment, he mouthed the translation. "The Acts of the Apostles."

He glanced through the rest of the pages, and other than a few singed edges, they were unharmed. But which New Testament books remained? Andreas held the manuscript by the binding and turned it from side to side. The back cover and the pages closest to it were gone, but the front cover now lay in his right palm. He flipped back two pages, and a new heading appeared: *EUANGELION IOANNIS*. The Gospel of John. He thumbed toward the front to verify.

All the Gospels had persevered through the fire.

Andreas closed his eyes and thanked God for His mercy. He held the manuscript for one more moment until he found his pack and slipped it in. It might not be everything, but it was still a gift from heaven.

Constanza, eyelids swollen and cheeks puffy, walked up and stood by Andreas's side. For the next few moments, she recounted her short time with Gedeon and her promise to his family.

Andreas shook his head. "God has delivered us from the hand of our enemy."

"I hope Gedeon knew the peace of Christ before he slipped away. He knew the truth, but I pray he finally received it."

A few Piedmontese families gathered around them. Some shook Andreas's hand, while others hugged Constanza. Andreas's head spun, and his gloom floated away like a waning fog. Again his life had been pushed to the edge of a cliff. By any standard, he, Constanza, and the children should be dead. The wind should have scattered the ashes from the manuscript. He gave his head an abrupt shake and looked to his future wife.

Her quick nod and reserved smile revealed both the shock and elation of what had happened—no, what had not happened. Neither Andreas nor Constanza spoke, but words were unnecessary. God had delivered them, and in the process had used them to reach some Piedmontese.

A few moments passed before Basile approached again. He looked at the Chanforans and said, "According to the law of the land, Addo Chanforan is now the rightful Lord of Luserna."

The Chanforans must not have heard Basile, for they remained huddled together away from the crowd. Addo was still young, but Marta would likely guide him in the years ahead, which lifted Andreas's heart.

Soon all twelve children crawled out of the cave opening and gathered around Andreas and Constanza.

Their courage is far beyond their stature.

Andreas's heart raced, but he was ready for anything. Why not tell them now?

"I'm going to tell the children about their new family," Andreas said.

Constanza's eyes widened, but a smile formed on her face. "I'm ready."

Andreas scanned the eyes of each child and admired their distinctive features: boys and girls, tall and short, quiet and boisterous. They would no longer live in an orphanage, but in a home.

"Boys, girls," Andreas said, giving a quick clap. "Everyone, listen. Madomaisèla Constanza and I have something to tell you." His voice quivered, but their curious gazes drove him to continue. "Your new home will be with us."

"At the Pavarin farm?" Ezio asked.

"No, at our home. Constanza and I will be your Mamà and Papà from now until forever."

Silvia's eyelids flew open. "What about Monsen Luca and Madòna Vitòria?"

Andreas took in a long breath. Not everyone had been delivered. In their struggles against Gedeon Chanforan, they had lost the selfless Grimaldis and the valiant Victor of Bricherasio.

Andreas's chin tensed with guilt. He, not the Grimaldis, deserved to die in a dungeon. He, not Victor, should have been slain at Castelvecchio. But for reasons far beyond his understanding, God had preserved him.

Constanza glanced at the children, then back at Andreas.

"Their souls are with God now," Andreas said, "but don't fret."

Irene immediately threw herself into Constanza's arms, and more children followed. Ave hugged Andreas on one side, and Guido on the other.

They spoke for a few moments while the tears tapered off. The older children said they had suspected the tragedy for months and had relayed their fears to the younger ones. Yet the current grief brought long-sought closure to the lives of those who had shown mercy to the children.

Silvia wiped her eyes and formed a little smile. "If you're adopting us, that means we're no longer orphans."

"Not anymore," Constanza said. "We're all family now."

Ezio stepped back and crossed his arms. "Not until you get married."

Andreas laughed, grabbed Ezio, and pulled him close. "And that will be soon enough."

45

To maintain the truth in their own mountains was not the only object of this people. They felt their relations to the rest of Christendom They sought to drive back the darkness, and re-conquer the kingdom which Rome had overwhelmed. They were an evangelistic as well as an evangelical Church.

—James Wylie
The History of the Waldenses, 1860

Three months later, April 1460

ANDREAS SAT ON A LEDGE at the La Torre market and spoke to a traveling merchant. The snow had vanished except for the white crowns atop Vandalino and Friouland. Narcissus bloomed in containers along the ledge and accented the bright spring morning. The market bustled with shouting merchants hawking their silks, gems, cookware, and seeds. Cattle mooed, chickens clucked, and newborn lambs bleated as the Vallenses bartered their goods with the visitors from the plains.

Andreas opened the cover of a little book and turned the pages, searching for a specific section. Constanza's precise and unornamented handwriting flowed across the page of John's Gospel, newly validated with the Greek text from Ioannis Argyropoulos. Andreas pointed to a line, read it in his mind, and translated it to Piedmontese.

Someday, all would have access to the Holy Scriptures in their own tongues, but for now, God had given Andreas enough. Though ink smudges, crossed-out words, and scribbles marked the pages, it was God's Word. Soon after the events at the cave, Johan had returned the old Romaunt Bible from the schoolhouse. Andreas and Constanza had begun the task of verification at once. But progress was slow—while Andreas compared the Greek manuscript with the lexicon, Constanza consulted the Romaunt Bible, verified Andreas's translation, and penned the words.

Andreas read the passage to the man sitting next to him. "'Verily, verily, I say unto you, He that heareth my word, and believeth on him that sent me, hath everlasting life, and shall not come into condemnation; but is passed from death unto life.'"

"It seems too easy," said the merchant, "And it goes against everything I've been taught."

"I thought the same once. In fact, not quite two years have passed since I was born again."

Andreas held his breath. He had once cowered at telling others about his lineage, but he concealed nothing anymore. Everyone in the Angrogna Valley knew, as well as many other Vallenses, and now he had found his story.

"Once, I was a prince of Savoy." Andreas held out his left hand and showed off the golden ring. "I had riches to last a hundred lifetimes and prestige to match it. I served as a Benedictine monk and aspired to become a famed scholar. But my soul was empty and lifeless. To fill the emptiness, I served the Roman Church, but only grew emptier."

The cavernous chambers of Sacra di San Michele echoed through Andreas's memory: midnight prayers, burning incense, Father Antonio, accusations, banishment. Then everything had changed.

Andreas gazed over the merchant's shoulder and quieted his voice. "But a man named Raimond Durand cared for my soul, and through him God showed me that Jesus finished the work of salvation on the cross."

The merchant examined Andreas's ring and tapped it with his fingernail. "It's real gold, and that is the symbol of Savoy. You stole it, or maybe it's an imitation. What are you trying to sell me?"

"I offer you the gospel of Jesus Christ and nothing else, but it's you who will either accept or reject it. Just as I don't deserve God's forgiveness, neither do you. But please know that it's the greatest treasure a man can possess—no gem, no coin, no castle can match its worth."

As the sun lifted itself higher into the clear sky, Andreas answered the merchant's questions. In time, he accepted the gospel and became a child of God.

Andreas couldn't restrain his smile, but a tear came along with it. He had come down to La Torre only to sell a few lambs and turn back quickly. But then he'd met the merchant. Though he hadn't planned on talking to anyone about spiritual matters, let alone the gospel, this was God's plan, and God had used Andreas—not because of his prestige, nor for his eloquence, but because he had submitted to the Spirit of God.

The merchant shook Andreas's hand and said he would seek out other believers in his hamlet. A church bell tolled in the distance, and Andreas's mind darted to the event for which he could not be late.

Andreas leaped into a jog and raced to the trail leading back into the Angrogna Valley. Birds chirped on branches filled with buds and blossoms. The freezing torrent rushed through the ravine on the left as Andreas wound his way uphill. Men gave him quick nods while they plowed their fields, and their wives grinned and waved. Children giggled and followed him before their parents called them back.

When Andreas came to the crossroads, he kept straight on the path, then veered right toward the farm. He, Nicolaus Pavarin, and the Piedmontese had reached an agreement soon after the events at the cave. A few of their shacks had since become proper houses, and the men worked to clear trees and remove stumps to make room for their own fields. The church was fuller now too, forcing them to teach the children outside while the adults remained indoors.

After a wash in the creek, Andreas reached the old Lauras farmhouse and opened the door. Everything was in its place—floors swept, walls scrubbed, linens washed, and vases filled with blue irises—perfect for the first member of his family. Plenty of work remained, but it would suffice until everyone came home.

He trimmed his beard, combed his hair, and changed into a fresh set of clothes. A mint leaf freshened his breath before he took one last look at himself. Andreas swallowed, let out a breath, and left the house.

Families streamed around him when he reached the crossroads. The women wore their traditional Vallense dress along with a white ribbon: the madònas had it draped in front of their shoulders, while the madomaisèlas let it fall behind them.

Johan joined Andreas just before the meetinghouse. "Do you feel senseless, or can you comprehend what's about to happen?"

"I'm grateful to be here," Andreas said. "Three months ago, I almost had my head dethroned. Now"—he shook his head—"it's almost a fantasy."

"Are you sure you want to do all of this?"

"I'm surer than anything."

"Wait a month or two, and you may say differently, especially about the children."

A crowd had assembled in the clearing outside the meetinghouse. Not only were Angrogna Valley natives present—noticeable by their distinct Vallense attire—but many Piedmontese were also in attendance. All eyes shifted to Andreas as he made his way toward the front. A light breeze swept down from the heights and into his sleeves, causing his shirt to billow.

Little Bino stood to the left with his hands clasped, followed by Ezio, Guido, Roberto, and Umile. To the right stood the girls: Irene, Fosca, Ave, Silvia, Alessia, Zama, and Prospera—each with a new outfit that would double as Sunday attire after today. Though the youngest few fidgeted, all their faces beamed.

Bertran Arnaldi stood in the front row of guests and gave Andreas a nod and a wide grin. Through all their adventures to Florence and back, Bertran had proved to be his most steadfast and like-minded friend. To the right, Johan leaned against a tree, and Basile stood near the front. *Without friends like these, I wouldn't be here.*

The crowd turned toward the meetinghouse and waited. The air stilled until only the chirps of sparrows remained.

At last the bride appeared. Constanza Pavarin stepped from the meetinghouse and entered the field with her father, mother, and nine siblings. They took methodical steps through the crowd as all stood and gazed.

Time passed like the twilight of a morning dream. Nicolaus and Armanda Pavarin stopped and embraced their daughter near the front, then stood back while she glided forward. Andreas's eyes latched onto Constanza's as they took each other's hands. His hands shook, and his breath was nearly gone.

The pastor's words entered his ears but didn't remain. The congregation sang a hymn, but neither he nor Constanza joined them—they were focused on each other.

"Will you take Constanza to be your wife?"

"Yes," Andreas said in an instant.

"Will you take Andreas to be your husband?"

Constanza smiled and said, "Yes."

Andreas blinked a few times, held Constanza close, and placed a long kiss on her lips.

The witnesses all cheered—most of all, the orphans. Constanza's hand gripped Andreas's, then she turned and kissed him again.

She pressed her nose against his and said, "Now I am wife to a prince."

"And I am married to a peasant heretic woman."

Fingers tugged on Andreas's coattail.

"The ribbon," Ezio whispered.

Andreas chuckled and reached over Constanza's shoulder. He pulled her ribbon up and let it drop in front of her. "Now we're official."

Constanza laid her head on Andreas's chest. "Silly formality."

Andreas scanned the witnesses' faces. Estève stood next Nicolaus and Armanda, laughing and throwing his hands together in hard claps. He nodded and mouthed two words: "Well done." Though they had spent only a few months together, Andreas would forever hold the white-haired barbe and his words of wisdom close.

Near the back, Gedeon's widow, Marta, stood by Claudia and Addo—Lord Addo, to be exact. With Marta's help, he had normalized the absurd tax bills and brought stability back to the valleys. Though the Chanforans had entered the Luserna Valley as tyrants, they were now welcomed as friends.

But at the fringes of the assembly, a pale man and a fair-faced woman clapped along with everyone else. They wore plain clothes, which likely hid their identity from all except Andreas and Basile.

Andreas pointed their direction with his nose and whispered in Constanza's ear. "My brother and his wife—Amadeus and Yolande."

Constanza jerked her head around and peered across the crowd. "Those aren't noble garments they're wearing."

"They don't want to be noticed."

Constanza grinned. "You should introduce me."

Amid the handshakes and well wishes, they struck the path toward the honored guests. Midway through the crowd, Constanza prodded Andreas's arm and pointed. "Elionor is here."

And like a phantom, there stood Elionor Janavel. A dark hood covered her head and cast a shadow across her dull eyes. She wore no smile or other hint of joy. Her gaze shot from Constanza to Andreas to the ground, then she spun and scampered to the road.

Constanza grabbed Andreas's hand and pulled him after Elionor. "Why does she run?"

"She has come to honor us but must not want to speak to us. We can't catch her, at least not at the moment."

"She doesn't look like the same Ellie I've always known. What happened to her?"

A hard life. But now wasn't the time to explain. Something had happened, but discovering what would cloud the joyous occasion. Elionor disappeared over a hill.

They turned back toward Amadeus and Yolande and approached with light steps. Amadeus gave a quick nod to Andreas. "*Toutes nos félicitations.* Congratulations, brother."

Constanza bowed. "*Mon . . . mon seigneur—*"

Yolande's eyes sparkled, and she gave a petite smile. "Your name is Constanza?"

"Yes . . . I . . . I am, my lady—"

"I bring greetings from our father," Amadeus said in a cool tone before Constanza could finish.

Andreas jerked his head back. "You've heard from him?"

"I'm afraid he has heard about all your deeds," Yolande said. "Duke Louis has summoned you to Chambéry and expects you there before summer."

Andreas looked up. That was only two months away, and it would take at least two weeks to travel to Savoy. He still had fields to plant, a well to dig—

"Your new wife will also be expected," Yolande said.

"We have children—" Andreas caught himself. "Adopted children, that is—twelve of them."

Yolande pursed her lips. "Do what you must, but do not ignore your father's demands. The duchy is in disarray. News of Gedeon Chanforan has reached the duke's ears, but he has done nothing to punish your brother. Instead, Philip asserts himself in the court and demands concessions from Louis. Also, the bishops have convinced your father to release the Dominican inquisitor, Marco Spada."

The name flew past Andreas's ear like an arrow.

"And my servant Basile Halphen told me you now possess the Greek Bible."

"Our arrangement stands," Andreas said with a curt nod. "We will return the manuscript to you before autumn of next year. Only the first half survived, though. I'm afraid the books after the Gospels are gone."

Gone, but not neglected. He might never see those beautiful Greek words again, but someone would. There was more than one manuscript in the world, and God would certainly guide others—perhaps in a different time and place—to collect them and translate the Holy Scriptures into common languages.

Constanza nestled close to Andreas and lowered her voice to a whisper. "We can speak of these matters later."

"Tell Father I have received his demands," Andreas said, "but I am a married man with a family now." He called for the children, and one by one, they gathered around him and Constanza.

Yolande's eyes suddenly brightened. She reached into her pocket, removed a booklet, and held it out to Andreas.

He didn't need to look twice. It was Raimond's Bible, the one Estève had given to Yolande in Turin. It didn't belong to Andreas, though; it belonged to whoever needed its truth.

"Please, keep it as a gift," Andreas said, "from our family to yours."

Epilogue

Over fifty years later

THE PEDDLER DROPPED the old pouch on the table. "I want ten Rhenish florins for it."

The Dominican friar opened the pouch and skimmed the pages. "Ten florins for only the Gospels?" He huffed. "I'll give you a single golden florin, otherwise you can skip it and show me the next item for sale."

"Dominus, this is a manuscript of the Scriptures." The peddler removed the codex, grabbed a page, and handed it to the friar. "Rumors say it escaped the ruin of Constantinople before falling into the hands of merciless heretics more than fifty years ago. The House of Savoy held it for a few years after, I heard, but now it is within your grasp."

The friar turned the codex from side to side and squinted. "I can't read these barbarian letters, so what use is it to Universitas Basiliensis?"

"I'll take two Rhenish florins, then."

The friar shrugged. "Perhaps someday one of our theologians will wish to examine it. We could rebind it and repair these burnt edges." He paused and eyed the manuscript. "I'll buy it."

The peddler rolled his eyes and opened his right hand. "I hoped to get more, especially since it came from the collection of a bankrupt princess. But two Rhenish florins are better than none."

The friar dropped the coins into the peddler's hand and accepted the bundle of parchment.

For the remainder of the morning, the friar bartered with the peddler for an assortment of higher priced items. Later that day, after the evening prayers, the friar placed the codex on a shelf with the other old books and forgot about it.

But it would not be long forgotten, for soon God would use scholars, laborers, queens, and dissenters to spread the words inscribed in that manuscript to every land.

Acknowledgments

First, I wish to express my thanks to the many readers of the first book in this series, *Heretics of Piedmont*. Their messages, letters, and conversations encouraged me to write *The Lord of Luserna* and made it a story worth telling.

It's common knowledge in the writing world to be careful about having family members read early versions of the story and offer advice, but I'm glad I wasn't too cautious. My wife, Andrea, was the first to read this book, and her insights were a tremendous help in making the characters more realistic, eliminating a few plot holes, and offering her wisdom throughout the writing process. Andrea's love of language and linguistics inspired me to dig deep into the languages represented in this story, and she also helped me understand what it feels like to be bilingual. Above all, Andrea is my encourager; whether I'm rambling on about Waldensians and Bible manuscripts or complaining about how tiring the editing process can be, she listens. *The Lord of Luserna* is a much better story because of her.

My mother, Vonda Murdock, offered excellent insights about the story early on. Together, my parents exemplify God's grace and comfort amidst the reality of grief and loss; they are ever an example and heritage to their children and grandchildren.

The beta readers who offered both valuable and distinct perspectives were Diana Wilbur, Brandon Starr, and Jenna Starr. I am thankful for the time they took to read and talk through their thoughts, and each had a part in making *The Lord of Luserna* better.

During the planning and writing stages, my friend missionary Bill Hardecker was home from the Philippines on furlough. He holds more knowledge about biblical criticism than anyone I personally know, and most importantly, his positions are sound. Several Sunday evenings while watching our children on the playground after church, I bounced questions and ideas off him; even if he didn't know the answer, he sent me resources and pointed me in the right direction.

The final steps of refinement came with the help of my editor, Jayna Baas. First, she evaluated the manuscript and offered areas to improve plot structure, characters, and language. After I addressed those points, she went through the manuscript word by word; not only did she correct my mistakes but she also taught me along the way. Her very relevant knowledge, expertise, and discernment are etched into every page of this book.

I am also grateful to the numerous institutions that have made their works freely available online. For example, the University of Basel in Switzerland has scanned the entirety of the Greek manuscript represented in this book and has made it easily accessible online.

The history of Bible texts can be a complicated and contentious subject, and I'm thankful for those who have taught me over the years. I know this area requires intense understanding and an investment of time. These men include but are not limited to Pastor Dan Armacost, Dr. Randy Starr, Pastor Chris Starr, and Bill Hardecker.

Lastly, there would be no story to write if it weren't for the men and women throughout history who have copied, protected, transcribed, translated, preached, and taught the Word of God. The Bible is more life-changing than I could ever describe, but God has chosen His children for the heavenly task of spreading it. May we never forsake the Holy Scriptures, and may we always be bold to preach them.

Historical Notes

The Lord of Luserna takes place in 1459 and 1460, about a year after the events in *Heretics of Piedmont*. At that time, Waldensians (Vallenses in this story, the Latin term) were prevalent in southeastern France and in the alpine valleys of western Piedmont. Oppression and persecution against them in the fifteenth century tended to come in waves, little of which is historically documented.

Most characters in this book are fictional, though several are a combination of Waldensian figures in different historical eras. Some characters, however, are based on real individuals.

Though Gedeon Chanforan is a fictional character, he represents the burgeoning class of burghers in the Duchy of Savoy in the mid-fifteenth century. The Black Death, which ended about a century before, hollowed out much of Europe's population, but it gave immense negotiating power to those who survived. One result was the rise of middle-class men like Gedeon Chanforan, who represents burghers with enough power to purchase their nobility.

Ioannis (John) Argyropoulos was a Greek scholar who fled from Constantinople before its fall to the Ottoman Turks in 1453. His teaching was a catalyst for the Aristotelian Revival in Florence during the Italian Renaissance; his students included Piero Cosimo de' Medici and Leonardo da Vinci. His stewardship of the Greek New Testament represented in this story, however, is entirely fictional.

Princess Yolande of Valois and her husband, Amadeus, are also historical, as well as the two children they had at that time: Anne and Charles. Yolande was highly interested in treasures from the East, and her residences were notoriously filled with these trinkets. The other members of the House of Savoy referenced in *The Lord of Luserna* are real, including the usurper, Philip.

Andreas, Constanza, and all Waldensian characters are fictional, though their life events are derived from dozens of sources spanning hundreds of years.

The first chapter in this book is based on an 1830 poem by John Greenleaf Whittier, titled "The Vaudois Teacher." Estève Malan represents the peddler in the poem, while Princess Yolande represents the noble lady.

In Chapter 42 of this book, the song Constanza pens in the cavern is adapted from an 1834 hymn by Felicia Hemans, titled "Hymn of the Vaudois Mountaineers in Times of Persecution."

The Manuscript

The Bible manuscript referenced in this story is based on Codex Basiliensis A. N. IV. 1 (also known as Minuscule 2), an eleventh- or twelfth-century Greek New Testament codex of the Byzantine text type. Along with most other New Testament manuscripts, its exact origins are unknown, allowing for some artistic license to craft a legend of how it could have found its way to the University of Basel by the sixteenth century. F. H. A. Scrivener (1894) only describes the Dominicans at the university purchasing the manuscript for two Rhenish florins after it appeared from the East. When it was purchased, it included only the four Gospels. *The Lord of Luserna* uses this fact to provide a reason that might have been the case. Minuscule 2 collected dust at the university along with similar New Testament manuscripts until a famous Dutch scholar used it to publish his most consequential work.

Desiderius Erasmus Roterodamus used the manuscript along with six others when he compiled the first published and printed Greek New Testament—*Novum Instrumentum omne*—in 1516. In subsequent decades, Erasmus's work was revised and corrected, until the printer Robertus Stephanus first titled it *Textus Receptus*—the Received Text—in 1633.

Six years after Erasmus published *Novum Instrumentum omne*, the scholar and linguist William Tyndale secured a copy and used it as his primary source to translate the New Testament into English. Other translations that originated from the Textus Receptus include King James (English), Luther (German), and Reina-Valera (Spanish).

During the same era, Pierre Robert Olivétan, a Waldensian pastor, used the Textus Receptus to translate the New Testament from Greek into French for the first time. His *la Bible d'Olivétan* was the forerunner to the popular *la Bible de Genève*.

This era of rapid Bible translation coincided with the spread of Gutenberg's printing press, and over the course of a few decades, the Bible went from being an enigma to being the most widely read book in history. Its impact is immeasurable, but its story has not ended.

Bible Renderings

For the benefit of English readers, I rendered Scripture quoted from the Romaunt Bible with the King James Version. When the literal Romaunt is quoted in *The Lord of Luserna*, I used facsimile copies of the Dublin manuscript housed at the library of Trinity College Dublin. Quotations from the Gospel of John were already transcribed thanks to *The Romaunt Version of the Gospel of John* (Gilly 1848), but others were my own transcriptions.

Where the Latin Vulgate is quoted, I did not use the King James translation; the difference between the Romaunt and Latin New Testaments was better represented by using the Douay-Rheims Version (1582). Douay-Rheims was a translation from Latin, in contrast to the King James Version being from Hebrew and Greek.

LANGUAGES

The Lord of Luserna uses words, phrases, and sentences from seven languages and dialects other than English. I am not a linguist, but I labored to represent how those languages might have sounded in the fifteenth century. Romaunt (the language of the Vallenses, today called Occitan) was perhaps the most difficult to represent because of its obscurity, but with the help of French–Occitan lexicons and the Romaunt Bible (Dublin manuscript), I feel the reader can gain an essence of how that medieval language sounded.

The Tuscan dialect spoken in Florence during the fifteenth century eventually formed the basis of modern Italian, so most translations are based on their modern Italian equivalents.

This story also uses Latin, French, Greek, Piedmontese, and Hebrew. There was some mutual intelligibility between dialects (for example, Romaunt and Piedmontese), but dialects could differ greatly between regions. Some of the mutual intelligibility, or lack thereof, is therefore based on historical conjecture and my own assumptions.

THIS STORY

It has always been fascinating to me that the most extant Greek New Testament manuscripts were brought west in the same era Gutenberg perfected the printing press. Add to that the Waldensians were thriving in Piedmont during that time, and this makes for an interesting hypothetical tale. The Waldensians were certainly involved in some Bible translation work, so what if they possessed one of the manuscripts from Constantinople, even for a short time? How might that have transpired? *The Lord of Luserna* explores those questions, and I hope it will inspire you to learn more about Waldensians and, even more so, the Bible.

Selected Bibliography

Allix, Pierre. *Some Remarks Upon the Ecclesiastical History of the Ancient Churches of Piedmont.* United Kingdom: Clarendon Press, 1821.

Baird, Robert. *Sketches of Protestantism in Italy.* Past and Present. Including a Notice of the Origin, History, and Present State of the Waldenses. Boston: Benjamin Perkins & Co., 1847.

Beattie, William. *The Waldenses: Or, Protestant Valleys of Piedmont, Dauphiny, and the Ban de la Roche.* United Kingdom: George Virtue, 1838.

Crowley, Roger. *1453: The Holy War for Constantinople and the Clash of Islam and the West.* Italy: Hyperion Books, 2006.

Gallenga, Antonio Carlo Napoleone. *History of Piedmont.* United Kingdom: Chapman and Hall, 1855.

Gilly, William Stephen. *The Romaunt Version of the Gospel According to St. John.* United Kingdom: John Murray, 1848.

Henderson, Ebenezer. *The Vaudois: Observations Made During a Tour to the Valleys of Piedmont.* United Kingdom: John Snow, Paternoster Row, 1845.

Jones, William. *The History of the Christian Church from the Birth of Christ to the Xviii. Century.* United States: R.W. Pomeroy, 1832.

King, Ross. *Brunelleschi's Dome: How a Renaissance Genius Reinvented Architecture.* United Kingdom: Penguin Books, 2001.

Lacroix, Paul. *Manners, Customs, and Dress During the Middle Ages, and During the Renaissance Period.* United Kingdom: Chapman and Hall, 1876.

Morland, Samuel. *The History of the Evangelical Churches of the Valleys of Piedmont.* United Kingdom: Henry Hills, one of His Highness's printers, 1658.

Muston, Alexis. *The Israel of the Alps: A History of the Persecutions of the Waldenses.* United Kingdom: Ingram, Cooke, 1852.

Scrivener, Frederick Henry Ambrose. *A Plain Introduction to the Criticism of the New Testament for the Use of Biblical Students.* United Kingdom: Deighton, Bell, 1874.

Todd, James Henthorn. *The Books of the Vaudois, the Waldensian Manuscripts Preserved in the Library of Trinity College, Dublin.* United Kingdom: MacMillan and Co., 1865.

Wylie, James Aitken. *The History of Protestantism.* United Kingdom: Cassel, Petter & Galpin, 1874.

Key to Foreign Words and Phrases

Fr.: French, spoken more formally and among nobility or clergy.

Fr.-Prov.: Franco-Provençal, the regional Romance language spoken in parts of Savoy and surrounding areas.

Ger.: German, the High German dialects of the Holy Roman Empire, spoken by soldiers, artisans, and merchants traveling south from the Swabian and Swiss territories.

Gr.: Greek, the language of the Byzantine East; studied by Western humanists and preserved by refugees fleeing the recent fall of Constantinople.

It.: Italian, specifically the Tuscan literary dialect popularized by Dante and Petrarch; used as a sophisticated lingua franca for diplomacy and commerce among the elite.

Lat.: Latin, commonly used in religious texts, services, and academic writing.

Occ.: Occitan, the vernacular language spoken by Waldensians and others in southern France and northern Italy; referred to as Romaunt in this story.

Pied.: Piedmontese, a Romance language native to the Piedmont region.

À quoi veux-tu en venir? (Fr.; ah KWAH vuh-TYOO ahn vuh-NEER): What are you getting at?

affrontements (Fr.; ah-frohnt-MAHN): clashes.

agapité (Gr.; ah-gah-pee-TAY): beloved.

alzarsi (It.; ahl-TSAR-see): get up.

amici (It.; ah-MEE-chee): friend.

amicus (Lat.; ah-MEE-koos): friend.

ampoas (Occ.; ahm-PWOH-ahs): raspberries.

angelet (Occ.; ahn-zheh-LET): angel.

approprié (Fr.; ah-proh-pree-AY): appropriate.

aprilo (It.; AH-pree-loh): open it.

aqual que fey mía èluy (Occ.; ah-KWAHL keh fay MEE-ah EH-lwee): he that shewed mercy on him.

archaïque (Fr.; ar-kah-EEK): archaic.

arché (Gr.; ar-KAY): archaic.

aspirante (Lat.; ahs-pee-RAHN-teh): aspiring.

belle dame (Pied.; bel DAHM): beautiful lady.

bien fondé (Fr.; byan fohn-DAY): well-founded.

bon a sèira (Pied.; bon-ah SAY-rah): good evening.

bona nuèch (Occ.; BOH-nah NWETCH): good night.

bonjorn (Occ.; bohn-ZHORN): good day.

boscarlas (Occ.; bohs-KAR-lahs): warblers.

bouleversant (Fr.; bool-vair-SAHN): overwhelming.

Buononimi delle Stinche (It.; bwoh-NOH-nee-mee DEL-leh STEEN-keh): Good Men of Stinche.

canaglia (It.; kah-NAHL-yah): scoundrel.

Carcere delle Stinche (It.; KAR-cheh-reh DEL-leh STEEN-keh): Stinche Prison.

cerea (Pied.; che-RAY-ah): hello.

cest à moi (Fr.; set ah MWAH): that's mine.

chiedi al prete di portarti sul fianco (It.; KYEH-dee ahl PREH-teh dee pohr-TAR-tee sool FYAHN-koh): ask the priest to carry you on his side.

chiudi la bocca (It.; KYOO-dee lah BOHK-kah): shut your mouth.

cinque fiorini per una balla (It.; CHEEN-kweh fyoh-REE-nee pair OO-nah BAHL-lah): five florins for a bale.

consegna le tue armi (It.; kohn-SEN-yah leh TOO-eh AR-mee): hand over your weapons.

convento (It.; kohn-VEN-toh): convent.

Cosa porti tra le braccia? (It.; KOH-zah POHR-tee trah leh BRAHT-chah): What are you carrying in your arms?

doleo (Lat.; DOH-leh-oh): I don't understand.

domicili (Occ.; doh-mee-SEE-lee): home.

dos se lus del mòt (Occ.; dohs seh loos del MOHT): ye are the light of the world.

Dov'è il tuo cavallo? (It.; doh-VEH eel TOO-oh kah-VAHL-loh): Where is your horse?

Dov'è la porta romana? (It.; doh-VEH lah POHR-tah roh-MAH-nah): Where is the Roman gate?

duomo (It.; DWOH-moh): cathedral.

écuyers (Fr.; ay-kwee-YAY): squires.

et rester ensemble (Fr.; ay res-TAY ahn-SAHM-bluh): stay together.

éternité (Fr.; ay-tair-nee-TAY): eternity.

eucharistie (Fr.; ur-kah-rees-TEE): eucharist.

euh (Occ.; ew): um.

fastigós (Occ.; fahs-tee-GOHS): repugnant.

felena (Occ.; feh-LAY-nah): little girl.

fermati (It.; FAIR-mah-tee): stop.

folet (Occ.; foh-LET): crazed.

Francese (It.; frahn-CHAY-zeh): French.

francese deficiente (Occ.; frahn-CHAY-zeh deh-fee-CHEN-teh): deficient Frenchman.

fugitiu (Occ.; foo-zhee-TEE-oo): fugitive.

grazie (It.; GRAHT-syeh): thank you.

guarda (It.; GWAR-dah): look.

Habesne ægritudines? (Lat.; hah-BES-neh eye-gree-TOO-dee-nes): Do you have any ailments?

Hai qualche disturbos? (It.; eye KWAHL-keh dees-TOOR-boh): Do you have any ailments?

hébergement (Fr.; ay-bairzh-MAHN): accommodation.

héritage (Fr.; ay-ree-TAHZH): heritage.

hilfe (Ger.; HIL-fuh): help.

homme (Fr.; uhm): one man.

Ich beiße dir die finger ab. (Ger.; ikH BY-suh deer dee FING-ur ahp): I will bite your fingers off.

imbécile (Fr.; am-bay-SEEL): imbecile.

Je fais ce que je veux, cathare. (Fr.; zhuh FAY suh kuh zhuh VUH, kah-TAR): I do what I want, Cathar.

la nuit dernière (Fr.; lah NWEE dair-NYAIR): last night.

la progéniture de Satan (Fr.; lah proh-zhay-nee-TYUR duh sah-TAHN): Satan's offspring.

lacai (Occ.; lah-KY): lackey.

le dôme (Fr.; luh DOHM): the dome.

logos (Gr.; LOH-gohs): word.

luna (Occ.; LOO-nah): moon.

ma maîtresse (Fr.; mah may-TRESS): my mistress.

madomaisèla (Occ.; mah-doh-mah-AY-lah): miss.

magnifique (Fr.; man-yee-FEEK): magnificent.

maman (Fr.; mah-MAHN): mom.

Mare Nostrum (Lat.; MAH-reh NOHS-troom): Our Sea (Mediterrean).

me dison (Occ.; meh DEE-zohn): my name is.

mémé (Fr.; may-MAY): grandmother.

mercé (Occ.; mehr-SAY): thank you.

merci beaucoup (Fr.; mair-SEE boh-KOO): thank you very much.

mère (Fr.; mair): mother.

mersi (Pied.; mehr-SEE): thank you.

mes amis (Fr.; may zah-MEE): my friends.

mi companhs (Occ.; mee kohm-PAHNS): my friends.

Mi im ës-ciamo Estève. Com-it us-cham-eh? (Pied.; mee eem uhs-CHAH-moh es-TEH-veh. kohm-EET oos-KAHM-eh): My name is Estève. What is your name?

mon seigneur (Fr.; mohn sen-YUR): my lord.

monsieur (Fr.; muh-SYUR): mister.

montagna (It.; mohn-TAHN-yah): mountain.

nescio (Lat.; NES-kee-oh): I don't know.

niente cavallo, niente letto (It.; NYEN-teh kah-VAHL-loh, NYEN-teh LET-toh): no horse, no bed.

non capisco (It.; nohn kah-PEES-koh): I don't understand.

non posso (It.; nohn POHS-soh): I can't.

non sum qualis eram (Lat.; nohn soom KWAH-lees EH-rahm): I'm not the man I once was.

Obsecro ne me occidas (Lat.; ohb-SEH-kroh neh meh ohk-KEE-dahs): I beg you not to kill me.

òm (Occ.; OHM): husband.

Ordo Prædicatorum (Lat.; OR-doh pry-dee-kah-TOH-room): Order of Preachers.

oui (Fr.; wee): yes.

Parlës-to Piemontèis? (Pied.; PAR-luhs-toh pyay-mohn-TAYS): Do you speak Piedmontese?

Perché hai smesso? (It.; pair-KEH eye SMES-soh): Why did you stop?

père (Fr.; pair): father.

pesta (Occ.; PES-tah): plague.

pietat (Occ.; pee-eh-TAH): oh, pitty.

précaire (Fr.; pray-KAIR): precarious.

prudéncia (Occ.; proo-DEN-see-ah): prude.

purgatorium (Lat.; pur-gah-TOH-ree-oom): purgatory.

que siá coma aquò (Occ.; keh SEE-ah KOH-mah ah-KWOH): so be it.

questa non è una casa di carità (It.; KWES-tah nohn eh OO-nah KAH-zah dee kah-ree-TAH): this is not a charity house.

Quomodo te adiuvare possum? (Lat.; KWOH-moh-doh teh ah-dyoo-VAH-reh POHS-soom): How can I help you, my friends?

rapina (It.; rah-PEE-nah): robbery.

rebut (Occ.; reh-BOOT): rejected.

rendetz-vos (Occ.; ren-DETS-vohs): rendezvous.

Repubblica di Firenze (It.; reh-POOB-blee-kah dee fee-REN-tseh): Republic of Florence.

salire le scale (It.; sah-LEE-reh leh SKAH-leh): go upstairs.

salve (Lat.; SAHL-weh): hail.

sas efcharistó (Gr.; sahs ef-kah-rees-TOH): thank you.

scomëtte (Fr.; skoh-MET): bet.

scusi (It.; SKOO-zee): excuse me.

se vos plai (Occ.; seh vohs PLY): please.

séparer (Fr.; say-pah-RAY): seperate.

sic (Lat.; seek): thus.

stai zitto (It.; sty DZEET-toh): shut up.

t'aimi (Occ.; tay-mee): I love you.

ta meta ta physika (Gr.; tah meh-TAH tah fee-zee-KAH): the metaphysics.

tanta (Occ.; TAHN-tah): aunt.

terrazze (It.; tair-RAHT-tseh): terrace.

Ti sento (It.; tee SEN-toh): I heard you.

tòta (Pied.; TOH-tah): young lady.

toutes nos félicitations (Fr.-Prov.; TOOT noh fay-lee-see-tah-SYOHN): all our congratulations.

trois (Fr.; trwah): three.

troisième heure (Fr.; trwah-zyem UR): third hour.

un vestito di seta per la tua signora (It.; oon ves-TEE-toh dee SAY-tah pair lah TOO-ah seen-YOH-rah): a silk dress for your lady.

vattene (It.; VAHT-teh-neh): be gone.

verum (Lat.; VEH-room): true.

Name Pronunciation Guide

Alessia (ah-LAY-see-ah)

Andreas de Bonomo (ahn-DRAY-ahs day bo-NO-mo)

Ave (AH-vay)

Basile Halphen (BAH-zeel hal-FEN)

Bertran Arnaldi (BAIR-trahn ar-NOL-dee)

Bino (BEE-noh)

Constanza Pavarin (kohn-STAHN-sah pah-vah-REEN)

Elionor Janavel (eh-lee-oh-NOR)

Estève Malan (eh-STAY-ve mah-LAHN)

Ezio (ETZ-ee-oh)

Fosca (FOS-kah)

Gedeon Chanforan (GED-ay-ohn shahn-for-AHN)

Guido (GWEE-doh)

Ioannis Argyropoulos (ee-oh-AH-neess ar-chi-RO-po-liss)

Irene (ee-RE-nay)

Johan Lauras (yo-HAHN loh-RAHS)

Luca Grimaldi (LOO-kuh gri-MAHL-dee)

Prospera (PROS-per-ah)

Roberto (roh-BAIR-toh)

Silvia (SEEL-vee-ah)

Umile (OO-mee-le)

Valeria (vah-LE-ree-ah)

Vitòria Grimaldi (vi-TOR-ee-ah)

Yolande of Valois, Princess Consort (YEW-lahn VAH-lew-ah)

Zama (TZAH-mah)

Gazetteer

Angrogna Valley (ahn-GROHN-ya). Narrow valley branching off from the Luserna Valley; central setting of the story.

Asti. Principal city in the March of Montferrat.

Bologna (bah-LOWN-yah). Largest city in Emilia-Romagna and major crossroads.

Bricherasio. Town near the mouth of the Luserna Valley; home of Victor.

Carcere delle Stinche. Prison for criminals and political enemies in Florence.

Castelvecchio (kah-stehl-VEK-ee-oh). Minor feudal castle near the mouth of the Luserna Valley.

Chisone Valley. Valley north of Angrogna with passes leading to France; has a large population of Vallenses.

Constantinople. Largest city in Europe; former capital of the Eastern Roman Empire; recently made capital of the Ottoman Empire.

Convento di San Marco. Dominican convent in Florence.

Emilia-Romagna. Region in Italy containing Parma and Bologna.

Florence. Principal city of Tuscany; birthplace of the Italian Renaissance.

Genoa. Wealthy maritime city-state on the Mediterranean.

Il Duomo. Florence Cathedral; largest masonry dome in the world; symbol of the Italian Renaissance.

La Torre. Principal town in the Luserna Valley; now called Torre Pellice.

Lombardy. Rival power to Tuscany, often sponsored by the King of France.

Luserna Valley. Wide, fertile east-west oriented valley containing several Vallense communities; now called Val Pellice.

Milan. Principal city of Lombardy.

Moncalieri (mon-kal-ee-EHR-ee). Summer home of Prince Amadeus and Yolande just outside of Turin.

Mount Friouland. Prominent mountain southwest of Angrogna, opposite of Mount Vandalino.

Mount Vandalino. Prominent mountain west of Angrogna.

Palazzo dell'Arte della Lana (peh-LAHTZ-oh dehl-ART-ay DEL-uh LAHN-ah). Palace of the Wool Guild, the most powerful political group in Florence.

Palazzo della Signoria (peh-LAHTZ-oh DEL-uh sin-YOR-ee-ah). Florence's seat of civil government; famous for its clocktower.

Parma. Major city in Emilia-Romagna; famous for its Parmigiano Reggiano cheese and Prosciutto.

Piacenza. Major city in Emilia-Romagna.

Piedmont. Principality administered by the Duchy of Savoy.

Pinerolo (PEE-nay-ro-lo). Principal town near Vallense lands; seat of Catholic diocese.

Pisa. Famous port city on the Mediterranean ruled by Tuscany.

Ponte Vecchio. Iconic bridge over the River Arno in Florence.

Reggio di Lombardia. Major city southeast of Parma; now called Reggio Emilia.

Rome. Capital of the former Roman Empire; seat of the Catholic Church.

San Lorenzo. Hamlet in Angrogna; home of Pavarin family; location of church meetinghouse.

San Martino Valley. Narrow valley north of Angrogna; now called Valle Germanasca.

Savoy. Duchy that once ruled parts of modern France, Switzerland, and Italy.

Studium Generale (STOO-dee-um jen-er-AHL-ay). University in Florence where Ioannis Argyropoulos teaches; works of the ancients preserved.

Turin. Principal city in Piedmont.

Tuscany. Wealthy duchy under the de-facto rule of the Medici family of Florence.

Venice. Famous maritime city-state built with many canals on the Adriatic Sea.

About the Author

D. J. Speckhals is the author of the Witnesses of the Light historical fiction trilogy, which transports readers to fifteenth-century Europe to explore the resilient faith of the Waldensians.

From a young age, Dustin has held a deep, lifelong passion for history and geography. He spent many school nights studying *National Geographic* and *Rand McNally* atlases, striving to capture a glimpse of the world beyond his home in Michigan. After receiving his B.A. in Pastoral Theology in 2009, he married Andrea and relocated to southeast Pennsylvania, where he has established a successful career as a software developer.

When not immersed in writing and research, Dustin enjoys serving in various ministries at his church, running, pursuing the perfect slice of pizza, and embarking on adventures with his wife and their four children.

www.djspeckhals.com
Facebook: @DJSpeckhals
Instagram: @d.j.speckhals
X: @DSpeckhals

If you loved this book, please give it a review online. Positive reviews help so much. Thank you.

If you loved *The Lord of Luserna,*
There's more!

Heretics of Piedmont: A Novel of the Waldensians
Witnesses of the Light #1

A monk banished for sins he didn't commit. A secret mission that could redeem him—or condemn him utterly.

Prince of Savoy: A Novel of the Waldensians
Witnesses of the Light #3

One man fights for his family against the darkest of evils.

The Outcast of Chivasso: A Novella of the Waldensians
Witnesses of the Light #0.5

His enemies want him to flee.
One little girl needs him to stay.